## LOEDICIA STOOD TREMBLING ON THE AUCTION BLOCK

She could hardly believe that only a few short years ago she had been a sheltered young girl living in an aristocratic paradise.

She could barely remember that but a few weeks ago she had been the most dazzling beauty at the year's most splendid ball, with the most eligible men of the colonies dancing attendance on her.

All had been swept away in the whirlpool of adventure into which she had plunged as she fled an unspeakable fate...

... to stand now as a prize to the highest bidder on the brink of a destiny she dare not imagine....

# THE RAGING WINDS OF HEAVEN

# THE RAGING
# WINDS OF
# HEAVEN

by

## June Lund Shiplett

A SIGNET BOOK

SIGNET
Published by the Penguin Group
Penguin Books USA Inc., 375 Hudson Street,
New York, New York 10014, U.S.A.
Penguin Books Ltd, 27 Wrights Lane,
London W8 5TZ, England
Penguin Books Australia Ltd, Ringwood,
Victoria, Australia
Penguin Books Canada Ltd, 10 Alcorn Ave., Suite 300,
Toronto, Canada M4V 3B2
Penguin Books (N.Z.) Ltd, 182–190 Wairau Road,
Auckland 10, New Zealand

Penguin Books Ltd, Registered Offices:
Harmondsworth, Middlesex, England

Published by Signet, an imprint of New American Library,
a division of Penguin Books USA Inc.

First Printing, August, 1978
19  18  17  16  15  14  13  12  11

 REGISTERED TRADEMARK—MARCA REGISTRADA

Printed in the United States of America

# DEDICATION

This book is dedicated to Charlie and the girls, Mo, Jill, Von and Laura, who sacrificed their time and energies for the sake of my dream.

To all my friends and relatives who gave me encouragement. There are too many to name individually, but they know who they are.

To my agents Elizabeth Pomada and Michael Larsen for having faith in me.

To my publishers for their confidence in my abilities.

And to God without whose help this book would not have been possible.

# 1

*Boston—May 14, 1774*

Waves lapped gently against the pilings of Long Wharf, causing the ships to rise and fall in a rhythmic cadence. Cool breezes floated down from the north and a lazy moon hung low amid a profusion of stars. Quiet had descended on the city, but it was a pregnant quiet, a quiet of unrest as the people of Boston simmered. With the appointment the day before of General Gage as the new Governor of Massachusetts there was no longer any question as to what was in store for the city. British soldiers roamed the streets two and three abreast, tense, muskets ready, prepared to enforce the king's law if need be.

In front of the British Coffee House a group of young officers crossing State Street laughed raucously and stepped aside as a closed carriage, drawn by a matched pair of bays, ambled toward them, then slowed down as it drew alongside. The carriage suddenly swayed jerkily as it hit a bump, and a woman's face appeared at the curtained window, her eyes wide, lips parted. The men pointed, smiling and bowing ceremoniously, attracted by the pretty face, then waved gallantly as the face was lost again in the darkness of the moving carriage.

Lady Loedicia Aldrich, her violet eyes laughing, one hand tucking a curl back behind her ear, looked across at her companions and smiled as she leaned back onto the cushioned seat.

"Why do men make such a fuss all the time?" she asked as the carriage rolled on. "You'd think they'd never seen a woman's face before."

Her aunt Agatha sighed. "If you'd refrain from looking out the window at every turn, you wouldn't get stared at," she replied sarcastically.

"Really, Loedicia," her uncle harrumphed, "why are you so brazen?"

"Brazen?"

"Ladies conduct themselves properly. They don't peek out carriage windows."

Loedicia frowned. "Oh, for heaven sakes, Uncle Thaddeus," she answered irritably, "don't be so stodgy."

Uncle Thaddeus was a pompous windbag so involved with the political situation in the colonies he barely had time for his wife, let alone a niece. He was always at meetings or with his nose stuck in a book or documents. Even tonight. He wasn't going to the party because he liked parties. He was going so he could feel out the new governor.

"Your uncle is not stodgy and I wish you'd refrain from using such colorful language," Aunt Agatha retorted.

Loedicia gave a sigh and rolled her beautiful eyes in disgust. "Heaven sakes is not swearing," she blurted. "Good God! You'd think I said damn or something."

Aunt Agatha gasped. "Loedicia!"

"Well, it seems ridiculous that people make such a fuss over a few silly words."

Aunt Agatha's eyes narrowed. "Nevertheless, as long as they do, you'll refrain from using them."

Loedicia sighed as she leaned her head back. It was dark in the carriage and she could barely see, but she knew exactly the expression that would be on her aunt's face.

When she had first heard the name Aunt Agatha she had conjured up a picture of a plump, middle-aged matron with gray hair and a motherly smile; instead she came face to face with a voluptuous woman in her late thirties with seductive amber eyes and coppery hair that tonight was coiffured into the latest fashion. How Uncle Thaddeus had managed to entice her to the altar was incomprehensible because he was at least twenty years older than she, with thining gray hair, an oversized paunch, and constantly watering pop eyes that reminded Loedicia of an overstuffed frog's.

Loedicia had no idea how a woman as pretty as her mother could have a brother like Uncle Thaddeus; she would have been happy had there been another relative she could have lived with after her father's death.

In India, where she had lived all her life with her widowed father, she had been pampered, spoiled, and fussed over by all the other officers' wives. The colonies were a bad enough change for her without Uncle Thaddeus's stuffy indifference and Aunt Agatha's animosity, for it was apparent from the start that the woman disliked her.

The carriage hit another bump, and Agatha stirred, turning toward her husband. "I'm so glad they decided to have a party for General Gage," she said, sighing a bit, her eyes bright with anticipation.

"They fuss too much," answered Thaddeus. "General Gage is here to stop this rebelliousness, not to cosset a bunch of dandies out for a good time."

"But we do need diversions once in a while," answered his wife, and even in the darkness of the carriage Loedicia could sense the exhilaration in Aunt Agatha's voice at the thought of all the available men who would be there tonight.

Loedicia didn't understand how Uncle Thaddeus could be so blind to the men who paid his wife compliments and wooed her right under his very nose. But then maybe he didn't care. Perhaps ten years ago when he'd married her he might have been a more vital man, but now he seemed dried up emotionally except for his zealous involvement in politics.

"Samuel Adams is overstepping himself," he said as the carriage started to slow down. "He and those ruffians of his have gone too far. By jove, General Gage'll nail his hide to the barn before this is over. They've gotten the whole city in trouble this time and the loyal citizens of Boston won't stand for any more of his arrogance. Him and his bloody tea party!" He spluttered a bit as he said it, and the carriage stopped, jolting him.

"Please, dear, don't get all worked up now," admonished Agatha. "I know all you've come for is to talk politics, but at least refrain from doing so while I'm around." She smiled at him coquettishly. "I do want to enjoy the evening, and politics is so boring."

"Nonsense," he countered. "Politics is the life blood of man. I'm glad everyone doesn't feel the way you do, my dear, or we'd be in a sorrier state than we are."

"I think it's ridiculous. All this fighting over tea."

"We're not fighting over tea . . ." he began excitedly, and she wrinkled her nose in distaste.

"Not now, Thaddeus, please!" She cut him short as the footman opened the door of the coach.

Loedicia saw the look on her uncle's face as he watched his wife descend with the footman's help and she had the distinct feeling that he cared little whether she enjoyed herself this evening or not. He hadn't even noticed the green silk dress she wore although it was new and had put him out quite a sum.

As she emerged from the carriage, Loedicia stared up at the hall where the party was being held. Lights streamed from every window; other carriages were pulling up, depositing their occupants and keeping the footmen and lackeys busy as a stream of people flowed into the building. But on the perimeter of the crowd groups of men in everyday clothes milled about, their movements watched by soldiers, and they looked none too happy. They yelled and made derogatory remarks, shouting to one another as they harassed the arriving guests.

Loedicia glanced over at them just as one man made an obscene gesture. Uncle Thaddeus, seeing it, grabbed her arm, ushering her and Aunt Agatha up the steps of the building as quickly as possible.

"Rabble, that's what they are," he harrumphed as they stepped inside and made their way to the cloak room where a lackey took their wraps. "I don't know why we have to be subjected to all this," he continued, mumbling breathlessly.

Loedicia sighed. She hadn't paid much attention to politics since she'd arrived here, but then, she had paid little attention to politics in India. All she cared about was that it didn't affect her in any way, although she had to admit it had begun to. Uncle Thaddeus was loath to let her go anywhere unaccompanied, even in the daytime, because of the soldiers and gangs of rebels overrunning the streets. She had pooh-poohed him at first, but tonight, seeing the angry looks on some of the men's faces, she thought perhaps Uncle Thaddeus was right. Maybe they were fighting over more than just tea. She shrugged. No matter. She was going to enjoy herself tonight regardless. It was her first big party in the colonies.

Soft music filled the air as she smoothed her hands over the soft folds of her new dress, then glanced down at herself. The bustle of her dress was trimmed with diamanté; the decolleté emphasized her firm breasts. She had chosen this material purposely, knowing the gold would set off her dark hair and violet eyes to full advantage, and the design would enhance her figure.

"Don't lag behind gazing at yourself," said Aunt Agatha as she took her husband's arm and started toward the archway that led into the partially filled hall, then turned to her husband as Loedicia followed hesitantly at their heels, gazing around curiously at some new arrivals by the door. "Why we should be saddled with a girl like that is beyond me," Agatha said as she glanced back quickly at Loedicia for a moment. "Why couldn't you have sent her to an orphanage or something?"

Her husband clucked softly. "Dear, dear, Agatha. You know the girl's too old. She's all of nineteen, and after all, it was my duty. She is my only sister's daughter, and her father had no relatives left."

"Well, I don't like having her underfoot," she whispered to him. Agatha had disliked the warm-eyed beauty the minute she'd gotten off the boat. She was far too pretty.

"Neither do I, my dear," he replied, "but duty is duty." Then he turned back toward Loedicia who was smiling coquettishly at a young British officer a few feet away.

"Come along, girl," he admonished. "You do have to be presented, you know. After all, there are many people here you haven't as yet met. One dinner invitation doesn't include all of Boston."

Shortly after her arrival she had dined at the home of
Governor Hutchinson where she had met a fair sampling
of Boston society, but Uncle Thaddeus was right. He took
her arm and she drew her eyes from the young man and
looked ahead.

A tall, distinguished-looking man stood at the head of
the receiving line with Lord Snow whom she remembered
meeting at the former governor's dinner party, because he
had reminded her a great deal of her uncle; he was just as
unappealing.

Lord Snow shook hands with Uncle Thaddeus, then introduced him to the guest of honor. "General Gage, may
I present Mr. Thaddeus Farrington, his wife Agatha, and I
believe, if I remember correctly, the young lady is Mr.
Farrington's niece, Lady Loedicia Aldrich, recently arrived from India. Am I right, Thaddeus?"

"Quite, quite," responded Thaddeus abruptly as they
shook hands and the ladies curtsied.

The new governor, resplendent in his uniform, was very
impressive. His hair was lightly powdered and his dark
eyes flashed as he relinquished Thaddeus's hand, then
nodded to the ladies, extending his hand. Loedicia could
already sense her aunt's eyes talking to the general in that
soft way of hers.

"I'm charmed," he murmured softly as he looked both
of them over, his dark eyes missing nothing. "I see you
have two beautiful women to share your home, Mr. Farrington," he said as he turned back to Thaddeus. "You're
to be congratulated, both on your wife and your niece."

"I dare say." Thaddeus accepted the compliment and
his protruding eyes almost twinkled; then his face grew
serious, reddening a bit as he changed the subject
abruptly. "But tell me, sir, I hear you plan to close the
port because of that stupid incident last winter." He harrumphed a bit irritably. "I agree these ruffians have to be
dealt with, but I'm in the shipping business. Is it fair for
men like myself to suffer for what a few unruly, dissatis-
fied hoodlums decide to do in a moment of haste?"

General Gage frowned. "Mr. Farrington, if I took into
account all the people who would suffer inconvenience,

including myself, I wouldn't be in the position I'm in at the moment. My orders are to stop this rebellion at all costs. Unfortunately, the innocent must suffer with the guilty."

"But I'm a loyal subject. What happens to my ships?"

Lord Snow smiled. "Surely you have enough friends, Thaddeus. There are alternatives."

"Alternatives?"

"You're ingenious enough to think of something. There are other ports, you know. You can sell the same goods in New York that you can sell here."

"But it's not the same."

General Gage's eyes flashed. "Nothing is the same anymore, sir," he offered. "And I doubt it ever will be unless these irresponsible fools and malcontents like John Hancock, Samuel Adams, and Joseph Warren don't stop instigating the people with their traitorous talk. Oh, yes, we know who they are. Dr. Franklin isn't helping, either, with his revolutionary ideas. There's even talk among some of a complete break with England." He laughed cynically. "As if a few scattered colonies could possibly govern themselves. The idea's preposterous."

He glanced toward the ladies and saw the disgusted look on Agatha's face. "But here now," he continued, "we aren't here to talk politics, we're here to enjoy ourselves and we're forgetting the ladies."

Thaddeus's face reddened. He didn't like being put off, but there was nothing he could do. He wanted the rebels punished, but to shut down the harbor—his pockets were going to be let for sure.

As the new governor and Lord Snow changed the subject, the three guests moved down the receiving line which was made up of city officials, soldiers of rank, and some of Uncle Thaddeus's old acquaintances.

Loedicia curtsied to all of them, then finally breathed a sigh as the receiving line was left behind. "Why do we always have to run the gauntlet?" she asked as they walked over to mingle with the other guests.

Uncle Thaddeus threw his head back and looked down his nose at her. "The gauntlet?"

She nodded. "Receiving lines are a curse of this generation. We never had them in India."

"Apparently there were a lot of things you didn't have in India, young lady," her uncle replied.

"Including manners," added Aunt Agatha.

Loedicia held her head up haughtily. "There's nothing wrong with my manners!"

Aunt Agatha sighed. "Loedicia," she said, "your father was far too lenient with you. You express yourself too freely in a manner most unbecoming to a lady of quality. A true lady conducts herself in a far more genteel way."

"And how don't I conduct myself properly?" Her eyes flashed angrily.

"You're far too forward in what you say and do. Like yesterday when Captain Chapman stopped by the house." Aunt Agatha's face reddened as she spoke. "No lady of quality talks of horse breeding with a gentleman."

"Why not? What's wrong with horses?"

Uncle Thaddeus glanced at her, his watery eyes a bit wider than usual. He hadn't heard of this latest transgression. "Have you no decency, lady?" he asked harrumphing, his lower chins vibrating as he shook his head. "What your father was thinking of bringing you up in that heathen country, I'll never know. You'll refrain from being so outspoken in the future, Loedicia, or I'll have to reprimand you severely."

She sighed in disgust. "Nineteen years old and I'm treated like a child," she said belligerently. She leaned closer to Uncle Thaddeus. "It may shock you, Uncle Thaddeus," she whispered sarcastically, "but I even know where babies come from and how they get there!" Her uncle's face turned white as he let out a gasp, his expression registering shock.

He was unable to retaliate, however, as a good-looking lieutenant had approached expressing his wish to be the first on Loedicia's dance card. Thaddeus made a mental note to speak to her on the way home.

Overhead, the huge hall was lit by the flames of over a thousand candles set in three crystal chandeliers, while mirrored ornaments beside the wall sconces caught the images of the candles and reflected them like tiny jewels. Plush overstuffed couches and chairs lined the walls, and at one side was a huge banquet table spread with an elaborate assortment of food, including a number of expensive delicacies. Huge bouquets of artificially grown flowers in every color imaginable, filled the hall, bursting from the tables, the corners of the room, and the musician's stand. Red bunting and ribbons of satin adorned the walls.

The evening was proving to be most interesting. Loedicia, charming and gay, flirted outrageously whether dancing or standing on the sidelines talking. Yet for all her outward appearances, she disliked men. They were merely a game with her. She had idolized her father and vowed she would never marry until she found a man who could equal him. Since there seemed no hope that another such man existed, she had decided she would probably never marry. Her father had felt the choice was hers; as far as he was concerned there was no man good enough for her.

She used to hear other girls giggling over stolen kisses and swooning at the thought of merely being near a man. Ridiculous! Men were men, nothing spectacular. In fact, except for her father, most men were comical, the greedy way they looked at her and the way they whispered in her ear when she stood beside them, their eyes fondling her bosom. It was great sport knowing what they wanted, yet knowing they'd never get it.

Then again there were the shy, embarrassed young men, falling all over themselves and her, awkward in their attempts at conversation and boring her to death. She loved to say outrageous things just to see them blush.

She was dancing with a rather nice but gawky young lieutenant when she heard a soft murmuring in the crowd. As the music stopped she looked toward the door where everyone else seemed to be looking and saw a tall, broad-shouldered stranger who had just arrived.

His red-gold hair was unpowdered and held back in a queue with a pale blue ribbon that matched his satin coat and the color of his eyes. The combination was striking against his deeply tanned skin. His right cheek was dis-

torted by a long vivid scar that ran from directly under
his eye to the corner of his mouth, almost touching his full
lips.

He began to survey the room arrogantly; then his eyes
caught her and held. She stood quietly staring back into
his cold eyes as they studied her from head to toe, and
gradually she saw the coldness replaced by a look she
knew only too well but had never encountered with such
intensity. She shivered involuntarily as her face turned
crimson.

He wanted her and she knew he wanted her. Although
she'd lived a sheltered life in India without a mother to
guide her, she had learned more than enough from one of
her promiscuous girlfriends. She knew exactly what that
look in a man's eyes meant, and in spite of this man's
clothes and gentlemanly appearance she had a premoni-
tion that he was someone to avoid.

"Who is he?" she asked her partner as the man continued to stare at her.

The young lieutenant shook his head. "I don't know,
Lady Loedicia," he answered slowly, frowning. "I've
never seen him before."

She reached up and put her hand at the base of her
throat, turning away self-consciously as Roth Chapman,
the handsome, dark-haired captain in his late twenties,
who had been coming to see her almost every day since
her arrival in Boston came to claim the next dance.

"I believe I'm next on your program," he said. The
young lieutenant bowed, then reluctantly walked away.

"Do you mind terribly if we don't dance?" she asked,
smiling sweetly into his dark eyes.

He smiled back. "Not at all. Perhaps you'd like something to drink?"

She sighed. "I'd love it." Then she glanced quickly
back toward the new arrival. "Who is that man who just
came in?" she asked. The captain glanced around; she
saw his jaw tighten a bit.

"You mean the tall gentleman with the red-gold hair?"

She nodded. "Do you know him?"

He looked back at her, studying her face a moment, his

dark eyes puzzled. "I've met him on occasion. He's Lord Kendall Varrick." He took her arm to usher her past a small group of people. "Any reason why you should ask?"

She shook her head and he felt her tremble momentarily. "No . . . it's just . . . something about him frightens me, that's all."

"He's not from Boston," he explained. "He came to the colonies from England some years ago and moved into the backwoods, living with the Indians. There are a lot of stories about him, some not too pleasant. I hear tell he fought against the French and put in a good account of himself. He has a vast holding on the frontier he hopes will someday be a city, but some people claim he acts more like it's a small empire all his own. He's a friend of Lord North's and Lord Snow's, however, and no one dares question his actions. Every now and then he heads east to see how the rest of the world is getting along."

"He seems to know Aunt Agatha and Uncle Thaddeus," Loedicia said as she motioned with her head, and the captain glanced across the room in time to see them shaking hands and exchanging greetings.

"I suppose you're anxious to meet him?" he asked, a bit put out, but she shook her head vigorously.

"No, thank you. I'd much rather have a glass of punch." She smiled at the captain, making his heart beat faster, but all the time she was aware that the man with the red-gold hair had turned around and was once more staring at her.

"Who is that lovely creature in the gold dress standing by the banquet table?" asked Lord Varrick, interrupting Thaddeus's complaints about the state of affairs in Boston.

Thaddeus stopped, harrumphing loudly, and glanced toward the table. "Where?" he asked, holding his head back and looking down his nose.

"The young lady with the dark hair and exquisite face. Her eyes are most arresting."

Agatha suddenly realized there was only one woman

wearing a gold dress near the table. "You mean Loedicia?" she gasped incredulously.

"If that's her name it fits her well," he answered. "Who is she?"

Agatha's eyes suddenly became evasive.

"By jove, Kendall," answered Thaddeus. "That's my niece, Lady Loedicia Aldrich."

His eyebrows raised. "Your niece?"

"Quite so."

"Then may I congratulate you, Thaddeus. She's a remarkably beautiful woman, and an aristocrat as well?"

"But rather young, wouldn't you say?" offered Agatha, envious of the smoldering looks he was giving Loedicia.

He straightened up, looking even taller. "She's old enough for marriage, I presume?" he asked, and both Agatha and Thaddeus looked at him sharply.

"I'm getting old, Thaddeus," he explained, noticing their surprise. "I want someday to leave an heir to inherit my holdings. After all, I can't have that cousin of mine trying to step in. But in order to have an heir I must first have a wife. Besides"—he smiled cynically, the scar on his cheek even more prominent under the candlelight— "it's time I settle down. That, my dear friends, is one of the very reasons for my visit this time. To find a bride to take back with me." His eyes gleamed as he continued to stare at Loedicia. "I never expected to find one so quickly."

Agatha gasped, hardly believing her ears. "You're jesting!"

His eyes narrowed as he watched Loedicia nibbling the pink frosting from a petit-four while she talked to Captain Chapman. "I was never more serious in my life," he answered.

"But you don't even know her."

"That can be arranged, I'm sure," he said, looking at Thaddeus who sputtered nervously.

"To be sure," he agreed, "but don't you think it's rather soon to be talking of marriage?" He harrumphed a few times. "Loedicia is a rather strange child—"

"Child?" interrupted Lord Varrick. "My dear Thaddeus, I don't believe you've taken a very close look at your niece lately . . . she's far from being a child."

Thaddeus blinked a few times as he tilted his head back and stared at Loedicia. "To be sure she has all the attributes of a woman, but she's been spoiled and pampered . . . I'm afraid she's far from being the lady her title demands her to be. Surely you could find someone more suitable."

Lord Varrick frowned and his eyes narrowed. "Do I understand you have objections to my asking for her hand?"

Agatha was mortified. "But . . ." Her hand flew to her breast, "but it's so soon. You've only set eyes on her tonight."

"My dear, Agatha," he answered as he finally drew his eyes away from Loedicia. "I have no time to waste. I must leave for home the first week in June. There's no time for a long courtship. I've found the woman I intend to make my wife and what better way to travel home than on a honeymoon."

"The first week in June? That's barely two weeks away."

"Exactly, dear lady, so if you and Thaddeus will kindly oblige me with an introduction" . . . He took a long, deep breath, straightening the ruffles on his shirt and inspecting the diamond cuff links at his wrists.

Agatha's first inclination was anger. Then, suddenly, she smiled knowingly. What better way to rid herself of a nuisance. As Lord Varrick's wife, Loedicia would be miles away from Boston and out of her hair.

"Well, don't just stand there, Thaddeus," she said anxiously as she took Lord Varrick's arm. "Shall we introduce him to Loedicia?" and she looked at him, waiting.

Loedicia wiped her mouth and fingers on a napkin, then took a sip of punch, her violet eyes laughing seductively at the captain. She liked Roth. He was one of the few men she did like because his straightforward manner reminded her a bit of her father.

"And when he leaned forward to retrieve the duck he went in head first," Roth was saying. "Needless to say, we had a horrible time keeping our faces straight." They both laughed, then stopped abruptly as Uncle Thaddeus's voice interrupted them.

"Loedicia, my dear," he said as he reached out and took her arm, turning her to face him. "Captain, if you'll excuse us," he addressed Roth. "I've brought someone over I'd like Loedicia to meet." She turned around and looked directly into those cold blue eyes that had stared at her so intently only a short time before. "Loedicia, my dear, I'd like you to meet Lord Kendall Varrick," Thaddeus turned to Lord Varrick. "Kendall, my niece, Lady Loedicia Aldrich."

Lord Varrick held out his hand as Loedicia began to curtsy and there was nothing she could do but put her hand in his. His fingers closed about hers, strong and hard, and he squeezed lightly as his lips parted and he smiled.

"At last I meet the most beautiful woman at the party," he said softly, and she trembled at the look in his eyes.

"You flatter me, sir," she answered.

"Flattery is merely sugar-coated words, my dear," he replied. "What I speak is the truth. You are the most beautiful woman I've ever seen."

Loedicia glanced at Aunt Agatha who stood beside Lord Varrick, a strange look on her face. "I'm afraid you're the only one with that opinion of me, sir," Loedicia said abruptly, then glanced toward a gentleman who was elbowing his way through the crowd now that the music had stopped. "If you'll excuse me," she said hurriedly, "I see my partner for the next dance." She turned to Captain Chapman to take her leave, when Lord Varrick reached out and took her hand, interrupting her.

"Ah, but the next dance is mine, Lady Loedicia," he said. "If everyone will excuse us."

She stared at him dumbfounded, then wrenched her arm from his hand. "I beg your pardon, sir!" Her eyes flashed angrily. "My dance is with Sir Giles." She addressed the gentleman who had just joined their small circle. "Isn't it, Sir Giles?"

Sir Giles never had time to open his mouth, for Lord Varrick's overbearing answer stopped him. "Sir Giles is an old acquaintance and I'm sure he won't mind relinquishing his right to this dance. Would you, Sir Giles?" he asked, and the arrogant tone of his voice was a warning that he wasn't about to be crossed.

Captain Chapman's jaw set hard, his teeth clenched together tightly; Sir Giles's mouth twitched nervously as he contemplated Lord Varrick's suggestion, but it was Loedicia who spoke.

"But I mind!" she answered heatedly. "I choose my own dance partners, Lord Varrick, and you, I'm afraid, are not on the list!"

Lord Varrick reached out carefully, took her arm, and deliberately tore the dance card from the ribbon about her wrist, then as they all stood watching, he ripped it up neatly, and shoved the pieces in his pocket.

"What on earth . . .?" Loedicia cried, her face white with rage. "You have no right! That belongs to me!"

Lord Varrick's eyes glared into hers maliciously, then he turned to Sir Giles and Captain Chapman. "There has been a change in Lady Loedicia's dance card for the remainder of the evening," he stated boldly, drawing himself up and looking down at them. "You will inform the rest of the gentlemen that the lady has decided to spend the remainder of the evening with me. If they disagree, I'll be happy to oblige and they may choose the time and place."

Everyone stared at Lord Varrick in hushed silence as the music started again.

"Shall we?" he said arrogantly, holding his arm out for her to take.

She stared at him stubbornly, anger blazing from her eyes. "I'll not dance one dance with you!" she cried vehemently. "You have no right to force—"

"No right?" he interrupted, laughing cynically. "As your future husband, my dear, I have every right," he said, and Loedicia was so astonished she had no answer for him.

She stared dumbfounded, hardly believing her ears as

he took her arm and led her away to the dance floor. There was an arrogance and self-centered egotism in his manner that frightened her, and his overbearing attitude added to her apprehension. The man was crazy to barge into her life and start running it as if he owned her. Who did he think he was? Her future husband indeed!

She gathered herself together and turned to face him as they stepped to their places. "I'm afraid you're laboring under a false assumption, sir," she said quite angrily as they started to dance. "I intend to be no one's future wife, least of all yours!"

He smiled and his tongue ran the length of his upper lip as he looked at her greedily. "I've already informed your aunt and uncle, my dear," he answered cunningly. "It will do you no good to argue. I have no time for the usual courtship, seeing as we must leave for home the first week in June." He leaned close to her as they held hands, pirouetting. "But I shall make it up to you after we're married, never fear."

"You're crazy!" she protested and jerked her hand from his, starting to walk away.

He reached out and grabbed her arm, his fingers pressing too hard into her flesh. "It will do you no good to create a scene," he whispered. "You'll only make a spectacle of yourself."

Loedicia glanced about her. The other couples on the floor were staring at them, and she could hear whispering behind her as she drew in a deep breath, her face white with rage. "You win the first round, sir," she spat at him, pretending to smile sweetly as she once more began dancing. "But I shall never marry you . . . count on that!" and she followed him in the intricate steps of the dance until the music stopped.

He pulled her up from her low curtsy as the last strains of the music ended and held her hand tightly, tucking her arm through his as she struggled to pull away.

"I like a woman with spirit," he said as he smiled at her. "It makes the taming all the better." Suddenly she realized he was enjoying her anger. The more she rebeled, the more it excited him.

"If you'll be so kind, sir," she said, trying to hide her anger and stay calm, "I'd appreciate it if you'd explain this whole affair to me." She glanced down at her arm which he was still holding in a viselike grip. "I come to a simple party and suddenly find myself facing the prospect of marrying a man I've never before laid eyes on. I believe you'll agree it is rather disconcerting, so I think I should be excused for taking the news so badly."

He hesitated and looked down at her, disturbed by this sudden change of character, then he eased his hold on her arm as he stared at her. "Need there be an explanation?" he asked lightly.

"How would you feel, sir, if you attended a party and suddenly some woman there, a perfect stranger, announced her intentions to marry you?"

"If it were you, my dear, I'd consent gladly," he replied.

She frowned. "But what if it were someone you couldn't stand?" she asked. "What if it was someone you would rather die than find as your wife. What then, sir?"

"Is that the way you feel about me?" he asked, and his hand once more tightened on her arm as they moved away from the other dancers. "You don't even know me yet, my dear," he whispered softly. "I can be quite charming when I want to be." His eyes bored into hers, making her cringe at the force behind them.

Lord Varrick seemed to find a sadistic enjoyment in her discomfiture, and Loedicia had to fight to hold her temper. "Are you prepared to hold me prisoner like this all night?" she asked, glancing down at her arm locked in his grip; he too glanced down, then caressed her bare arm with his other hand.

"What would you do if I let go?" he asked, and her eyes narrowed.

"Are you man enough to find out?"

His eyes were wary as he loosened his hold on her arm, but she didn't run away. Instead she rubbed her arm as if to rub away the feel of his hands on her skin; then she looked up at him.

"Now, will you please tell me what all this nonsense is about?"

"Nonsense? I assure you, my dear, it's far from nonsense. I've already spoken to your aunt and uncle. I must have a wife in order to produce an heir, and I've chosen you."

"And my feelings don't count?"

He smiled cynically. "Let's say that as your guardians they know what's best for you."

"I hate to disappoint all of you," she answered after a brief silence, "but I haven't the least intention of marrying anyone."

"Then I'll have to change your mind for you," he said, and she knew by the look on his face that he was as determined to marry her as she was for him not to.

Although she was rude and sarcastic to him for the rest of the evening, she was unable to get away from him except for a few stolen minutes in the powder room. And by the time the party was over everyone was whispering about their forthcoming marriage.

As she left the hall at the end of the evening, Loedicia didn't look back when she entered the carriage and leaned back against the seat, but she knew he was standing on the steps watching her, an insolent smile on his face. She couldn't stand the man, and most of all she was afraid of him. He was a strange man of varying moods, and she had a strong feeling that few people ever crossed him.

As the carriage moved forward, away from the crowd that was leaving the party, Loedicia looked over at Aunt Agatha and Uncle Thaddeus. Well, it was now or never.

She took a deep breath, then exploded. "Of all the backhanded . . . exactly what did you tell that man?"

Aunt Agatha's eyes widened innocently. "You don't like him?" she asked innocently.

"Like him? I hate him!" she stated.

Agatha shrugged. "How ridiculous," she replied. "He's a wonderful catch. Wealth, a title. Any girl would be pleased. And besides, we've already given our consent."

Loedicia stared at her, a sudden strange feeling in the

pit of her stomach. "You're jesting," she said slowly. "You have to be . . . this is some sort of a jest."

"I never jest about such important matters, my dear," Agatha said firmly and Loedicia's face went white.

The more she had been with the man the more her first impression of him had deepened and the more he frightened her. She lifted her head haughtily. "Well, I don't intend to marry anyone," she stated. Aunt Agatha laughed, a soft, tinkling laugh.

"Since when did you think you had a choice in the matter?" she asked vindictively, and Loedicia gasped.

"But I won't!"

"Oh, but you will!"

"I will not marry him or anyone else!" she cried. "I don't even know the man!"

Uncle Thaddeus, who was well in his cups, his eyes at half mast, harrumphed a few times, waving his hand as he belched. "There'll be no more said on the subject," he answered lazily, his voice slurred.

But Loedicia wasn't to be brushed off. "No more said? My whole future's at stake."

Thaddeus tried to straighten himself as best he could in his inebriated condition. "As your guardian, young lady," he drawled, "I shall have the last say as to whom you shall marry. And as your aunt has informed you, we have already given our consent."

"But why?" she almost shouted across the darkened coach. "This is insane. Why are you trying to do this to me?" She glanced quickly at her aunt. "Are you so anxious to get rid of me you'd give me to the devil himself?"

Thaddeus harrumphed a few times. "I have no choice," he snapped irritably, the drink making him even more disagreeable. "Lord Varrick is a friend of General Gage's, and the general is going to need local ships to help bring in supplies to his troops during the blockade. If I consent to this marriage, there's every chance I can get those commissions. And without them, my dear, I stand to lose a great deal of money."

So that was it. If she married Lord Varrick, he would use his influence on General Gage, and Uncle Thaddeus

wouldn't have to worry about the port being closed. It
was plain to her now; she had quickly learned on her arrival that no one stands between her uncle and his money.
He liked the better things of life and spent lavishly.

"I might have known it would hit you in the pocket
somewhere," she answered bitterly as she realized he was
far too drunk to make sense in an argument. "But I don't
care if he promises you the world. And there's nothing
you or anyone else can do to make me change my mind!"

A pregnant silence filled the coach; Loedicia held her
breath waiting for another outburst from Uncle Thaddeus, but this time it was Aunt Agatha who spoke.

"I wouldn't be too sure about that, my dear," she
answered softly, deliberately, her voice, ominous. "There
are ways . . . and there are ways," and again there was
silence.

Loedicia turned and stared absentmindedly out the
window into the darkness. Maybe tomorrow she could
think of a way to make them change their minds, but
tonight it was hopeless. She leaned her head wearily
against the side of the carriage and listened to the horses'
hooves echoing through the quiet street.

# 2

The next morning she tossed and turned in bed. She
hadn't slept well at all. How could she possibly marry a
man whose very presence made her flesh crawl. Never before had she experienced such a sudden dislike for anyone
as she had for Lord Varrick. Regardless of his wealth and
the fact that he was a man of some consequence, she was
determined he would never lay hands on her.

"We'll just see who gets married!" she whispered to
herself as she turned over in bed and bunched the pillow
up beneath her head.

Her bedroom was small but cozy, with a lace-canopied

bed, brick fireplace, imported Persian rug, and lace-ruffled curtains. Uncle Thaddeus's house was considered one of the better homes in the neighborhood, and he had spared no expense in its furnishings.

As the clock in the hall struck ten, there was a knock on the door. Loedicia pursed her lips stubbornly. Marie, the house girl, entered and crossed the room, to stand at the foot of the bed. "Your aunt says as how you're to come downstairs," she said softly. "The gentleman is here to see you."

Loedicia pulled the covers tighter against her chin. "Tell my aunt I don't intend to leave this room until they forget about this whole stupid affair," she grumbled. "And nothing they can do or say will make a bit of difference. I wouldn't marry Lord Varrick if he were the last man on earth!" She turned her back on the servant girl and settled more comfortably into the covers.

Marie frowned but didn't say a word as she turned and left the room to return to the parlor where Agatha was entertaining Lord Varrick. Agatha was wearing a beautiful dress of gray silk with white lace trimming that complimented Lord Varrick's gray riding coat, gold vest, buff breeches, and highly polished riding boots.

"Excuse me, ma'am," Marie interrupted hesitantly as she entered the room, "but Miss Loedicia says she won't come down."

Agatha was disconcerted. "She. . . ?" She turned quickly to Lord Varrick. "Excuse me, Kendall," she apologized, "I'll see what the trouble is." She left the room hurriedly with Marie in tow.

"Now what is all this?" she asked the girl, keeping her voice barely above a whisper as they walked toward the stairs.

Although Marie's face was expressionless, she disliked Mrs. Farrington and was secretly pleased with Loedicia's defiance. "Miss Loedica says she isn't coming down until you change your mind about her marrying that swell what's in the parlor," she answered, and saw Agatha's eyes narrow viciously.

"Oh she did, did she?" Agatha kept her voice low, but

by the time she reached the bottom of the staircase her rage carried her up them on the run, her gray silk skirts held high.

A few minutes later the door to Loedicia's room swung wide and Agatha stepped inside. Her face was livid and her amber eyes flashed angrily as she slammed the door behind her and walked over to the bed.

"Just what do you think you're doing?" she demanded. Loedicia opened her eyes lazily and gazed up insolently, not even bothering to move from her comfortable position in bed.

"Marie told you," she answered calmly. "I meant what I said last night. I intend to stay right here in my room until you and Uncle Thaddeus come to your senses and tell Lord Varrick you've changed your—"

She never got to finish, as Agatha reached out, grabbed the covers, and ripped them off her. "You ungrateful little snip!" she raged. "Get up! Get out of that bed this instant!"

Loedicia rolled over as the covers were pulled from her and slid out of bed on the opposite side, then stood facing her aunt. The pale blue flannel nightgown with its high neck and long sleeves trimmed with lace made her look almost childlike but her figure, quite apparent under the cloth, left no doubt that she was a woman.

"You can push me out of bed all you want," she said firmly, "but you won't get me out of this room. Not until you call off this ridiculous farce."

"Do you realize what you're doing, young lady?" Agatha cried in frustration. "What this will do to your uncle?"

"And how about me? You don't care what happens to me, do you? You don't care if I'm hurt!"

"Hurt? Lord Varrick wants you for his wife. How could that possibly hurt you?"

"How?" Loedicia leaned across the bed. "Because I don't want his filthy hands on me. Because the thought of him making love to me is sickening and I won't do it!"

Agatha stared at her silently for a few moments; then her eyes narrowed. "Won't is a hard word, Loedicia," she said, suddenly composing herself. She threw the covers back on the bed in disgust and walked toward the door, then turned back. "For the moment I'll tell Lord Varrick the party was too much for you and you're a bit indisposed." Her voice was hard and cold. "In the meantime we'll go ahead with the wedding plans and set the date." She eyed Loedicia contemptuously. "Since you insist on staying here, fine. Perhaps a few days without food will make you change your mind, because I don't plan to have anything served to you until you come downstairs to the table." She reached down, took the key from the lock, then closed the door swiftly behind her; Loedicia heard the key turn in the lock.

Downstairs Lord Varrick stood in front of the fireplace, his hands behind his back, staring at the picture of Agatha that hung over the mantel. She was a sensuous woman, and at first he had wondered why she hadn't been irritated by his attention to her husband's niece until he realized it offered her a way of eliminating the competition. After all, he wasn't the only man with whom she had had an affair. Women like Agatha needed men around them, varieties of men, and they usually went from one man to another quite readily.

He remembered his last visit to Boston. Thaddeus had been out of town and Agatha had entertained him in her inimitable way. He had almost hated to return to the backwoods and those Indian wenches. This time he would have Loedicia with him, and the prospect intrigued him as he remembered the previous night.

"You're very engrossed." Agatha interrupted his thoughts, and he turned away from the fireplace as she entered the room.

He smiled a knowing smile, his blue eyes boring into hers. "I was remembering," he answered softly, and her face reddened slightly as she tilted her head coquettishly, then returned his smile.

"Too bad your marriage to Loedicia will change all that," she replied, a bit piqued, and this time he grinned.

"I do believe you're jealous, Agatha," he said, and saw the flash of her amber eyes.

"Well, you must admit you seem rather smitten with the girl."

He laughed. "You *are* jealous." He walked over and took her hand in his. "My dear Agatha, no matter whom I marry, there will always be trips to Boston."

She fully understood his meaning. Loedicia was merely a conquest for him—a fascination, and he would tire of her in no time. Agatha drew her hand from his, expertly letting her fingers caress his palm, and the look in his eyes told her everything she wanted to know. They were alike in so many ways.

He released her hand hesitantly and glanced toward the door. "Loedicia isn't coming down?"

"She's not feeling well this morning," she explained as she turned away and looked out the window. "I guess the party was too much for her."

He frowned. It was what he had expected. She was a high-spirited female; perhaps it was the fire in her eyes that had attracted him. He enjoyed a challenge, especially in women. It excited him and made the conquest all the sweeter.

"You lie well, Agatha," he said. He watched her face turn crimson, then waved his hand in protest. "No, don't deny it, my dear. Loedicia was very adamant in her opinion of me last night and I imagine she hasn't changed her mind this morning. But she will. With a bit of persuasion from you and Thaddeus there should be no problem. So I'm sure we can set the date without further delay."

He walked over to stand beside her at the window. "She'll need a trousseau, bridesmaids . . . you'll see everything's taken care of . . . the wedding will be June first at the Old South Church. I stopped before coming over this morning and made the arrangements. The banns will be announced this Sunday from the pulpit."

"You're sure of yourself, aren't you?" she asked.

He smiled cynically. "I'm sure of your gentle art of persuasion, my love." He hesitated. "Oh, yes, and tell Thaddeus when he returns this afternoon that I dine with General Gage this evening. That fact should please him."

Agatha glanced at him sharply. "Did you really mean what you said last night, Kendall?"

"Indeed," he answered. "The day I walk up the aisle to make Loedicia my bride, Agatha, your husband can be assured he'll suffer no discomforts from the king's blockade." He returned her glance, his eyes dancing wickedly. "You know, it amuses me immensely," he said as he started toward the door. "After all we've been to each other it must be hard for you to persuade Loedicia to consent to be my wife, yet I know how much you love money . . . you're rather torn between two evils, aren't you, my dear?"

He retrieved his hat and opened the door, then turned as she spoke.

"As you said yourself," she replied, and her eyes spoke far more than her words, "this isn't your last trip to Boston."

He reached out and took her hand, raising it to kiss her fingertips. "That's what I like about you, Agatha," he whispered softly. "You play the game well." He was smiling when he left, very pleased with himself.

Upstairs Loedicia sat on the edge of the bed and stared angrily at the door, tears welling up in her eyes. All right, she could do that too. She could go forever without food and die of starvation if that's what they wanted. She'd rather die than marry Lord Varrick.

For the next three days she refused to leave her room and she refused to relent. Finally, on the third evening, quite late, Aunt Agatha unlocked the door, and she and Uncle Thaddeus entered the room.

Loedicia was in bed, the covers pulled up to her chin. She wasn't really weak but she had to pretend to be. Marie had been sneaking food to her when she came in to dust the room, and Loedicia couldn't let her aunt and uncle get suspicious.

"Are you ready to admit you're being foolish?" Uncle Thaddeus asked as he stood beside the bed and looked down at her, his watery eyes bloodshot.

"And if I say no, are you content to let me starve to death?" she asked.

He frowned. "Be reasonable, Loedicia, dear. We've set the date for June first. The marriage banns have been announced. What good will it do you? You're only making matters worse."

"Besides," added Aunt Agatha, "you really have no alternative, do you?"

"What do you mean?" she asked as she sat up in bed.

Aunt Agatha's face was like granite, her eyes hard and cold. "If you persist in this foolish attitude we'll have no alternative but to have you locked up."

"Locked up?" Loedicia could hardly believe her ears.

"After all, you're showing a definite lack of mental stability," she sneered, knowing Loedicia understood full well what she meant. "It would be a shame if it was suddenly discovered that you had contracted some rare disease in the heathen land you came from. A disease that affects the brain and leaves it addled." She smiled a sickeningly sweet smile. "You do understand, don't you, dear?"

Loedicia stared at her dumbfounded. "You'd have me committed to one of those horrible places?" she gasped. "You're insane!"

Agatha shook her head. "On the contrary, my dear. It is you who are insane. At least that's what your uncle and I will attest to, unless you stop this foolishness."

Loedicia looked at her uncle, her face white. "You'd be a party to this?" she asked, incredulous.

He harrumphed and looked away toward the fireplace, unable to face her. He put his hands behind his back and walked away, to avoid seeing the pain in her eyes. "You don't seem to understand, Loedicia," he said, his back still to her. "Lord Varrick has already spoken to General Gage, and he and Lord Snow have agreed to give the commissions to me." He finally turned to face her. "If you don't marry Lord Varrick, they'll back out, and I can't afford a setback. I need those commissions."

"You'd put money above my happiness?"

He gestured helplessly. "Happiness? Don't be fanciful, child. Marriages have been arranged for centuries." He walked back to the bed. "Your aunt and I have talked the whole matter over and there's no way you can change our minds, so you might as well be resigned to becoming Lord Varrick's wife."

Anger and frustration were apparent on Loedicia's face as she glanced first at one, then the other. They were serious. Dead serious. The whole thing was like a nightmare. Things like this just didn't happen . . . but it was happening. Her mother's own brother . . .

She bit her lip and turned over in bed, pulling the covers up to her chin, burying her face in the pillow.

"We'll give you until morning," offered Aunt Agatha. "I'll leave the door unlocked, and if you're not at the breakfast table tomorrow, we'll know what course you've chosen." She put the key to Loedicia's door on the mantel, then turned back toward the bed where Loedicia still had her face buried in the pillow. "And don't think of running away, my dear," she warned. "You'd be picked up before you got out of the city."

After they left the room, Loedicia lay still for a long time with her face in the pillow. Then slowly she turned over and stared up at the lace canopy above her. Tears rolled down the side of her cheeks onto the pillow. What was she to do? She shivered as she thought of Lord Varrick with his lust-filled eyes. She wouldn't marry him . . . but what choice did she have?

It wasn't fair! She threw the covers off furiously and jumped out of bed. For a moment she stood in the middle of the room, simmering, anger turning her lips white. There had to be a way. She walked to the window and stared out. Then she opened the window, letting in the cool night air, smelling the night as it surrounded her. Oh, God! There had to be a way!

Suddenly, as she stared at the top of the back porch roof only a foot beneath her window, tracing its outline in the moonlight, an idea began to form, and she smiled. It would work . . . it had to work, because there was no way under heaven that she would ever marry Lord Varrick.

The next morning she sat at the breakfast table, eating

sparingly, a sullen look on her face. She couldn't look too pleased or they might become suspicious.

Agatha hesitated as she stood in the doorway and watched Loedicia. She had expected to see her red-eyed and hostile, with her clothes thrown on haphazardly as if in defiance of what she was being forced to do, but instead, she looked beautiful. Her hair, pulled up on either side, cascaded halfway down her back onto the deep green velvet of her dress, and the blush on her cheeks enhanced her sullen violet eyes and pouting mouth, the only visible signs of her hostility.

Agatha felt a pang of jealousy as she thought of Lord Varrick wanting this inexperienced young girl, but she brushed it aside quickly as she approached the table. "Well, I see you've come to your senses."

"You gave me little choice," Loedicia countered as Agatha sat down.

"I'll send a note to Lord Varrick to let him know that your brief illness is over," Agatha said, smiling. "I'm sure he'll want to come calling."

Loedicia frowned but said nothing.

"You don't mind?"

"Why should I mind," answered Loedicia. "It wouldn't do me a bit of good if I did, would it?"

"Now you're being sensible. And I can promise you that once you get to know Kendall Varrick, you'll laugh at how foolish you've been."

Loedicia eyed her skeptically. "I doubt that!"

"So young and you know all about love I suppose."

"I know that what Lord Varrick feels for me is not love," she replied. "I could put another word to it."

Agatha's eyes narrowed. "The point is he wants you, that's all that counts."

"So I've found out," Loedicia replied as she finished eating. "Now that I've accepted my fate, what happens next?"

Agatha stared at her, then laughed cynically. "You are a paradox, Loedicia," she said as she watched the girl rise and push back her chair. "One minute swearing you'll never marry the man, the next almost anxious to get it over."

"When a man's condemned to hang, why prolong the agony," she retaliated and left the room. Agatha stared after her, wondering just how Kendall Varrick thought he was going to tame this wildcat he had set his heart on marrying, and she almost laughed out loud.

Rain beat against the window in a solid sheet, driven by a cold wind that bent the trees. Loedicia stood in her room, lit only by the flickering flames from the fireplace, and stared at the rain, listening to the drumming tattoo it made against the glass and the sound of the wind as it howled past the corner of the house. Raising her arms, she lifted her long, dark hair from the back of her neck, letting it fall slowly through her fingers. If only the rain would stop.

The clock in the hall struck twelve, and she shivered. Turning, she crossed the room and dropped to the floor in front of the fireplace. She had to get away! She had to!

The cold seemed to penetrate every nerve in her body, and shutting her eyes, she leaned toward the fire. Its warmth reminded her of the sun in Calcutta when she had sat on the veranda and watched her father's troops parade. She could almost smell the horses and hear the shouts of command as the men marched past in review, their heads held high, eyes right.

She stared into the fire. Lord Varrick had come courting almost every day for the past few weeks, and now the wedding was only three days away. Her time was running short. The trousseau was ready, all plans made. She cringed as she remembered his parting words of endearment when he had left earlier that night. He hadn't touched her before, but tonight, made bold by the wine Uncle Thaddeus had given him and left alone with her at the door, he had drawn her into his arms and kissed her, a kiss she hated. She wiped her mouth as if to erase the kiss from her memory.

She stood up quickly and walked back to the window. She had been sitting in front of the fireplace reminiscing

longer than she had meant to. The worst of the rain had
let up and was now a hard drizzle, and the wind had died
down considerably. She took a deep breath as the clock in
the hall struck two, then she walked over to the dresser,
opened a drawer, and took out a small, neatly tied
bundle. Rain or no rain, she could wait no longer.

She opened the window as quietly as possible and
slipped out onto the roof of the back porch, feeling the
rain as it penetrated her clothes. The rain was cold, and
the driving wind made it seem even colder. Moving with
the bundle in her hand was awkward, and the rain made
the roof slippery so that she had to make most of her
descent on her knees. She almost slipped off the edge of
the roof as she tried to find the pillar that held it up.
Once found, she wrapped her legs around it, swung all
the way over the side, and shinnied down.

Her clothes were plastered against her, her hair soaked,
as she reached the ground, ran across the yard, and
slipped into the old shed in the back yard. The shed was
used by the hired man as a shop. It was where he fixed
furniture and took care of all the small repairs about the
house. He had been a joiner by trade and still loved to
work with wood.

The shed was redolent of pine, mahogany, and
beeswax, and at the moment it smelled very strongly of
black walnut as well. It was the black walnut that she had
been counting on. The hired man made his own walnut
stain, and there was always a tub with walnuts floating in
it in a corner of the shed.

She had planned everything carefully. A few days earlier she had stolen some boy's clothes from a clothes line
a few doors down the street and had hidden them in her
room along with a pair of scissors from a sewing basket in
the house.

The shed was pitch dark, and she knew she would have
to work mostly by touch, but there was no alternative.
She set the bundle on the workbench amid assorted pieces
of furniture and began to undress hurriedly. The weather
was cold for the end of May, and she began to shake so

badly she could barely unfasten the hooks at the back of her dress.

Rain still drizzled outside, and she prayed it would stop. Her teeth began to chatter as she slipped out of her bloomers and chemise and stood naked in the small shed. She wasn't about to give in even if she caught a fever.

She spread her petticoat out on the dirt floor, then picked up the scissors. Her long hair was hanging in tendrils about her face, sopping wet. She sighed; the thought of what she was about to do almost brought tears to her eyes.

"Well, there's no choice," she sighed to herself in a whisper, and began cutting.

Ten minutes later a pile of black, curly hair lay nestled in the center of her petticoat as she reached up to feel the shaggy mass on her head. It wasn't too bad a job—below the ears and above the collar. Being wet, it had already started to form ringlets about her face as she pushed it back.

She dropped the scissors in the center of the pile of hair, picked up her chemise, and walked gingerly over to the tub of soaking walnuts, which she could barely see. If only she had a light, but she didn't dare.

Using her chemise as a rag she dipped it into the walnut stain and began washing herself all over, holding the rag tightly against her skin. It took almost an hour to make sure the liquid had done its job well. She even ran it along the part in her hair and around her ears. A mirror would have helped. The liquid burned and made her skin tingle at first, but after a while, the burning let up.

She walked back to her petticoat and dropped the stained, wet chemise in the center of the pile of hair. Using her dress as a towel, she blotted herself dry all over, then began dressing in the boy's clothes.

They had belonged to a thirteen-year-old boy down the street; the pants were a bit big on her slim hips, but they would do. She started to put on the shirt, then stared down at herself. Even in the dark there was no hiding the fact that she was a bit too well endowed. Her breasts were full, the nipples high and firm, and she stopped, wondering what to do.

Then she remembered the dress, and she reached down where she had thrown it and ripped a large, long strip from the skirt. Making a binder she wrapped it around her chest as tightly as she could without being uncomfortable. It flattened her breasts enough so that when she put the shirt on, buttoned to the collar, with the jacket over it, her chest looked almost flat. Since both jacket and shirt were loose, she should be able to get away with it.

Her only problem now was shoes. She had forgotten socks, and the only shoes she had were her own, which had silver buckles and heels. Her feet were frozen, but it made no difference, she would have to go barefoot.

She dropped her shoes and several other bits of clothing into the center of the petticoat with the hair, then stood looking about, trying to see in the dark. She needed something heavy. She remembered a small anvil at the back of the workbench and reached for it among the debris. It was just what she needed. She pulled it out, walked over, and dropped it in the center of the petticoat, then wrapped the whole bundle up, tying it with the string she had used to hold the boy's clothes together. It made a neat, heavy bundle.

This done, she went back to the bench, got down on her knees, and reached back for an old crock tucked against the wall behind some wood. Removing the board that lay across the top, she reached inside and pulled out two hunks of bread and a large piece of cheese, stuffing them into the pockets of her jacket.

She stood for a minute taking inventory, making sure everything was picked up. Then, satisfied she had left nothing behind, she picked up the bundle and headed for the door. It was still raining as she opened the door cautiously and stepped out into the dark night. She felt the oozing mud squish between the toes of her cold, bare feet, making her even colder. She hesitated for a moment, then headed for the front gate and out onto the dark street.

# 3

Everyone in the tavern was asleep except for one man. He bent his gray head low as he ascended the steps, water dripping from his coat and hat. He shuffled along with an easy gait, the two wooden buckets, one in each hand, swinging close to the floor with their burden of rags. With a sigh, he opened a door at the top of the stairs and moved slowly inside, then shut the door quickly.

As he straightened up and leaned against the closed door, the slow, lazy movements were replaced by an attitude of alertness as he listened for any sounds. Nothing. He walked briskly but quietly to the far side of the room, his movements fast and sure, no longer the tired old man who had dragged up the steps.

After removing his coat and hat and setting them and the buckets down on the bed, he walked over and began washing his hair in a basin of water he had set out earlier. The powder that had made it look gray washed off easily, revealing a shock of blond hair as gold as dandelions on a hillside in the summer sun. He rinsed his hair, wiping soap from his eyes, and he began to wash his face. As he did so, the dark lines of dissipation disappeared quickly as the makeup washed off, revealing a beautiful bronze skin turned copper from the sun; the eyes that stared back at him from the cracked mirror over the washstand were sky blue.

He was glad he had left the candles burning in the room before he had gone out earlier so that he hadn't had to stumble about in the dark. Thank God it had almost stopped raining. That had been a help. There was a slow fire going in the fireplace, and he stripped down next to it, feeling its heat on his buttocks as it began to warm him. There was no time to lose, however: he walked over, and reaching under the bed, pulled out a large black bag. He opened it and took out a black suit, white shirt, and hat. Within minutes he was completely dressed, the clothes he had on before crumpled at his feet where he had piled them.

He made sure the white collar was turned around straight, then leaned over and threw the rags from the top of the buckets into the fireplace. He reached into the bottom of the buckets and hefted two bags, one from each bucket, shaking them and listening to the jingle. They were heavy all right. Almost too heavy. Filled with enough Spanish silver dollars to pay off half the British Army. He grinned as he heard a light tapping on the door.

He walked over and opened it cautiously; a dark-haired man slipped inside.

"Made it," the newcomer whispered as he set an identical black bag on the floor beside the first one.

"Anybody see you?"

The man grunted. "Not a soul."

"Good."

The newcomer was also dressed like a man of the cloth. Together they worked hurriedly, stuffing a sack of coins in each black bag and putting some clothes on top, dividing the clothes between them.

"Ready?" asked the younger of the men as they secured the locks on the bags.

"Ready," the other replied. They checked to make sure nothing was left behind, then slipped from the room, down the stairs, and out the door as the voice of the town crier sounded in the distance: "Four o'clock, and all's well. . . ."

Loedicia huddled crouching in the dark shadows of some packing boxes, rubbing her bare feet, which still hurt from the cold. If she could only have found a pair of boy's shoes. She was soaked to the skin. She let go of her feet, and reaching up, grabbed the stocking cap from her head, wringing the water from it, then pulled it back over her crowning mass of dark, wet curls.

She felt ridiculous, but it had to work. Her bundle of

clothes with the anvil inside already lay at the bottom of the harbor. She didn't even resemble a girl anymore, let alone Lady Loedicia. She breathed a sigh, then shivered, watching her breath as it caught, misting in the cold morning air.

She stared at the ships tied up at the wharf. Most of them were British men-of-war, but one, *The Golden Lady,* was sailing this morning at dawn, and she had to sail with it. The blockade of Boston Harbor that Governor Gage had ordered for June first, the very day she was to have been married, was just two days away, and she had no intention of waiting until the last minute.

She straightened a bit and peeked from behind the boxes, squinting her violet eyes in the semidarkness of the fading night. Whoever would have thought when she left India a few short months ago that she would come to this. She stared at *The Golden Lady,* contemplating. There was no question of swimming out, climbing aboard, and stowing away because she couldn't swim, but maybe she could sign on as a cabin boy. But what if they wouldn't take her? After all, she was rather short and puny for a boy. Maybe they'd think she couldn't do the work—and maybe she couldn't. Maybe they wouldn't want a black boy; she rubbed the back of her hand, staring at the dark brown hue of the walnut stain. Maybe they already had a cabin boy and didn't need another. Her heart sank. She had to get away. She had to!

She glanced up and held her breath, stiffening back against the boxes as the sound of horses' hooves echoed on the morning air, mingling with the shouts of the men loading cargo. She pushed wet ringlets from in front of her eyes, staring as a carriage turned the corner, raced down the street, and pulled up a few feet away from a sailor who stood guarding the gangplank.

The horses pawed and snorted friskily, splashing water on the cobblestones as two men in black emerged, paid the driver, then watched as he drove off. Both men were preachers, their straight white collars visible as they turned toward the ship, and each one carried a large black bag. They were so far away that she could barely hear the conversation as they spoke to the man at the gangplank, but she strained her ears, listening intently.

"Reverend Wainscoat and his assistant, the Reverend Burlington, sir," one of the men said, his voice low and quite pleasant. "We should have a cabin reserved."

The seaman checked his passenger list, then nodded. "Below quarterdeck, first cabin on the left," he said, and as both men walked slowly up the gangplank, an idea struck Loedicia. She frowned. It was a chance, a dangerous one, but she would have to take it. Time was running out and there was no turning back now even if she wanted to, which she didn't. She would rather die first. She rubbed her feet, trying to get some feeling into them, without much success. She still had a while to wait.

Day was just breaking and the last of the cargo was being loaded aboard when the sailor guarding the gangplank turned his back and Loedicia made her move. She slipped quietly out of the shadows, hesitated a moment, but only for a moment, then ran up to the man, trying to sound breathless as if she had been running. He turned at her approach, frowning as she spoke.

"Please, your kindness," she said in stilted, broken English trying to deepen her voice to sound more like a boy. "I have a message for the two reverends who sail on your ship. I am pleased to take it to them, sahib?"

The sailor eyed her warily, squinting one eye. "I'll see they gets it, lad," he said and reached out his hand, but she shook her head vigorously as she clutched a piece of paper in her fist. It was just a slip from one of the packing boxes she had been hiding behind, but she treated it as if it were gold.

"Oh no, but no, sire," she protested, her eyes wide. "His Grace the Bishop said I must give it into the Reverend Wainscoat's own hand. I cannot do less," and she finished her sentence with a protest in Hindi, a language she had spoken fluently all her life.

This was enough to convince him. "All right, lad, but mind you get off afore we sail. And make it quick. It's the first cabin ter yer left 'neath the quarterdeck." She bowed, thanking him in English and Hindi as she backed partway up the gangplank.

She had it all thought out. Once she talked to them and had a chance to play on their sympathy it shouldn't be too hard to convince them. After all, what good Christian preacher would deny helping a poor, homeless, mistreated orphan boy far from his native land. Then when they made the first port, she would elude them and get lost in the crowd. It had to work. She would make it work, but first she had to hide someplace until the time was right.

As her feet hit the deck she glanced about quickly and spotted the two preachers standing at the railing in the bow of the ship, their bags at their feet. Evidently they wanted to watch the departure. Well, fine; she headed for their cabin, her brain working rapidly. She would hide there until they were out to sea, then they would have to help her.

The cabin was small and dark with two built-in bunks at one end behind a pair of drapes and a built-in bench against the outside wall with cushions on it for comfort. There was a table with two chairs fastened securely to the floor, but other than that the cabin was bare. This was definitely a cargo ship and carried few passengers, but it would serve the purpose. At least she was out of the wind and cold. Now to hide. She pulled back the drapes and popped into the top bunk happy to discover warm blankets, a pillow, and a feather mattress. She burrowed down and pulled the blankets up, feeling their warmth against her half-frozen feet; she let the warmth start to penetrate her whole body, and suddenly tears glistened in her eyes as she thought of the torturous weeks she had been through.

Well, she wouldn't have to marry Lord Varrick now, but she did have one regret. Roth Chapman. The day after her forthcoming marriage to Lord Varrick had been announced in the newspapers Roth had stopped by for a visit. To congratulate her, he said, and wish her well, and also to let her know he was being promoted, but she knew that wasn't the real reason. It was to say good-bye, and she didn't want to say good-bye.

She wished she could have told him the truth—that she didn't intend to marry Lord Varrick, that she planned to run away, that she wasn't going to marry anyone. But she couldn't. Aunt Agatha had stayed at her side during his entire visit, watching her every move, and all she could do was force a weak, nervous smile to her lips and accept his congratulations.

Later as he kissed her hand at the front door, his troubled eyes looking down at her, tears filled her eyes. He was the only real friend she had found in the short time she had been in Boston, and now she was losing him and there was nothing she could do. Nothing!

He tried to smile as he stood on the top step still holding her hand, his eyes compelling. "Good-bye," he whispered huskily and squeezed her fingers, then dropped her hand reluctantly. "Until we meet again," and he lifted his head high and sighed, turning away from her. The tears spilled over onto her cheeks, running slowly down them, and she watched helplessly as he walked away, out of the yard and out of her life.

She felt empty inside now as she settled deep in the covers thinking of Roth. The same kind of emptiness she had felt when her father died, worse because now she was more alone than ever. She would have to forget, to wash away the unhappy memories of the past few months. She forced herself to dwell on what lay ahead, of what she would tell the two preachers when they returned.

She pulled the blanket up tighter under her chin; it felt wonderful against her half-frozen feet, and she snuggled down ever farther as the warmth began to penetrate her body. Her eyelids grew heavier and heavier, and the last she remembered was hearing the waves pounding against the side of the ship and the shouts of the men above deck as they finished loading the cargo. Then, exhausted from the strain of the past few weeks, and drowsy after being up all night, she relaxed and fell into a deep sleep.

Up on deck, the two clergymen watched the wharf, their eyes moving slowly from one end to the other as if casually watching the loading, but in reality neither pair of eyes missed a thing. They didn't talk much, just stood watching until the last box was loaded, the gangplank pulled up, and the anchor hoisted, then they looked at each other and smiled knowingly as the ship took sail and headed out of the harbor. The first rays of the gray, clouded sun creeping up over the horizon silhouetted His Majesty's fleet as it continued to form the blockade, but *The Golden Lady* slid quietly past, one of the last ships to leave Boston Harbor before the blockade was complete.

Loedicia had no idea how long she'd slept, but she vaguely heard voices as she opened her eyes and snuggled under the covers. For a minute she had to get her bearings and she'd forgotten where she was. As she came fully awake she listened closely to the voices and realized the only thing separating her from the men was the curtain.

She recognized one voice as that of the man who'd called himself Reverend Wainscoat. His voice was deep and resonant, one she couldn't easily forget.

"Well, we did it," he was saying as she snuggled deeper into the covers. "I'd love to see his face when he shows up empty-handed."

"They'll have every road out of Boston watched," answered the other man. "I have to give you credit, Quinn," he said softly, "I never thought you'd get away with it."

"Damn fools!" he exclaimed, and she suspected he was grinning. "They'll be looking for a wizened-up old man while I sail leisurely down the coast with all their money."

"Let's hope your dear cousin doesn't get wise or we may find a reception committee waiting for us at the next port."

"I changed my mind about stopping in New York," offered the one named Quinn. "This ship's bypassing New York and setting a load down in Jersey. They'll have to go some to travel that far ahead of us."

"I hope you're right."

"Cheer up, Burly," said Quinn. "We just stole a fortune in silver from under the nose of the British Army and they won't suspect a thing for two days. Not until they try to pay their men."

"Then all hell's gonna break loose."

Quinn laughed. "God damn, Burly. I'd love to see his face. It'd be worth getting hung for."

The other man muttered, "Speak for yourself."

She heard the man named Quinn slap the other on the back. "Come on, Burly." His voice was more serious. "We've got a two-day start and as I said, they'll be looking for one bent-over old man, not two preachers. Now, what's say we get some sleep. Our night's work made me a bit weary." Loedicia cuddled deeper in the covers, cringing as she saw the drapes start to move and a pair of hands begin to pull them back.

She closed her eyes tightly, holding the covers for dear life, waiting for the explosion, but instead there was a dead silence as the two men stood staring at the small head barely showing above the covers.

"What the. . .?" blurted Quinn softly, and Loedicia popped her eyes open. She looked up from the covers into the most beautiful pair of blue eyes she'd ever seen, with thick, dark lashes. She'd never before seen a man with such eyes.

"What are you doing here?" he asked, a frown settling on his tanned face. His shirt was open halfway down the front, revealing a soft mass of curly hair on his chest, and the collar he'd worn earlier was thrown on the bench with his coat and hat. A thick shock of blond hair, the color of dandelions faded in the summer sun, curled lazily above those blue eyes as she stared up at him.

She was unable to utter a sound as she looked behind him to the other man. They were both about six feet tall; the older man was stockily built with massive shoulders and a thick waist but not a pound of fat on him. Black curly stubble clung to his cheeks and chin and above his mouth, and his dark, piercing eyes stared at her under bushy brows.

He too had discarded his coat and collar and unbuttoned his shirt and his torso was completely covered with hair. He reminded her of an animal and her heart started pounding. He looked frightening.

"I'm waiting," said Quinn, and his eyes narrowed as he stared at her. "How the devil did you get here?"

She had no way of turning back now and she could tell by the tossing of the ship that they had cleared the harbor and were out to sea.

Her first words were in Hindi, then she lapsed into a stilted English. "Please, sires . . . I will be no trouble!" She scooted up on the bunk and sat cross-legged, staring at them wide-eyed. "You will help, yes?"

Quinn stared at the slightly built lad with the dark skin and big violet eyes. He couldn't be much more than thirteen or fourteen and he looked scared half to death.

"What's that language?" he asked. "It's not any Indian dialect I've ever heard."

She smiled and nodded. "I am from India, sahib," she answered softly, trying to sound as masculine as possible. "But I was raised by missionaries, so I speak English too good."

"You speak English terrible," countered the one with the beautiful eyes, and he continued to stare at her menacingly. "But you didn't answer my question. How did you get here?"

Her face reddened under the walnut stain as both men stared at her. She could tell they were angry. "I see you get on the ship. I tell the man I have a message from the bishop, so he let me come."

Quinn's frown deepened. "Why?" he asked.

"Why, sahib?" she asked hesitantly.

"Yes. Why did you say you had a message for us?"

She hung her head. "Because I run away."

"From where?"

She flashed a big smile and began to jabber in Hindi.

"In English," he demanded curtly, and she nodded.

"I was bought in India by a big man to wait on a lady. The lady die on the ship when we come across the water. The big man he sell me to a mean man. He beat me. I will not stay!"

"Let's see now . . . you were bought in India?" She nodded. "A slave?" She nodded. "They brought you to America, but the lady you were to serve died on the way, right?" She nodded. "Your new master beat you, so you ran away . . . right so far?"

She nodded, smiling, spouting off another exhortation in Hindi and gesturing with her hands.

"Jesus Christ," the big blond man, Quinn, exclaimed. "You don't speak good English, but at least I can follow it. Will you stop the gibberish."

She quit smiling and frowned.

"I presume you want us to help you," he stated.

She nodded.

He turned and looked at the big man he'd called Burly. "What do you think?"

"I think we turn the lad over to the captain," he answered sternly, and Loedicia sat up straight.

"No!" she shouted stubbornly.

"Why not?" asked Quinn as he grabbed her left wrist with his right hand, making sure she stayed put.

Her eyes narrowed warningly. "If you tell the captain I run away, I tell the captain you steal from the British."

His eyes grew dark and his fingers pressed harder, biting into the flesh on her wrist, and she flinched.

"You'll what?" he asked.

"You stole the silver," she whispered through clenched teeth. "I heard." Suddenly her eyes widened and the blood drained from her face as he slipped his left hand behind his back and brought a knife from its concealment, deftly placing the blade against her throat while still holding her wrist and forcing her arm behind her.

"One slice and you're shark bait," he answered viciously.

"Please!" she pleaded, her voice shaking. "Please!" She used every argument she could think of to keep the knife from doing its work. She could feel the sharp edge against her soft flesh and once it bit too close, making her jump and cry out. Then she lapsed into Hindi, begging him in a mixture of both languages.

"I can help you. You said they would not look for two preachers . . . they would look less for two preachers with a servant boy. I would do anything you ask. Please, yes?" She let her big violet eyes stare up into his, then closed them as she waited for an answer.

"You told them you had a note from the bishop?" he asked.

"Yes," she whispered, her eyes closed.

She felt the knife at her throat ease slightly and opened her eyes.

"It might work at that," he said, and his fingers eased about her wrist, but he still made no move to release her or take the knife away. He turned to his partner. "If you thought two preachers weren't preachers and started investigating, wouldn't you take the word of a sailor who said they had to be preachers because even the bishop knew they were aboard?" he asked.

Burly eyed the lad. It might be just what they needed. Who would suspect two preachers and a servant boy? "We'd have to think of something to tell the captain. Can you keep your mouth shut?" he asked her, and she nodded. "If you don't . . ." His eyes bored into hers as he put pressure on the knife and she began to protest in Hindi, then he released her.

There were tears at the corners of her eyes as she rubbed her wrist, then felt her throat where the knife had caressed it. She'd gotten herself into a real mess this time, but it was better than getting married, especially to Lord Varrick. She'd thought these men were real preachers. She never dreamed they were thieves, and not very friendly ones either, and she glanced over at the one called Quinn.

Now that she wasn't quite so frightened she realized he was really very handsome. His blue eyes were set in a bronzed face and there was almost a classic, genteel look to his features, but at the moment he was still a bit upset as he spoke to his partner.

"We can tell the captain that the bishop insisted we bring the boy to assist us at our new church." He turned to Loedicia. "What's your name?" he asked, and she had it ready for him.

"Dicia, sahib," she answered softly. It was a nickname her father had often used for her.

He grinned, but the grin held a touch of malice. "All right, Dicia, for now we'll help you and you help us, but mind you, one word, just one to anyone, and you're dead. And don't expect to share in the money," he added firmly. "I have its use all planned."

She shook her head. "I don't want money, sahib."

"What about money to pay the captain?" asked Burly. "The lad can't sail for nothing."

"We'll pay his fare and he can work it out," said Quinn. "It'll be nice having someone to wait on us for a change."

Burly grinned, large white teeth showing amid his curly black beard. "The devil take it. I always wanted me own gentleman's gentleman, but I never expected it to be a lad no bigger than me shoulders."

"I just hope he's strong and healthy," said Quinn. "He looks a bit puny to me."

Burly reached out and grabbed her arm, trying to feel the muscle. "Where's your strength, me lad?" he bantered, and she pulled away, sticking her lip out defiantly and telling him off in Hindi.

"Get down," ordered Quinn, and she slid her legs to the side of the bunk and slipped to the floor, standing in her bare feet as he walked over and put his coat and collar back on and picked up his hat.

"Let's go see the captain," he said, and he opened the door, waiting for her.

She walked over to him and he motioned for her to go out the door first, then he followed. As they reached the top deck Loedicia saw that the day had not cleared off well. The sky was almost white and the air exceptionally cool. Huge whitecapped waves tossed the ship defiantly and there seemed to be a dullness to everything without the sunshine, as if a veil of gray had been painted across the world.

They headed for the mizzenmast and found the captain by the wheel, barking orders to the crew. He was a short man, compared to Quinn. About five seven or eight, a bit paunchy, with a full set of whiskers and dark, deep-set eyes that looked watery and bloodshot most of the time.

"What can I do for ye, Reverend?" he asked as Quinn stood waiting.

Quinn put his hand on Loedicia's shoulder as he spoke. "Seems I'll have to pay you another fare," he answered in a gentle voice oozing piety. "The bishop asked if we'd take the lad along to help and I'm afraid one doesn't refuse his superiors, Captain."

The captain eyed Loedicia skeptically. "Sort of measly, ain't he?"

"We'll toughen him up," answered Quinn. "A little hard work and a lot of prayers and the lad'll grow up straight."

"Aye," agreed the captain, and Quinn reached in his pocket, pulling out some coins, and paid the fare.

"See the lad doesn't get in the way," warned the captain, then turned and started toward the forward deck to check the rigging.

"You'd better stay below most of the way," offered Quinn as they headed back toward the quarterdeck. "In fact, I'd feel safer with you below." This was all right with Loedicia because the fewer people who saw her, the better.

It started raining again in the late afternoon and the sea became even rougher, giving her stomach a few hours of trouble before she managed to find her sea legs. Ordinarily no ship would have sailed with the threat of strong winds, but the captain was afraid if he hadn't left that morning the blockade would become impenetrable. Already they were stopping all ships from entering the harbor.

Loedicia spent a restless night on the seat at the side of the cabin while the men relaxed peacefully in the bunks. Twice she slid off, being used to a large bed, but managed to scramble back on without waking them. She talked as little as possible on the whole trip, going on deck only occasionally for a breath of fresh air.

She had three duties on board ship: bringing water to them each morning for washing, seeing that their food was brought from the galley, and emptying the slop jar. The last mortified her. Most of the time she made excuses and went on deck when she realized one of the men had to use it, but a few times she was caught, unable to flee, and she rolled over on the bench with her back to them, pretending to sleep.

She always made sure they were both up on deck when it was her turn. The situation was not only embarrassing but humiliating. But she didn't dare let on that there was anything unusual about it.

It was the second day when Quinn mentioned her feet. At first when he looked at them with that queer look on his face she thought he was going to make some remark about how dirty they were because she'd purposely avoided washing, afraid she'd wash off some of the walnut stain, but instead he asked, "Didn't they give you shoes, Dicia?"

She had stepped into the cabin from a walk on deck and her feet were exceptionally cold.

"I was, as you say . . . slipping out not to wake anyone and I dropped them."

He frowned. "Aren't your feet cold?"

"They are numb, sahib, but I will cover them with the pillow from the bench for a while to warm them," she said, and walked to the bench where she slept.

"Wait," he said. He'd been sitting at the table and stood up, walking over to one of the bags that held the money. He opened it, reached inside, and took out the leather weskit he'd worn when he'd dressed as an old man. It was soft doeskin, a bit worn and dirty, but sturdy.

Removing his knife from its sheath at the back of his pants, he began cutting as he talked. "I'm pretty handy at this sort of thing. Besides, I shiver every time I look at your bare feet. Come here."

She walked over to stand beside him and he put the large piece of leather he'd cut on the floor. "Put your foot down," he continued, "to see if it fits."

She set her foot on the scrap of leather and he measured, then she stepped back and sat in the other chair, watching him shape the leather.

His hands worked deftly and in less than an hour she was tieing the moccasins on her feet.

"I wouldn't advise you to wear those on deck, though,

lad," cautioned Burly from the bunk where he'd been resting.

"Oh?"

Quinn glanced over at him.

"You're supposed to be a man of the church, Reverend Wainscoat," he reminded him. "No preacher'd know how to make a pair of Indian moccasins."

"The days will be warmer," she stated. "I will wear them only in the cabin until I leave the ship. I wish to cause no trouble, sahib."

"You're a strange one," mused Quinn. "Where'd you live in India?"

"Calcutta."

"No brothers or sisters?"

"I was an orphan, sire."

"Probably half starved too," he added. "I've seen them huddled together, children without parents, trying to live by their wits."

"You've been there?" she asked, surprised.

"A long time ago. The ship I was on stopped in Calcutta for a time and I met an old friend of my father's. Wanted me to join his regiment, but I had my heart set on coming to the colonies."

She stared at him apprehensively as he continued.

"Besides, who wants to live in that godforsaken land. I'd go crazy."

She shook her head. "Oh, no, sahib. It's a beautiful land. The days are hot, nights are cool with the scent of jasmine and hibiscus." She closed her eyes, remembering.

"And the constant smell of dung on the streets from those stupid cows," he added sarcastically. "And the dirty monkeys chattering incessantly all day long. I never saw such a place to get on one's nerves."

She opened her eyes and stared at him, almost forgetting for a moment everything but her love for the land where she was raised.

"You did not truly see India," she answered softly. "She is passionate and warm. Did you ever ride on the desert at night among the moon-shadowed mountains of sand or sit quietly in the jungle and listen to the songs of

the birds in the mangrove trees or walk among the ruins
of some ancient temple, listening to the past?"

"Have you?" he asked, surprised.

She blushed under the walnut stain. "I have done many
things, sahib," she answered softly, then thanked him for
the moccasins and returned to sit on her bench as he
stared at her, frowning, and she realized she'd almost said
too much. It was hard trying to act an age she'd already
outgrown and doubly hard trying to act like a boy. Boys
weren't ordinarily sensitive to the effects of moonlight or
the trill of songbirds. She'd have to watch herself more
closely from now on.

# 4

They sailed down the coast, past Cape Cod and through
the islands of Nantucket Sound, but kept their distance
from the shore, watching the lights as they passed Long
Island. After the first stormy day the rest of the trip went
well, with sunny skies and brisk breezes. They passed two
other ships, both British men-of-war on their way to the
blockade, but other than that the journey was without incident.

On the fourth day they passed the lighthouse at Sandy
Hook and headed for the Jersey coast. Loedicia expected
to see another city like Boston and was surprised to see,
not a city, but a small wharf and only a few scattered
buildings.

"This is Monmouth?" she asked as they stood at the
rail, waiting for the ship to drop anchor and tie up.

"This is the landing," answered Quinn. "Port Monmouth is farther inland a mile or so." He was glad there
was a wharf and they didn't have to go ashore in a long-
boat. That's why he'd picked Monmouth. Anyone hefting
their bags around would know there was more in them

than a few clothes and he couldn't take the chance. This
way they'd carry their own bags from the ship.

As they walked down the gangplank Loedicia looked
cautiously about, wondering how far the news of their escape had traveled. Apparently no one here knew one
tittle, because they passed among the crowd unmolested.
Loedicia stayed close beside them. She would like to
leave, but they'd made it clear to her that she knew far
too much for them to let her out of their sight.

They started to walk toward town when an old man
with a wagon offered them a ride, seeing they were
preachers. But there was no room for Loedicia on the
seat, so she sat atop the boxes in the back of the wagon.

As soon as they were out of sight of the ship she
slipped the moccasins from her pocket and put them on.
Here, away from the ship, there was no way for anyone to
know she hadn't always had them and there'd be no questions asked.

It was so good to get out in the fresh air and away
from the confines of the cabin, knowing the ground was
under her and not water. She gazed around, taking everything in. The hills were covered with freshly greened trees
and there were still a few flowering shrubs, although the
lilac had faded and died and honeysuckle had yet to
bloom. Wild roses completely covered one hillside, and as
the wagon passed she breathed in their sweet fragrance,
which reminded her of the sachets in Aunt Agatha's side-
board drawers.

She stared at the dusty road behind them, wondering
what was going on back in Boston. Uncle Thaddeus must
be furious at what she'd done. The commissions would be
lost to him and if the blockade lasted any length of time
his finances could be sorely depleted. Even if he used
other ports he'd never be able to make up the revenue
he'd lose, but she didn't care. Not after what he'd tried to
do to her. It would serve them right. She hoped they'd
both suffer for what they'd done.

Aunt Agatha no doubt was mortified and she hoped
Lord Varrick would be so red-faced and humiliated he'd
put his tail between his legs and head back to the woods.

The thought of how embarrassed he must have been when the wedding was called off made her smile wickedly. The guests would have to be notified, the minister, her attendants. And what explanation had he given? Boston society had been talking about the wedding as the biggest social event of the season.

He'd be furious and he was so sure of himself and arrogant. Well, just let him find her now if he could. She'd lose herself in the colonies as soon as she could get away from Quinn and Burly.

She glanced behind her at the seat where the old man and her two cohorts were sitting. Burly had frightened her at first, not only with his appearance but with his gruff manner, but he really wasn't too bad a sort. His talk was rough and coarse, but he had a samaritan attitude toward people, which had been displayed one day on board ship.

She'd gone up for some fresh air in time to catch sight of one of His Majesty's ships as it sailed by at close range. The captain had a cabin boy some fifteen years of age. A husky, broad-faced lad with thick lips, a squashed nose, and a foul temper. Since the only person on board ship smaller than himself whom he could bully was Loedicia, he'd taken to taunting her.

This morning was no exception. She was standing near the foremast, looking out toward the jib boom as the man-of-war approached, marveling at the full sail caught in the gold of the morning sun.

"Hey, scrud," the cabin boy addressed her as he walked up and leaned on the foremast.

Her eyes were drawn from the ship and she glanced his way quickly, then back to the other ship.

Her silence served only to infuriate him. He straightened up and grabbed her arm, whirling her to face him.

"When I talks to you, you listen, understand, scrud?" he exclaimed, and Loedicia stared at him, her eyes narrowing, then called him a few choice names in Hindi, which made him even angrier because he couldn't understand what she was saying.

"You're about the puniest critter I ever did see," he snarled, twisting her arm as she tried to push against his

hand. "I s'pose them preachers knows what they's doin'."
Then his eyes lit up. "Hey, now . . . I never did think of
that b'fore," he exclaimed, grinning and lowering his voice
menacingly. "I hear tell some preachers ain't as God-fear-
ing as they looks. I knowed one once what liked young
fellas like you. Better'n any stupid gal, he said. Showed
me his private room, he did." His fingers bit into her arm
harder. "That why they got you with 'em, scrud?" he
asked. " 'Cause if it is, I just might get some of that stuff
myself. Ain't no females on board and I'm learnin' to like
it."

Loedicia's heart was pounding as she understood what
he meant. She'd never come up against this before. He
was asking her and he knew she was a boy . . . at least
he thought she was. The thought sickened her, but she
couldn't let him know she was trembling inside.

"Let go of my arm," she whispered through clenched
teeth, but he held it all the tighter and began to twist it
behind her back, forcing her to her knees as Burly
stepped out of the shadow of one of the sails.

"Something bothering you, Gipper?" he asked as he
stared angrily at the cabin boy, who slowly began relinquishing her arm.

He stammered and backed off. "Nothin' at all, Reverend," he answered. "We was just watchin' the man-o'-
war." He pointed to the ship, which was now in full view,
but Burly never took his eyes from the cabin boy's face.

He took two strides and grabbed the front of the boy's
shirt, lifting him almost a foot off the ground.

"You might as well know, boy," he offered angrily.
"Before I started preachin' I did some fightin' and I can
break you in two with one hand." He motioned with his
head toward Loedicia. "And if I ever see you so much as
talkin' to the lad again, the captain'll be waitin' on you
the rest of the trip. Is that understood?"

The boy nodded as he looked into the fiercest face he'd
ever encountered and he spluttered, "I'm sorry, Reverend,
I ain't even gonna look at him no more. You can have
him all to yourself."

"And that's another thing," snarled Burly. "If I want a

woman I'll take a woman, not no boy. You get that in
your perverted little brain!" Then, as if remembering who
he was supposed to be, he added, "The bishop asked us
to take care of the lad and that's what we intend to do, so
keep your hands and your propositions to yourself." Burly
set him back on deck with a shove that probably shook
his teeth.

Without another word Gipper turned and walked off
hurriedly, trying not to look too obvious as Burly
straightened his clothes.

"That wharf rat. I saw him eyein' you the other day,
but don't you worry, lad. He won't try any of his tricks.
Not anymore."

She'd watched Burly, suddenly realizing there was more
to him than met the eye. A man with fewer principles
would have merely laughed over the situation, but he was
genuinely angry and her face reddened under the stain as
she realized he'd heard the cabin boy's intimate overtures,
and she looked away to watch the British ship glide past
them and lose itself in the distance.

Later, down in the cabin, Burly told Quinn about the
encounter and Quinn decided it was time Loedicia learned
the art of self-defense.

As she rode along on the back of the wagon now, she
glanced at Quinn, his back straight as he sat beside Burly,
then she reached up and touched the side of her face,
which still hurt. All the rest of that afternoon she'd tried
to dodge Quinn's hands as they snaked out at her. He was
a quick fighter, alert and deadly, and he gave no quarter
as he taught her, although she knew he wasn't using his
full strength. But it still hurt and she still was black and blue.

Burly had cautioned him once when Loedicia ended up
on the floor, having ducked a bit too late, but he'd countered, "The only way to teach is by experience and he
can't fight something that isn't there."

She'd learned, all right. Although her blows barely
ruffled Quinn, she knew enough when the lesson was over
to take pretty good care of herself. And she'd learned
something else she'd never known. She glanced back
again at Quinn and smiled to herself as she remembered

how he'd doubled over, cursing her, when she'd accidentally belted him too low and landed her fist in his groin.

Actually it was the blow that put an end to the lessons and she snickered now, remembering, because if the lessons hadn't stopped they'd have learned something too. She'd felt the binder that flattened her breasts begin to slip and as soon as the lesson stopped she found a quiet corner on board ship and fixed it.

It was late afternoon when they rode into Port Monmouth and made their way to the Herald Inn.

"We need two rooms, some decent food, and a hot tub," Quinn told the innkeeper, and they were given all three in that order.

The food, a mutton stew served with black bread and dried apple cobbler, was washed down with a bitter ale Quinn swore tasted as if it had been aged in rotted wood. They made Loedicia drink a mug of milk with her meal, which she hated, then they carried their bags and followed the bondwoman to their rooms.

They left Burly at the door to his room and Quinn grabbed her by the shoulder, ushering her ahead of him to his room. The bondwoman dropped the key in his hand after opening the door, then turned and left.

They were not fancy rooms. Plain wood floors without even a throw rug on the floor, a big double bed with straw ticking, pillows, and a blanket. A washstand with a mirror hanging lopsided over it, one large chest of drawers, a straight-back chair, and a window with a built-in window seat minus the usual cushions.

Loedicia stood in front of him as he shut the door and she eyed the tub of hot water set up in the middle of the room.

"Well," he said as he walked past her and set his bag on the floor beside the bed, "at least the service is good." He walked over and stuck his finger in the water. "And it's hot."

She stood rooted to the spot, staring at the tub of water.

"What's the matter with you?" he asked as he started removing his coat.

She shook her head and walked to the window seat and sat down, curling her legs beneath her. "Nothing," she answered softly.

"Then see if they have any soap and towels in the commode," he ordered. "Just because we've left the ship doesn't mean you can forget you owe us for your passage."

Her eyes snapped his way and she regarded him for a minute, then stood up and walked quickly to the washstand. There were a bar of soap and two large towels, which she brought over and set on the bed.

He'd stripped to his underwear already and she hastily looked away as she started back to the window seat.

"May I go for a walk?" she asked, swallowing hard as she stared toward the window, her back to him. She'd never dreamed something like this could happen and she knew he was completely naked as she heard the water splash behind her.

"Not by yourself. I don't know whether I trust you yet or not," he answered. "Besides, I want my back washed."

This time her face went white under the walnut stain before it turned red. He started whistling as he splashed in the water and her heart sank. If she refused to wash his back he'd probably hit her and want to know why and if she did wash it . . . The thought made her feel strange inside. She'd seen her father without a shirt on and some of the little native boys ran around naked, but to see a grown man in the altogether was something else. Especially such a virile, handsome one.

She sat down again on the window seat and glanced sheepishly toward him, remembering some of the conversations he and Burly had had about women during the voyage. Her ears had burned as they'd expounded on the merits of the feminine anatomy and its varied uses and she wondered if all men talked about women the same when there were no women around. If her promiscuous girlfriend in India hadn't completed her education on the subject of men, her journey from Boston did.

Quinn's voice interrupted her thoughts. "What the devil's the matter with you, Dicia," he called. "I said come wash my back now."

She took a deep breath. There was nothing else she could do, so she slipped from the window seat and walked slowly up to the tub.

He'd soaped up the washcloth and held it out to her and she tried not to look, but it was impossible. Her hand trembled slightly as she took it from him.

Kneeling beside the tub, she reached up gingerly and touched the cloth to his back and suddenly she was very much aware of his masculinity. Of his broad shoulders, slim hips, and flat stomach. He had a physique like those of the Greek gods whose statues she'd seen once when she'd visited Athens with her father.

As she moved the washcloth across the breadth of his shoulders he leaned his head back and sighed contentedly. "Ah, Dicia, you have the gentle hands of a woman." She swallowed hard and began to scrub more vigorously.

"Hey, what's the matter? You don't have to take off the hide!"

"I am not a woman!" she protested. "I am Dicia!"

"All right," he answered. "No need to argue the point."

She finished getting the past four days' grime off his back, then dropped the washcloth from his shoulder and it slid down his chest.

"Thanks," he said, and she started back toward the window seat. "Check the bed, will you," he ordered.

She stopped and looked back at him. "For what?"

"Since when don't they have bugs in India?"

"Bugs?"

"Those nasty little things that like to pester a man when he's trying to get a good night's sleep."

She glanced toward the bed as he continued talking and washing.

"Check along the seams of the mattress and shake it a bit. If they're there, you'll know it."

She shook the mattress vigorously, told him there was no sign of bugs, then set the mattress down, not knowing he'd stood up to leave the tub.

"Hand me the towel," he said, and she reached out, grabbing one of the towels, her back still to him, then turned with the towel outstretched and froze, her eyes glued to his naked body.

He reached out. "Well, hand it here," he demanded.

She took a deep breath, stepped forward a bit, and handed him the towel, staring at him wide-eyed. When he was in the tub the water had covered him sufficiently, but now. . . .

He frowned as he took the towel from her. "Is something the matter with you, Dicia?" he asked as he began to dry off, then stepped from the tub.

"No . . . no." She gulped, then fled to the window seat, turned her back to him, and stared out the window. My God! How strange she felt inside and there was a quickening in her loins she couldn't understand. He'd looked magnificent. His bronzed body dripping with water, every muscle taut and rippling, his hair tousled. She'd never dreamed . . . then she realized he was talking to her.

"I should be back in about an hour," he was saying, "so it won't do you a bit of good to try to leave. I can track a snake over solid rock if I have to, and get yourself a bath while I'm gone. You smell like that goddamn ship."

"Where are you going?" she asked, her back still to him.

"That, young man, is my business," he answered. "Now do your work and help me on with my boots."

She turned toward him gingerly. He was completely dressed now and she sighed with relief as she left the window seat hurriedly and helped him on with his boots.

"And remember to get clean," he said again, and hit her on the rear as she finished slipping on his last boot.

She straightened up, rubbing her rear end as he stood up, bid her good-bye, and left, locking the door behind him.

After he was gone, she walked to the window again, climbed onto the window seat, and looked out. There was a narrow ledge separating both floors and a back porch with a roof she could easily reach, and he'd left the black bag with the money in it. It would be easy to get away even with the door locked. Then she remembered what he'd said about tracking snakes and decided against leaving. At least for now. Besides, they could help her lose herself, that is, if they didn't get caught first.

He'd told her to clean up and she left the window and stood looking at the water in the tub with longing. But what about the walnut stain? It was already beginning to wear away where her clothes rubbed it. How much would wash off? But if she didn't wash he'd know it. He was probably right when he said she smelled. Four days on that dirty ship without so much as washing her face.

She stripped down hurriedly, climbed in the tub, and washed, scrubbing as lightly as possible, but even at that the water turned a faint brown color and she could tell when she was through that she was a shade lighter. Well, she'd have to take that chance.

When she was finished, she dressed quickly, then sat on the window seat to wait. There wasn't much of a view here, only a back alley and some houses, but her waiting was shortened when he got back about fifteen minutes earlier than expected and evening shadows were beginning to darken the room.

He lit the candles right away and had her call someone to haul away the tub, then locked the door securely.

"We leave in the morning for Princeton," he said as he walked to the bed. He sat down and called her to pull off his boots. "I managed to get us three horses, so it'll save some of the miles on our feet and we can travel faster."

Loedicia knew very little about the colonies. "Where is this Princeton?" she asked as she set his boots beside the bed.

"It's inland about forty miles or so."

"We have to go there?"

"Burly and I do and as long as you know enough to get us hung, my lad, you'll be going with us." He swung his legs onto the bed and stretched out. "Now blow out the candles and come lay down. We've got a long journey ahead of us."

She stared at his long form stretched out on the bed. Earlier he'd taken a pistol from his black bag and set it beside his pillow. Now he checked it to make sure it was in readiness.

"Well, don't just stand there, do as you're told," he ordered as he set the pistol down. He put his hands under his head to cradle it and sighed. "Shits fire, I don't know what's got into you since we got off that ship," he said nastily. "Is something bothering you?"

She shook her head as she hurried over and blew out the candles, then approached the bed in the dark. She had to crawl across his feet, as he'd instructed her to sleep on the inside, and her knee hit his shinbone and he cursed.

"You could be a bit careful," he said. "Now settle down." She moved as close to the wall as she could, then he reached down and pulled the blanket up over them because the night air was cool.

She huddled under the blanket. Both slept with their clothes on and at least that much was on her side. She was almost afraid he was going to sleep in the raw, as her girlfriend back in India said most men did. She imagined that having all that silver to guard necessitated being prepared at all times because even on board ship both men had slept with their clothes on. Then again, these covers didn't look any too clean.

She could hear him breathing steadily and suddenly smiled to herself, wondering what Lord Varrick would think if he knew his precious Lady Loedicia Aldrich was sleeping with a thief, even if the thief did think she was a boy, and the thought struck her as funny and she went to sleep with a smile on her face, very conscious of the nearness of this man known to her only as Quinn.

# 5

The next morning found them heading out of town before the sun rose. Two preachers dressed in black and a small black servant boy who knew she was a shade lighter this morning and hoped it wouldn't be noticed. The road between Port Monmouth and Princeton was not much of a road. More like a wide trail cut out of the countryside with settlements along the way to relieve the monotony of hills, woods, and fields.

Loedicia enjoyed the ride even though she was not used to straddling a horse. She was proficient in the use of a sidesaddle, but this was different and a bit awkward at first.

She followed behind, letting them lead the way, and it wasn't until they stopped sometime in the afternoon to eat the bread and cheese they'd brought with them that she learned their plans.

Quinn was stretched out beneath a small oak tree resting while Burly finished eating. "I sent word I'd be there by the ninth of June if all went well," he was saying. "There's an inn, the King's Pride. He said he'd go there every night and wait."

"But can he get away? I hear tell Nassau Hall is strict about the students' curfew," added Burly.

"Joseph Wickham could steal out of the best jail His Majesty had if he had a reason, and five hundred pieces of silver should be reason enough."

"But the five hundred isn't his," stated Burly. "He knows that, don't he?"

"He knows the men along the line are waiting for it, yes. Without arms, Burly, we're not a match for anyone, but with a Kentucky rifle and ammunition in the hands of every patriot we can lick the whole British Army if need be and he leaves for home on the twelfth with enough silver to spread along the way."

Loedicia had curled up in the grass, pretending to take a short nap, but was listening to every word. So they weren't just ordinary thieves. They were the kind of men Uncle Thaddeus was always railing against and they were preparing to fight against the crown. According to the conversation as she listened to it, rebels were arming in all the colonies and money was needed to buy arms and ammunition. Also money was needed to send supplies cross-country to Boston to help alleviate the hardships the king's blockade would make on the people of Boston. Food had to be paid for, and what better way then with British silver? Plans for this little venture had been made months in advance and so far things were going well.

"You realize before we reach the Appalachians they'll be onto us, don't you?" stated Burly.

"Maybe," answered Quinn.

"It stands to reason sooner or later they'll discover your hand in this. One description of the preacher on *The Golden Lady* and Lord Varrick's going to have you dead to rights."

Her ears pricked up at the mention of Lord Varrick's name.

"He has to get to Port Monmouth first," answered Quinn. "And I think he'll be busy enough with that wedding of his to delay things awhile. After all, you don't leave a new bride at the altar to go traipsing cross-country, money or no money. He'll send his men and by the time they report back to him we'll be halfway home."

"What if he decided to take his bride with him?"

"From what I hear of Lady Loedicia Aldrich he'll be lucky if he gets her to the altar. Sam Adams said she was a reluctant bride, new to the colonies. One of the servants in her uncle's house is loyal to the cause and she said they locked her in her room for three days when she refused his proposal."

Burly laughed. "At least she's got spirit."

"Married to that pervert, she'll have to have more than spirit," answered Quinn. "I've met some of the women my dear cousin has discarded and I feel sorry for the woman he makes his bride."

Loedicia's heart was pounding. They were talking about her. And what was it Quinn called Lord Varrick? His cousin? What irony.

Quinn stood up, stretching, then kicked her lightly with the toe of his boot. "Come on, Dicia. We're wasting time. We'd better be on our way."

She rolled over, pretending she'd just woke up, and hurried to her horse, anxious to keep her distance from them, as she'd done all day, hoping neither one would notice her lighter complexion.

When night came they tied the horses securely and stretched out on the ground. They'd bought some buns and cold mutton at the last settlement they'd gone through and while they rested, ate a late meal, then settled down for the night.

Loedicia watched as the two men stretched out, unconcerned about lying on the bare ground without even a pillow.

"The ground is hard," she said as she looked at the men, one on each side of her. "And there are crawling things. . . ."

Quinn raised himself on his elbow and glanced over his shoulder at her. "You're bigger than they are, so who's afraid of who?" He laid his head back down, cushioning it with his hands. "For a boy, Dicia, I swear you're worse than an old woman. Now lay down and get some sleep."

She shrugged her shoulders, curled up between the two, and tried to fall asleep, her mind alert to every sound in the dark woods about them, and only the thought that both men slept with pistols close at hand let her finally doze off.

It took them three and a half days to reach Princeton and Loedicia was pleased to see a city of some size emerge out of the countryside. The King's Pride was at the far end of town and they reached it a few hours before sundown on June 9.

The rooms were better here, with a rug on the floor, feather mattress, pictures on the wall, a fireplace, and overstuffed chairs to sit in. The arrangements were as before and when the bags were locked in the rooms, they entered the taproom to look for Joseph Wickham.

"That's him in the far corner," said Quinn as he drank his mug of ale.

Loedicia glanced over and saw a young, dark-haired man in his early twenties with dark, bushy eyebrows and a broad forehead. He was sitting alone drinking ale and a few minutes later, when Quinn nodded to him, he stood up and left, followed a short time later by Quinn.

She glanced at Burly, sitting beside her drinking his ale. "Sahib," she asked, "what is Quinn's real name?"

He glanced at her quizzically. "His real name, lad?"

She nodded. "You call him Quinn, but I have discovered that unlike India, men in the colonies have more than one name."

"Aye," he said, then leaned close to her ear. "He's Captain Quinn Locke, that's who he is," he whispered. "But mind you, don't say his name aloud. He has enemies everywhere."

"But what has he done, besides stealing the silver?" she asked softly.

Burly grinned. "He's spoken for a break with the crown," he whispered back, "and there are those who'd have him hung for insurrection if they could catch him."

There it was again. Politics. What Uncle Thaddeus was always mumbling about.

"I don't know about all of which you speak," she whispered, "but I do thank you and him for helping me."

It was at that moment fate, in the form of an old acquaintance of Burly's, walked into the taproom of the King's Pride. He was an older man with a hard face and cruel eyes and Loedicia knew by the look on Burly's face they hadn't been too friendly in the past.

He spotted Burly right away and walked directly to him. "It can't be, but it is," he exclaimed as he pulled the chair from the table and sat down. "What the hell you doin' wearin' them clothes, you old reprobate?" he asked.

Burly stared in awe at the man, unable to put him in these surroundings. "What you doin' here, Krueger?" he asked in a low tone.

"I come east to find me a woman."

"A woman?"

"My old lady died last winter. I been tryin' to get on by myself, but it ain't workin'. I gotta have someone to cook, sew, all them things. I tried a squaw." he shrugged. "She's all right in bed, but she don't know how I like things . . . but you didn't say. How come the clothes and this dark boy?" he asked, pointing to Loedicia.

"The clothes is so nobody'll guess who I really am, so

keep your mouth shut," said Burly, and Krueger's eyes lit up.

"You with that Quinn again?"

"I didn't say that."

"You didn't have to." Krueger leaned closer. "I know a man'll give me a hundred pieces of eight if I tell him where he can put his hands on Quinn."

"So?" asked Burly as he continued to sip his ale.

"So how much you gettin' workin' with him? Nothin', I'll mind you."

"Keep talkin'," said Burly.

"What's Quinn ever done for you but get you in trouble? We could split a fat reward, not only from this fella I know but Lord Varrick's willing to pay a small fortune for proof he's dead."

Burly bent toward the man, taking in every word as he plied the man with ale. And as Loedicia sat, mortified, he made arrangements with the man to turn Quinn over to the man's friend.

"But first I want to meet this friend of yours," added Burly. "Maybe if we talk to him right he'll give us more than his first offer."

Krueger downed his ale and stood up. "Well, let's go, then," he said, and both men started for the door, then Burly remembered Loedicia and came back, grabbed her arm, and shuffled her outside with them.

It was pitch dark out and Krueger led the way down the street, Burly's arm slung about his shoulder. Burly's other hand held Loedicia tightly, dragging her along so there was no chance to escape.

They'd walked about two hundred feet when Burly suddenly stopped. "Listen!" he said, and shoved his mouth close to Krueger's ear.

"Listen to what?" asked Krueger.

Burly motioned toward a dark alley on their right. "Somethin's goin' on in there, friend. I heard scufflin' noises. Maybe somebody's hurt."

Krueger tried to peer into the dark alley, but the ale he'd drunk and the darkness made it impossible for him to see anything.

"Come on," urged Burly, and swung the man easily into the alley.

The rest happened so fast Loedicia hardly had a chance to take a breath. The arm Burly had around Krueger's shoulder tightened viciously about his neck and Krueger never had time to utter a sound. Burly was as strong as five men and she heard the crack as Krueger's neck snapped, then his body went limp and Burly heaved it away from himself, farther into the alley, as Loedicia stared wide-eyed.

He'd killed the man! With one arm Burly'd killed the man! She started to say something in protest, but by then Burly'd tightened his hold on her arm and was ushering her away.

She began to tremble as they reached the door of the King's Pride and Burly stopped, turning her to face him. "Hey, lad, perk up. I didn't mean to put feathers in your stomach. I'm sorry you had to see what you saw, but there wasn't anything else to do. He was a no-account anyway. Slimy as they come. I wouldn't hurt nobody lest I had to. But I won't let Quinn hang!"

She stared at him incredulously. "You killed him!" she whispered.

"And I'd do it again to save our necks," he answered, and took her by the shoulders, straightening her up. "Now look, lad, don't think of squelchin' on us. You're in this as far as you can go, so you might as well accept it."

"But—"

"Just go in the King's Pride with me, sit back down at the table, and act like nothing's happened. Think you can do that?"

She sighed breathlessly, then realized the mess she was in. "Yes," she whispered, her voice quivering.

They walked into the taproom together, sat down, and Burly ordered two mugs of ale. "Drink up, lad," he offered as he set one of the mugs in front of her. "I think you need it."

She closed her eyes and lifted the mug, taking a big swig of the honey-colored liquid, hoping it'd stay in her stomach. It burned all the way down and she felt as if it

had set her throat on fire, then she felt its warmth spread
through her body. She'd never tasted spirits of any kind
before and although it tasted bitter, the sensation was de-
lightful. Especially when she began to lose all sense of
guilt over the death of Mr. Krueger.

She was on her second mug of ale, drinking the last
drop, when Quinn walked into the taproom. The minute
he saw the stupidly relaxed smile on her face and the
drooping eyelids he knew she was drunk.

"What the hell have you done to him?" he asked Burly
as he stuck his hand under her chin and raised her face,
looking down into it.

"The lad was upset," answered Burly. "Somethin' happened."

"What?"

"We'd better go upstairs to your room," suggested
Burly. "I can't tell you here."

He finished his ale quickly, stood up, and they both
ushered Loedicia between them toward the stairs. She
wasn't so drunk that she didn't know what was happening. She was just tipsy enough not to care.

The weather was a bit cold for June and the first thing
Quinn did when they reached his room was to start a fire
in the fireplace.

"Now," he said as he lit a fire and the candles, then
turned to face Burly. "What happened?"

"There we were, minding our own business, when who
walks in but Krueger."

"Krueger?"

"Aye. From Meekham's Swamp."

"Holy Jesus!"

"That's what I figured and he knew that where I was,
you were too."

"Where's he now?"

"Two or three blocks down in an alley with his neck
broke. That's why the lad's drunk. He looked sort of
green around the gills."

Quinn glanced over at Loedicia, who'd dropped to the
floor in front of the fireplace and was staring into it. She

started singing a song in Hindi, something soft in a minor key, and Quinn shook his head.

He wished Dicia hadn't seen it. He was young, impressionable, and he could give them trouble, but at the moment he didn't seem very concerned. Then, suddenly, she turned and looked at Quinn and her eyes narrowed.

"He snapped his neck like paper," she said, pointing to Burly, her words slightly slurred. "No one will find us now. Not Uncle Thaddeus or Lord Varrick."

Quinn's eyes flashed as he stared at her. "What do you know about Lord Varrick?" he asked, and she smiled secretively as she pointed her finger at him.

"He's your cousin and he's supposed to get married. . . ." Then she stopped, put her hand over her mouth, and began to giggle.

Quinn looked at Burly. "He must have heard us talking," he explained.

"But what's he laughing at?"

"He's got a snootful. He'd probably laugh at anything right now. We'd better get him to bed."

He walked over and reached down, pulling her to her feet. "Come on, Dicia, let's get your things off," he said as he started to peel the coat from her shoulders, and suddenly she turned on him.

She'd been laughing over the thought of Lord Varrick's being left practically at the altar and now she remembered she was supposed to be a boy and they wanted to take her clothes off.

"No!" she yelled, and pulled away from him. "No!" She wrapped her coat tighter about her and lurched away from them toward the bed. The room was all hazy with a soft glow and the bed looked as if it were animated, moving up and down like a ship. It was set in the middle of the floor and she hurried around it, hanging on to the bedpost to help steady the floor, which kept trying to come up and hit her right between the eyes.

She couldn't let them take off her clothes and she heard Quinn's voice penetrating her woozy head. "You can't sleep on those clean sheets with your dirty coat and pants on." She pulled back the covers, fighting against the uncoordinated movements of her hands.

She took a deep breath and turned, lowering herself gingerly onto the bed, making sure she wouldn't end up on the floor. One at a time, she took off her moccasins and dropped them, then stood up again and dropped her pants, her back still to them. The boys' underwear she had on was baggy, cut off at the knees, and both men stood quietly now, grinning as they watched her progress.

She stepped from her trousers, reached down, and piled them on top of the moccasins, then reached up, slipped hurriedly out of her jacket, and dropped it on top of her pants. Then she sat on the bed, leaned back, and stretched out, pulling the covers up to her chin.

"Good night, sahibs," she said, a smile on her face, and closed her eyes, pretending sleep.

"If that don't beat all," exclaimed Burly. "I think he's passed out."

Quinn studied Loedicia silently a minute. "I wish he wasn't involved in all this," he said, then he walked over and stared out the window. "Joe Wickham says the grapevine has it Varrick's wedding didn't come off and word's out there were two preachers on board *The Golden Lady* who didn't act much like preachers. I guess that cabin boy's getting even with us."

"So we shed the black suits?"

"We shed Dicia someplace too. He stands out like a sore thumb. And all because of a stupid cabin boy with a perverted mind. He thinks he's being cute, giving us trouble with the authorities. He probably has no idea he's hit on the truth."

"But what'll we do with the lad? He knows too much."

"Don't you think I don't know that?" Quinn replied, irritated. He'd begun to like the boy. He was pesky at times and asked fool questions, but there was something about him, the way he looked at them with his big violet eyes and the warm smile that seemed to light up his face.

"You can't kill the lad!" protested Burly.

"Yet we can't take him with us and we can't leave him here."

"I don't mind killin' some bastards," argued Burly, "but this is different."

"Pray, what do we do with him then?"

"How the hell should I know?"

"Maybe if we sleep on it," Quinn answered, and walked back to the bed, looking down at Loedicia.

Although she'd had enough ale to make the room spin, she was still conscious and had heard every word the two men spoke. They were debating whether or not to kill her. Good Lord! She'd said she'd rather be dead than married to Lord Varrick. Now she wasn't so sure. Death was so final and she remembered Mr. Krueger in the alley.

Quinn assured Burly he wouldn't do anything drastic until morning and maybe they could think of some way out.

"We meet Joseph Wickham at the bridge west of town at daybreak," he said. "We can lock Dicia in the room and maybe Joseph knows a place we could leave him until we're well on our way. I'd rather know he's tied up someplace for a few days than have to slit his throat."

Burly grinned at him sheepishly. "I think you're as fond of the lad as I am," he said, and glanced over at Loedicia, who was still feigning sleep. "He sort of grows on a person. You wouldn't have the heart to slit his throat."

Quinn grinned. "You know me too well, Burly," he said. "Now suppose we call it a night and I'll see you early."

He bid Burly good night, then walked over, his back to the bed as he started undressing. Loedicia opened one eye barely a slit to see what was going on.

He was taking his clothes off, was down to his underwear, and she knew he'd be getting into bed any minute. He blew out the candles and as she felt his body slip into bed next to her she rolled over on her side with her back to him. Thank God he had no idea she was a woman, but she knew he was a man and the thought made her quiver inside. She could feel the warmth of his body next to hers and moved as close to the edge of the bed as possible without falling off.

She lay for a long time thinking, her mind still muddled but clear enough to know what they were planning. They didn't have the heart to kill her, that is, if they could find another way out, like tying her up somewhere for a few days. Well, nobody was going to tie her up if she could help it. They were going to leave her alone when they went to meet Joseph Wickham. Fine. She'd see to it she wasn't here when they got back. But for now she was sleepy and a bit sick, so she closed her eyes and went to sleep, conscious all the time of Quinn sleeping next to her, especially when he moved in bed and rested his buttocks against her backside.

She took a deep breath and said her prayers, hoping God would hear them.

# 6

The next morning brought sunshine, birdsong, and a hangover for Loedicia. She woke up when Quinn slipped from the bed, but feigned sleep until they were gone, then she slid from the covers, put on her clothes, and walked to the window.

She knew the door would be locked, so there was no use trying it. The window was on the second floor and there was no ledge or roof, only a tree that was set far enough away from the window to be useless as a means of escape.

She turned around and studied the room. There was only one way she could escape. She took the sheets from the bed, ripped them into big, long strips, then tied the strips together, fastening one end to the back of the rocking chair that sat in the far corner of the room. After securing it tightly, she pulled the rocking chair to the window. The sill was wide and she stood on it, in the center of the window, balancing herself by leaning against the frame.

She glanced behind her, saw no one in the yard below, looked back around, then reached out and pulled on the chair and the sheet both at the same time until the chair was wedged across the opening in the window. She pulled her weight on the sheet, saw it would hold, and slowly lowered herself out the window to the ground below.

It took her only minutes to leave the King's Pride behind her and get lost in the city streets. She hadn't taken any money with her, not wanting to steal from them, and her main concern now was staying out of their clutches.

They'd be looking for a boy, had no idea she was a woman, so the obvious thing to do was to discard the boys' clothing. That meant she'd have to find a dress somewhere.

She'd been wandering around for about half an hour when she sat down on a tree stump to think. She was toward the edge of town, where there were more houses than shops, and she glanced up and down the dusty road, wondering what to do next, when her eye caught a dash of color up the road a bit. She slid from the stump and walked into the field at the edge of the road and glanced toward the patch of color she'd seen through the trees. It was a red dress hanging on a clothesline with a wash load of other clothes and was obscured from the view of the small house by a clothesline full of sheets that almost touched the ground.

There were bushes surrounding the small yard but no fence, so she began to edge closer to it. She ducked down behind some chokecherry bushes and eyed the dress. A petticoat, chemise, and a pair of bloomers were hanging on the same line and it looked as if all were about the right size for her.

The clothes she had on had been stolen off a clothesline and it seemed that her change of clothes would have to be too. She glanced about carefully. Not a soul was in sight and the large sheets hanging on the line closest to the house hid the second line from view.

It took her only minutes to grab everything she needed

and dive back into the bushes, her heart pounding. She stayed quiet for a few minutes, waiting for any shouts that might prove she'd been seen. There were none.

The clothes were still a bit damp, but she rolled them in a ball and headed for the road again to find a place to change. She wanted to get as far away from this part of town as possible. When they'd ridden into town yesterday they'd crossed a bridge and she headed for it now, remembering its approximate direction.

An hour and a half later she emerged from the river another shade lighter and hid in the bushes while she donned the women's clothes. It felt good to be free of the cloth that bound her breasts and she marveled at the way the dress was filled out. It was a bit tight, rather shabby and worn, but it would do. The boys' clothes she took off were rolled up in a ball and tied into a neat bundle with the jacket sleeves in case she had to use them again, but she kept the moccasins on her feet.

Her short hair felt strange with a dress on and she breathed a sigh, knowing she didn't have to talk in clipped English like a Hindu anymore. She was still exceptionally dark, but people would think she was a light-skinned Negro woman.

Now her only problem was food. It was already way past noon and she hadn't had even one bite to eat. She picked up her bundle and wandered back into town with it slung over her shoulder, trying to think of a way to get at least a piece of bread or a bun, but without money there was none.

Then fate stepped into her life again. This time it was in the form of a garrulous woman of about forty. She was sitting on a low brick wall that surrounded a rather nice house and she was eating some biscuits alternately with slabs of cheese she was cutting from a small block of cheese set beside her. After each bite she tilted a bottle of red wine to her lips and washed down the food and Loedicia licked her lips as she stood watching.

"Hey, you girl!" called the woman, her mouth full of food. "What you starin' for?" Loedicia winced.

"I didn't mean to stare," she said as she boldly approached the woman, "but I'm terribly hungry."

The woman stopped chewing and eyed her a minute, then grinned. "The fine gentlemens ain't paying much lately for the likes of you when they can get the swells for free, is they, dearie?" she said, and Loedicia frowned.

"I don't know what you mean," she answered, swinging the bundle of clothes in front of her.

"Aw, come now, dearie. No need to pretend with me," the woman said, taking a slug of wine. "No decent girl walks the streets of Princeton hungry. Come have a bite. I've more to share than I need. It don't matter to me how you gets your money."

Loedicia suddenly realized what the woman meant, but at the moment she didn't care. She walked over, dropped the bundle at her feet, and sat down, letting the woman hand her a slab of cheese and a biscuit. They tasted heavenly on her empty stomach. She could have asked the woman where she got the food because it didn't look like the average fare someone would be carting around for a picnic, but one didn't question what seemed like manna from heaven.

While they ate she learned the woman's name was Meg, but that's all she learned about her except she had no family and was originally from Philadelphia.

"I don't like it here in Princeton, the people's too uppity," Meg offered as they finished eating. She wrapped the food up in a soiled cloth, then finished the wine and tossed the empty bottle into the bushes in the yard behind her. "Where you headed?" she asked, looking Loedicia over. "You're a mighty pretty wench. Prettier than most of the rich bitches in town. 'Course that dark skin of yours probably keeps the high-payin' gentry away."

Loedicia ignored her remarks. "Where you headed, Meg?" she asked.

"Anyplace I can get for a decent night's sleep tonight," she answered. Then as she looked past Loedicia, down the road, she suddenly let out a shriek. "Lord save us!" she yelled. "He's brought the whole damned regiment!"

She picked up the bundle of food, climbed over the brick wall, and started across the lawn toward some bushes.

Loedicia looked in the direction where Meg had been looking and saw a rotund man with gray hair, mutton-chops, and a bulging stomach accompanied by four of His Majesty's lobster backs, as Quinn called them, and a large Negro about six feet tall with a shiny bald head, no shirt, and earrings dangling almost to his shoulders.

The unruly group was converging on her with a ferocity that sent her reeling after Meg, almost tearing her skirts as she scooted over the low brick wall.

Running did no good, however. The soldiers were faster and the big black was two strides ahead of them. He dived into the bushes at the side of the house, pulling Meg out by her hair. She was fighting mad, her eyes wild, nails scratching.

Two of the soldiers grabbed Loedicia and held her tightly as the black dragged Meg across the yard toward them and a woman came to the door of the house.

"What's all the racket?" the woman called from the top of the steps.

"Just a couple runaway bond slaves," called one of the soldiers. "No need for alarm. Sorry we disturbed you."

The woman eyed Meg and Loedicia, then turned up her nose. "Trash!" she exclaimed haughtily, then went back in the house.

"I thought you said there was only one," said one of the soldiers as the fat man reached them.

"Did I say that?" he asked, and his eyes fell on Loedicia as he huffed and puffed, trying to catch his breath. Running did nothing but make him weak and winded and he ran so slow he might as well have walked. "I forgot to mention the young one." He panted as he looked her over.

"They're both yours, then?" asked the soldier.

"Aye," answered the fat man. "We can take care of them ourselves now." He pulled a rope from his pocket.

Loedicia started to struggle to get away and the fat man slapped her hard across the mouth, cutting the side of her lip, and she let out a shriek.

"Keep your filthy hands off me," she yelled as blood began to trickle from the corner of her mouth and her eyes flashed angrily. "I'm not your bond slave or anyone else's!"

"Then who are you?" asked one of the soldiers who was holding her.

Loedicia stared at him, her eyes narrowed. She didn't dare tell them. If she told them she was Lady Loedicia Aldrich they'd send her back to Boston, to Lord Varrick, and she didn't dare tell them about Burly and Quinn. She was hoping they wouldn't pay any attention to the bundle of clothes she'd dropped by the wall. If they did they'd start asking more questions.

"There, what'd I tell you," blustered the fat man as she kept silent. "She can't tell you anything else because she belongs to me. Now hand her over and we'll see the two of them don't run off again."

Loedicia was flustered. There was nothing she could do but go along with them. They probably wouldn't believe her even if she did tell them the truth.

The soldiers helped the fat man and the Negro tie their hands in front of them, then fasten both to the end of a rope.

"We won't need any guard," said the fat man. "But I want to thank you all for the help."

"Anytime, Mr. Pittman, anytime at all," answered one of the soldiers, and the four of them walked off toward the center of town.

Mr. Pittman, the big black he called Sam, and the two women walked back across the lawn, out the front gate, and headed back, following some distance behind the soldiers. Sam dragged the two unwilling women behind him on the rope and passersby paid little attention even when Meg burst forth with some choice gutter language Loedicia had never heard before. She felt she knew the meaning, however, and blushed under the walnut stain.

It was close to dinnertime when Mr. Pittman threw open the door of the barn and shoved the two women inside to join an assortment of milling men, women, and children. All the people in the barn were tied in one way or another and there must have been at least twenty. They were both black and white, but all were slaves, whether by indebtedness as bond slaves, which was the lot of most of the whites, or because they or their ancestors were unable to outrun the slave traders.

The barn smelled rankly of sweat and human excrement soured in the heat of the day and Loedicia felt her stomach churn as she tried to take a deep breath. They tied her to a horse stall with Meg beside her, then Mr. Pittman stood staring at her as she dropped down on the pile of straw.

"You know, you're a beauty for a black," he said. "Must be some white in you somewhere. You're too light to be a true blood. You a virgin?"

Loedicia wasn't about to answer him.

The man grinned broadly and nodded to Sam and within minutes, against her flailing protests, they had her spread-eagled in the straw, her skirt to her waist, while his fingers probed. Satisfied, he grabbed her chin, forcing her to look at him. God, she was a beauty and virgin too. He could use her in his own bed, but the thought of the money he could get for her untouched was more intriguing. His hand pushed at the bulge in his pants as he stood up and nodded for Sam to let her go.

Loedicia's face was flushed, tears in her eyes as she pulled at her skirts, trying to hide what his filthy hands had done.

"You'll bring a pretty price in the morning, wench," he said, sneering. "A pretty price." He dropped his hand, then turned and walked away with Sam at his heels.

Loedicia turned to Meg. "He can't sell me!" she protested. "I'm not a bond servant."

"You got papers sayin' you're free?" asked Meg.

"I don't need papers."

"Where you been, dearie?" asked Meg. "No black runs around this country free less'n they got a paper with 'em says they are."

Loedicia knew the woman was right. She'd forgotten the status of most blacks in the colonies and because of the walnut stain, although it was fading, she still looked part black. People called them mulattoes, if she remembered right. She could tell him she wasn't black. She could tell him she was from India. . . . She shrugged. That wouldn't help either. He was a cruel man with cruel eyes and it would be impossible to appeal to his better nature because he had none.

"What did he mean, I'd bring a pretty price in the morning?"

"There's a slave auction tomorrow," stated Meg, "and he's been gathering us up for the past week."

"Why are you here?"

"My husband died owing debts so I was sold into bondage to pay them off. I didn't mind that so much except I paid them off two years ago."

"But you should be free then."

"Free?" The woman spat on the floor. "I would be if I'd had decent owners. I can see you never been owned by nobody before." She gave her a sideways glance. "Everytime somethin' goes wrong they tack a few more months onto your service. Mine says I got six more to go, but I'll be safe in sayin' that unless I get someone decent this time I'll still be a bond servant a year from now. Believe me, dearie, they ain't gonna get much work out of old Meg." She grinned at Loedicia, her wrinkled face, old for its age, looking like parchment. "Maybe you'll get lucky. With a face and figure like yours it don't always matter if your skin's black. 'Sides, I think old Pittman was right when he said you was part white. And I made a mistake, dearie." She frowned. "I never dreamed you was a virgin." She stared at her intently. "How come a wanderin' tart like you ain't never had a man?"

Loedicia blushed at the thought. Why should she tell this woman anything? "I think that's my business," she answered curtly, and the woman shrugged.

"Have it your way, dearie," she said belligerently. "Either way you ain't got a choice. Pittman has all sorts of forged bills of sale. He'll sell you in the mornin', all right, nice and legallike." She eyed Loedicia curiously. "I don't know where you come from, dearie," she said knowingly, "but I hope you ain't got no family around 'cause you

sure ain't gonna see 'em again for a long time." Loedicia
stared at the woman angrily.

Then she looked away as she heard a strange sound a
few feet away. The smell in the barn continued to
nauseate her and now her eyes bulged as she realized the
noise was made by one of the blacks relieving himself
without even bothering to stand up and it was splashing
on the side of the stalls and the edge of the straw. She
turned quickly away and proceeded to vomit into a pile of
straw next to her, losing the food Meg had given her so
generously, then she moved as far from the vomit as possible and leaned her head against the side of the stall,
tears streaming down her face. Her escape had taken her
from bad to worse and she began to pray harder than
she'd ever prayed before in her life.

# 7

Quinn was whistling lightly as he and Burly walked along
the street toward the King's Pride. Things were going
pretty well. They'd met Joseph Wickham as planned and
he assured them the silver was safe until he left college at
the end of the week. He also had news that delegates
were to meet in Philadelphia in September to organize the
colonies. Things were really moving along. They'd let the
crown know exactly what their feelings were. Franklin
was still in London and Parliament wasn't paying much
attention to him, so if war came . . .

Quinn didn't like the thought of war, but what else was
there? Unrest was everywhere and the British were becoming more and more arrogant with each passing day.
He smiled as he thought of the coup he and Burly had
pulled off. Of course they weren't safe yet by any means
and now there was the boy, Dicia, to worry about.

They'd all three agreed that Dicia would have to be
kept prisoner and guarded until Burly and Quinn were

well on their way again and Joseph agreed to lend a hand. He had a friend, loyal to the cause, who'd look after the boy, then when Joseph left to return to Virginia he'd take the boy with him and drop him off on the way with some friends.

They turned in at the door to the inn, went through the lobby and on upstairs. "Let me tell him," suggested Burly as Quinn unlocked the door. "Maybe if we tell him the right way he'll go along without us having to tie him up."

"Give it a try," answered Quinn, and swung the door open and the two men stepped inside.

The first thing their eyes fell on was the bed shorn of its covers and the shreds of leftover sheet crumpled on the floor.

"What the hell!" Quinn walked over toward the rocking chair sprawled beneath the open window and he picked up the strips of sheet attached to it and followed their trail out the window. "He's gone . . . damn!"

"What do we do now? The lad knows too much. What if he goes to the law?"

"Let's hope not," answered Quinn as he pulled the dangling rope of sheet up into the room. "He probably heard us talking last night when we thought he was asleep and he wasn't about to hang around to have his throat cut."

"Then we just let him go?"

"Not on your life," answered Quinn. "If we can find him we bring him back and carry out our plans. If we don't find him we'll just have to hope he doesn't decide to tell somebody everything he knows."

Burly frowned. "Let's get looking, then," he said. "He's got a head start on us, but it shouldn't be too hard to locate a lad like Dicia."

By sundown that evening, however, Burly'd retracted his brash statement. They'd hunted from one end of Princeton to the other without a sign of the boy and they had to be careful asking questions because they had no proof who the boy was and why they were looking for him. No one, however, had seen a slightly built black boy in a dark blue jacket, brown pants, gray shirt, and with a blue stocking cap on his black curly head. It was as if he'd dropped from the face of the earth.

It was almost dark as they stood at the edge of the dusty road and glanced about at the fine house behind the low brick wall, then suddenly Quinn's eyes froze on something in the weeds and grass at the foot of the wall some distance from the front gate. He walked over, Burly at his heels, and picked up the bundle of clothes, untying them as Burly watched.

"What's the lad wearing?" asked Burly.

"He sure as hell isn't wearing these," said Quinn as he held up the blue coat and brown pants she'd had on. "Probably stole some from a clothesline somewhere."

"Fine," answered Burly. "Now we'll never find him."

"Well, at least he hasn't gone to the authorities," offered Quinn. "If he had we'd be in jail by now." He put the bundle under his arm. "Let's sleep on it," he said. "It's getting too dark now to see much of anything."

Burly nodded and the two men gave up their search and headed back to the King's Pride.

The next morning they were up before dawn. Joseph had given each of them a change of clothes and there were two dirty, worn brocade carpetbags to replace the two black bags carrying the money. It took only a short time to dress and put the silver in the new bags. They left the other clothes and the black bags in the room and left by the back stairs, having already paid their bill the night before.

"If we don't find him on our way through town this morning we're just going to forget the whole thing and hope he keeps his mouth shut," said Quinn as they headed down the street.

"But you can't leave a helpless lad like that to wander about Princeton," protested Burly. "He don't have no money. He could get in all kinds of trouble."

"If he hasn't already," answered Quinn. "There's one place he'll probably head this morning, especially if he didn't make it there yesterday."

"The market?"

"He'll need food and the best place to steal it is where there's plenty. It's not as easily missed."

They moved from booth to booth and cart to cart, buying some food to take with them, keeping their eyes open for a head of curly black hair. A din hit them as they turned a corner and Burly winced.

"Slaves," he said bitterly. "I hear Georgia's tryin' to stop the slavers."

"No man should be a slave," stated Quinn, and suddenly stopped dead in his tracks as he stared at a young Negro woman the auctioneer was dragging to the center of the slave block.

"The men went first! Now we get to the women!" Mr. Pittman shouted as he pulled the rope.

The woman on the other end pulled against it reluctantly, trying to keep from being put on display, but it did no good. Her flashing violet eyes narrowed viciously as she yelled at him in a language no one in the crowd understood. He reached over and grabbed her arm to make her stand erect, warning her to quit her caterwauling, and his fingers bit hard into her flesh.

"She's a beauty, gents!" the fat man yelled, displaying his prize. "She'll not only warm your food, but she can warm your bed!" He leaned closer to the men standing in the front row. They were already looking her over greedily. "And she's a virgin, gents. Mark my word." He let go of her arm and reached out to cup her breast in his hand, but she saw the move and turned quickly, aiming her knee at his groin. She missed only because his fat stomach protruded so far.

Furious at her outburst, he backhanded her and called Sam, who pinned her arms behind her and tied them.

"She's a wildcat for the man who can tame her!" he yelled as he looked at her cruelly, then looked back at the crowd. "Who'll make the first bid?" A man down in front raised his hand.

"Look at that woman, Burly," said Quinn, his face dark, his jaw set firm.

"The one on the block?"

Quinn nodded. "Where'd you see eyes and hair like that before?"

Burly stared and suddenly his face fell. "Oh, my God!" he gasped. "It's Dicia!"

Quinn laid his hand on his friend's arm. He moved closer until he was among the bidders and then raised his hand.

"You crazy, bidding on her?" asked Burly.

"I aim to take that she devil away when I leave here, Burly," he answered through clenched teeth. "She's got some explaining to do." He raised his hand again as the bidding rose higher.

Loedicia felt sick to her stomach. The humiliation! The degradation! To be sold as a slave, and what next? To be ravaged by some unfeeling man? Would it have been better to have stayed in Boston? Would Lord Varrick have been worse than this?

A greasy, dark-haired man reached up from in front of the block and grabbed her ankle, trying to run his hand up her leg. She kicked at him with her moccasined foot, which only excited him, and he raised the bid.

Then suddenly she heard a voice from the crowd, low and vibrant, and she jerked her head up to stare at the new bidder. It was . . . it was Quinn! Beside him was Burly and they were both staring at her with an intensity that frightened her.

They knew! My God! they were here and they knew who she was and Quinn was bidding on her. She wanted to die! Anything! all she could remember was hearing his voice talking about slitting her throat and now, since she'd run away, he'd probably take no more chances. She was between two evils and had no way out of either.

Suddenly the bidding was over and everyone was staring at the blond giant of a man who'd paid one hundred fifty Spanish silver dollars for this beautiful black woman, who shrank from him as he approached.

Burly followed Quinn and he walked up, set down his bag, and reached inside, bringing out, a few at a time, one hundred and fifty silver dollars, handing them to Mr. Pittman, who handed him the rope tied to Loedicia's arms.

But instead of grasping the rope, Quinn reached down, picked the woman up, slung her over his shoulder like a sack of corn, and elbowed his way out of the crowd.

Loedicia was scared to death. What did he have planned?

He carried her through the marketplace, away from the noisy crowds, and neither of them spoke, nor did Burly, who followed behind Quinn.

When they were sufficiently away and the road widened with fields and trees, he walked over, stood for a minute, took a deep breath, then set her down, leaning her back to stand against a tree.

"Now!" he said, his eyes flashing. "Who the hell are you?" Tears cascaded down her cheeks, leaving streaks, yet she didn't answer.

He looked as if he could kill her. "Did you hear me?" he asked.

She nodded.

"Well?"

"I told you before," she sobbed, her body quaking. "I'm Dicia."

"And you're a woman, not a boy." He thought back. "No wonder you looked so wide-eyed when you handed me that towel. Why the masquerade?"

She leaned her head over, trying to wipe the tears on her shoulder, licking the rest with her tongue. They were wet and salty.

"Would you have let me stay if you had known I was a woman?" she asked. "And how far do you think I would have gotten the night I ran away if I hadn't been dressed like a boy?" She still couldn't tell them who she really was. "Didn't you think it strange a boy was bought to wait on a lady? When my mistress died I thought perhaps I'd be set free, but her husband had other things in mind," she lied. "I had to get away."

"Then you're really from India?" asked Quinn.

"Yes," she answered. "I was born and raised in Calcutta."

"And your name is really Dicia?"

She nodded, sniffing, wiping her nose again on her shoulder.

Quinn stared at her, remembering the nights she'd slept in the same bed with him and when she'd washed his back. She had nerve, he'd say that for her.

"Why'd you leave us?" he asked, and she let out a deep sigh.

"What would you do if you had a choice between being killed or tied up and held prisoner for two or three days? I didn't want either, so I figured if you couldn't take me with you I'd better go it alone."

"Didn't get far, did you?"

"That's not funny," she answered, and a new tear fell down her cheek.

"Well, what do we do with her now?" asked Burly from behind Quinn.

"We tie her up as planned," answered Quinn, and Loedicia began to protest.

"Please! I couldn't stand that!" she pleaded, and took a deep breath. "Take me with you," she begged. "They're looking for two preachers and a servant boy." She looked at their clothes. They were dressed like farmers. "They wouldn't be looking for two men and a woman. Please!" Tears again rolled down her cheeks.

"Damn it anyway," exclaimed Quinn. "You don't have to cry. I hate women who cry."

She sniffed, trying to stop. "I wouldn't cause you trouble," she said softly. "And I could help you."

"And who do we say you are?" asked Quinn.

She bit her lip. "Your slave?" She paused, then continued hesitantly. "Your mistress? Whatever you wish me to be."

Burly put his hand on Quinn's shoulder. "Why not, Quinn?" he asked. "They won't be looking for you with a woman."

"You really want to go with us?" he asked her.

"Rather than stay here," she stated softly, and he looked deep into her eyes. She was beautiful, but he'd never remembered seeing a black woman with violet eyes. But, then, she was from India and maybe she wasn't all native. If they left her here she'd probably end up back on the auction block and he wouldn't wish that on anyone, let alone a woman.

"All right, you can go with us," he answered after a few moments, and he saw her shoulders droop with relief. "But you'll have to keep up," he said sternly as he reached out, turned her around, and began untying the ropes on her wrists. "I sold the horses, so the going may be rough."

"I can do it," she said, her voice once more alive, and she turned around to face him. "Thank you," she offered as she rubbed her wrists, only Quinn frowned.

"Don't thank me," he answered, hating to admit he had any feelings in the matter. "Thank Burly. If I'd had my way you'd have had your throat slit back on *The Golden Lady* the first time I set eyes on you." Then he picked up the brocaded bag from the ground. "Shall we go now?" he asked, and Burly had a twinkle about his eyes and a grin for her as Quinn stepped out to the edge of the road.

"Don't worry, lass," he said, winking. "His bark's worse than his bite." The two of them followed Quinn out to the road and the three of them made an incongruous picture as they left Princeton.

The sun was high as they left the houses and city behind and for the first time in days Loedicia felt a little more at ease. At least now she didn't have to keep pretending to be a thirteen-year-old boy. She could be herself . . . well, almost.

By late morning she was starved, having heaved up the cheese and biscuits the day before and having had nothing for breakfast. But she wasn't about to complain. She'd show them. She'd fall over before she'd ask for food and her stomach curled up to her backbone all morning as she shuffled along beside them, taking in the scenery, listening to the two of them talk.

When she finally did get food in the early afternoon she relished the hard cooked sausage, round bread, and hard-boiled eggs washed down with some wine. She didn't even mind drinking out of the same bottle Burly and Quinn used. Something she'd never have done before.

She eyed Quinn as she peeled one of the eggs, trying to figure out how he could possibly be related to Lord Varrick. He had similar features, she had to admit, but they were put together so differently. She thought he must be close to thirty, maybe a bit younger, and from the talk she'd heard aboard *The Golden Lady,* although he enjoyed the charms of many women, he had little use for them except to fill his bed occasionally when the need arose. She had to admit he was handsome even if he did treat her rather harshly most of the morning, yelling at her to keep up and admonishing her for wasting time picking wild flowers.

Burly whispered to her once that Quinn had his nose out of place because she'd managed to fool him, but she wasn't at all sure. He probably hated the sight of her. Well, that was fine, because she hated him too. Coming along with them was merely accepting the lesser of two evils.

With their stomachs full, they started out again. Small settlements were few and far between and they passed few people on the way. Some places the road was no more than a wide trail. By dusk they'd left a good many miles behind them.

"But we've still got a long way to go," said Quinn as Loedicia sat down in some soft grass at the side of a pond where they'd stopped for a few minutes' rest. "So don't make yourself comfortable."

"But the grass is so soft here," she protested. "It'd be the perfect place to sleep tonight."

"Far from it," he said abruptly. "We'll go on up there." He pointed some distance away to a hilly, rock-strewn area.

"He's worse than a fakir," she grumbled to Burly as they left the pond.

"What's a fakir?" he asked, and she proceeded to explain.

Burly laughed when she'd finished. "I could just see Quinn trying to sleep on a bed of nails. He may use a rock for a pillow occasionally, but his hide's not as tough as it looks."

"What are you two gossiping about?" asked Quinn as he stopped to wait for them to catch up.

Loedicia blushed and Burly grinned. "The lass was telling me about Indian fakirs," he answered, and Quinn frowned.

"Fakirs?"

"Those fellas who sleep on nails."

"I know what a fakir is," he snapped irritably, then turned and walked away.

"What's wrong with him?" she asked, looking at Burly. He shrugged. "Don't ask me, ask him," he said.

"I'd rather talk to a cobra," she said stubbornly, and they followed behind Quinn as he made his way a good half mile farther to the top of a hill, where he dropped his bag and stood looking around.

"This ought to do," he said. "We're far enough off the trail and we shouldn't have to build a fire tonight."

"Why don't we ever build a fire?" asked Loedicia as she sat down on a mossy plot of ground she was surprised to find among so many rocks.

"Fires can be seen," he answered curtly. "And as long as we have the silver with us we take precautions."

"That's why you came up here?"

"Exactly. There were a lot of people at the market this morning and one of them might get the idea that there's more money to be had by following us."

"You've seen something?" she asked anxiously.

"You ask too many questions," he answered.

"But did you? Is that why you didn't want to stay by the pond?"

"That and the mosquitoes. As soon as it gets dark that place'll be swarming with the little bastards."

Burly was standing next to him and nudged him in the ribs, motioning toward Loedicia. "We have a lady present, Quinn," he suggested, meaning he should watch his language, and suddenly Quinn let out a loud guffaw.

"Ha! Now that's rare!" he said sardonically. "That's really funny. She spends a week with us and now suddenly we have to be careful she might hear something that'll curl her ears." He stared at her angrily. "She's probably heard more than enough already."

She stood up quickly. "Is that what's bothering you?"

"What do you mean, bothering me?"

"You're mad because I heard you and Burly—"

"Heard what?" he asked sternly, and her face turned red. "I knew it, damn it!" he exclaimed. "All those times you pretended to be sleeping and on board ship . . . Do you know how it makes me feel, knowing what you know about me? Knowing you emptied our slop jar and the things we talked about and seeing me naked!"

Loedicia smiled coquettishly. "I'm sure, from what I've heard, I'm not the first woman to see you in the altogether."

"That was different," he snapped, then set his jaw firmly. "That's what I mean . . . Oh, hell! You're with us, so just forget the whole thing."

"I will if you will," she answered.

"Good," exclaimed Burly as he eyed the two of them apprehensively. "For a minute there I thought you two were going to get violent."

"Oh, shut up!" ordered Quinn, and he opened a small bundle he had hanging from his belt and they finished the last of the food.

"What do we do for breakfast?" asked Loedicia as she nibbled at the hard, dry sausage.

"We get drunk," answered Quinn as he held up the half bottle of wine they had left.

"Oh, good," she answered flippantly. "I like getting drunk. It's a fascinating experience."

Quinn eyed her rather strangely, remembering the ale she'd gotten drunk on that night at the tavern, but he kept silent and she became self-conscious under his scrutiny.

"Why are you staring at me?" she asked finally as her face reddened.

"Is it my imagination or are you a few shades lighter than you were when I first laid eyes on you?" Then he reached over, grabbed her under the chin, and tilted her face up so he could get a better look. It was almost dark, but he was sure he wasn't mistaken. "Your nose is sun-burned."

She tried to pull her face away, but his fingers gripped her chin too tightly. "I didn't say I was a full-blooded Indian woman," she said stubbornly. "Even dark people sunburn."

"Pink?" he asked.

"Oh, you're impossible," she answered.

"I just want to know what I've gotten myself into," he retorted.

"I assure you again. My name is Dicia and I'm from India." She spouted off some Hindi to prove it.

He loosened his fingers slowly, not knowing whether to believe her or not. He'd take a better look in the light of morning. He turned to Burly.

"She sleeps between us with the bags," he said firmly. "I don't want her disappearing during the night." Burly glanced at Dicia as she got up and walked a bit away, straining her eyes to look out over the valley below them into the gathering night.

It must have been well past midnight when she wakened, aware of the exceptional darkness. There was no moon tonight and she could barely make out the shape of Quinn's back next to her with the bag of money between them. She could hear his deep, steady breathing, which she'd become accustomed to the past week, and she sighed.

The ground was hard and she was suddenly chilled. Before, she'd always had on a jacket or been in a bed with sheets, but the dress she'd stolen had short sleeves and the air had turned cool.

She was contemplating what to do when suddenly Quinn yelled, "Now!" and with a savage leap, shooting as he went, he jumped from his position and she heard a loud thudding noise.

Behind her, Burly too had rolled aside as he fired his pistol. Then she heard the crunch of bone against bone.

Heart pounding, unable to comprehend exactly what was going on, remembering what Quinn had said earlier, she sat up, grabbed both money bags, put them under her, and sat on them, then reached about, hunting for a piece of branch she'd seen on the ground earlier.

She heard bodies thudding about in the dark and curses, then someone yelled, "Hell, it's Captain Locke! You didn't say it was Captain Locke!"

"I didn't know!" squealed a voice in return. "I never seen Locke b'fore." Then the voice became strangled in the violence of the onslaught.

"Get the silver!" another voice yelled, and instinctively Loedicia braced herself.

She vaguely saw the form before her but knew somehow it wasn't Quinn or Burly, and she swung the heavy club with all her might, catching the man unexpectedly across the face.

"Jesus! My nose's broken!" he yelled as he sprawled on the ground, blood splattering all over him in the dark.

She saw another vague form move toward the man and all the while she could hear the grunts and groans of battle as Quinn and Burly, both skillful fighters, tried to outmanuever their attackers.

"It's that damn nigger woman!" gasped the man on the ground, and she saw the vague shape beside him start to lunge at her.

She'd seen the natives fight with sand and since the soil here was rather sandy she'd reached down and scooped a handful of dirt in preparation. Now she threw it toward the man's head and saw him stop abruptly and grab at his eyes. While he did this she pummeled him with the heavy hunk of wood until he backed off, cursing.

He grabbed toward the other man, who was standing up now, and the one with the broken nose led the other down the hill and they melted into the darkness.

She sat in the dark, listening. The fight was still going on with shouts and curses, then someone screamed, "I'm cut," but she couldn't tell who it was. A few seconds later there was a rustling sound, then silence, and all she could hear was the beating of her own heart as she sat poised with the stick in one hand and a handful of dirt in the other.

She had no idea who'd won. It was too dark to see anything but vague figures and there were two of them coming toward her out of the darkness, then she heard Quinn's voice, a bit winded but steady.

"You're sure one hell of a fighter," he said as he sat down beside her and let out a sigh.

Burly joined them, dropped down on her other side, and seemed to be wiping off his knife in a small patch of grass. "One of them won't be eating much for lunch tomorrow," he said as he stuck the knife back in its sheath.

"And one won't be blowing his nose, thanks to Dicia," said Quinn.

"You heard?" she asked. She thought they'd be too busy fighting to know what was going on around them.

"When you fight Indians you learn not only to know what's going on in front of you but on all sides," answered Quinn. "It's a habit."

She took a deep breath. She'd been brave during the fight with little thought of fear, but now that the whole thing was over she suddenly began to shake almost uncontrollably and Quinn saw it. He stood up, grabbed her hand, pulled her to her feet, and put his arms about her, holding her close.

The action startled her, but as he held her she could feel the warmth of his body against hers and slowly, a little at a time, the shaking began to subside. His arms seemed a cocoon wrapped around her, until he felt her body stop trembling and stand still against him.

"Are you all right now?" he asked.

"Yes," she answered against his chest. "Will they be back?"

"I doubt it. I think they've had enough for one night." He began to loosen his arms from about her. "Will you be all right now?"

She nodded. "I think so," she whispered, and looked up into his face. It was so dark she could barely see his features, but she'd swear he really looked concerned. She'd felt safe and warm in his arms and it surprised her because she'd felt something else too. A strange quickening inside she'd never felt before.

"We'll sleep the same way," he said as he released her,

then reached over, picked up the bags, and set them apart. He looked around to make sure the men were really gone, then they laid back down again on the moss-covered ground and stretched out.

It was cold and damp and dew had fallen where their bodies had been warm before. She pressed as close to the bags as possible, trying to get warm, but it did no good. It didn't seem to bother Quinn and Burly, but they were probably used to it.

The longer she lay there, the colder she became, and suddenly her teeth started chattering. She clenched them tightly, trying to stop, but it seemed impossible.

"What's that noise?" asked Quinn as he raised his head, secure in the knowledge that it wasn't their unwelcome visitors again but unable to pinpoint the sound.

"My teeth," she answered softly, her voice quivering.

"You're cold?"

"Frozen!"

He leaned on one elbow, turned toward her, grabbed one of the brocade bags, and hefted it over her, plunking it down next to the one behind Burly.

"Come here," he said firmly, but she just stared in the dark, not realizing what he meant. "Well, if you won't," he said, and moved close to her, then reached out, pulling her into his arms.

She started to protest vigorously, but he held her all the tighter.

"Stop it!" he cried angrily. "I'm only trying to keep you warm." Slowly, little by little, unable to fight him, she settled down.

Her head rested on his arm and she felt his lips brush her hair as he said, "Now go to sleep," and there was nothing she could do but stay there.

She had to admit it was better than freezing and she moved closer in his arms, feeling his long, muscular body next to hers. It made her feel strange and warm, deep down inside. She'd never let a man get this close to her before and for a moment it frightened her, but then she brushed her fear aside. There was nothing to it. He was merely being sensible.

He couldn't stand her. He was only doing what he'd do for anyone else under the circumstances, then suddenly his hand moved up her back, his fingers caressed her neck, his body pressed closer to her, and she felt his body responding to hers, something she'd never experienced before, and her heart started pounding. Then, just as suddenly, he relaxed, pressed her head close to his chest, and whispered huskily, "Good night, Dicia."

She answered softly, "Good night," and closed her eyes against his chest, wondering why he'd changed his mind, because she was sure he'd wanted to kiss her and she was sure he hadn't wanted to stop with a kiss. Men! She sighed as she settled down and the heat of his body made her drowsy and she dropped off to sleep quickly.

# 8

The next morning came warm and steaming after the cold night and for a moment before opening her eyes she'd forgotten where she was, then she felt the strength of Quinn's arms and opened her eyes slowly to find him staring directly at her face.

"Good morning," he said softly. "Sleep well?"

She started to move, to get out of his arms, but he stopped her.

"Wait," he said sternly. "I want the truth from you."

She tried to relax in his arms, very aware of his nearness and the strange effect it seemed to have on her. "The truth about what?" she asked, trying to be calm.

"I was right when I said last night that you were a few shades lighter than you were a week ago. I've been watching while you slept. You're a white woman. What did you put on your skin?"

Her eyes stared into his and she didn't answer.

Suddenly he smiled cynically. "Walnuts," he whispered

softly. "That's the smell I always associate with you. You put on black walnut stain!"

Her eyes narrowed. He'd guessed the truth.

"Who are you?" he asked, and his eyes looked deep into hers. But still she didn't answer. The smile left his face and his arms tightened about her. "Who are you?" he asked again, and this time his voice had a touch of malice in it.

"You're hurting me," she gasped, and he leaned his head forward, his mouth coming down on hers hard and demanding, setting her lips on fire.

She fought against him, managing to pull her head back as he pressed his body close against hers, and she felt him once more responding as he had last night.

"Thief . . . murderer . . . now you'd ravage a lady?" she asked venomously against his mouth.

As suddenly as he'd kissed her, he rolled her from his arms and leaped to his feet, leaving her lying on the ground.

"Since when are you a lady?" he asked cynically, looking down at her, his eyes hard and cruel.

She scrambled to her feet hurriedly, neither of them aware that Burly was awake and had stretched out, watching them, his elbow bent, head propped on his hand.

"I've always been a lady!" she cried indignantly.

Quinn let out a sarcastic laugh.

"I am!" she yelled louder, goaded on by his laughter. "I'm Lady Loedicia Aldri . . ." She got no further, realizing suddenly that in her anger at his insolence he'd goaded the truth from her. Her hand flew over her mouth and her violet eyes became round and full as she saw the expression on his face.

He reached out and grabbed her wrist, pulling her toward him. "What did you say?" he asked, hardly believing his ears, but she only stared at him wide-eyed. "Say it again," he demanded, his jaw set hard as his hand gripped her wrist tighter.

There was no use pretending anymore. "I'm Lady Loedicia Aldrich," she answered slowly. "But I didn't lie to you . . . my father always called me Dicia and I am from India."

"And you were supposed to marry Lord Varrick," he finished, and suddenly saw the irony of the whole thing. "By God," he exclaimed as he looked at her dumbfounded. "We not only stole his money but his wife!"

"I'm not his wife," she stated emphatically as his fingers eased from around her wrist and she pulled her arm from his grip. "I'd rather die first!"

"And you almost did," he said as he remembered holding the knife to her throat back on board ship.

She reached up and put her hand on her neck and he knew she knew what he was thinking.

Burly had gotten to his feet when she'd confessed her real name and now he walked over and put his hand on Quinn's arm.

"What do we do now?" he asked. "If Varrick finds out we have her, Brant's Indians'll be waiting for us by the time we reach the foothills."

"Who's going to tell him?" asked Quinn, and Burly grinned as he looked at her. Quinn motioned toward her. "Tell me, Mr. Burlington, would you have any suspicions at all that the dark-skinned woman staring at me with fire in her eyes is really a genteel lady of high breeding?"

Burly held up his hands as if to frame her and closed one eye, cocking his head as he looked. "Can't say as I would. She looks more like a camp follower."

"What's a camp follower?" she asked belligerently.

"A camp follower," answered Quinn, "is a young woman who follows the soldiers about, selling her favors."

Loedicia's eyes narrowed. "You think I'm like that?" she yelled angrily.

"I didn't say you were," apologized Burly. "I said you looked like one. And what better for us?"

"Aye," said Quinn. "That way we can get you back to Fort Locke without anyone the wiser." He looked at Burly. "I hear my dear cousin was quite smitten with Lady Aldrich. Her disappearance must have left him extremely embarrassed. I wonder how much he'd be willing to pay to get his little lady love back?" He looked back at

Loedicia and reached out, grabbing her under the chin so she had to look at him.

She jerked her head away. "What do you mean?" she cried. "You'd turn me over to him?"

"For the right price," answered Quinn. "I'm in a bargaining position," he said calmly. "If I've got something my dear cousin wants he's going to pay high to get it."

"I won't go!" she cried. "You can't make me go to him!"

"But I can," he stated firmly. "And you won't run away either," he continued as he saw the look in her eyes, "because I'll be with you every minute from here to Fort Locke. You're not getting out of my sight if I have to tie you to me with a rope. Do you understand?"

She stared at him, her eyes blazing. "I hate you!" she cried, and lashed out at him with both fists.

He caught her wrists and held them tightly, keeping her from hitting him.

She began kicking and yelling like a wildcat and suddenly he let go of her wrists, pulled her into his arms, and grabbed her hair with one hand, holding her head back. She tried to avoid his mouth, but it was no use, his hand held her like a vise. As his lips touched hers she opened her mouth and started to sink her teeth into his lower lip, but he was too quick and drew his head back a few inches.

"Close your mouth!" he demanded, but instead she started pounding him again with her fists. His hand tightened on her hair and she thought he'd pull it from her scalp.

This time his lips met her closed mouth and he kissed her long and hard, his mouth never leaving hers until the fight was gone from her and she melted against him, her hands no longer pounding but clutching his coat weakly.

After long moments he drew his lips from hers and looked steadily into her eyes.

Loedicia felt weak inside from her outburst and from the utterly alien feeling that he'd aroused within her. She never knew a man could make her feel like this and she hated him for it.

She stared straight at him, looking into those beautiful blue eyes of his, and it was the first time Quinn had ever known a woman's eyes to be filled with such intense hatred.

"You'll do exactly as I say and there'll be no more fighting," he whispered softly. "Do you understand?"

She never took her eyes from his. "Yes," she murmured through clenched teeth, and slowly he loosened his arm from about her and she backed away.

"Now let's get our things together," he said as he walked over and picked up one of the bags. "We've got a long way to travel."

Burly walked over, picked up the other bag, and glanced over at Dicia. She'd turned her back on them and was staring off into the morning as the first rays of the sun came up over the horizon. So she was a lady, high bred and high toned. Well, to him she was still Dicia and he felt sorry for her. Quinn wasn't treating her anything like a lady.

Loedicia wouldn't let them know she was crying. She brushed the tear from her cheek furtively, then turned and followed as Quinn started down the hill back toward the main trail. Burly waited to help her over some rough stones and the strength of his hand and his assurance and friendliness made her start to forget what had happened only moments before. She couldn't stay mad. Not when that big ugly face of his with the overabundance of hair broke into a massive grin. His good humor was contagious.

Besides, what good would it do to rebel? Quinn had meant every word. He'd never let her out of his sight. Her only hope was to talk him out of ransoming her to Lord Varrick or maybe, better yet, she'd pray that Lord Varrick wouldn't want her back. He might be so angry at her for running out on him he'd never want to see her again. Either way, there was nothing for her to do but go along with them. One thing for sure, she couldn't make it anywhere on her own. She'd already tried that.

After a few hours' walking they stopped by a farm and bought some bread, butter, cheese, and milk, filling their stomachs and wrapping some of the bread and cheese to take with them. It'd probably be all they'd have for supper, since Quinn was determined not to build any fires.

They reached the Delaware River early that afternoon and by now Loedicia seemed to have completely forgotten her animosity toward Quinn. She was tired and dirty and her first look at the water brought a gleam to her eye.

"Oh, Quinn, it looks so inviting," she said as they stood at the edge of the water. She could feel sweat trickling between her breasts and down her legs and she knelt, leaning over, putting her hand in the water.

"You can swim?" he asked.

"No, but I'll try."

"You may have to," he answered. "The water's over your head here."

She looked up at him. "This is the only place to cross?"

"The only place that isn't over my head."

"But how do I get across?" she asked as she stood up. She was barely up to his shoulder.

"I'll carry you across," he answered, and saw the expression on her face. "Burly has to carry the boots, food, and bags," he explained.

She eyed him suspiciously for a minute, then smiled impishly. "You sure you won't drown me halfway across?"

He looked down at her and a smile played about the corners of his mouth. "Don't tempt me," he answered, then bent over and started taking off his boots. He took his jacket off and set it on the ground and they tied the boots and food inside, then fastened it in the middle of a stick with the bags of money, one on each side.

"I'll go first," said Burly, and he picked the stick up, hefted it over his head, and slipped quietly into the water. It was waist-deep as he hit bottom and started slowly across with Quinn and Loedicia watching. As he moved farther out the water deepened until it was up to his chin. He held his head high and turned around to face them. "So far, so good," he yelled, and Quinn held his hand up to acknowledge that he'd heard.

Loedicia watched in awe as the slowly moving water

moved above his chin and licked at his mouth, then slowly, as he moved forward, it began to recede until it was below his shoulders. In minutes he walked out on the other side and waved to them from the bank. It looked terribly far across.

Quinn turned to Loedicia. "Ready?"

She swallowed hard. "Ready," she answered, and he stepped down into the water, then held his hand up to her.

"What do I do?" she asked.

"Give me your hand and we walk until the water gets too high, then let me handle the rest."

She took his hand and stepped into the water slowly, feeling its coolness against her feet and legs. She'd taken off her moccasins and the muddy river bottom felt slimy between her toes.

"What's the face for?" asked Quinn as she wrinkled up her nose.

"The mud feels terrible."

"It's better than rocks. Wait till we get out farther, the rocks are covered with slime and one slip is all we need."

She clung to his arm as they started to walk slowly and she felt the water getting higher and higher, even covering her breasts. When it was up to her shoulders Quinn reached out, pulled her toward him, and picked her up in his left arm so she almost faced him.

"Put your arms around my neck and hold tight," he said.

She did as he told her and her cheek pressed against his.

He stepped slowly forward, gauging his steps more carefully now. Ordinarily he was as surefooted as Burly whether in water or on land, but with the extra burden he carried it wasn't so easy.

Water crept higher on them both and now it was caressing her chin.

He stopped for a minute. "I'm about a half inch or so shorter than Burly," he explained against her ear. "If the water covers your mouth, keep it closed and breath through your nose."

She looked about her at the deep water and felt strangely afraid. Although the water wasn't flowing too fast, she could feel its pull against her clothes and she held on all the tighter as she answered him, her lips pressing against his ear.

He began moving forward again, trying to pick his footing. About three steps farther and his foot came down on a rock he thought was solid, then suddenly it slid from under his foot and they both went under.

The sudden movement caught Loedicia by surprise and there was no time for her to get even one breath before she was completely submerged. Her hands slipped from around Quinn's neck as she panicked and she started to drift away from him in the muddy water.

He groped in the water frantically, trying to catch her before she drifted too far, and suddenly his hand struck her arm. He grabbed hold and pulled hard, reaching out with his other hand.

They were both still underwater as Burly plunged back in, but before he could reach them Quinn's head emerged first, then Burly breathed a sigh as a gasping Loedicia popped her head up beside Quinn's.

She was sputtering water and hanging on to Quinn for dear life and Burly stopped where he was and waited.

Quinn held her tightly against him, his cheek pressed close to hers, making sure her head was high above the water, and he started slowly continuing across the river, feeling every step carefully.

"Hang on," he whispered softly, and she breathed in the taste of the sweet clean air, trying to forget the nightmare she'd experienced as the river water tried to force its way into her lungs. Stark terror had engulfed her and she'd felt as if she'd been buried alive.

Fear that it might happen again made her grasp him all the tighter until slowly, as the water level moved down his body, she began to relax, knowing they were safe.

As the water reached his knees and he reached Burly he swung her up so he was carrying her in both arms and he saw her face for the first time, tears streaming down her cheeks.

He stopped and looked down at her. She looked rather small, her curly hair wet and straggling, her eyes large and misty.

"You didn't do very well on your first swimming lesson," he said as he continued toward shore with Burly beside him.

Her face reddened. "You weren't supposed to slip," she answered breathlessly.

He reached the bank and set her on the edge and she made no effort to get up. He sat down beside her and looked back out over the water as Burly got out and went to get their bundle and bags.

"Are you all right?" he asked as he saw her taking deep breaths.

"I will be when I get the taste of the river water out of my mouth and my knees quit shaking."

He watched her as she lay back in the grass, breathing deeply, trying to relax. She closed her eyes and he studied her face.

Even with the walnut stain on he should have realized . . . She was a beautiful woman, warm and vibrant, and he imagined what she must have looked like back in Boston. Her hair would have been long and full, there would be a slight blush on her lips . . . yes, he could see why Varrick had been smitten.

She felt his eyes on her and sat up quickly as Burly walked over. "Did you two give up?" he asked as he knelt beside them.

"Not yet," she answered. "I needed a breather."

"I don't think she likes swimming," offered Quinn.

"I think you did it on purpose," she added, but there was a touch of mischief in her voice.

He scrambled to his feet, picked her up before she had a chance to say a word, and stood holding her poised as if to throw her back in.

"Did I now?" he asked.

"Don't you dare!" she cried as she grabbed the front of his shirt, hanging on, her eyes wide.

Suddenly all three started laughing and Quinn hollered,

"Catch!" and threw her to Burly, who caught her deftly, then set her on her feet.

"We'll dry out on the way," Quinn said as he walked over, picked up his bag, and threw his jacket at her. "Put this on until you dry off a bit so you don't catch a fever." She grabbed the jacket, putting it on.

She wondered if it was his way of apologizing for his behavior this morning, but then again she wasn't sure. He was a strange man and hard to understand. One minute laughing and teasing like a young boy, the next vicious and cruel as he had been that morning. But, then, had he been cruel? He hadn't beaten her, only kissed her, and her lips burned and her face turned red as she remembered the strength and fire in that one kiss and it angered her that he'd made her feel as he had.

She raised her head to the warmth of the afternoon sun and fell into step between Quinn and Burly and they headed away from the river.

That evening, as dusk fell, they ate their bread and cheese and settled down for the night. They'd found an old burned-out farmhouse with the barn intact, hay and all, and climbed up into the loft. Burly settled down by the broken hayloft door so he could see out.

Loedicia started to climb across the hay toward him when Quinn stopped her.

"Dicia?"

She turned to look back at him. It was dark in the loft and she could barely see him. He'd settled in what looked like a comfortable spot in the corner of the hayloft.

"Come here," he said, but she sat on the pile of straw, staring at him. "Come here!"

"But I won't run away," she protested as she saw him stretch his arm out in the straw, motioning with his head for her to lie down beside him.

She moved forward slowly, reluctantly. "I promise you I won't," she pleaded. "Please . . ."

"Lay down," he whispered softly but firmly as she reached the spot beside him.

Cautiously she stretched out and put her head on his arm to use it as a pillow, only he didn't let her stay so far away. He pulled her closer against him, both arms around her.

"Now I know you won't leave unexpectedly," he whispered as he tried to look down into her face in the darkness of the loft. "Settle down now and get some sleep."

She was furious as she lay against him, her heart pounding, fighting the emotions his nearness always aroused in her. "It's too hot to sleep like this," she said softly, but he ignored her.

"Good night, Dicia," he whispered stubbornly as he nestled her close in his arms and there was no use arguing.

For the next few weeks they plodded along for miles, fording rivers and creeks where they stopped long enough to wash off some of the dust, borrowing, begging, stealing, and sometimes paying for food along the way. Quinn seemed to know the country well and could single out the farmhouses where they'd be welcome. They slept in fields, caves, and abandoned barns and farms, never building fires at night, and always Loedicia reluctantly slept in Quinn's arms.

"But where could I possibly run to?" she protested one evening as he held her close, but it did no good. When he said he wasn't about to let her out of sight, he meant it.

Loedicia, in spite of the hardships, had enjoyed the journey. Her two companions were fun to be with, even Quinn when he wasn't being stubborn and bossy.

# 9

They trudged into Reading early one night the last week of June, tired and a little thinner, with a drizzle of rain to accompany them.

"And where do we go from here?" asked Loedicia as they walked into the quiet village.

"To see a man named Basque," answered Quinn, "Adam Basque, and to get rid of the rest of the silver."

She looked up at him as they walked, feeling the light rain on her face. "I thought you were taking the money to Fort Locke."

"Afraid not. We're building an army, Dicia. An army that'll hold back the British and let them know we mean business. This money's going to buy arms. We're building an arsenal here in Reading and we're going to do it with their own money."

"But you said the money was Lord Varrick's."

"It was. Lord Varrick owned property in the Indies, but he'd rather own a part of the colonies. He sold the property, bought more land from the crown, and this was supposed to pay for it. The crown in return was to use it for the June payroll. One of those under-the-table transactions where Varrick gets twice as much as he's entitled to. I'd like to know how he explained the missing money to General Gage."

"Why do you hate him so?" she asked.

"You hate him."

"That's different."

"How?"

"There's something about him. The way he looks at me. As if he couldn't wait to get his hands on me. As if he was the devil himself."

"Which he is," answered Burly from her other side.

"But why?" she asked again. "If he's Quinn's cousin . . ."

But Quinn changed the subject and before she knew it they were at the door of Adam Basque's house.

He was a short man, compared to Quinn and Burly, muscular and red-faced, with a pudgy wife, but his daughter was the one who caught Loedicia's eye as she stepped in.

She had eyes for Quinn only. Suggestive eyes that reminded Loedicia of Aunt Agatha's, the way they talked to a man, and Loedicia knew what they were saying. Quinn had obviously been here before and Roxanne knew him.

She was blond, taller than Loedicia, maybe four or five

years older, and wore her hair long and straight. Her figure was full and she used it to advantage as she walked, holding her breasts high, hips swinging.

Adam Basque was a carpenter and wagon maker and his house was one of the better homes in the village. He greeted Quinn and Burly enthusiastically.

"Captain Locke, Mr. Burlington, I didn't expect you for a few more days," he said jovially. "Come in out of the rain. Come in." Then his eyes fell on Loedicia as she stood, wet and bedraggled, between the two men. "And who do we have here?" he asked, surprised.

Quinn stepped back and ushered Loedicia in. He'd confiscated for her an old black jacket a few days back and she hugged it about her as she stepped into the warmly lit room, the smell of fresh bread and spices filling her nostrils.

"This"—Quinn introduced her with no other explanation—"is Dicia."

Adam stared at her, frowning, as did his wife. "How do, young lady," he finally said, and turned to Mrs. Basque. "The poor thing looks tired and hungry. Put out some of that leftover stew. They could all use some hot food." Then he turned to his daughter. "Put some water on so they can clean up."

"Did Ramsey arrive with our clothes?" asked Quinn, and Adam nodded.

"A week ago. After you eat you can take a bath and clean up."

"Maybe we should change before we eat," suggested Quinn. "I hate dripping water all over the kitchen."

"Nonsense," exclaimed Mrs. Basque. "It won't hurt a thing. You folks set right down and get something warm into your stomachs first."

So Quinn ushered Loedicia ahead of him and they sat down at the table.

"Where are you keeping the supplies?" asked Quinn as Adam pulled up a chair and sat down with them.

"Lapham has a farm a short way out of town since he's married, so we put a false floor in with enough space under it for a small arsenal which we're slowly building and the money you brought'll help fill it up."

"You men," added his wife from the fireplace, where she was reheating the stew. "The only way you know how to settle things is by fighting."

"We have no choice if they won't listen to reason," answered her husband.

"No one likes war," said Quinn, "but we can't just sit back and let them bleed us to death. America's rich, not only in people but resources. We've got the best land in the world, plenty of timber. There's nothing we can't do with this country given the time and money. Why should we fill the king's purse while ours goes empty and our land goes undeveloped?" He looked back at Adam. "Joseph Wickham said word's out that they're going to ask Washington to take command of the army if war comes."

"I heard," agreed Adam. "The men followed him before. They'll follow him again."

"Aye," answered Burly. "Right around Georgie's bloody throat."

"Boston's bad," stated Adam. "The governor's given orders to shoot anyone trying to run the blockade. Everyone's sending supplies who can, but we know they aren't all getting through. It's a long way by land and it doesn't take much to waylay a wagon load of rice or grain."

"It can't last much longer," said Burly as Mrs. Basque set the food in front of them, and they went on talking while they ate.

The beef stew was delicious and the bread was hot, letting the butter melt into it. If it hadn't been for her wet clothes and the constant chatter, Loedicia could almost have fallen asleep here in the warm kitchen. The men were still talking as she finished eating and sat back self-consciously. She'd sensed whenever Roxanne came in and out of the room with the water and each time she looked up she was met with hostile eyes and Quinn still did nothing to explain her presence to them.

The walnut stain had almost left now, leaving her a dusky, suntanned hue, and she felt she must look any-

thing but attractive, especially compared to Roxanne's
clean, scrubbed look.

Quinn finished eating and turned to Dicia as if he'd just
remembered she was there. "You look tired," he said.
"We'll find a place to sleep as soon as we've cleaned up."

"You'll sleep right here," said Adam. "Take a bath,
climb into bed clean. We have two extra rooms now with
both Lapham and Michael gone." He turned to his
daughter. "Take the young woman and help her bathe.
Lend her one of your nightgowns. She can use Lapham's
room. Burly and Quinn can bed down in the other."

Roxanne came over, took Dicia's arm, and she stood
up, following Roxanne across the room, then she stopped
and looked back at Quinn. Was she going to get a
reprieve tonight? He wouldn't dare . . . or would he? She
saw the look in his eyes and her heart sank.

"Dicia and I will sleep in Lapham's room," he stated
boldly, and Adam's eyes bugged out, his wife's mouth
flew open, and Roxanne stopped at the door, whirled
around, and stared. "And Burly will sleep in Michael's
room," he finished as he reached out for another slice of
bread.

Loedicia looked at him and their eyes met. There was
complete silence in the room and she wished she could
crawl under the table.

"Captain!" gasped Mrs. Basque in surprise.

"We can always sleep in the barn," he suggested coldly,
but Adam spoke up.

"No . . . no," he protested hurriedly, looking at his
wife. "No need . . . Mrs. Basque was just surprised." His
face reddened. "You never brought a . . . a . . ." He
cleared his throat, embarrassed. "Well, you never did, you
know."

Quinn never flinched. "I account to no one for my actions," he said. "If you prefer, the barn will do just as
well."

"I won't hear of it," said Adam, and turned to
Roxanne. "Take the young lady upstairs."

"But don't let her out of your sight," added Quinn.

"Find her a robe and take her to the parlor when she's cleaned up and remember, keep her with you."

Loedicia fumed as she stared at him. If he was trying to embarrass her he was succeeding, but she wasn't about to give him any satisfaction. She held her head high and tried not to blush under the tan and her eyes flashed as she smiled at him seductively.

"Don't worry, darling," she answered sensuously. "I don't think anyone here's about to run off with me." She turned to Adam Basque, rolling her eyes. "Now, would you, Mr. Basque?" she asked softly, and he stammered, his face turning crimson, his wife's turning white.

Quinn's eyes narrowed.

"I'll see you upstairs, darling," she added to Quinn, and turned to Roxanne. "I am terribly tired, if you don't mind," she said, ignoring the look Roxanne was giving her.

They left the kitchen before Quinn had time to retaliate.

"Do you mind if I pick out the nightgown before I bathe?"she asked Roxanne as they started down the hall.

Roxanne shook her head. "If you want," she answered, and guided Loedicia to the stairs. "How long have you known Quinn?" she asked, and Loedicia tipped her head back, closing her eyes for a second as if thinking.

"I met him in Boston," she answered truthfully as she opened her eyes. "You might say we've been inseparable ever since."

She saw Roxanne become tense. The woman was overly upset over the whole affair. Then Loedicia remembered the conversations on board ship between Quinn and Burly. That's where she'd heard the name Roxanne. Her face flushed and she looked away as she remembered what they'd said about her.

When they reached Roxanne's room and she opened the drawer there wasn't much choice. There were two flannel nightgowns with long sleeves, a cotton one a bit worn, with short sleeves and a rounded neckline, but as Loedicia pulled it aside something colorful caught her eye. She pulled out a bright blue thin cotton gown with a plunging neckline trimmed with lace. Something special for rainy days, she presumed.

"This should do fine," she said, picking it up, holding it in front of her. "It's a bit big, but I guess I can't be too choosy," she said purposefully, and Roxanne flinched as she gave Loedicia's petite but curvaceous figure a quick evaluation.

"Why are you going to the fort with Captain Locke?" asked Roxanne as they headed back downstairs toward the back of the house, where the bath water was set up.

"Isn't it obvious?" answered Loedicia.

"Obvious?"

"Why, Quinn can't let me out of his sight for one minute," she said, lying to her. "He's so terribly jealous." She saw the crestfallen look on Roxanne's clean, scrubbed face.

That was ironic too. Her mouth should have been clean scrubbed with soap, from what she'd heard Quinn and Burly tell. Roxanne looked as innocent as a newborn babe, but Loedicia knew differently and she was enjoying knowing that her presence tonight was taking the wind out of Roxanne's sails.

Loedicia couldn't resist. "Don't worry, Roxanne," she said solicitously. "When I'm through with Quinn and tired of him you can have him back."

"What do you mean?" she asked sharply, and Loedicia smiled that wicked, coquettish smile that so often got her in trouble.

"Oh, come now," she answered, "don't be coy. Quinn told me how you practically raped him the first time he came here. I believe it was in the cornfield, wasn't it?" Loedicia knew she'd been right by the deadly look on Roxanne's face.

"Oh!" she cried as her face reddened. "How could he . . . and to you!" She stalked off, leaving Loedicia to bathe herself. Something Quinn had given specific orders for her not to do.

Loedicia smiled as she climbed into the tub. Two could play at Quinn's game and she slid down into the warm water.

An hour later she sat on the edge of the bed, contemplating. Maybe she'd gone too far? Maybe . . . but, then, so had he! He'd made her feel like . . . what? A whore? Yes. His mistress? What else? But hadn't she told him when she'd asked him to take her with them? Hadn't she said she could pretend to be his mistress? She should have controlled her temper. After all, what did it matter what these people thought? She'd never see them after today.

She got up and started to walk to the window when she heard a noise outside the door and walked over to listen. She heard voices and put her ear to the door.

"But, Quinn, you can't," Roxanne was pleading softly. "I've been waiting for months. Why are you doing this? You knew I'd be waiting."

"Be sensible, Roxanne," he answered irritably.

"You never worried before," she whispered.

"Who's worried?"

"Quinn, I love you. I need you."

"No. You need a man, Roxanne. Any man. You always have. The only reason you want me is because I don't come to you. You came to my room, remember?"

"But you took me, didn't you?" she pleaded. "Take me again and this time make it complete!"

Loedicia heard the doorknob turn and started to move away from the door as Quinn said, "It's over, Roxanne. That's all there is to it. There wasn't ever anything in the first place except a stopover. Be content with that." Loedicia made a mad dash for the window and was standing quietly looking out, her back to him, as he entered the room and closed the door behind him, locking it.

He breathed a deep sigh and walked over to the bed. He was barefoot. He set his boots on the floor, then looked toward Loedicia.

"Is it still raining?" he asked, and she nodded.

"Who . . . who sleeps on the floor?" she asked. "You or I?"

"Neither!" he shot back, and she knew he was angry. He stood up and walked over to her. "What did you think you were doing down there?" he asked angrily, and she bit her lip.

"Nothing," she answered, and started trembling nervously. "I was only taking your lead, that's all."

"Oh, yes." He mimicked her. "Darling, Quinn! And what did you tell Roxanne?"

Her eyes widened. "You mean your lady love from the corn patch?" She saw his eyes take on a new depth.

"Damn you!" he blurted. "You know everything, don't you?"

"I know she had to practically rape you to get a rise out of you. At least I'm better than she is!"

He stared at her, his eyes dark and forbidding. "So you've noticed, have you?" he said with malice, and she couldn't answer. The look on his face frightened her. She'd pushed him too far.

He turned abruptly, walked to the bed, slipped off all his clothes except for his underwear, and climbed in.

"Blow out the candles and come to bed, Dicia," he ordered, and she took a deep breath, her knees shaking. "Blow them out!" he ordered again, and she walked to the dresser, her legs hardly supporting her, and blew out both candles.

"Now come here," he said in the darkness, but her feet wouldn't carry her.

"I can't," she whispered. "Not tonight, Quinn. Please, not tonight . . . not in the bed."

She was standing with her back to him and suddenly, before she realized it, he'd left the bed, walked up behind her, and picked her up, cradling her in his arms.

"Please . . . Quinn," she begged. "Not tonight. I'm afraid of you when you're like this."

"Like what?" he asked huskily as he held her over the bed.

"You're angry," she whispered.

"Am I really?" he asked cynically, then leaned over and gently laid her on the bed.

She felt him lie down beside her, then, just as before, his arms reached out and he pulled her to him and her whole body became tense as she felt him responding once again.

"You know me pretty well, don't you," he whispered,

and she put her hand on his chest, trying to keep him
away.

There was something different about tonight. Maybe it
was the soft bed or the rain outside or how sweet she
smelled, all clean and soft, her hair curling about his finger, but tonight was not like any other night.

Quinn let his hands move through her hair, then down
onto her neck, and he felt her body quiver.

"Quinn, please," she pleaded, realizing too that tonight
was different. It was like no other night. Tonight he
wasn't just holding her.

"Shhh!" he whispered softly, and his lips brushed her
cheek, then her mouth, and he kissed her passionately,
drinking in the new, strange feeling the touch of his lips
had brought to her.

He took his lips from hers and bent down, kissing her
neck, his hands gently caressing her body as it trembled
beneath his fingers, and Loedicia thought she was going
mad.

She'd never felt so alive in her life as she felt him
stroke her sensuously, bringing her whole body to life, yet
she fought against her emotions, trying to keep her sanity.

"Dicia! Dicia!" he murmured against her ear, and
kissed her again, and it was no use. She was lost in his
embrace. There was no turning back and she gave in to
him, surrendering not only her body but her soul as he
made love to her, taking her, not once, but twice before
the night was through, and she responded each time with
a violent passion that surprised them both.

She had fallen asleep in his arms, but the next morning
when she woke, the other side of the bed was empty and
she sat up quickly. Quinn was staring out the window,
completely dressed, only now he wore buckskins and
moccasins. He turned as he heard her stir.

"Your clothes are on the chair in the corner," he said
matter-of-factly. "I was about to wake you. It's almost
time to leave."

There was something about him this morning. A cold
indifference. She stared at him, unable to speak, pulling
the covers to her chin to hide her nakedness, and she

vaguely remembered his slipping the nightgown off her during their lovemaking.

His eyes looked at her almost cruelly as he glanced at her, then he turned and looked back out the window.

She slipped from the bed and walked to the chair in the corner. "Where did these come from?" she asked as she held up buckskins and a new pair of moccasins.

"I had Adam get them last night."

"You've been downstairs already?" she asked as she got into the clothes.

He shrugged. "I had business to attend to this morning."

She glanced past him out the window. Well, at least today it wasn't raining, but somehow a cloud seemed to have fallen over Quinn.

"I'm ready," she finally said, and Quinn turned to look at her. For a moment she thought she saw pain in his eyes, but it passed quickly.

"Let's go, then," he said, and walked to the door.

"Quinn?" She stopped him and he turned to face her. "Quinn, last night . . . I want to explain about last night."

"Forget about last night," he snapped irritably. "Forget everything about it."

Her mouth fell. "Forget it?"

"That's right. It was something that happened, that's all."

He might as well have slapped her across the face and she looked at him, stunned, as tears of shock began to gather in her eyes. My God! It meant nothing to him! The warmth, fire, passion, and later the ecstasy. She might have known. Hadn't her father warned her? She felt dirty and ashamed. She'd let him do to her what she vowed no man would ever do and she felt humiliated. But she felt anger too. It began to stir in her loins, spreading into every fiber of her being. Anger at herself and anger at Quinn.

"How could you!" she gasped, her face livid. "After what you did to me!"

His jaw tightened and his eyes flashed cynically. "Well,

at least this morning you won't have to pretend you're my mistress, will you?" he said, and his eyes bored into hers.

"I hate you, Quinn Locke!" she cried through clenched teeth. "Don't you ever touch me again or so help me, I'll kill you." The last word was more of a sob.

"Let's go," he said roughly, opening the door and ushering her out.

Burly was waiting for them in the kitchen and the minute he saw them, he sensed something had happened. There was a depth in Loedicia's eyes that hadn't been there before.

Adam and Mrs. Basque were there too, as was Roxanne, who stared daggers at Loedicia, who ate breakfast silently as the men talked.

"Did you get the rifles?" Quinn finally asked Burly, who leaned over, hefted two Kentucky rifles off the floor, throwing one to Quinn as he stood up, then held out a sack to him. "There's powder and ball in the pack."

"Good," answered Quinn. He turned and looked down at Loedicia, who'd finished the last of her eggs. "Have Mrs. Basque give you enough food for a day or two . . . bread, cheese, you know what to get."

She nodded and went to the larder with the woman while the men said good-bye and she returned with a sack of food to find Quinn and Roxanne missing from the room.

"Roxanne went with Quinn to get the horses," explained Burly when he saw the look on Loedicia's face, but she didn't answer, only walked to the window and stared out toward the barn.

When they returned she expected to see Roxanne smiling over her triumph at getting Quinn off to herself, but instead Quinn came back to the house alone and she saw Roxanne walking off toward the patch of garden at the side of the house, kicking at the ground with the toe of her shoe as if in anger, and she wondered what might have happened.

There were no saddles on the horses this time and Loedicia looked at them apprehensively. "I've never ridden bareback," she said to Quinn as he handed her the reins.

"Then it's time you learned," he answered, and picked her up gently, setting her astride the horse.

She held up the bag of food. "What do I do with this?"

He took it from her, tied it to another bag he was holding, and slung it across in front of her. "Make sure it doesn't slip off."

They told the Basques good-bye and Quinn told Adam to keep in touch. "Joseph Wickham's going to Philadelphia for the meeting," he said as they shook hands. "Jefferson's a friend of the family, he'll let him know what goes on and you can get word to me. I'll send Telak and some warriors in before the snow flies."

Adam agreed and both men jumped easily astride their horses and the three of them cantered out of the yard as the early-morning sun began to dry up the wet earth.

A short distance out of town, Quinn left the main trail and headed for the distant hills. Loedicia, not used to riding without a saddle, slid all over the horse's back and by noon she was stiff and sore. They stopped to rest rather late and she declined to sit down to eat. Quinn grinned.

"Can't take it, can you?" he quipped.

"I can take anything you can give!" she answered angrily, and stalked off, not hearing his quiet answer, "I doubt it."

Burly gave Quinn a disgusted look. "What are you trying to prove, Quinn?" he asked.

"What do you mean?"

Burly watched Loedicia's back as she wandered among the trees, stretching her legs, munching on a piece of bread and cheese.

"You didn't have to sleep with her last night. Or the past two weeks for that matter," he said. "What are you trying to do to her?"

"Maybe I like it."

"Oh, I don't doubt that, but she's a lady, Quinn. She's not like other women."

"I'll agree there," answered Quinn. "She'd run away at the slightest chance . . . and take a good look at her,

Burly, the walnut stain's gone. She wouldn't have to worry this time about being mistaken for a slave. An Indian maybe, with the suntan, but not a slave."

"You know very well she wouldn't go now. She didn't have to go to that room last night and wait for you."

"But she did."

"That's right, she did," argued Burly. "She could have walked out the front door of Basque's house and never come back—"

"You're blind, Burly," interrupted Quinn. "Dicia doesn't do things on impulse. She plans things, like when she ran from Varrick. She must have had that planned for days."

He stood up and watched her as she leaned against a tree, her hair brushed back from her face to feel the sun as it reached through a hole in the branches above her.

"If the opportunity was right she'd leave now, but she knows she doesn't have a chance. I know what she has in mind," he said as he watched her, knowing the gracious curves hidden under those buckskins and the soft curve of her neck where his lips had caressed it. "She figures if I fall in love with her before we reach the fort I won't turn her over to Varrick." He turned to Burly. "She waited for me last night, all right." His voice became hard and cynical. "She waited for me with her sweet-smelling hair and wearing a nightgown Roxanne's probably worn to entice half the male population of Reading."

"And you took advantage of it?" asked Burly.

"Why not? She asked for it, didn't she?"

"You fool!" blurted Burly. "She was trying to impress Roxanne. Any damn fool could tell that Roxanne expected you to share her bed last night and you as much as told them Dicia was your mistress. She was only playing your game."

Quinn flinched, then his face became hard. "The hell she was!" he exclaimed. "She was playing her own game and it won't work. Quinn Locke gives his heart to no woman, not now or ever!" He brushed the crumbs from his fingers. "Now let's get the hell out of here. We're los-

ing time," he said, and hollered for her. "Dicia! It's time
to go."

Loedicia walked slowly over and stood leaning against
her horse. How can a person's rear end get so sore? She
rubbed it lightly, feeling the sore spots, and tears came to
her eyes. What if she got blisters?

Burly walked up behind her. "Dicia?"

She turned, biting her lip. "I'll put you on," he said.

"Thanks," she answered softly as he reached down to
pick her up.

"I'm sorry," he said, his bristly face worried.

"Sorry?"

His face reddened. "For what Quinn did to you last
night." He picked her up and set her on the horse gently,
handing her the reins. "I don't know what's got into him.
Last night . . ." He put his hand over hers as it rested on
her thigh. "He never forced a woman before, lass. . . .
He never did. . . . I know him. They always gave
willingly."

Her face turned crimson. "So did I, Burly," she answered softly. "That is, I didn't fight him, but it wouldn't
have done me any good if I had, would it?"

"Lass . . ."

"Don't fret," she said. "Only tell me. How can he do to
a woman what he did to me last night, then act like nothing happened? What is Captain Quinn Locke?"

Burly sighed. "He's a bastard, lass." He saw the astonished look on her face. "Not figuratively, but literally. His
father never married his mother. Not that he didn't want
to. But you see he already had a wife. A mad one, true,
locked away from the world, but very much alive. He
would have had what Lord Varrick has now if it hadn't
been for two women, his father's wife and his mother. He
never knew his mother. She died when he was two and
his father took him to the estates at Locksley, hoping
Quinn's grandfather would accept him. But he never did.
He let him take the name of Locksley, which Quinn shortened to Locke when he left, but when Quinn's father
died his grandfather let it be known that his only daugh-

ter's son, Kendall Varrick, would be his heir. That's when Quinn decided to leave."

"How do you know all this?"

"Because I grew up with Quinn. I worked on the Locksley estates and left England with him. We've been together ever since."

"And he's taken it out on women ever since, right?"

He looked at her sheepishly. "In a way. Trouble is, they find him irresistible and he's taken advantage of it."

"What are you two gabbing about?" called Quinn as he mounted his horse and rode toward them.

"I was helping her on," answered Burly as he squeezed her hand.

"Thanks," she said, and tried to smile, but it didn't come off too well as her horse moved forward a step and she winced with pain.

Quinn reached out and caught her mount's bridle as Burly moved off toward his horse. "Is it really that bad?" he asked.

"Why should you care!"

He leaned forward, picked her up, and sat her in front of him on his horse as she protested violently.

"Will you sit still!" he yelled as the horse became skittish. "If you ride with me until you get used to it you won't be as sore and I'll teach you how."

"Don't do me any favors," she answered sarcastically as she quit fighting him and sat stiff and straight-backed in front of him.

He called to Burly. "Put the sacks on your horse and lead Dicia's," he said. "She'll ride with me until she learns it. I can't have an amateur with us for the next three hundred and fifty miles."

She turned to look at him in surprise. "Three hundred and fifty miles?"

"This is big country," he answered, a grin on his face. "And the part where we're going I call my country."

For the rest of the day she rode with Quinn, listening to his instructions, learning the ins and outs of riding bareback. At first she balked, but when she realized he wasn't doing it to irritate her, she settled down to learning and she had to admit the day went better.

That evening when they stopped, she was still able to walk when she got off the horse and she was no more sore than she had been that morning. There was such a difference when you knew what you were doing.

"Tomorrow you'll ride with me again, then the next day we'll try you on your own," he said. "By that time you should have a few calluses." He hit her on the rump as she started to walk away and she looked back at him in surprise.

He'd made no mention of last night, yet sometimes while they were riding she'd look back at him and he'd be looking at her in the strangest way.

They built a fire that evening for the first time and Quinn showed her the rudiments of fire making in the wild. While they gathered wood and got the fire going Burly took off and came back a short time later with two rabbits, which they barbecued on a spit Quinn had set over the fire.

The evening went well, but as it neared time to bed down for the night Loedicia felt her stomach tie up in knots. If he forced her to sleep in his arms tonight he'd have a fight on his hands, but he didn't. Instead he stretched out on one side of the fire, his rifle at his side, bid them good night, and closed his eyes.

Burly was sitting next to Loedicia and she looked at him in surprise as she sighed, "Thank God," then she crawled to her own little corner in front of the fire, as far away from Quinn as possible, curled up, and tried to sleep, but sleep wouldn't come.

She'd been used to sleeping between them, first as Dicia the native boy, then in Quinn's arms every night, and now as she lay on the hard ground alone she heard every little sound. The screech owl, the nighthawk, her horse's whinny, and rustling sounds as some animal passed near her head. The night seemed to have a thousand sounds, all of them louder in the darkness about her.

First she turned this way, then that, then lay quiet as something, probably a bat, swooped down in the darkness, then made off through the trees. Over an hour later she still tossed and turned and lay awake. The fire was only a faint glow and it was pitch dark.

Suddenly she heard movement beside her in the darkness, but before she could scream, Quinn's hand went over her mouth and he whispered. "Shhh . . . I can't sleep either." His hand moved from her face to the back of her neck and on down her back as his arms went around her and he pulled her close to him.

She wanted to protest, but couldn't. He said nothing more, only held her close against him, and the warmth and security in his arms made her drowsy and before they realized it they were both asleep.

# 10

Loedicia learned quickly and in two days she was riding well. By the end of the week she had it mastered. Quinn even took time to teach her how to load and shoot his rifle, how to make a cup out of a wild gourd. He took time to teach her about the different plants and the medicines that could be made from them and which were good to eat. By the time they reached Fort Locke she was going to know survival in the wilderness as if she'd been born to it.

Burly never interfered; in fact, he helped and sometimes he'd eye the two of them curiously. They seemed to get along all right most of the time, but once in a while the tension would build up and they'd fight like wildcats. In spite of this, each night when they settled down to sleep Loedicia found herself in Quinn's arms, but not once did he make love to her, although almost every night she knew he fought the natural responses of his body and as much as she hated what he'd done to her, she couldn't forget it. Nor could she forget the feelings it aroused in her and many a night as she lay in his arms she wondered if she really would fight him if he tried to make love to her again and she'd fall asleep aching inside.

Two days from Reading, they slipped past one of the forts in the Blue Mountains and rode on toward the foothills of the Appalachians. The fort still garrisoned British soldiers and Adam Basque had warned Quinn that the British were onto him, so from here on they rode light and avoided anyplace where they might come in contact with redcoats.

They lived off the land, hunting, fishing, putting rugged miles behind them as they crossed the mountains, avoiding people as much as possible and, when it was necessary, making their stops in the small settlements on the way brief ones.

"Varrick'll figure you'll head for home," said Burly one afternoon about ten days from Reading as they made their way along an old Indian trail overgrown with weeds.

"But he has to catch me first," answered Quinn.

"He could do that too. We lost time back there between Princeton and Reading."

"I wonder which he'll look for first, his money or his bride." Quinn laughed and he glanced over at Dicia, whose face turned scarlet under the suntan.

She was quite a woman, he had to agree. She'd taken to the wilderness like a duck to water and there was never a complaint from her even when the rain beat down on them and the sun was so hot you could fry an egg on a rock.

For a titled lady, brought up in drawing rooms, spoiled and pampered, she proved most interesting to watch because Quinn swore she looked as if she were enjoying the ordeal. She was laughing and gay most of the time, except when she was arguing with him, and then she had a temper like a bobcat's.

Burly watched them with a gentle acceptance, but he knew better than to mention anything to either one about their relationship. He'd just nod and shake his head, especially at night, when they always ended up in each other's arms.

"What happens if he catches us?" she asked as they rounded a bend and started down a small slope.

"He'll kill me," answered Quinn, and she looked at him, startled.

"Why should he do that?"

"Because I'm a thorn in his side."

"But he can't just kill you."

"Why not?"

"He has no proof you've done anything."

"He doesn't need proof."

"But he'll have to take you back to the authorities."

"Dead or alive?"

"Don't be silly," she said. "Alive."

"You're a dreamer, Dicia," answered Quinn. "Out here we make our own laws."

"But you can't."

"Who's to stop us?"

"They have troops here, don't they?"

Quinn looked at Burly as they continued to ride along the trail. "Hear that, Burly?" he said.

Burly laughed. "Fort Niagara has troops, but they look the other way when Lord Varrick's on the prowl."

"He lives at Fort Niagara?" she asked.

"He lives about eight or ten miles east of Niagara," answered Burly. "Smack dab in the lap of Joseph Brant's Iroquois."

She reined her horse around a boulder, using leg pressure as Quinn had taught her. "Who's Joseph Brant?"

"He, little nosy," answered Quinn, "controls the other half of the league of Iroquois."

"Half?"

"The Mohawks, Onondagas, Cayugas, Senecas."

"But they're Indians."

"So is Joseph Brant."

"But what do they have to do with Lord Varrick?"

"Varrick's a friend of Brant and his Indians. Brant's about the only man Varrick doesn't dare cheat, except maybe Sir William Johnson. They fought together against the French and I know if war comes the Indians'll side with Johnson and back the king and so will Varrick."

"But why will the Indians fight against you?"

They came to a small stream and Quinn went across first, followed by Loedicia, then Burly.

"Because," he said as he waited for her to rein up beside him, "the British promised them permanent land. A promise they'll never be able to keep, with settlers moving in. Brant believes everything Sir William and his son Guy tell him. That's fine for Sir William." He paused as if thinking. "He believes he's told Brant the truth, but I'm afraid he's a dreamer. I'll give him credit. He loves the Indians. He's lived with them the same as I." They continued along the trail, leaving the small stream behind. "But," continued Quinn, "he's too close to the crown and blinded by England's shadow. He believes everything the king's envoys tell him and his son Guy has always been dazzled by royalty. That gives Lord Varrick an edge and he takes advantage of it. He's already playing his own game. Naming his price for scalps."

She looked at him sharply. "Scalps?"

"They're taking them from the Mississippi to Niagara."

"But why?"

"The less settlers to rebel against the crown, the better. With war almost inevitable, my dear cousin wants to make sure he's on the winning side, at least on the frontier. If he can stir up enough unrest . . . He's lived with the Indian too and he, Brant, and Johnson have vowed the Indian will fight for the crown, but mine won't."

"Yours?"

"The Tuscaroras and Oneidas. There's not a British soldier at Fort Locke. In fact they'd like to find it. It's my land, not the crown's. I bought it with blood and sweat and I'll kill any man who tries to take it from me, and Telak and his braves will back me all the way."

He laughed a bit and smiled at her. "Varrick's had a price on my head for years, but they've had quite a time trying to collect it."

"Quit bragging," called Burly from behind them. "One of these days they'll catch up to you and it'll be your scalp he's handing out prize silver for."

Quinn ruffled his blond hair, bleached even lighter from

the sun. "You take all the fun out of everything, Burly," he answered. "Only one thing wrong, though. Varrick won't pay for my scalp. He's got to have the whole body and I don't plan to go easy."

The three of them were so busy talking they'd become a bit careless and none of them noticed the slight movement in the bushes up ahead until Burly suddenly said, "Stop, Quinn," and Quinn reined up, reaching over to grab the bridle on Loedicia's horse.

He was too late. The Indians came swooping like hawks out of the slopes on either side of the trail, shooting as they came and swinging tomahawks.

Loedicia's horse bolted forward, breaking Quinn's grasp as a shot rang out, and she saw blood spatter on Quinn's face and he started to fall. She screamed as Burly rode up, hit Quinn's horse on the rump, then pulled up beside him, grabbing him so he wouldn't slide from the saddle.

Quinn and Burly broke through the Indians ahead, Burly's tomahawk biting the wind and anything that got in its way. But Loedicia, trying vainly to fight them off, was overpowered and dragged from her horse and the horse went on into the brush riderless.

She screamed and fought as she watched the two men up ahead, blood covering Quinn's hair and face, and she knew he was dead as he slipped from his horse.

Burly jumped down quickly, picked Quinn up as if he were paper, threw him sideways across his horse, hopped on behind, and disappeared in the trees ahead as another shot rang out after them.

It all happened so quickly and now Loedicia looked about her at the strange bronze faces staring into hers. An Indian held each arm and there was no use struggling anymore. They were too strong. Her skin prickled as she looked at their tomahawks, expecting them to grab her hair and start scalping, but they didn't. Instead they spoke back and forth, then took some rawhide and tied her hands behind her, and her long journey began.

"What are you doing?" she yelled frantically after a few forced steps. "Where are you taking me?"

One Indian seemed to be in charge and he turned back to look at her, his sloe eyes steely. "You lady be squaw Lord Varrick. He say we bring, we bring." She stared at him, her face livid.

But how? How could he possibly have known where she was? No one knew except Quinn and Burly. She was dumbfounded.

The Indian wasn't giving her any more information. Instead he motioned to the men behind her and they pushed her forward again and Loedicia knew her freedom was over.

Meanwhile, Burly pulled his horse to a halt and looked about. He'd ridden over a mile and he slid from the back of his horse, pulling Quinn behind him and stretching him out on the ground.

Blood covered his face and Burly took a cowhide flask from a strap at his belt line, poured some water in his hand, and wiped the side of Quinn's head, then sighed.

Thank God the ball had only creased him, but he was still out cold. He stood up and took his bearings. He had one horse and if he was right they weren't too far from the Susquehanna River, where old Hickory Pete and his squaw had a cabin.

He picked Quinn up again, put him gently over the horse, climbed on behind, and headed toward the banks of the Susquehanna.

A day and a half later, he rode into the yard of the log cabin, scattering the pigs and chickens, a feverish Quinn slung across the horse in front of him.

Hickory Pete was a scraggly man, lean and wiry, his squaw the opposite, soft and plump with laughing eyes and a perpetual smile. They both greeted Burly with enthusiasm, clucking over Quinn as they carried him into the log house and stretched him out on a cot.

"It will take time," said Pete's woman in her slow English. "I will need herbs." She began undressing him and instructed Burly and Pete to wet down rags in the cold river water and begin bathing him while she brewed some special tea to help fight the infection.

By evening the fever had broken and Quinn had regained consciousness with a head that felt as if it'd been scalped and he reached up, grabbing his blond hair, just to make sure.

"Dicia?" he said almost as soon as his eyes were open, and he tried to sit up as his head began to clear.

"They got her," answered Burly. "There were about ten of them and the lass didn't have a chance."

"Damn!" he exclaimed softly as he touched the side of his head where the ball had grazed him, close to the temple. "Why?" he asked as he looked at Burly. "Why?"

"Hickory Pete said he just got back from Albany two days ago and Varrick went through there with his whole entourage. Those men that jumped us outside Princeton made it through to him and when they gave him a description of Dicia he went into a rage and put a price on her return."

"Does Pete know how they got wind of us?"

"Since *The Golden Lady* was the last ship to leave, they checked the passenger list carefully and the bishop knew nothing about a Reverend Wainscoat and Reverend Burlington, and with your description it was easy."

"But how did they know who Dicia was? Surely the description didn't do it."

Burly frowned. "Not many people can speak Hindi fluently, but evidently one of the men on the dock heard Dicia talking to the sailor before she boarded the ship. It was all he needed and when the men who attacked us reached Albany he had his confirmation. Seems when Dicia was wielding her club at those men, she cut loose with a few choice words in Hindi and unfortunately one of the men had been to India and recognized the language. Pete says Varrick's more determined to marry her now than ever. What she did was a blow to his ego."

Quinn frowned. "Those were probably Brant's warriors under Varrick's orders and there's only two of us. How do we get her back?"

Burly eyed him suspiciously. "You want her back?"

"I still have a score to settle with Varrick," explained Quinn, "and what better way than through the woman he's intent on marrying?"

"I thought maybe you wanted her back for yourself," offered Burly, and Quinn scowled.

"Myself?"

"Why not?"

Quinn stared at him, then slowly a cynical smile moved his mouth. "You know, Burly, you're right," he suddenly said, and his eyes lit up. "Why not? What better way to get even with Varrick? He's taken everything away from me all my life. Why not take the one thing away from him that he wants more than anything else?" He settled back on the covers, a grin on his face. "Besides, I'm kind of getting used to having her around."

Burly looked at him, pleased. "You intend to marry her?"

"Hell! Who said anything about marriage?"

Burly stared at him and his face showed the anger he felt. "Oh, no, Quinn! I won't be a part of it," he exclaimed, shaking his head. "I've seen you break women's hearts and treat 'em like dirt. I've seen you do some rotten things in your time, but you aren't gonna hurt that lass. She isn't the kind of woman you can take to bed at night and forget about in the morning. You hurt her enough back in Reading. She's a lady clean through and I won't help you in any way if you've a mind to force her to be your mistress. I won't be a party to it. I don't intend to sink that low."

Quinn tried to sit up in bed and he scowled as he watched the expression on his friend's face. "You want me to marry her?"

"Marry her or leave her be!"

Quinn didn't answer. He looked away, unable to face the contempt in Burly's eyes.

"You could do worse, you know," suggested Burly. "She's got a title and all the charm to go with it, if need be, yet she's one hell of a woman! There aren't many women who'd take what you've been dishing out the way she has."

"You're serious, aren't you?" asked Quinn.

"You're damn right I am. You're thirty years old and what have you got to show for it?"

"I've got Fort Locke."

"A fort full of Indians and someday when this mess is cleared up it'll probably be a town, so who takes over when you're too old? Even Sir William's got sons to leave his heritage to, such as they may be."

Quinn looked up at his friend. He was sincere and what he said made sense. Besides, it'd be one hell of a way to get even with Kendall Varrick after all these years.

"Will you help me get her back?" he asked Burly.

The big man sighed. "Aye, Quinn." He took hold of Quinn's hand and squeezed it. "And I know you'll never have any regrets." As Quinn closed his eyes he could see Dicia's big violet eyes looking at him and almost feel the caress of her body as he had that night in Reading. Burly was right. She was quite a woman.

# 11

For the next few days Loedicia knew nothing of comfort. Her moccasined feet were sore from walking, her hair became matted and tangled, and she felt dirty. At least Quinn and Burly had stopped as often as possible to bathe in the nearest river or water hole, but these braves seemed to think it unnecessary. After the first day, however, they did untie her hands, at least during the day. At night she was tied to a tree and she'd lean against it, trying to sleep, remembering Quinn's arms about her, and she'd cry until she cried herself to sleep.

The next morning she'd wake up stiff and sore, only to repeat the same long trek again, and each day things seemed more hopeless. Quinn was dead and maybe even Burly and there was no one to help her.

She lost track of the days and was so tired she could have screamed. They fed her as well as they could, but she was so upset there were many times when she went without supper because she was unable to hold anything in her stomach and each day the gnawing suspicion kept growing on her.

If she was pregnant she'd kill him! Then she'd start to cry. How could she kill him when he was already dead? At this thought, she'd cry all the harder. Her suspicions were almost a certainty when her time of the month went by and her breasts suddenly became sore and sensitive to touch. It was all she needed. It was bad enough they were taking her to Lord Varrick, but to take her there with another man's child growing inside her . . . He'd kill her. She wished she could die, but she was too much of a coward.

Then she became angry, not only at Quinn for what he'd done to her but at herself for being such a coward. So she was pregnant, so Quinn's mother didn't have a husband either and she lived through it. Each day she became more weary and things seemed more hopeless, but she was determined to face anything that came.

Over a week had passed since she'd been captured. They'd already crossed both branches of the Susquehanna River and were deep along the Appalachian Trail when they stopped for the night in a valley. As usual, the Indians tied her to a tree with a piece of rawhide, after an upsetting supper of half-raw pheasant, which she proceeded to vomit up as soon as it hit her stomach.

She slumped over against the tree's roots, leaning her head against the bark, listening to the grunting sounds the men made as they stood about their campfire talking. Everything seemed so useless.

Meanwhile, Burly and Quinn were flat on their stomachs, elderberry bushes with half-ripe berries dangling above their heads. Three horses were hidden about two hundred feet back in the brush, as the crow flies, and everything was set.

They watched the group of Indians as they talked among themselves and Burly turned toward Quinn, whispering as low as possible.

"I told you they'd get careless if we gave them enough time. They're sure you're dead now and that big one poking up the fire's complaining because he doesn't have your body so he can collect his reward."

"He'll collect a reward, all right," Quinn whispered back.

They waited silently, watching the Indians as each one settled down for the night; one stayed awake to watch their prisoner. But, assuming that Quinn was dead, the man wasn't too intent on his job.

The moon was high and the stars filled the sky as both men crept silently from their hiding places. Quinn held tightly to the small pouch of gunpowder he held in his hand and thanked the good Chinese who'd showed him how to use it; he crept closer until he was hidden in the middle of some bushes about five feet from Dicia. Each step was mastered carefully, so not a sound was heard.

He put one hand to his mouth and let out the soft call of a night heron and seconds later heard the faint answer from the other side of the camp.

The Indian guarding Loedicia glanced toward the woman, grunting sleepily, then his head jerked to attention as a slight rustle was heard from the other side of the fire. He stood up slowly, his rifle pointed, and walked stealthily around his sleeping comrades, who were as close to the fire as possible because the night was exceptionally cold.

While the Indian was occupied watching a rabbit scurry into the underbrush, a rabbit Burly had conveniently let loose, Quinn took his advantage.

"Dicia?" His voice was barely a whisper, yet he saw the startled jerk of her head as she recognized it. She hadn't been asleep. It was what he'd prayed for. "Try to slip as far behind the tree as possible, but toward me," he whispered softly, "and when all hell breaks loose be ready to run as soon as I cut you free."

She nodded and he knew she'd heard him and he ducked back in the bushes as her guard returned to his post. He sat down a few feet from Quinn and in minutes he was resting his head forward lazily on the barrel of his rifle.

Quinn saw him nod forward, then let out another soft

call, which was answered from directly behind him. He stood up cautiously, swung his arm carefully, easily, and let the pouch in his hand sail through the air. It landed exactly in the middle of the fire and its plunking noise made the Indian stir a bit and he apparently thought a piece of wood had popped because he rested his head back against the rifle barrel.

It didn't stay there long, however, as the air was rent by an ear-splitting explosion that tore into the sleeping Indians and scattered pieces of them and firewood about the camp.

Burly moved forward quickly and shoved his knife between the ribs of the startled Indian who'd been guarding Dicia while Quinn quickly cut the rawhide holding her.

A few men on the perimeter of the fire staggered to their feet, dazed and bloody, trying to comprehend what was happening, but Burly, Quinn, and Dicia were out of sight in the trees before the Indians could fully recover.

Loedicia's heart was in her mouth as she held tightly to Quinn's hand and stumbled behind him in the darkness as they circled the camp. Her ears were still ringing from the force of the explosion and she felt sick to her stomach, but she was holding his hand. She was holding Quinn's hand and he was alive!

She fell over a small log, crashing into the underbrush, and Quinn reached down, hurriedly picked her up, and carried her the rest of the way to the waiting horses as the shouts of the Indians could be heard behind them.

"They don't even know where we went," offered Burly. "And by the time their ears stop ringing we'll be gone."

Quinn set Loedicia on one of the horses. "We ride easy," he said. "They're on foot, they won't catch us." He set the reins in her hand.

Within seconds she was following Quinn farther away from the sounds of the angry Indians who'd survived the attack and they were lost in the darkness among the trees.

They rode for well over an hour before they stopped and Quinn took their bearings. They were following a small stream now and he knew he was moving in the right direction as he dug his horse in the ribs and they kept on.

Three hours later they reined in before the ruins of a burned-out fort and Quinn guided his horse deftly across the rotting boards that were once a gate.

He sat his horse for a minute and looked around, trying to see into all the shadows to make sure, then he slid to the ground and walked over to Loedicia as Burly too slipped silently from his horse.

He reached up and put his hands on her waist, gently lifting her from the horse's back. "They won't come here," he said softly. "It's taboo. They think it's haunted."

"Are you sure?" she asked slowly as her feet touched the ground.

"Positive." He turned to Burly. "Bring the horses to what's left of the stables. We'll sleep there the rest of the night," he said, and took Loedicia's hand, leading her across the deserted ruins.

The moon cast shadows about them as she held tightly to his hand and her eyes took in the burned-out buildings.

The stable door lay partly on its hinges and they stepped over it into the silent ruin. There was still hay in the corners and Quinn found a comfortable-looking spot and sat down, pulling her down beside him as Burly settled himself in a good position for seeing anyone trying to cross the open space between them and the broken gate.

"Now," asked Quinn, "are you all right?"

She sighed as a tear rolled down her cheek. "Yes," she murmured softly. "Only I'm terribly tired."

He lowered himself, resting his head back in the straw, and held his left arm out, motioning for her. She stretched out beside him and he reached out, his arms engulfing her as he rolled over in the musty hay and held her close.

"Go to sleep, Dicia," he whispered. "It's all over." He stroked her hair as she began to sob uncontrollably, her body trembling.

He cradled her in his arms gently and let her cry herself to sleep, then he leaned his bandaged head on top of her dark, matted hair and slept too.

When she woke in the morning the sun had yet to

come up and it was barely light in the stable. Neither
Quinn nor Burly was anywhere in sight and for a minute
the old fear returned, then suddenly Quinn stuck his head
in the doorway.

"Ah, you're awake," he said, and stepped inside. He
was holding an old pewter cup and it was steaming in the
cool morning air. "A bit of brew to warm the stomach,"
he said, and knelt on one knee beside her as she pushed
herself into a sitting position. It was then she noticed the
bandage on his head and she stared at it as he handed her
the cup, but she didn't say a word.

She took the cup from him and sipped at the liquid. It
was strange-tasting, not exactly bitter, but pungent and almost sweet.

"What is it?" she asked.

"Tea," he answered. "Not East India tea, of course,
but a special brew the Tuscaroras taught me to make."

"Why did you come after me?" she finally asked as she
avoided his eyes and looked down into the cup.

The muscles in his jaw tightened. "I couldn't let Lord
Varrick get away with that, now could I?" he answered.
"I told you I had plans for you. They've changed a bit,
but you're still included."

"Changed? Then you're not going to ransom me back
to him?"

He laughed a bit cynically. "Not now. After all, why
should he have all the fun?" His voice became hard and
bitter. "He wants you so bad he'll turn hell upside down
to get you, so why should I give you to him?"

Her eyes widened at the harshness in his voice. "Then
what are you going to do with me?" she asked breathlessly, and his eyes narrowed.

"I'm going to marry you, Dicia," he stated arrogantly.
"Then I'll have the last laugh for a change. For once I'll
have something my dear cousin wants and he won't be
able to get it." Loedicia stared at him dumbfounded as he
stood up and walked outside.

She stood up slowly, staring after him, hardly able to
believe what he'd said. She started to simmer and her fingers clenched tightly about the cup in her hands. He was

going to marry her! Just like that! Not because he loved her, oh, no, not Quinn Locke! He couldn't love anyone! He was going to marry her for revenge, to get even because he felt cheated out of what he felt should be his. Well, she wasn't about to marry anyone. Not Lord Varrick, not Quinn!

She tossed the last bit of brew into the straw and stomped out of the stable after him.

"What did you say?" she shouted from the doorway, her eyes flashing angrily.

He was halfway across the parade ground, headed toward Burly, who was keeping his eye on some trout baking over a slow fire, and he turned back to her. "I said I'm going to marry you!" he stated emphatically, and turned again to walk away.

"By hell you are!" she screamed, and the cup she'd been drinking from missed his head by barely two inches as she threw it with all her might, then she reached down and picked up the nearest thing, which happened to be a rock, and it came hurtling toward Quinn.

He ducked and it hit one of the half-rotted boards of one of the burned-out buildings and sent the wood flying in all directions.

"By hell I will!" he yelled back, determined. "So you might as well get used to it!" Her face turned livid as she reached down and picked up another rock, only Quinn was faster.

He closed the distance between them in seconds and before she could throw it he had her wrist in his hand and bent her arm over until she dropped the rock.

"Let me go," she yelled, and began to beat her fists against his chest. "I'll kill you."

He reached up and grabbed her hair as he'd done once before and he pulled her head back until she winced with pain, then he looked down into her face and the sudden fire in his eyes stopped her fists as she stared at him.

"You haven't much choice, Dicia, darling," he said softly, arrogantly. "Either you marry me or become my mistress. . . . Which will it be?"

She bit her lip as his fingers tightened on her hair.

"Neither!" she whispered, her eyes blazing, and suddenly he leaned his head forward and his mouth came down on hers, soft and caressing, and his lips moved against hers, sipping at them lovingly, tasting the sensuous warmth that began to surge from deep inside her.

His hand relaxed in her hair and his arms went around her as he pulled her closer, his lips still on hers, and he felt her tremble as he began to respond to her.

Suddenly he pulled his head back and stared into her eyes and neither of them said a word, then from behind them Burly called and Quinn took a deep breath.

"Which will it be?" he asked softly, and she shuddered.

"I hate you, Quinn Locke," she answered through clenched teeth. "I hate you!" He only smiled cynically, released her, turned, and walked toward Burly, who was dishing up their breakfast on some confiscated tin plates that had been lying around the ruins for years.

The only one who talked while they ate was Burly and even he was silent at times. The baked fish tasted better than what she'd been used to with the Indians, but morning sickness claimed her again. She used the excuse that she had to relieve herself and ducked behind one of the buildings and vomited up not only the fish but the brew Quinn had given her earlier.

When she returned Quinn looked at her rather oddly. "You're losing weight," he finally said, and she sneered.

"I've had such marvelous cuisine this past week I can't understand why," she answered sarcastically, but he only continued to stare at her.

"You could use a bath too," he added, and this time she laughed.

"You're marvelous," she said. "Just marvelous. I could probably use a new dress and a manicure and a hairdresser too, don't you think?" She stopped for a minute and looked at him. "And just where can I get a bath around here?"

"Show her, Burly," said Quinn, "while I finish eating." Burly stood up and ushered her toward the broken gate.

The stream they'd followed the night before widened just past the fort and beavers had created a small dam.

"A bath for the asking," said Burly as he gestured toward it, and Loedicia could hardly wait to get into the water even though it was cold.

Burly sat on a rock above her, his back to her, keeping watch as she undressed.

She stared down at herself as she shed her buckskins. The deeply tanned skin, dirty hands, swelling breasts. She patted her stomach. It was still flat, but then she had to expect that. Nothing would show for at least four or five months. Some women didn't show until seven or eight. She stood for a moment, a strange feeling prickling inside her as she lay her hand on her stomach and felt the flesh beneath it.

She was pregnant, really pregnant! One night with Quinn and she was pregnant! She kneaded the skin and tears came to her eyes. This wasn't supposed to be. Not like this! When she thought Quinn was dead she'd been determined to have the baby and face whatever Lord Varrick or anyone else had to say, but now that he was alive . . . how could she tell him? She couldn't, not now. It was bad enough he was intent on marrying her to get even with his cousin; she wouldn't give him the satisfaction of knowing she was carrying his child, not until she had to.

She stepped into the cold water and it felt like heaven after the days of dirt. When she emerged a short time later, she felt clean and she looked with distaste at her dirty old buckskins. Well, she had no choice. She was a far cry from Boston and the drawing room and she sighed as she slipped the fringed shirt over her head.

One thing for sure, she told herself as she pulled the shirt down and flattened it over her stomach, maybe Quinn could force her into marriage, but he'd have a fight getting into her bed again, and she turned, calling to Burly and waving, her mind made up. She'd marry him, if that's what he wanted, because by doing so she'd give their child a name, but that's all she'd do.

Burly climbed down when she called and they returned to the fort to find Quinn waiting with the horses and

ready to move on, all signs that they'd been there over-
night gone.

"Well, you do look more presentable now, don't you,"
he said facetiously as she patted her horse's nose.

"Will one of you help me on?" she asked, ignoring his
remark. She had yet to master getting on an unsaddled
horse.

"Let me," said Quinn before Burly could move, and he
stepped up beside her, put his hands on her waist, and
lifted her into the air, but instead of putting her on the
horse, he leaned forward and nuzzled her neck below her
ear, nibbling at her earlobe.

"Ah, you smell sweet," he whispered, and kissed her
neck, sending shivers down to her toes. "And that's for
the rock you threw at me," he said, then gently lifted her
the rest of the way to the horse's back and grabbed the
reins, handing them to her.

Burly looked at them sheepishly as he saw Loedicia's
face redden and her eyes flash angrily. The rest of the trip
looked as if it would be as interesting as the first part and
he smiled to himself, shaking his head as he followed
Quinn's lead and easily swung onto his horse.

Some days it rained, others were scorching, the wind
blew hard, and the sun beat down like fire, but still they
moved on, day after day penetrating deeper into the Alleghenies. Three times they came on burned-out home-
steads, everyone dead and scalped, and Loedicia knew
now that Quinn had told the truth.

"Mohawks," he said after looking over each scene, and
he and Burly always buried what was left of the people.
Some had been dead so long all Quinn and Burly could
do was throw stones over them to keep the scavengers
from finishing off the little that was left. Some of the victims had been tortured before they were killed and Quinn
shielded Loedicia from the worst, but one day, when
they'd come upon a lone cabin, isolated and silent and
with the door broken in, he'd thought the only victims
were in the house, so he left her outside.

She walked along the side of the house, wondering how
long she'd stay alive in such wild country and what she

was doing here at all, when she stopped abruptly and stared toward a tree in the backyard. Her hair stood on end, tears flooded her eyes, and she let out an agonizing shriek that brought both Quinn and Burly flying.

"There!" she wailed, pointing at the tree by the back shed, and as Quinn saw it he grabbed her head and pulled her into his arms, burying her face in his chest.

A baby no more than nine or ten months old was suspended against the side of the tree, a lance through its chest, and its small head was caked and dried with blood where the scalp had been torn from it. Flies and maggots swarmed over the decaying mass and any resemblance to the laughing child it had once been was almost gone.

"My God!" she sobbed against his chest. "It's only a baby! A baby!" Then she thought of the child she was carrying and her stomach began to churn as she forced her hand to her mouth. "I'm sick!" she gasped, and pulled away from him, but it was too late. She'd taken only two steps when her lunch came up and she grabbed hold of the back fence to help support herself.

Quinn looked at Burly helplessly, but Burly only shrugged, so he reached out and grabbed her shoulders, helping support her until she was through.

Her face was a mess. Her nose was running, her eyes red from crying, and her mouth tasted like vomit. "I'll be all right," she sobbed, turning her head, trying to avoid him so he wouldn't see her like this. "I'll be all right!"

Burly had dashed into the cabin and he came out with a cloth in his hands and threw it at Quinn, who handed it to Loedicia.

"Here, wipe your face," he said, and she reached out and took it from him, blowing her nose, wiping her mouth and eyes on the musty rag.

"I want to get as far from here as possible," she said, her voice trembling. "If I see one more dead body I'll go insane."

Quinn took her by the arm and led her out front to a wooden bench near the cabin door. "Sit here," he said, "until your stomach's settled."

She looked at him, her eyes misty. "But why, Quinn?

Why a baby? A beautiful little soul who never hurt any-one."

He knelt down on one knee and reached out, cupping her chin in both his hands. "Dicia, please. It isn't right, I know. Why anyone, for that matter? Not just the baby. Why can't people understand?" His blue eyes looked deep into hers and she saw something strong and vibrant in them, something she'd never realized was there before. "Why do men and women have to die before the world realizes all they want is to be themselves, to live their life to its fullest. But if we must die and we all must someday, let it be swift like the baby rather than tortured as his parents were. The baby's gone, his soul's with God, Dicia, all that's left now is the shell. Forget it or it'll drive you crazy. Whether the baby died of sickness or the lance, it's dead and we can't bring it back."

She nodded. "I know."

He kissed her lightly, then let go of her face and reached out, squeezing her hand. "I'll go finish helping Burly," he said, and stood up, walking into the cabin.

She sat on the bench, trying to erase the sight of the dead baby from her mind and remembering the look in Quinn's eyes. Burly and Quinn walked back and forth from the yard to the house, carrying stone after stone, and she knew why. The bodies were too decomposed to bury and the cabin was too close to the woods to burn. If they tried, they'd set the whole forest on fire.

After a while Burly walked up and stood beside her. "Quinn's finishing up," he said, and she looked up at him, her eyes veiled with sorrow. He put his hand on her shoulder. "Take good care of the wee one inside you, lass," he said softly, winking as he bent forward a bit. "It may be all my friend Quinn ever gets to leave behind him in this crazy world at the rate he's going." Her mouth fell open as she realized what he was referring to and she was still staring at Burly's grizzly, bristled face as Quinn walked up.

"Let's get out of here," Quinn said quickly. "I want to put distance behind us between now and dark. The far-ther we get from here, the better." They headed for their horses, grazing a short distance away, and Burly walked behind the two of them, a faint smile on his face as he looked at Quinn's back and sighed. He had a lot to learn, did Quinn, an awful lot, and as Burly leaped to the back of his horse and they moved out of the clearing, back into the wild, Burly was grinning a knowing little grin and whistling a little tune Loedicia could have sworn sounded very much like a lullaby.

# 12

More than three weeks later, well into August, they rounded a bend in the river they'd been following, which Quinn said the Indians called Ashtabula, the fish river, and he reined his horse to a stop. They were on a slight rise overlooking the mouth of the river and he pointed to the right.

Loedicia nudged her horse forward to be beside him, where the bushes wouldn't obstruct her view, and she let out a gasp. The late-afternoon sun hung above the largest body of water she'd seen since they'd left the Atlantic Ocean and it flooded the horizon, turning it to fire as the river they'd been following emptied lazily into it, its dark waters mixing with the blue waters of the lake.

"The Indians call it Okswego, but we call it Erie," said Quinn as he breathed deeply, taking in its vast horizons once more. He pointed to a spot along the lakefront and Loedicia followed his finger. "My house is on the beach, you can see it from here." She made out a large log house nestled beneath some drooping willows almost at the edge of the sand. "And there's Fort Locke," he exclaimed as he pulled her toward him a bit to peek through the trees.

She looked down to the left of his house and saw the stockade, its wooden spikes pointing toward the sky, a blockhouse at the four corners. Surrounding the walls were dozens of bark and hide houses and teepees of all sizes, made into a regular village, and mixed among them were a few other dwellings, including a gristmill along the river.

"I don't see any houses except yours," she said as she craned her neck, trying to see it all.

"There aren't any," he said. "Mostly Indians. I came here to trap and liked it so well I decided to stay around for a while. Little by little the Indians moved in closer around me until we had a regular village and we built Fort Locke for protection against hostile tribes."

He nudged his horse and moved on through the trees with Loedicia and Burly following and as they made their way down the slope Loedicia heard a long-drawn-out call coming from the direction of the fort and before they reached the first wigwam a chattering group of Indians, old and young, converged on them.

Quinn held up his arm and spoke to them in a language new to Loedicia, then he turned to her.

"They saw us coming last night," he said. "The food's ready and the house is clean."

Loedicia was surprised. "But they couldn't have seen us last night. We slept without a fire."

He sat straight and tall as the hands of his Indian friends reached up to greet him and the smiling faces made way for him. "Telak and his warriors don't need a fire to spot anyone," he answered. "He's the one who taught me to track snakes over rocks." He smiled as she gave him a half-amused look.

"Do any of them speak English?" she asked as they stared at her, backing away, then exuberantly greeted Burly.

"A few, but not too well." He nodded toward an old man with an elaborate headdress of horns that protruded from what looked like a hat of sheep's wool. "That man is the shaman," he said, "the witch doctor. He's very important, so smile at him as we go by." Loedicia did as he told her.

They rode through the village and Quinn stopped before a large bark hut that looked impressive. A tall, well-built man stepped from the doorway as Quinn slid from the back of his horse and the two men greeted each other warmly, talking awhile in the Indian's dialect, then Quinn turned and walked to Loedicia, holding up his arms to her.

She hesitated and he reached over, lifting her from the horse's back and setting her on the ground. "He wants to meet you," said Quinn.

She looked up into his blue eyes. "Why?"

He smiled. "I told him you were to become Mrs. Locke."

"You had no right!"

He continued smiling, a false smile, as he warned in a whisper, "Don't start anything here, love, unless you want to get yourself scalped." He saw the shocked look on her face. "Don't look like that," he offered as he took her arm and started ushering her toward the man, who stood waiting. "They are Indians, you know."

They stopped directly in front of the man and Loedicia looked up at him. He was tall and impressive, his face expressionless as he looked at her.

"This is Lady Loedicia Aldrich," he said as he looked down at her. "Lady Aldrich, may I present my friend Telakonquinaga. I call him Telak, which makes it much simpler."

Telak nodded and held out his hand for her to shake. "Is good to meet squaw of friend Quinn. We are pleased you here."

She smiled weakly, not knowing what to say at first, then, "I'm pleased to be here," she answered softly, and she reached out, taking Quinn's arm. "You are Quinn's friend. I hope you will be mine." The Indian's face broke into a big grin as he looked at Quinn.

"She is good, yes," he said, still speaking in English, then returned to his own tongue.

A short time later, after being introduced to Telak's four wives and numerous children, Quinn, Dicia, and Burly continued on to the fort with everyone staring as they rode the short distance.

The gates to the fort were open and as they rode in, Loedicia looked about her in amazement. More than a hundred men, all in uniform, were standing at attention in the parade ground and one man, obviously an officer, stood in front of them, his hand raised in salute. Their uniforms were much like those of the British, but their coats were green instead of red and they made an impressive sight as the three riders moved forward abreast of them and Quinn turned, looked them over, then saluted and spoke to the officer in charge. "Everything go all right while I was gone, Lieutenant Holmes?"

The man was nice-looking with sandy hair, a rather square face, and deep-set brown eyes. "Aye, Captain," he answered. "A few skirmishes here and there. We ran into a few Mohawks two, three days ago. They'd been raising hell hereabouts. They won't anymore."

Quinn nodded. "Good. I think we saw some of their handiwork." He looked out over the men. "I see a few new faces," he said as he spotted some men in the back. Quinn knew all his men. Knew them personally. He looked back at Lieutenant Holmes. "I'll be back later to meet them and go over a few things, but first"—he reached around and grabbed the bridle on Loedicia's horse, pulling her up next to him in full view of the men—"I want to introduce someone to you," he said, raising his voice so they could all hear. "This is Lady Loedicia Aldrich." He looked at Loedicia, her hair windblown about her face, which was tanned brown almost like an Indian's, and his eyes crinkled, amused. "I know at the moment she doesn't look much like a lady, but I assure you she is. She's come all the way from Boston with us and as soon as we get settled I intend to make her my wife."

Loedicia saw startled looks on many of the faces, although hardly a man moved a muscle.

Quinn grinned. "I thought I'd better warn you ahead of time so none of you ladies' men would get any ideas."

Lieutenant Holmes looked at Loedicia, then at Quinn again. "Congratulations, sir," he said, "but haven't I heard the lady's name somewhere?"

"News travels fast," answered Quinn. "We'll talk about

it later, after I've cleaned up." He saluted again, then nodded to Loedicia.

They started to turn their horses toward the gate when Burly moved up close to her. "This is where I leave you, lass," he said. "My quarters are at the fort."

She reached out and put her hand on his arm, squeezing it. "Thank you for everything," she said gratefully.

He put his hand over hers. "It was my pleasure," he said, his eyes twinkling. "But remember what I said." He winked as her face reddened and Quinn gave them a curious look.

As they rode out of the fort Loedicia saw for the first time a small group of women standing in the shelter of one of the buildings. "Who are they?" she asked Quinn as she motioned toward them.

Quinn waved to them as if he'd just realized they were there. "Some of my men are married," he answered as they moved on out through the gate. "I've discovered they work and fight better if their women are with them."

She glanced sideways at him as if to get a better look at this man who'd become such a vital part of her life. "When you mentioned your fort . . . I never dreamed," she exclaimed. "All those men. . . . It's a small army."

"Small, yes," he said as they rode toward the rambling log house on the edge of the beach. "But an army no less and an effective one. Those men are the best woodsmen and Indian fighters in the territory and when war comes, which I'm sure is inevitable even though Franklin's trying his damnedest, we'll be ready on our end."

She was amazed. She'd had no idea that so many people looked up to him. He was a leader and as she glanced over at him, tall and straight on his horse, she wondered how she could have mistaken him for an ordinary thief. He'd said there was a price on his head. Now she understood why.

The house was more than a cabin. A long veranda stretched across the back, which faced the lake, and Quinn said he often sat there in the evenings and watched the sunsets. The furnishings were made of logs, but on the chairs were plump cushions made from fabrics the Indians wove, filled with the down of a thousand geese. Thick, colorful braided rugs graced the floors, and there was a fireplace, made of stone hauled from the riverbank, in every room, the one in the main room taking up the whole inside wall and extending into the kitchen, where it was used for cooking by an old Indian woman, Moneola, his housekeeper.

It was rustic and very comfortable and Loedicia fell in love with it the minute she stepped through the door.

Quinn saw her eyes light up. "You like it?"

She stood in the middle of the room and looked around her. After the long days on the trail it looked like heaven, but she didn't want him to know. He was too sure of himself already.

"What, no velvet chairs or Persian rugs?" she asked sarcastically. "And what happened to the brocade drapes and crystal chandeliers? After all, you are nobility, aren't you?"

His eyes snapped as he walked up behind her. "You're not amusing," he said angrily, and she whirled around.

"I didn't mean to be amusing. I meant to be cruel!"

He nodded. "So Burly told you . . . and you hate me that much?"

She threw her head back defiantly. "What do you think?"

His eyes bored into hers and suddenly her defiance began to weaken. "I think you need taming," he said slowly, and he reached out, pulling her to him. His lips found hers and he was kissing her long and hard, making her head spin. He released her quickly, scooped her up in his arms, and walked across the room, entering a long hall and then kicking the door at the far end open.

She was too startled at first to do anything, then she began to kick and squirm. "Let me down!" she yelled as she started to thrash about, only he held her all the tighter until he reached the bed in the center of the room, then he flung her onto it.

She lay back, her head on the huge feather pillow, her eyes wide. "What are you going to do?" she asked.

His mouth formed a half smile as he stared down at

her. "You get a reprieve for today," he said viciously, his eyes hard and cold, "but tomorrow, after we're married, you'll be waiting for me as you were in Reading. Do you understand?"

She stared at him breathlessly, unable to say a word.

He turned from her abruptly and walked to the window, staring out for a second, then, without saying another word, he left the room, slamming the door behind him.

Loedicia lay on the bed and closed her eyes, putting the back of her hand to her mouth. The memory of Quinn's kiss burned on her lips and she swore softly to herself because she knew tomorrow night when he came to her, no matter whether she fought or not, Quinn would have his way. There was something about him. She could fight him just so far, then it was as if there were no fight left in her.

Quinn hunted through the house until he found Moneola in the back larder and hurried the plump woman out to fetch his uniform while he washed up, then gave her instructions to heat water for Loedicia and see she got a bath.

"Who is this Dicia, Captain Quinn?" she asked as she checked the corn bread baking on the hearth.

"She's the woman I'm marrying tomorrow," he said as he took a basin from the shelf and walked over to the fireplace, took a hot pad, and picked up a copper kettle. "I'll find some clothes for her at the fort and have someone bring them out. See she puts them on."

"Why I have to see she puts them on?" she asked, puzzled.

He winked at Moneola. "She's slightly temperamental, but pay no attention to what she does or says. Just make sure you duck if she throws anything."

Moneola raised her hands in consternation. "She throws things?"

"Mostly at me."

"But why you marry woman who throws things?"

He stood for a minute, staring at the basin in front of

him. "That, Moneola, is my business," he said, and Moneola shook her head as she went to get his uniform.

Not quite an hour later Captain Quinn Locke rode back into the fort wearing the uniform his men were used to seeing on him. It was a green coat with white facing worn over a buff-colored waistcoat and white ruffled shirt with buff-colored breeches tucked into highly polished riding boots. His tricorn hat was decorated with a medallion of the Locksley crest, which held up short red, white, and blue feather plumes. His hair, minus powdered wig, was held back with a green ribbon.

A scabbard and sword that had once belonged to his father hung on the left at his waist and his rifle hung from his saddle. He rode tall and straight, proud of his fort and the people who trusted him.

He rode in, dismounted, and walked to a building in the center of the fort. Minutes later, in his office, his sword set aside, he sat down at his desk and faced Lieutenant Holmes.

"It's true?" Lieutenant Holmes asked. "She was supposed to marry Lord Varrick?" Quinn leaned forward across the desk.

"That's right." He leaned his head on his hands as he held them folded in front of him. "I only wish I could see the look on his face when he finds out."

Lieutenant Holmes stood up. He'd been with Quinn a long time. "He's got his scalp hunters out again," he said, and Quinn nodded.

"And they're getting farther south all the time."

"I wanted to send some men to Johnson, but it wouldn't have done any good. Sir William died some weeks ago and Guy is so tied up with Butler and Brant he wouldn't listen if we did. We'd be lucky to get our men back alive. And you might like to know the price on your head's gone up."

"I figured as much after Boston," he answered, then stood up and walked over to a map on the wall. He pointed to an area below Fort Niagara near the great falls. "Get ten braves, Telak's best. Have them infiltrate as far as the falls. Dress them like Senecas, Mohawks.

You know what to do. I want them to move into the camps and find out what they can and I don't want a camp missed or a man lost. I want all the information they can find. I want to know if they're bringing any more soldiers toward the frontier. I want any news from England that might come their way, whether official or unofficial."

"What's happening in the East?" asked Holmes.

"Representatives of all the colonies are getting together in Philadelphia at the end of summer to talk things over."

"Talk!" snapped Holmes. "You can't talk to them. Franklin's been talking his head off. They won't listen. England wants us subordinate. I say it'll come to a fight."

Quinn shrugged. "I think it's a certainty," he said, "and they're already eyeing Washington to take command, but it won't come for a while. The people aren't angry enough, but they will be. Give them time. . . . Meanwhile His Majesty, good King George, keeps sending in more and more troops." He sighed. "So all we do is wait and make plans so that when the time comes we're ready. There's going to be a hell of a big job for us out here and every white man and Indian we can get on our side helps." He walked back to the desk and sat down. "When you leave go tell Lizette I want her and send someone to find the parson."

"That's all the orders, then?"

"For now, yes." Lieutenant Holmes, who'd followed Quinn to the map, then back to his desk, saluted and walked out.

Lizette was the wife of one of Quinn's best men. She'd elected to come with her husband and fortunately for the fort she was an experienced seamstress. Her skill with the needle soon made her indispensable about the camp. She was a dark-haired snap of a woman in her late twenties with a touch of gray in her hair and eyes that sparkled mischievously.

"So you finally did it," she clucked as she closed the door behind her. "And of all the women, you have to pick this one."

"And what's wrong with this one?" asked Quinn. He was used to her disregard of formalities.

"Ooh, la la," she exclaimed. "I see it in her eyes, *mon capitaine.* She will be hard to tame. Already you have the trouble, *non?*"

"You see too much, Lizette," he answered. "She was to marry Lord Varrick on the first of June, now she's to marry me." Lizette's hands flew to her face as she sat in the chair opposite him.

"Oh, but, *mon capitaine,* you are asking for trouble. He will try to kill you for sure this time."

"If he catches me."

She crossed herself. "Mother of God, I don't know why François insists you are a genius. You have cotton in your head for the brains!"

"Speaking of cotton," he said, ignoring her remark, "how is our stock of material in the storeroom?"

She looked at him quizzically. "We have enough."

"Enough for a wedding dress?"

"A wedding dress?"

"Use the material you use for our shirts," he said, touching the edge of his ruffled shirt. "I want her to have a dress to match her station. Nothing will be too good and I want it done by six tomorrow evening even if you have to stay up all night."

She shook her head. *"Sacré bleu!* I have only two hands, *mon capitaine,* not eight like the octopus."

"Then find someone to help you. Sara should do. She sews a fine seam."

"Sara? *Ah, oui, mon capitaine,* she is just the one if you want the dress to look like a rag."

Quinn's face reddened slightly.

"Every time you go away she eats her heart out hoping this time you come home you'll come home to her. Now, instead, you bring a woman to take the place she wants and expect her to help make her wedding dress? *Mon ami,* you are heartless and cruel."

He said in a lowered voice, "I never made any commitments to Sara and you know it. There was nothing between us."

Lizette shook her head. "She is not a good one to make an enemy and she is in love with you."

"Bosh!"

She waved her finger in his face. "No, no bosh! You watch that one, *mon ami*. I saw her eyes this afternoon. She did not like what she saw."

He laughed. "Lizette, you have the strangest way of making me feel like a little boy." She smiled. She was fond of Quinn. "Now, as I was saying," he continued, "find some decent clothes. Surely someone in the fort has something to fit Dicia so she can get out of those dirty buckskins. Take them to the house and you can get her measurements then, and personally," he added, sighing, "I don't care who helps you with the dress, just so it's finished by six tomorrow."

She nodded, they talked a bit longer, and she left, passing the parson as she went out.

Loedicia sat in the tub of hot water, a stubborn look on her face. The Indian woman who called herself Moneola practically had to drag her off the bed. If she had just told her what she wanted her to do she'd have gone willingly, but when Moneola walked brazenly into the bedroom with that ferocious look on her face, as if she were about to skin a bear, Loedicia'd fought like a tiger. How was she to know the woman spoke English so well? If she'd said, "The bath water's ready," she'd have come without a fight and Loedicia wondered just what Quinn had told the woman.

Loedicia stepped from the tub and Moneola held up a large towel and wrapped it around her. "Captain Locke will send clothes from the fort soon," the Indian woman said as she ushered her into the sitting room, took the towel from her, and wrapped a big robe around her. It had to be Quinn's, because the sleeves dangled to her knees and it bunched up on the floor at her feet.

She and Moneola were getting along fine now that they understood each other and Loedicia knew she wasn't going to be boiled in oil and she walked outside and sat on one of the chairs on the veranda, looking out over the lake, wrapped up in the big robe, and it was there Lizette found her.

Lizette was enchanting with her lilting tongue, French accent, and mothering nature and Loedicia was pleased.

She dragged Loedicia into the house, into the bedroom, and insisted on helping her into the clothes she'd brought with her. One look at Loedicia's bronzed skin and she protested, sending Moneola all the way back to the fort to get a bottle of lotion she'd made herself, the recipe taught to her by her *maman*.

"Your skin will be soft like the petal," she exclaimed when Moneola returned, and she rubbed it generously on Loedicia's brown, dry skin. A few minutes after the application it felt soft and smooth.

"You're a genius," exclaimed Loedicia, and Lizette agreed.

"You are much in love with *mon capitaine*?" Lizette asked as she measured her, then helped her into the blue cotton dress she'd brought for her.

Loedicia sneered. "Is that what he told you?"

Lizette shrugged. "No."

"What did he tell you?"

"That you were to marry Lord Varrick, now you are to marry him."

"He didn't tell you anything else?"

Lizette's eyes sparkled mischievously. "There is more to tell?"

"Much more," answered Loedicia, "but I don't want anyone else to know." Over a cup of Indian tea brewed by Moneola, Loedicia confided much of what had happened from the time she left her uncle's house, but purposely left out the intimate details and the fact that she was pregnant.

Lizette nodded. "Then he marries you to spite his cousin," she said. "I thought as much the minute he tell me." She shook her head. "I don't like it. It's not like Quinn."

"Oh?"

"To fight with his cousin, yes. They have fought for

years. His cousin hates him, not only because he threatens his place in the world but because of the scar."

"The scar?"

"*Oui.* The scar that runs the length of Lord Varrick's face was inflicted by *mon capitaine* when they were boys. It was Varrick's fault they were fighting, but he's never forgiven Quinn and it only makes matters worse." She frowned. "But he's never forced anyone to join his fight before. All of us—my husband, François; Lieutenant Burlington; Holmes; the others—are here by choice."

"Except me!"

The woman examined Loedicia carefully. Even in the buckskins she had been attractive. There was a sensual quality about her that would attract men and she was sure it had probably attracted Quinn, but knowing him, he'd fight his feelings all the way. She had seen him look at the girl earlier when they rode in and he had a look in his eyes she'd never seen before. He may think he is marrying her solely to wreak vengeance on his cousin, and Loedicia may think the same, but Lizette was sure there was more to the relationship than either wanted to admit.

She reached out and took both of Loedicia's hands, squeezing them. "Marry him, *ma petite,* and give him sons," she said. "Perhaps that's what he needs and one day—who knows?—you may grow to love each other."

Tears filled Loedicia's eyes as she thought of the child growing inside her. "Don't worry, I'll marry him," she answered bitterly. "I have no choice, but I shall never love him, never! He's cruel. Cruel and heartless . . . and I hate him!" The last words were said with such vehemence that it startled Lizette.

She squeezed Loedicia's hands again. "Well, *ma petite,* I must get started on your dress or Quinn will skin me alive." Loedicia smiled at her newfound friend. "I promise to tell no one what you've told me. That is between us, *n'est-ce pas?*" Loedicia walked to the door with her.

Quinn arrived back from the fort shortly before dark and Loedicia stared at him dumbfounded as he came around the corner of the house and stepped onto the veranda, where she was standing. She hadn't seen him in his uniform as yet and he made an even more handsome picture than he had in buckskins.

He swept off his hat, unbuckled his sword, and called into the house for Moneola to come fetch them, then joined her at the edge of the veranda.

"What are you staring at?" he asked, and she blushed.

"I've never seen you in uniform," she said. "I never realized you were a man of such importance. I should be honored to be your wife, I suppose." The last was said with an air of sarcasm.

"Some women might think it was an honor."

"I'm not some women."

"That I realize," he said, and she blushed again as he looked directly into her violet eyes.

She had looked pretty before in the buckskins, earthy and sensuous. And before that when she'd had on the threadbare red dress she'd stolen with the dark stain on her skin there was an animal magnetism about her, and now her bronzed skin shone like velvet and in spite of the weight she'd lost she still looked round and firm and he remembered what it had been like to make love to her.

He reached out and put his hand on the side of her face, moving it back through her dark curly hair, and gently pulled her head toward him. "I don't think I've ever met a woman quite like you," he said honestly. "One moment fight and fire, the next warm and desirable. You're a vixen, Dicia. A vixen sent to try my soul." He bent over, touching her lips with his, gently this time, and she felt her heart start pounding, her knees became weak, and a strange yearning filled her loins as his lips moved softly against hers.

Suddenly they were interrupted by Moneola's voice calling them to eat.

He drew his mouth from hers and pulled his head back, looking into her eyes. Her lips were warm yet from his kiss, her face flushed, and she looked exquisitely alive. Damn her for doing this to him! He couldn't seem to help himself. His body was responding to her as it always did.

"Go in the house," he whispered harshly. "I'll be in in a minute."

She pulled away from him and went inside while he stood for a minute breathing in the clean air, waiting for the effects of her nearness to pass. All he'd have to do is walk into the room and she'd know right away. He didn't know what the hell difference it made, though, she probably knew anyway. She'd had her body pressed close to his. She couldn't help but notice and he swore to himself as he paced back and forth across the veranda a few times, then turned and went into the house.

That night Loedicia slept in a bed by herself for the first time in months and she felt strangely lonesome.

# 13

The next morning when she woke he'd already left the house and she was glad. Moneola made her breakfast and waited on her like a princess, yet she couldn't keep the wedding out of her mind. He had talked about it all through dinner as if he were enjoying making her squirm. The day went abominably slowly and Quinn made himself scarce all day.

It was close to six o'clock when Lizette arrived, carrying Loedicia's dress. She helped Loedicia bathe and get into her clothes and when she slipped into the white gown, she was quite amazed. Only a few tucks were needed here and there; otherwise it fit her perfectly.

"You have a beautiful bosom," said Lizette as she smoothed the dress across it, making sure the tucks and shirring were in place. "It is so full and firm." Loedicia's face reddened. She wasn't about to tell her it hadn't been quite that full and firm until she became pregnant.

The dress was beautiful. The fancy bodice was attached to a skirt of billowing white flounces, caught into a bustle in back, and bows of white lace, with which Lizette trimmed the men's dress shirts, were tucked about the bustle, streaming down the back. The sleeves were short and puffed with inserts of the same lace, and bands of the lace were sewn together to make a veil that touched the edge of her shoulders and was gathered on top to form a tiara across the top of her dark curls.

"You should be in Paris," exclaimed Loedicia as she saw herself in the mirror.

Lizette shrugged. "A bit of cotton and some lace, *ma petite*. It is nothing."

The white dress was striking against her tanned skin and Lizette backed away to get an overall look. "You are exquisite," she murmured. "*Mon capitaine*, I feel sorry for him."

"Oh?" Loedicia said as she looked at herself in the mirror. "Why? Because I have a bad temper?"

"Because you are so beautiful." She winked. "He will have a hard time keeping the men away."

"I don't think he'll care one way or the other," remarked Loedicia. "I can't imagine Quinn being jealous over anyone, especially me."

"Don't be too sure. I saw the way he looks at you, *ma petite*. He has never looked at a woman so before."

"I imagine there have been enough of them in his life."

"Women?"

"Yes, women!"

Lizette's face grew serious. "I must tell you something. As a woman I speak to you." She waved her hand. "And sometimes it is hard to speak of these things, but I feel you must know what kind of a man you marry, *n'est-ce pas?*" She leaned toward Loedicia furtively. "My François tell me *mon capitaine* never go to a woman, they come to him. And always he . . ." Her face turned crimson. "He try to avoid them every way possible. . . . Do you see? And when he cannot he spill his seed on the ground. He tell Burly he will bring no bastard into the world as his father did." She waved her finger at Loedicia. "But Burly say one day *mon capitaine* will fall in love with a woman and bury his seed deep when he cannot control his emotions. So it is good he marry. *Oui.*"

Loedicia stared at her, suddenly understanding something Roxanne had said outside their bedroom door that night in Reading, about making it complete, and now a strange feeling crept through her as she looked down at herself. Could it be? Could Quinn possibly love her? The thought gave her a vibrant feeling all over. He had taken her twice that night and both times he'd buried his seed deep.

"You are sure of this?" she asked, and Lizette nodded.

"*Oui, ma petite.* Quinn has never gone to a woman yet, but I have a feeling he will come to you." Loedicia smiled knowingly. He was already coming to her.

The ceremony took place at seven that evening on the parade ground at the fort with Parson Townley officiating. The parson had been removed from his pulpit back east for speaking out against the king's abuses and had allied himself with Quinn and Burly, coming to the fort to minister to the needs of the men. He was a thin, gangly man with gentle eyes and a soft voice, and Sara was his daughter.

The fort was crowded with Indians and soldiers, all craning their necks to get a look at the bride and groom. Quinn had dressed at the fort and sent Burly to bring Loedicia and now they stood, with Burly and Lizette as witnesses, exchanging their vows, and to Loedicia it seemed like a dream. She couldn't even remember half the words she repeated or Quinn's putting the ring on her finger, but it was there, a plain gold band. Then, when it was all over and Parson Townley said, "You may kiss the bride," her knees almost buckled under her as Quinn turned her toward him, put her face between both his hands, and kissed her softly, gently as he had last night on the veranda and the whole place erupted in wild, gleeful shouts.

She stood beside Quinn, shaking hands, accepting congratulations from everyone. The celebration was a sight to behold. Indian and soldier mingled together, laughing and drinking. One of the few times Quinn allowed the Indians to drink. The Indians did ceremonial dances, fertility dances, "To make many sons," said Telak as he shook his friend's hand.

One of the soldiers had a fiddle and Quinn turned to Loedicia as the soldier started playing a minuet.

"The first dance is ours," he said, and stood up, holding his hand out to her. She didn't dare refuse and it was strange to be going through the intricate steps of the ballroom dance here on the dirt of the parade ground with the stars overhead. And Loedicia was surprised to discover that Quinn was an excellent dancer, smooth and accomplished.

He watched her closely as they danced and it made her self-conscious. He held her hand at the end and she curtsied as the music stopped, then she raised her face to him and something in his eyes made her gasp.

He drew her up, pulling her hand, and she was suddenly engulfed in his arms and he was kissing her passionately as the crowd urged him on.

Her face was crimson and she was flustered as he released her and she stared into his eyes, then suddenly he broke into a grin as his friends crowded around them once again and they were separated as the men pulled him away.

The women took her aside and for the next half hour she had to listen to their chatter as they cautioned her about all the do's and don'ts of being a happy bride. There were about ten women who'd come with their husbands and then there was Sara, the parson's daughter.

Loedicia had been with the women less than ten minutes when she felt Sara's eyes on her, staring at her with an animosity that frightened her. She was a rather attractive woman, taller than Loedicia, with thick light brown hair she wore braided into a coronet about her head and large brown eyes with flecks of gold. She looked perhaps in her mid-twenties, a bit on the hippy side but well built. Her face was broad and her mouth a bit large, but nevertheless she was pleasing to look at. Her gaze was so intent Loedicia's face reddened under her scrutiny.

Lizette saw Loedicia's discomfort and eased close to her ear. "Pay no attention to her, *ma petite*," she whispered softly. "She has been chasing Quinn since she got out of pigtails and she is disappointed, that is all." But Loedicia still felt ill at ease under the woman's gaze.

Then suddenly Sara stepped up to her. "So you're the straw that's supposed to break Lord Varrick's back," she said sarcastically, and sneered. "I must say Quinn's putting on a good show."

Lizette bristled. *"Sacré bleu!* It is no show!"

"Come now," Sara answered. "The whole fort knows by now that he's married her for one reason. To get even with Varrick. It was a drastic measure to take, I admit, but then Quinn hates Kendall Varrick so much nothing is too drastic."

Loedicia's face was livid as she stared at Sara. So he had told them! Everyone knew he hadn't married her because he loved her but because he hated Lord Varrick. How could he do this to her? How could he make such a fool of her and humiliate her like this?

She tried to keep her composure and held her head up, looking haughtily at Sara. "And who might you be?" she asked as if Sara were of no importance.

"I'm the parson's daughter, Sara Townley," she answered confidently. "You mean Quinn hasn't told you about us?"

Loedicia smiled sweetly. "Perhaps he felt it wasn't important enough to bother with," she said, and Sara's eyes narrowed as Lizette clucked to herself and the women glanced about from one to the other.

"Don't underestimate me," answered Sara, her eyes flashing. "Quinn knows where to find me when he needs me." She walked off toward where the men were raising a ruckus and a short time later Loedicia saw Sara and Quinn laughing together at something one of the men said.

The rest of the evening she seethed with anger but kept it inside so no one would know. She could feel the stares and her heart sank, knowing these people were probably pitying her for being forced to marry him. She hadn't minded Lizette's knowing—Lizette was different—but she didn't want the whole fort to know.

By the time Quinn had one of the men bring a horse to take her back to the house her anger had almost reached the boiling point. He didn't seem to notice, however, and acted exceptionally pleased with himself as he lifted her up and set her on the horse with the good wishes of his friends ringing in his ears, and the short distance to the house was traversed in silence except for Quinn's whistling softly most of the way.

He lifted her from the horse, only this time he cradled her in his arms and carried her toward the house. She made no protest but lay passively in his arms, smoldering with rage.

Moneola had left candles lit in the sitting room, but he didn't stop in the sitting room. Instead he walked to the bedroom where Loedicia had spent the night and set her on her feet in front of him, just inside the door.

"Now, my dear Dicia," he said smartly as he chucked her under the chin, "was that such a hard thing to do?"

Her eyes flashed as she stared at him and her voice suddenly became venomous. "Get out of my room!" she ordered through clenched teeth, and saw the surprised look on his face. "I wish I never had to set eyes on you again! You told all of them, didn't you?"

She whirled and walked farther into the room and picked up a fancy nightgown Moneola had evidently set at the foot of her bed and she threw it at him. "Here!" she yelled. "Take your nightgown, take all your clothes!" She reached down, her hand on the bodice of the wedding dress, and ripped it down the front, throwing the torn remnant at him.

"You had to tell them, didn't you!" she screamed. "See my lovely bride," she mimicked sarcastically, tossing her curly head, "I didn't marry her because I love her. I made a fool of her. I married her to get even with my cousin!" She'd become hysterical with anger and she saw the startled expression on Quinn's face change as he walked toward her. "At least you could have left me some pride!" she sobbed, half yelling, half crying, "or don't I even have a right to that?"

He reached out to touch her and she cringed.

"Don't you dare touch me!" she whispered, sniffing, tears rolling down her cheeks. "Don't you ever touch me again." Suddenly she saw anger in his eyes as he reached out, grabbing her arm, pulling her toward him.

"I'll touch you whenever and wherever I please," he answered passionately. "And I want to now!" His arms went about her, crushing her against him as his mouth came down on hers.

She could taste the salty tears between their lips and then she felt the tip of his tongue as it caressed her and a flame shot through her as if she'd been burned.

He didn't wait to unfasten her dress, but ripped it off her the rest of the way as his mouth continued to caress hers. His hands, once more touching her soft flesh, lost control and he picked her up, carried her to the bed, his mouth never leaving hers, and set her down gently and let his hands continue to fondle her.

He drew back his head and looked down into her face, flushed and warm, her violet eyes filled with desire. She wanted this, he knew. She fought him all the way, but in the end she'd enjoy it as much as he would, as she had before, and he hurriedly slipped from his clothes and climbed in beside her.

"No, Quinn," she protested weakly as he bent over her, kissing her once more. Then, unable to conquer the vibrant yearnings of her own body, she yielded to him with a violent passion, running her hands through the soft hair on his chest, feeling the hidden wonders of his body, kissing him back passionately, moving with him motion for motion until he moved on top of her and all the world was ecstasy, all the anger forgotten.

The next morning Loedicia was in a foul mood when she woke up, angry because she'd let him get the best of her again, but this time he was still beside her and as she opened her eyes she saw he was leaning on one elbow and looking down into her face.

"Good morning," he said softly, and there was a hint of amusement in his eyes.

She turned her face away from him, ashamed of her weakness.

He bent down and kissed the hollow at the base of her throat and she trembled. "Don't do that," she exclaimed breathlessly, and he laughed lightly.

"You know you like it."

"That's beside the point," she said, looking back into his face.

He lifted the sheet from her breasts and leaned over, kissing each on its rosy tip.

"And you like that too," he whispered, and she closed her eyes.

"Why do you do this to me?" she asked. "Do you enjoy torturing me?"

He bent down and kissed her. "I enjoy making love to you," he said softly against her mouth.

"Why?"

He drew back and looked at her. "I was trying to figure that out when you woke up," he answered, rather amused. "After all, you're not the most beautiful woman in the world. You're two different colors." He put his hand on her shoulder, where the suntan stopped. "And you're too short, and your hair's too curly, and your eyes . . . Who ever heard of violet eyes?" He laughed softly. "And you've got a foul temper. Look what you did to that beautiful dress Lizette took such pains to make." She blushed.

"I didn't mean to," she apologized. "It's just that sometimes I get so angry with you."

"Why?"

"Why?"

"Yes. Why do you get angry with me?"

She stared at him, at this new Quinn, and for some reason there was an intimacy in his nearness that frightened her. He made her do and say all the things she vowed never to do or say and she looked at him stubbornly.

"Do you know how I felt when that Sara said the whole fort knew you were marrying me merely to spite Lord Varrick?" The old hostility began to rise inside her. "A woman wants to be married for love . . . and even if she's not, she at least wants the world to think so. But you took even that away from me."

"Then I'll give it back to you," he answered softly.

"And how, pray tell, can you do that?" she asked. "They all know you're not in love with me."

He was looking into her eyes and she felt that strange quickening inside. "Oh, do they, now? And who said I wasn't in love with you?"

"Well, you're not, are you?"

He laughed, a soft, relaxed laugh. "I haven't decided yet." He leaned down and kissed her. "Maybe if I kiss you often enough I'll be able to make up my mind," he said, his mouth close to hers.

"Let me know when you do," she answered, and he laughed out loud.

"Dicia, you're precious. Now suppose we see if Moneola has some breakfast ready." He slipped from the bed and reached for his clothes, which he'd dropped on the floor the previous night. He put on his underwear, pulled up his pants, then stood staring at her. "Well, are you going to stay there all day?" he asked.

"And what do I wear?"

He sat on the edge of the bed and reached out, pulling her into his arms and kissing her passionately, then released her and looked down into her face.

"Mmmhmm . . . it gets better every time," he whispered, licking his lips sensuously, then let her fall back on the bed. He grabbed the ends of the sheet and pulled them, rolling her up inside as she protested, laughing. Then he brought the end up and tucked it in the top as she frowned, confused as to what he was doing. When he was finished, he picked her up, to her surprise, and slung her over his shoulder like a sack of flour.

"Put me down!" she yelled. "You're crazy!"

But he only laughed and carried her into the sitting room, calling for Moneola.

The Indian woman emerged from the kitchen, a spoon in her hand, and her eyes widened at the sight.

Loedicia was yelling and Quinn smacked her across the rear. "Shut up!" he said, amused but sounding stern. "Bring breakfast out on the veranda," he ordered Moneola. "I'm going to teach Dicia how to swim." He headed out the door and toward the beach.

"Stop it!" she cried, and started beating on his back. "Quinn, you're crazy. . . . Put me down!"

But he kept on going across the sand and waded into the surf until it was up to his waist, then he slid her from his shoulder and held her tightly against him.

"I take a dip every morning before breakfast," he said. "And now that I have a wife I don't intend to swim alone." Before she had a chance to protest, he held her high, then threw her away from him into deeper water.

She took a quick breath and went under, bobbed up, sputtering water, tried to take another breath and got a mouthful of water, spit it out as he hollered, "Kick! Move your arms! Come on!" Much to her surprise, she wasn't sinking anymore. She was staying up in the water and she no longer panicked. "Longer strokes," he called, and she lengthened them and within seconds she was swimming through the surf toward him.

Then, aware that she'd mastered the water, she kicked and moved her arms, turning from him, heading back toward shore.

"Hey!" he yelled, and dived headfirst after her, his lean body reaching her as she stood up in the water.

He grabbed her leg and she went down on her knees, clutching the sheet as it started to slip.

"Quinn, stop it," she yelled. "Are you trying to drown me?" But he pulled her down as a wave broke over them and she came up, sputtering, Quinn's arms around her, and the wave washed them onto the edge of the sandy beach. Water still lapped at their legs and she lay breathless in his arms, her back on the sand.

He leaned over and kissed her passionately and his hand moved down her body, caressing her affectionately. This time her arms went about his neck and she held his mouth on hers long and hard.

He pulled his head back and looked down at her, then rolled over beside her in the sand and stared up at the sky, reaching out to take her hand, holding it in his.

"Will you come with me every morning?" he asked.

"Yes," she whispered, and sat up, leaning on one elbow, staring down into his blue eyes. Then she saw a movement out of the corner of her eye and glanced toward a small hill a short way down the beach and she let out a gasp.

"What is it?" he asked as he saw the look on her face.

"Someone's watching us."

He raised himself a bit, then smiled. "Yes, didn't you know?"

She stared at him for a moment, mortified, then leaped from the sand and began to run toward the house, struggling, clutching the falling sheet about her.

Quinn jumped to his feet and ran after her and as he caught up to her and scooped her into his arms she let out a squeal, then he carried her into the house.

"You're insane!" she cried angrily as he set her on her feet in the kitchen, dripping water all over the floor.

"You wanted me to take it back, didn't you?" he asked, and she stared at him, puzzled, as he continued. "When those busybodies get back to the fort they're going to say Quinn Locke's in love with his wife."

Her eyes flashed. "Oh, they are, are they? Or are they going to say, 'Well, he may have married her for spite, but at least he's enjoying himself'?"

He looked amused. "Moneola will get you some clothes. Get dressed and come out on the veranda for breakfast. I'll go change." He left her standing in the kitchen, fuming.

Late in the afternoon they were sitting on the veranda eating lunch when Burly stuck his head around the corner. "Honeymoon's over," he announced as he stepped onto the veranda and walked over to them. They looked up from their food.

"Never," answered Quinn as he glanced at Loedicia, and her face reddened.

"It is for today," said Burly. "We've got company."

"Who?"

"A young friend of yours from Virginia."

Quinn leaned forward anxiously. "George?"

Burley nodded.

"What the hell's he doing up here?"

"Says he's headed back toward Kentucky soon and came on up for a little talk."

Quinn looked skeptical. "George never goes out of his way just for a little talk."

"He's waiting at the fort," offered Burly. "Says if I don't bring you back with me he'll come after you himself. I didn't tell him you were married. I thought you'd want to surprise him yourself."

Quinn grinned. "He's really grown into quite a man, hasn't he, Burly?" Burly nodded.

"Aye. And there's a fire in his eyes that matches his hair, that you can be sure."

Quinn pushed back his chair and stood up. He was shirtless, with a pair of old breeches on, and barefoot. He glanced down, realizing he looked like anything but the leader of more than a hundred men.

"I guess I'd better put on my Sunday best," he answered casually, excusing himself and leaving Burly and Loedicia alone.

"Who's George?" asked Loedicia, wiping the crumbs of corn bread from her fingers. She was wearing a blue calico dress, the only one she had, but there was a glow about her that pleased Burly.

"He's a young upstart we've known since we first hit the shores of Virginia," answered Burly. "The lad followed Quinn into the backwoods as soon as he could shake his family and grabbed ahold of Quinn's coattails. He's a rare one, is George Clark. A woodsman like myself and Quinn. Moves fast when there's somethin' on his mind." He hesitated. "Speaking of having things on one's mind . . . have you told Quinn yet, lass?"

She blushed. "No. And don't you tell him either."

"Why not?"

"Because I won't give him the satisfaction."

"But he's in love with you."

"Oh, is he, now?" she retorted. "Then why hasn't he told me so?"

"He hasn't?"

"He's done everything but." She stood up angrily,

walked to the edge of the veranda, and looked out toward the lake. "And he'll never know about the baby until the day he does," she said stubbornly. "At least until I can't keep it a secret any longer."

Burly shook his head. Like a mule she was, and just as ornery he thought as he waited for Quinn.

A short time later, Quinn with Burly at his heels strolled into his office, took off his hat and threw it on his desk, and greeted his friend, shaking hands vigorously.

"By God, George, you're as tall as I am," he blurted out as he looked eye to eye at the younger man.

It had been two years since they'd last seen each other and Quinn was pleased at how the lad had filled out. He was lean but muscular, trim from the miles he'd put behind him.

George grinned. "Told you I'd catch up to you one day."

Quinn put his arm about the other's shoulder and led him to the chair by the desk.

"Burly, bring us a drink," he said. "I'll guarantee the lad hasn't had a drop since he was up here last time."

"Not that rotgut you serve anyway," replied George. "One swallow of that stuff's enough to last a lifetime."

"Well, tell me now," said Quinn as he sat down opposite his friend. "What brings you to my little domain?"

The man's face reddened a bit. He and Quinn had been friends a long time and besides, you didn't try to tell a man eight years your senior how to manage his affairs.

"Hey," exclaimed Quinn as Burly walked in and set three mugs and a pitcher of ale on the desk, "what is it, old friend? It can't be that bad."

Burly poured a drink for George, who took a big swallow before addressing Quinn. "This wasn't my idea. Tom Jefferson asked me to come by."

"For what?" asked Quinn.

"The whole country's talking, Quinn," he finally confessed. "It wasn't bad enough you had to steal the money, but did you have to take the woman too?"

Quinn frowned.

"They don't like it," added George.

"They?" questioned Quinn.

"I saw Tom just before he left for Philadelphia to attend the congress. Since your little escapade some of the people who were on the fence have fallen all the way over. They call you an outlaw, Quinn. Not only the British but the men who are trying to put some semblance of order into this land. Taking the money can be overlooked, but to kidnap a titled lady . . ."

Suddenly Quinn's eyes twinkled as he looked at the young man he'd taught to survive in the wilderness. A smile played at the corners of his mouth.

"Just what are they saying, George?" he asked, and George took another swallow of the potent brew, shut his eyes, and shuddered.

"They say you stole the British payroll."

"I stole what should have been mine," answered Quinn. "That land Kendall sold in the Indies had belonged to my father before he died. Kendall had it by default. It was coincidence that it was to be used for the June payroll. A nice coincidence, but a coincidence no less."

Burly was at the other side of the room, mug in hand, and he leaned against the wall where the maps hung as he watched the two men talk.

"All right," agreed George. "You felt you had a right to the money, but what about Lady Aldrich? You didn't have any right to her."

"From what I heard, Kendall didn't either," answered Quinn. "She hated him."

"But that gave you no right to kidnap her."

"What makes you think I kidnapped her?"

"She was with you, wasn't she, when you went through Reading and according to the tales that filtered back, she's here with you now."

For the first time Quinn looked irritated. "Didn't it ever occur to anyone that she might have run away?" he asked, the muscles in his neck flexing involuntarily.

"Two days before her wedding?"

"Two days, two weeks. Does it really matter?" He leaned across the desk. "She was being forced into a marriage with a man she couldn't stand. What girl with any guts wouldn't have run away?"

George leaned back in his chair and sipped at the ale as he watched Quinn, then took the mug from his lips. "Where is she?" he asked.

Quinn emptied his mug and stood up, grabbing his hat. "Come along, I'll show you," he answered, and Burly shook his head as he followed the two men from the room.

# 14

❦

Loedicia was sitting on the beach, barefoot, her skirt spread about her, sifting sand through her fingers. She watched the terns diving at the water, landing and bobbing on the waves, skimming the surface, calling raucously to one another, and she was oblivious of the three men as they approached her across the sand.

"You'll get burned," offered Quinn from behind her, and she turned abruptly, then jumped hurriedly to her feet, pushing the short curls from her face.

"I'm already burned, or have you forgotten?" she retorted flippantly as she eyed him.

She looked at the three of them, her eyes resting on the red-haired stranger standing between Quinn and Burly. He was perhaps twenty-one or twenty-two years old with a face wise for his years and a body as disciplined as Quinn's from living in the wild. His buckskins were well worn.

"Loedicia, my dear, I want you to meet a friend of mine," Quinn said. "This is George Rogers Clark. George"—he put his hands on Loedicia's shoulders—"my wife, Loedicia Locke." He saw his friend's face fall.

"Lady Aldrich?" he asked, staring at the tanned beauty with the violet eyes.

"Not anymore," answered Quinn. "We were married yesterday."

George frowned.

"You disapprove, Mr. Clark?" asked Loedicia, and he shrugged as he glanced at Quinn, at the look on his face.

"May I congratulate you both," he answered, then sighed. "But I'm afraid the rest of the country isn't going to agree with me, especially Lord Varrick."

Quinn laughed aloud. "*Touché*, my friend," he agreed. "Now, you didn't say, did you come alone?"

George shook his head. "I have three men with me. The rest are at Fort Pitt. We headed for Roanoke as soon as the skirmish with the Indians was over, then moved back into the Ohio Valley to do some surveying. We're heading for the Kentucky River territory soon's I get back to Fort Pitt."

"Then you'll stay the night and eat with us," suggested Quinn, and his hands tightened on Loedicia's shoulders. "Go tell Moneola, my love," he said as he leaned close to her ear, kissing it as he spoke. "And include Burly too."

She turned and glanced up at him. He was looking at her in such a strange way and it made her heart beat faster. She smiled as she ducked from under his hands and headed for the house, excusing herself to George and Burly.

George's eyes followed her as she walked across the sand, kicking it with her bare feet. He'd never seen the woman before and he tried to imagine her in a drawing room with all the frills and pomp of a titled lady, and he frowned.

"What's the matter?" asked Quinn as he saw the puzzled look on his friend's face.

"She married you willingly?" he asked, and Quinn glanced quickly at Burly, then looked back at George.

"And why shouldn't she?"

"Because you're not the best catch of the year, that's why," he answered, and Quinn laughed.

"Did she look like she was forced?" he asked, and George had to admit she looked quite happy.

"So what happens now?" he asked Quinn. "Tom Jefferson sent me to tell you to send her back." Quinn looked at him sharply.

"Impossible!"

"So I see," said George as he watched the look on Quinn's face as he watched his wife reach the veranda and go inside. "I'll tell him what's happened and he'll understand."

Quinn looked at his friend. "No one will ever understand," he answered, "but that's between Dicia and myself."

"Why should Tom Jefferson be so concerned about Lady Aldrich?" interrupted Burly as they started back toward the lane that led to the fort.

George sighed. "A lot of reasons, Burly, but mostly . . . until now no one back east has paid much attention to what Quinn's been doing out here," he said, "except Lord Varrick, that is, and few people have paid much attention to him. At least you didn't have the British Army breathing down your necks. Before this they only heard of Captain Quinn Locke like a willo'-the-wisp, a rumor here, a rumor there. Word filtered back that he was out here somewhere and talk was that he was building a small army in case of a break with the crown, but it's all been hearsay and no one's been interested enough to come take a look. A few have nosed around, but nothing serious."

He stopped as they reached the lane and headed toward the Indian encampment. "Taking the money was bad enough," he went on, "but when you took Lord Varrick's bride . . . You've got the entire country up in arms and now the whole British Army will be heading this way."

"But I'm not on British land," protested Quinn. "The French still claim this land, and technically it doesn't belong to the French or English. It belongs to the Indians."

"But the redcoats aren't going to give a damn who it belongs to. I have a sneaky feeling they're going to come after you regardless."

"Then let them come," remarked Quinn, and George

eyed him stubbornly. "You planning to start a revolution all by yourself?" he continued.

"Don't worry, George," Quinn said soothingly. "We can hold our own here."

"That's not the point," argued George. "If things aren't settled in Philadelphia we may need you out here. Tom told you how he feels about this land. He's got dreams, Quinn, big dreams. And it's not only the colonies that are a part of those dreams, it's this wilderness and the miles of land stretching to the west beyond the big river and the mountains."

The three of them were at the edge of the Indian village and George stopped, staring ahead as if his mind were miles away. As if the Indians weren't in front of him and he was looking at faraway mountains and hills beyond the horizon.

"Could you imagine a nation that large, Quinn?" he asked breathlessly, as if he were actually seeing it in his mind's eye. "A nation spread from sea to sea . . . a nation so large . . ." He shook his head as if shaking himself awake, then looked at Quinn. "You've heard Tom Jefferson talk."

Quinn nodded. "I've heard," he acknowledged. "And I agree with him. That's why I intend to stay here and fight if need be." He put his hand on George's shoulder. "Don't fret, George. Let me worry about Loedicia." His face grew serious. "Tell them I haven't lost my mind and captured a screaming, unwilling victim, no matter what Kendall Varrick labels me, and as for the money . . . it went for a good cause. Adam Basque's barn in Reading should be well stocked with rifles by now."

"I'll see they hear about it," answered George.

"Tell them I'll run things my way out here and be damned with what the rest of the country thinks. I'm accountable to no one but myself."

"Don't you think he knows that already?" retorted Burly, interrupting the two men. "He's known you long enough to know nobody tells you what to do or when to do it."

Quinn gave Burly a sharp look. "Meaning I'm bull-headed, I suppose."

"It's like this, George," said Burly, ignoring Quinn. "Quinn's sure war's coming regardless, so it don't matter to him what the British think of him and as for the rest of the country, he figures he's Quinn Locke and that's the only explanation they need."

George eyed Quinn knowingly. "I told Tom it wouldn't work," he said, glancing back toward the house, remembering the sight of Loedicia with the sun in her hair and the warmth in her eyes. "But then Tom never met Lady Aldrich or he'd never ask you to give her up."

"And I never will," stated Quinn, and his eyes suddenly grew hard, then softened as he sighed. "Shall we go visit Telak," he suggested, dismissing the subject, and the three of them walked toward the chief's tent as Telak stepped out to greet them.

About an hour before dinner that evening, Loedicia stood in the bedroom holding her mended wedding dress in her hands. She had worked all afternoon piecing it back together and although some of the stitching showed, it would look better than the faded calico that made up the rest of her wardrobe.

She'd taken a warm bath and was wrapped in Quinn's robe again with its sleeves rolled up and the bottom dragging on the floor. She laid the dress across the bed, then walked to the dresser and began opening the drawers one at a time, but they were empty.

"Looking for something?" asked Quinn as he stepped through the open doorway, then reached back and closed the door behind him.

She sighed. "I thought maybe there might be a scarf or a ribbon . . . something I could put on the dress to hide the big tear in front," she answered. "But the drawers are empty."

He glanced at the dress on the bed. Most of it had mended well except for a spot in the middle at the neckline where the material had practically shredded.

"You're wearing the dress tonight?"

"We're having company, aren't we?"

He stared at her, his blue eyes looking deeply into hers, then he threw his hat on the bed and walked slowly toward her.

She reached down automatically and tugged the sash on the robe tighter, grabbing the lapels, pulling it closer over her bare breasts.

"I don't want company tonight," he whispered softly, and reached out, putting his hand behind her head, pulling her toward him.

"They're your friends, not mine," she answered, and he felt her quiver at his touch.

His face was inches from hers as he stared into her violet eyes and his breath came quickly, his body suddenly alive with desire.

"Who needs friends when they have such lovely enemies?" he said cynically, and she pulled her head away, wrenching it from his grasp, starting to walk away, but he was too quick for her. His hand shot out and he grabbed her arm, pulling her back, his other hand grasping the sash at her waist, pulling it apart, letting the robe fall open.

She stood poised and rigid, her head high as his eyes traveled down her naked body, caressing it warmly, then he reached out and cupped one of her breasts, massaging it tenderly, feeling the nipple stand taut and firm. Her eyes slowly closed and unconsciously, aroused by his actions, her hips moved seductively, invitingly, thrusting forward as if searching for him.

His hand left her breast and moved to her waist, encircling it as he drew her toward him.

She opened her eyes and looked into his and she held her breath.

"You know what you do to me, don't you, my little vixen?" he whispered passionately against her lips, then he groaned hopelessly. "My God, will I never get enough of you?" His mouth covered hers, smothering her small cry of protest as he lifted her and carried her to the bed, appeasing his hunger for her the only way he knew how.

Their guests were due any minute, but he didn't care as he took the medallion with its feathers from his tricorn hat and fastened it to the front of her dress to cover the tear, then let his hand move, cupping her breast, letting his hand rest, holding its fullness, and surprisingly, her face reddened.

"You blush, Mrs. Locke?" he questioned lazily, and her eyes fell under his gaze.

He was so infuriating. He made love to her and made her feel loved and wanted even though he never said the words, and merely by looking at her he could stir her deep inside, making her surrender to him even when she fought against it. The thought embarrassed her.

She reached up and pushed his hand down, then turned toward the mirror, flicking her fingers at the medallion to make sure it looked right. "You never did say, what was it your friend wanted to talk about?" she asked.

"You."

She looked up at him in the mirror, her eyes meeting his. "Me?"

"My orders were to take you back."

Her eyes widened. "Orders from whom?"

He leaned forward and kissed her neck. "It doesn't matter," he answered. "I never was one for taking orders."

She leaned back against him. "What happens to us now?" she asked softly, and he shrugged. For the first time as he looked into the mirror he saw bewilderment in her eyes. "Please, Quinn," she begged as he straightened up, "be serious. What happens now?"

"All right," he answered as he walked toward the bed and picked up his coat, slipping it on over his buff-colored shirt and vest. "It seems the whole country thinks I captured you and dragged you away from your betrothed. Something a gentleman of breeding doesn't do."

"But I ran away."

"They don't know that."

"The fools!" Her eyes flashed angrily. "Who ordered you to send me back?"

"Tom Jefferson."

She frowned. "It seems I've heard my Uncle Thaddeus mention him once or twice."

"I haven't seen him for two years," answered Quinn. "George, Burly, and I attended his and Martha's wedding back in '72. I met him when I first arrived in the colonies and we've been friends ever since, but Tom has a moral code that doesn't hold with scandal and what we did, my dear, is scandalous."

"But why should it matter to Mr. Jefferson what we do?"

"Let me enlighten you," he answered. "You were to marry Lord Varrick, who is a friend of General Gage, who is not only the governor of Massachusetts but one of the leading generals in the British Army. Also, Varrick's an intimate friend of Lord North, the king's minister, as well as Lord Snow and a number of other dignitaries, and you, my dear, are a titled lady and Tom's afraid I'm going to end up with the whole British Army out here on the frontier. Something we've been trying to avoid."

"Then it isn't exactly my welfare he's been worried about."

"He knows me better than that," stated Quinn, but Loedicia didn't agree and eyed him sheepishly.

"Your Mr. Jefferson's naive."

He reached out and took her hand, pulling her gently to him, and then put both arms about her.

"Are you in that much danger from me, my love?" he asked lazily, and she stared at him, unable to speak. "They say I'm a bounder and a cad. A despoiler. I've taken an innocent maiden and corrupted her. I'm an outlaw and a rebel. Tell me, Dicia . . . what do you say I am?"

His blue eyes bored into hers and she felt the strength of his arms about her. Those arms that only a short time before held her captive as he made love to her, setting her whole being on fire.

"I say you're crazy," she whispered softly, and he leaned forward, his lips touching hers, warmly, lovingly.

"Shall we go wait for our guests, Mrs. Locke?" he asked against her mouth, and she pressed her lips fervently against his, kissing him back.

Their guests arrived on time and they sat on the

veranda in the dusk with a dozen candles lighting the table. Moneola had outdone herself with venison steaks, baked squash, vegetables sautéed in herbs, and corn bread dripping with honey. Dessert consisted of rhubarb pie, about which George and his companions raved, and Indian tea sweetened with honey.

Loedicia was fairly quiet and listened to the men recounting past experiences they'd shared. George and his companions related their recent bloodcurdling adventures defending the frontier in Virginia.

"They're already calling it Lord Dunsmore's War," exclaimed George as they went into the gory details.

There was a fierceness about these men, a fierceness she'd recognized in Quinn also, and sometimes it frightened her. They spoke of killing as if it were an everyday affair and she remembered how nonchalantly Quinn had killed the Indians when he and Burly had rescued her and she glanced at Burly, remembering how unconcerned he had been that night in Princeton when he'd snapped the life from a man as if he'd been a twig.

How could you explain men like this? So gentle at times, yet with a violent nature that controlled most of their waking moments.

As they pushed back their chairs and retired to the veranda steps to relax and smoke, listening to the lake as it gently caressed the shore, Loedicia excused herself and joined Moneola in the kitchen to help with the dishes.

Sometime later, the dishes cleaned and put away, Loedicia sat in the sitting room reading a book. She'd felt it best to leave the men by themselves. There were times when men appreciated not having a woman around.

Quinn somehow had managed to accumulate a small library and Loedicia loved to read. She was well into *Poor Richard's Almanack* when George appeared at the doorway.

"Excuse me," he said, and she looked up from the book. "But Quinn said if I step inside I can talk the cook into parting with another piece of her rhubarb pie. Is she about?"

Loedicia smiled. "I'm not the cook, but I'll gladly get

you some pie," she answered, setting the book down, and he followed her into the kitchen.

Moneola was busy preparing dough for bread to be baked in the morning and Loedicia told her to continue her work, she'd take care of Mr. Clark herself.

George watched Loedicia closely as she took out the dish, then reached for the pie. She was even lovelier this evening in the white dress and he smiled to himself as his eyes moved to the medallion with its feathered plumes pinned to her bosom. It was the Locksley crest and it was as if Quinn had deliberately put it there as a brand, warning others to keep hands off.

She set the piece of pie in front of him and he looked up, then nodded for her to sit down. "Let's talk," he said casually as he poked at the pie with his fork, then took a bite, and she had the feeling the pie wasn't his real reason for coming inside.

She sat down opposite him as Moneola stood at the end of the table kneading the dough, humming to herself.

"Quinn says you ran away."

"I did."

"Why?"

She cocked her head as she looked over at him. "Did you ever meet Lord Varrick?" she asked.

He shook his head. "No, but I've heard stories."

She leaned forward. "Ah ha . . . then tell me, Mr. Clark. Assuming the stories you heard about him were true . . . if you were a woman, sir, would you have been willing to marry him?"

He stopped eating, his fork poised in midair. "If I were a woman?" he mused, surprised, thinking, then, "No . . . if I were a woman I guess I wouldn't," he answered. "But then neither would I have married Quinn Locke." Loedicia smiled, a wicked little smile.

"But then again, you aren't a woman, are you, Mr. Clark?" she whispered softly, her voice low and seductive. "Because only a woman would know the difference." George smiled.

"You're in love with him, aren't you?" he asked as he downed the last of his pie, and she frowned.

"Don't you think that's between Quinn and myself?"
she asked, then stood up. "Tell your Mr. Jefferson I came
of my own free will and I stay of my own free will, regardless of what Lord Varrick has said. I wouldn't have
married him if he'd been the last man on earth. I was
being forced into the marriage and I took the only way
out left to me. And as for Quinn Locke . . ."

George grinned as he stood up and reached across the
table, putting his hand over hers. "No need to set me
straight there," he said. "I think I know all there is to
know." He squeezed her hand, then turned and walked
from the room, a pleased look on his face, satisfied with
what he'd found out.

George and his friends left late the next morning and
life at the fort swung into its usual routine. Quinn divided
his time between the fort and the house and he and Loedicia alternately fought and made love as Moneola shook
her head in consternation when they battled, then sighed,
holding her hand over her heart, when Quinn carried
Loedicia to the bedroom and slammed the door, both of
them emerging hours later warm and flushed from their
lovemaking.

Some days they rode from camp and he proudly
showed her the wilderness he'd grown to love and each
day she learned more about the men under him and the
Indians he called his friends. While he was busy in the
fort she kept herself busy learning as much as she could.

A week after George's departure they were sitting on
the veranda eating breakfast, their hair still wet from their
morning swim, when Burly strolled up the steps and stood
gazing at them, shaking his head.

"Swimming before breakfast." He laughed. "I knew
Quinn was crazy, Dicia, but you too?"

She smiled as her face reddened, and Quinn answered.

"It pleases me," he said softly, and looked directly into
her eyes, making her blush all the more, then he glanced
at Burly. "What brings you out so early, my friend?" he
asked. Burly pulled up a chair and sat down.

"Ramsey's back," he answered, and Quinn frowned.

"Already?"

"You'd better come."

Quinn excused himself and went into the house to get into uniform. Ramsey had dropped their clothes off in Reading, then gone on to Boston to look things over, and Quinn was surprised he was back so soon.

Fifteen minutes later Quinn took off his hat as he walked into his office and shook hands with Ramsey. "You sure made good time," he said as he sat down behind his desk, setting the hat in front of him.

"The Senecas and Mohawks made it a bit easier," Ramsey said, rubbing his balding head. "I ain't got much hair left, but I sure don't want those bastards to raise it."

Quinn smiled, then grew serious. "What did you find out?"

"Plenty." The man's gray eyes were alert, his unshaven graying beard moving nervously in his partially toothless mouth. "Boston's like a powder keg. Gage is bringing in soldiers by the hundreds and with no quarters to be had they're forcing their way into every home in the district and the people don't like it. There ain't many jobs and food's scarce. They're bringin' in what they can smuggle after dark, but it ain't enough and the people are mad as hell and I don't know as they're gonna stand for it much longer without hollerin'. They got ammunition and supplies hid someplace up by Cambridge and Charlestown and it sure won't take much for 'em to get used. Adam's warned them off, though, and everybody's waitin' for the congress to settle things in September, but if it don't, all hell's gonna break loose. It sure don't look good no way you look at it. Old George is gettin' ready for a fight, that's for sure."

"So are we," stated Quinn.

"The British are sendin' ships farther down the coast to other ports," continued Ramsey, "but the merchants there are refusin' to buy. It's like a tinderbox."

"Anything about Varrick?"

Ramsey laughed. "He's yellin' foul all the way and he's talked the governor into puttin' a price on your head, so it's not just Varrick's money that'll be payin' for your scalp. You're an outlaw, Quinn, plain and simple, and

Gage'd give his right arm to get his hands on you. And bringin' Lady Aldrich here ain't helped."

Quinn frowned. "You run into any of my men on the way down?" he asked, and Ramsey shook his head.

"I stayed clear of everything and everybody once I hit the woods."

"Then you don't know that I married Lady Aldrich three days ago."

"Jesus Christ!" exclaimed Ramsey. "Varrick's headed this way to get her back. When he found out she was with you he convinced Governor Gage you'd kidnapped her."

"He's on his way?"

"Aye," answered Ramsey. "With about fifty of his best Mohawks and about ten handpicked soldiers. I passed them up by the Allegheny country."

Quinn stood up and walked over to a map. "Where were they when you passed them?"

Ramsey stood up too and eyed the map, then pointed. "Right about here," he said.

Quinn stared at it and rubbed his chin. "Is he traveling fast?"

"Not too fast. The soldiers are slowin' him up, but I guess he figures bringing them with him makes it legal as far as the British are concerned."

"I wonder why so few men," mused Quinn. "He knows I have a small army here. He must know it."

Ramsey shook his head. "Don't know unless they plan to sneak in and out again with the lady. He knows you ain't got the silver no more, so they have to be after the lady."

Quinn walked back to his desk and sat on it, thinking, then turned to Ramsey, who still stood by the map. "Think you could find him again?" he asked, and Ramsey nodded.

Quinn stood up, opened the door, and called to Burly in the outer office. "Get Telak and about fifty or sixty warriors. Tell them we're traveling light. We'll leave at dawn, so they'll have all night to say their good-byes."

"Where we goin'?" he asked, and Quinn frowned.

"I don't want Kendall to reach the fort. I intend to stop

him," he said, walking over and putting his arm around Ramsey's shoulder. "Get yourself some food and a good night's sleep and replenish your gunpowder. We'll leave an hour before daylight."

He said good-bye to Ramsey and spent the next half hour giving Lieutenant Holmes instructions on what to do while he was gone, then Holmes left.

He'd been gone only a few minutes when Sara walked in. Quinn had been studying the map and turned, startled, as she stepped in and shut the door behind her.

"I knew you wouldn't mind," she said, stepping forward. "I heard you were leaving again."

"For a short time, yes," he said. "But why should that concern you?"

"Oh, come now, Quinn," she answered seductively. "You don't have to pretend now. There's no one else here."

"Pretend what?"

She walked over to him and pressed her breasts against his chest, putting her arms about his neck. "I know you only married her for spite," she whispered. "We can pick up where we left off before you went away." Her fingers were entwined behind his neck. "I waited years for you to notice me, Quinn," she went on, "and when I told you I'd been saving myself for you I meant it, every word."

Quinn remembered that last night in camp before he'd left. He'd talked to Sara, but that was all, always avoiding any hint that he might be interested in her. He knew she liked him, but the feeling was far from mutual. She was a nasty little bitch. That night, however, he'd been celebrating his journey to Boston and had had just enough ale to make him agreeable to almost anything and when she followed him to the house he hadn't put up an argument when she'd forced herself on him. Thank God he'd been sober enough to know she hadn't been saving herself for anyone and he'd pulled away at the last minute. Now the thought of succumbing to her the least bit angered him.

He reached up, pulled her arms from about his neck, and stared angrily into her face. "I'll forget you said that," he said, and she looked chagrined.

"What do you mean you'll forget?"

"I happen to be a married man. Now . . . unless you intend to try to force yourself on me as you did before so that I'll have to use violence, I suggest you leave before I really lose my temper."

Her eyes narrowed with rage as she stared at him. "Force myself on you?"

"That's right. You came after me, I didn't come after you. It was my bed you crawled into, or have you forgotten?"

"But you didn't struggle, did you?"

"Struggle? Why should I struggle? If you want a man that bad why shouldn't I oblige?"

"But you didn't," she answered spitefully. "You didn't oblige!" Her eyes were filled with hatred as he rejected her. "You quit," she said venomously. "The great Captain Quinn Locke and he couldn't even give me what I wanted."

"Why should I give you what I was keeping for my wife?"

"Your wife? You mean the woman you forced into marriage so you could get revenge on your cousin? I wonder if you'll ever give her what she wants!"

He sneered. "I gave it to her long before I married her," he answered arrogantly.

"Ha! That's a lie!" she yelled. "You don't have the guts to really take a woman. You're too afraid of having a bastard, Quinn Locke. A bastard like you are!"

She'd gone too far and his face grew dark as his hand shot out instinctively and struck her across the face, leaving its imprint on her fair skin. She let out a gasp of pain.

Tears of anger filled her eyes. "You'll regret that!" she retorted viciously, putting her hand up to her face. "I'll get even with you and that bitch you married if it's the last thing I do." She whirled, stalking out, slamming the door, leaving him standing in front of the map, his face livid with rage.

# 15

❧

It was still dark as Quinn stirred. Loedicia was on her stomach, one arm across his chest, her head on his shoulder, sleeping peacefully. With his right hand he brushed the hair from her face and she began to stir.

"Dicia?" he whispered. "Dicia?"

She murmured something and nestled closer.

His arms went around her and he held her close as she opened her eyes. "It's time for me to leave," he said, and she turned her face to his.

"You have to go?"

"Give me something to take with me," he whispered softly, and kissed her passionately as his hands caressed her.

Half an hour later he rolled out of bed and began getting into his buckskins. She raised herself, leaning on her elbow, her head resting in her hand, and watched him in the darkness. She could barely see him, but she could still feel the effects of him in her body and she trembled.

When he was all ready, he slipped a knife into the sheath on his belt, walked over and sat on the edge of the bed, looking down at her. He reached out and cupped her chin in his hand.

"In case I've forgotten to tell you, Dicia, my darling," he said softly as he bent over and kissed her lovingly on the mouth, "I love you very much." He kissed her once more, dropped his hand, stood up, and left the room before she had time to recover from the shock of hearing him say those words.

Suddenly she jumped from the bed, wrapping the sheet about her naked body, and ran through the house to the sitting-room door. "Quinn!" she called into the darkness outside. "Quinn!"

She saw him heading for the lane that led to the fort.

"Quinn!" she yelled again, and he turned and waved. "I have something to tell you!" she called desperately. "Please, Quinn!" He laughed as he hollered back to her.

"Don't worry. You can tell me when I get home." He threw her a kiss, then disappeared around the corner of the house.

She sighed as she leaned against the doorframe. "I intend to," she whispered softly to herself, and wiped the tears from her eyes. She went back to the bedroom and curled up in bed with her arms about his pillow. He had to come back to her now. He had to!

Everyone was still sleeping as the men moved silently out of camp. Sixty-odd warriors, Telak, Ramsey, Burly, and Quinn. They moved fast and light and by daybreak were well over five miles from the fort. Ramsey led the way as they quickly put the miles behind them.

Close to noon they slowed down a bit, eating on the run, and Burly moved up close to Quinn, who was following at Ramsey's heels.

"Notice anything peculiar about Ramsey?" he asked as they trotted through a grove of scrub maple and started down an incline.

Quinn nodded as he raised a piece of dried venison to his mouth and tore off a piece, chewing it methodically as he ran. "Seems a bit nervous, doesn't he?"

"You think something's wrong?"

"It better not be."

"I'd keep him in sight if I were you," suggested Burly. "I don't trust him. He spends too much time out of the woods on women and ale."

"You think he'd sell us out?"

"Something's making him jumpy."

"I'll keep watch," answered Quinn, "but just to be sure, maybe you'd best keep a jump ahead of him. I don't care to move into any ambush." They quickened their pace as Ramsey disappeared around a large boulder up ahead.

They never stopped till dark, then took off again before daylight, moving continually, eating dried meat on the run.

They were four days out as dusk began to settle and they were looking for a place to bed down when Burly, who'd moved up in front of Ramsey, hollered, "Hold it!" and as they all hit the ground and looked down into the small ravine visible through the trees they spotted about ten or so warriors spread out, ready to make camp.

Burly motioned to Quinn, who nodded.

"Think it's a trap?" asked Burly, but Quinn only stared hard.

"There's only a few. Where are the others?" His eyes shifted as he turned to look around. "And where's Ramsey?"

Burly whirled around, suddenly realizing he hadn't seen Ramsey since he'd complained earlier about having something in his moccasin and had fallen back. Burly motioned for Telak and sent word along the line, but Ramsey'd dropped out of sight and no one seemed to know exactly when.

Burly hugged the ground, still looking at Quinn as Telak slithered up to them.

"Is not ambush," he said stoically, and Quinn's hair stood on end. If it wasn't an ambush, then what was it and why had Ramsey taken off?

"Let's find out," he whispered grimly, and gave a nod to Telak, who silently signaled his men.

Within fifteen minutes Telak's men had surrounded the unsuspecting band of Indians and were stealthily moving in. Burly and Quinn stayed out of the fray and let Telak's warriors handle it. A few minutes later there were nine dead Mohawks and two survivors as the two woodsmen moved swiftly into the ravine.

"Where's Varrick?" Quinn asked one of the captives in the Indian's dialect, but he held his mouth tight.

Quinn nodded to Telak, who was holding the man, and Telak disappeared in the bushes with the Indian. There was a sharp grunt, silence for a minute except for a low mumbling, another noise, which sounded like a stifled scream, and then Telak returned alone.

"What did he say?" asked Quinn. Telak looked puzzled.

He motioned with his hands as he spoke. "Him say leave Niagara on way to big river Ohio pass white lord and Mohawks few days back heading down shore Okswego. Soldier redcoat with him. No like soldier redcoat, rather raid settler down valley."

Quinn stared at him, stunned. Now it fell into place. He'd been prepared for an ambush, but this . . .

"Damn it!" he cried viciously, his teeth clenched, face white. "Damn Ramsey to hell, the son of a bitch." He threw his head back in anguish and closed his eyes. "And we're four days from the fort. We can never get back in time and he's got over fifty men with him, counting the soldiers."

"Maybe he won't attack," said Burly, but he knew better.

Quinn didn't seem to hear him but he straightened up, a determined look on his face. He turned to Telak. "If he gets to the fort before we do and manages to take Dicia I think he'll head up the shoreline again. You and your warriors head cross-country to the lake and try to head them off." His face was dark with anger. "I'll take Burly with me and try to make it to the fort before they do."

"They have a four-day start," exclaimed Burly.

"And a bunch of clumsy soldiers. I'll travel without stopping."

"We'll never make it."

"I can go alone!" snapped Quinn, and Burly frowned.

"Damn it. You know better than that. I won't let you do that."

"Then let's move," said Quinn, and he gave Telak his instructions, then he and Burly headed up over the crest of the hill, headed out of the ravine. They hadn't gone fifty yards when there was a garbled scream behind them as the surviving Mohawk took his last breath.

Quinn didn't especially like the Tuscaroras' methods of taking care of their prisoners, but it was one thing with which he never interfered. As long as they were his friends they could do what they wanted with their prisoners, even if it did give him some restless nights sometimes.

They were a strange people, suffering anything for a
friend but giving no quarter to an enemy.

Quinn stopped and listened one last time, then took off
at a fast run with Burly close behind.

The first four days Quinn was gone, Loedicia tried to
fill her days with as much as she could to keep busy. She
knew now that she was in love with him and he had told
her he loved her. Was there anything more wonderful in
the world, to love and be loved? She was no longer bitter
toward the child she carried or the man who had fathered
it and she waited impatiently for his return.

Lizette came every day with material and they worked
on some clothes for her. Not that she didn't need them.
They made her nightgowns, petticoats, bloomers, and a
few dresses.

She spent hours walking along the beach, watching the
water as it lapped the shoreline, sometimes angrily, sometimes gently. She helped Moneola cook and clean house,
getting soot and ashes all over her as she cleaned the fireplace against Moneola's wishes and covering herself with
flour and cornmeal as she tried her hand at baking.
Moneola smiled and shook her head at Dicia's stubborn
insistence that she wanted to learn how to do everything
so Quinn would be proud of her.

She visited the fort and made friends with Telak's
wives and children and was delighted when they tried to
teach her some of their weaving skills and she fell in love
with one of his children, a little boy of three whose
mother had been half Indian and half French. His eyes,
deep green, and his hair, black as ebony, contrasted and
he looked nothing like his brothers and sisters. She spent
hours playing with him. Everything was interesting to her
and she began to understand why Quinn loved this quiet
wilderness. It was beginning to become a part of her.

Sara too was keeping busy. Trying to think of some
way to get even with Quinn. She had wanted him ever
since that day she'd set eyes on him when she was fifteen
and her father had brought him home to dinner. The next
day, they'd left for Fort Locke and she'd vowed that
morning that someday she'd marry him, but he'd never

looked at her with desire in his eyes as had the other men at the fort and ten years had been a long time to wait to share his bed, so she'd accepted the favors of other men, substituting them for Quinn until that night before he'd left for Boston. Now, to have him humiliate her as he had done and for that snip of a girl, barely a woman. It was too much. All she could think of was revenge, and the chance for revenge came sooner than expected.

Guards had been posted day and night at the fort and the house, and even the Indians were on edge. One afternoon Sara strolled through the Indian village, not paying much attention to what was going on around her or to anyone in particular. She left the encampment and went to the fort, where she talked one of the men into letting her take one of the horses, having promised to share his bed that evening, and in no time at all she was galloping along the river, the sun and wind in her face. She paid no attention to how far she'd gone. She was angry with herself and the world around her. She hated Loedicia more than she'd ever hated anyone else.

She'd ridden hard from the fort and now she slowed her mount to a walk, then stopped him and slid to the ground. She stood at the edge of the river, looking down into the water and contemplating how enjoyable it would be to hold Loedicia's head under until there was no more breath in her body, when suddenly she heard a step behind her and whirled around.

The Indian was tall and lean, his sloe eyes glistening as he stood in the center of the path she'd ridden on moments before. But he wasn't a Tuscarora, he was a Mohawk, and her face went white. A movement behind him caught her eye, then another and another, and before she could utter a sound she was surrounded by Indians. Then from behind them, as they stepped aside, came a man, tall and broad, his red-gold hair glistening in the sun, and instinctively, even before seeing the scar, she knew who it was.

Lord Varrick wore buckskin breeches and moccasins, a fringed shirt of buff, and his hair was tied back with a black ribbon. "And you are?" he asked as he approached her.

She bit her lip, shaking, her knees quivering. She had heard so many stories about him. "I'm Sara Townley, the preacher's daughter," she answered nervously.

He looked her over from head to toe, taking in the light brown crowning braids and gold-flecked brown eyes. She wasn't unattractive. A bit of a handful for a man who liked his women small and he thought of Loedicia and the scar on his cheek grew red in anger.

"You're from Fort Locke?"

There was no use trying to lie. "Yes."

"You know Lady Aldrich, then, I presume."

Her eyes narrowed. "I know her."

He grinned sardonically. "You're friends?"

"Hardly!" she answered, and saw the gleam in his eyes as he noticed the hurt in hers.

"Ah ha! I see you have little love for the lady."

"Why should I?"

A sneer formed at the corners of his mouth. "Then perhaps the two of us can strike a bargain," he said. "Unless you're too devoted to my cousin, Captain Locke."

She studied his face. It was a hard, cruel face and she had heard of the fate of others who'd had dealings with him, then she realized this was her chance. She had to take it.

"I hate him!" she answered angrily, and Kendall Varrick smiled, pleased with himself.

A woman scorned! What could be better? He was amused at the scheme he was hatching as he stared at Sara and within minutes they had their heads together and were working out a plan.

It was close to midnight the next evening when Sara slipped from her bed and put on her dress. She'd been preparing things all day. She was getting revenge, all right, and she sneered as she thought of Loedicia's fate and what Quinn was going to say when he came back and discovered his precious Dicia gone.

It was exceptionally dark as she worked her way to the

catwalk, keeping in the shadows until she reached the ladder. She waited until the sentry passed above her on his way to the other blockhouse. The gates were closed and two sentries stood watch, and she had only minutes before the sentry on the catwalk would march back along his post.

She'd stolen some rope from the storeroom and now she crept up the ladder silently and tied it to one of the spikes, throwing it over the side, then she climbed over, holding on to it, and lowered herself to the ground. All the hatred that had built up over the past few days as she watched everyone around the fort accepting Loedicia, treating her like someone special, exploded inside her. Maybe without her Quinn would come to his senses. At least she'd have a chance then.

The sentry passed above her and she hugged the wall, then moved away from the fort into the shadows. A few yards farther and she heard the call of a night heron. Only it wasn't a night heron, it was one of Varrick's men. They found her easily and ushered her to where Lord Varrick waited in the bushes beyond Quinn's house.

"You've got the bottle?" he asked softly, and she nodded.

"It's here in my pouch," she whispered, and held up a beaded leather bag. She reached inside, pulling out a bottle of wine. "My father's been saving the wine for Christmas communion services," she said, and handed it to him.

He reached in his pocket, removed a small packet and opened it, pouring its contents into the bottle of wine, then he shook it vigorously.

"It won't kill them, will it?" she asked. "I don't want anyone hurt." Her eyes narrowed. "Except Loedicia. I don't care what you do to her."

"Don't worry," he whispered. "It's a bit of laudanum. It'll just put them to sleep."

Two men guarded the house and she knew them both. She and Lord Varrick, the Mohawks close behind, crept close along the lane, keeping to the bushes. She tucked the bottle under her arm and headed for the guard by the veranda.

The night was hot, not a breeze stirring as she stepped out of the shadows in front of the guard.

"Hello, Harry," she whispered as he stared dumbfounded.

"What the hell are you doin' here, Sara?" he asked anxiously. "You're supposed to be in the fort."

She wrinkled her nose. "That stinkin' place. It ain't fit for pigs. It's nice out here and I thought maybe you'd like some company. Join me in a drink or two."

The private's eyes squinted in the dark as she held up the bottle. "Jesus, what'd you do, steal some of your father's best stuff?"

She laughed. "It's wine he was savin' for Christmas. Want some?" She held the bottle toward him.

He licked his lips. "I really shouldn't."

"Just one?" she coaxed.

He sighed. "One swig," he whispered softly. "I'm on duty, but one swig ain't gonna hurt none and then maybe we can have a kiss or two before you leave, eh?"

When she left Harry he was unconscious, his head resting at the foot of the veranda steps, then she slipped around to the back door and treated the guard by the kitchen to the same fate.

Emerging at the shore side of the house, she walked to the edge of the sand beside the lane. "She's all yours," she said softly. "Just see she doesn't come back." She started to walk away when Varrick caught her arm.

"I'm afraid you can't go now," he whispered. "You see, my men are using the rope you so kindly left down the outside wall of the fort and by now at least forty Mohawks are crawling about inside it, doing what damage they can before we leave."

"You said you wanted her," she said, pointing toward the house. "You said no one would be hurt."

"I lie a lot," he answered casually. "If my men can find the powder storeroom," he retorted, "Quinn'll have nothing to come back to except cinders."

She stared at him, horrified. She'd wanted Loedicia out

of the way, but not like this. He'd promised. Now she knew why so many people feared him. She'd heard Quinn say the only man he'd never cross was an Indian. What a stupid fool she'd been.

"My father's in that fort," she cried, raising her voice, "and all those people! I didn't want them hurt, I only wanted Quinn hurt!" She turned hurriedly and made a lunge to get away, but it was too late.

Varrick nodded and an arm shot out of the darkness behind her, covering her mouth as she felt the knife slide between her ribs, then her body felt warm all over and the last thing she heard was Moneola's voice calling from the house.

Moneola squinted into the darkness, trying to see. If it was Quinn he'd make more noise to let them know he was coming. "Who's there?" she called into the darkness, but all she heard was the call of a night heron. A few seconds later she heard an answering call and her heart started pounding. She shut the door quickly, threw the bolt across, ran to the kitchen as fast as her plump body could go, secured the bar across the back door, then ran to the bedroom.

Dicia was sleeping soundly, her arms wrapped around Quinn's pillow. The night was cool and without Quinn to keep her warm she'd put on one of the nightgowns Lizette had made for her.

Moneola nudged her awake and Loedicia sat up, startled.

"What is it?"

"Shh!" she whispered. "There is no guard at veranda and no guard by kitchen. Something is wrong."

Loedicia slipped from the bed and walked to the window. It was already open and she stuck her head out, only to find herself staring directly into the face of the man she'd come hundreds of miles to escape from.

She let out a gasp, pulled herself back in, and tried to shut the window, but it was no use. The curtain ripped and hit the floor as he climbed through and she grabbed the nearest thing, a book off the stand, to throw at him.

Moneola screamed as Loedicia bumped into her in the

dark and they both fell against the dresser as the room was overrun with Indians. Loedicia fought, scratching, biting, and kicking, almost breaking her toes against their shins, but it did no good.

She heard Moneola let out an agonized scream and she knew without seeing that they'd killed her. She stopped fighting and gasped for air. "What have you done?" she screamed breathlessly at the man whose shadow she couldn't mistake as he stood a few feet from her. "My God! What have you done?"

"I've come after my bride," he answered angrily. "No one makes a fool of Lord Varrick. No one! You're going back with me and we're going to be married just as we planned." His voice sounded triumphant. Sara had purposely kept Loedicia's marriage from him, afraid if he knew he'd never take Loedicia with him. He went rambling on, arrogantly acknowledging how her uncle and everyone else were waiting. Nothing would be changed. Her trousseau was still intact, everything would go as planned, then suddenly her words cut across his voice and he stopped abruptly.

"What did you say?" he asked sharply.

She cried almost hysterically, "I said I can't marry you. Don't you hear me or are you too deaf to listen? I'm already married!"

He reached out and grabbed her wrist, pulling her toward him in the dark as the Indians stood motionless, watching them.

She sneered. "That's right. I'm already married!" she repeated vindictively. "I'm Mrs. Quinn Locke!" She felt his fingers bite into her wrist.

"You lie!" he whispered through clenched teeth, and his fingers tightened.

"No," she answered, trembling. "I'm telling you the truth. Quinn and I are married and I'm expecting his baby. I—"

The back of his hand tore across her face and she let out a moan, then slumped forward, and he caught her before she hit the floor.

He picked her up and held her to him, then nodded to

the Indians, and they went ahead of him through the house and out onto the veranda. He carried her against him as they walked through the sand, along the shore, and on into the underbrush.

They must have gone two hundred yards or more when she started to moan and he knelt down, putting her on the ground, her back against a tree trunk.

Her head hurt and everything was black as she opened her eyes and tried to focus them, then suddenly, from back at the fort, the air turned crimson as a loud explosion tore through the sky and timbers flew every which way. As agonized screams and shouts from Quinn's men and the Indians rang in her ears Loedicia, dazed, her lip bleeding, head pounding, felt herself being lifted up and slung over someone's shoulder like a sack of grain, then all went black again.

# 16

Quinn and Burly were about a mile off when they saw the smoke, knew something was wrong, and quickened their pace. They'd been running almost day and night, stopping an hour or so at a time to get a second wind and a short nap, then kept going. But it hadn't been fast enough and Quinn, with a burst of energy brought on by panic, traveled the last mile in minutes.

As he rounded the bend and got his first glimpse of the fort he felt sick at the sight before him. Burly tried to keep up, but Quinn was moving like a man possessed. He ran through the trees into the clearing, between the teepees and bark houses, hardly looking left or right, then stopped abruptly and stared at what was left of the fort, a hollow feeling in the pit of his stomach.

He looked quickly up the lane toward the house and he felt as if his heart stood still inside his body. No one came to meet him and he stopped, looking around at the faces staring at him in silence, then with a heavy heart he slowly walked what seemed like an endless walk until he reached the door.

Silence greeted him as he entered the kitchen, then walked from room to room. He went out onto the veranda, walked down to the sand, and stood staring at the lake, his face dark and ominous.

He whirled around as Burly came up behind him. "What do you want?" he asked irritably, and Burly sighed. He'd hung back and talked to the survivors.

"She's alive, Quinn," he offered. "Moneola's dead, but Dicia's alive."

He saw the flicker in Quinn's eyes.

"She's not here," he explained quickly. "Varrick took her away the night before last." He saw the agony in Quinn's eyes, then he saw them narrow cruelly.

"Get the men that are left," he said savagely. "We're going after her. I'll see Varrick dead for what he's done to me!" Burly winced. He'd seen Quinn angry before, but not like this.

Quinn didn't even sleep. He tried to reconstruct what had happened, took inventory of what was left, then without more than an hour's rest took off again, heading up the shoreline in hot pursuit with as many able-bodied men who could be spared. He left Lieutenant Holmes with a small detail of men and a few Indians to help clean up, a job the women and children also shared, and he was gone before they hardly realized he'd returned.

Dicia was cold. She'd been cold for days. Since the night Kendall Varrick had come back into her life. They'd trudged for endless miles, along sandy beaches dotted with poplar saplings, small fluttering leaves twisting to and fro in the breezes blown from the lake. Through groves of silver birch, white bark glistening in the sun. Along trails so dense they had to cut their way through.

One of the soldiers had given her his coat to wear the first day and she'd wrapped it tightly about her, but it did little good, since she was still wearing the flimsy cotton nightgown. And her feet, encased in moccasins provided by one of the Mohawks, were sore and blistered. She was weary and hungry and although she'd cried endlessly those first few days, now only bitterness was left.

She cringed every time Kendall looked at her and her sad eyes would suddenly become hostile when the soldiers tried to be friendly. She wanted no part of them and her heart ached for Quinn. It had all been so unnecessary. All those people dead because Lord Varrick couldn't stand the thought of Quinn's getting the better of him.

"I don't know what good it's going to do to take me back," she said as they sat around the fire trying to keep warm. "You'll only make a fool of yourself."

He turned and looked at her. "Oh, I don't think so," he answered cynically, and she eyed him suspiciously. The scar on his cheek was prominent in the light of the fire and she thought that if it hadn't been there, perhaps his hatred of Quinn wouldn't be so strong. But then again he was a proud man, too proud, and he was cruel. It showed in his eyes and the way he smiled.

"What do you mean?" she asked gingerly.

"You said it yourself, my dear," he remarked calmly. "Since you already have a husband marriage is out of the question. But you'll still go back with me, Loedicia. Not to Boston, but to my settlement near the Niagara . . . as my mistress." She stared at him dumbfounded.

"You wouldn't dare!"

His eyes hardened, dark and somber. "Don't push me, Loedicia," he said, and he ground his teeth angrily. "When I'm through with you Quinn won't want to dirty himself with you and as for his bastard child, because that's what it is—father a bastard, child a bastard—I'll decide what to do with it when the time comes."

"He'll kill you," she cried as she pulled the coat tighter about her to stop the chills that were starting to make her shake.

"On the contrary, I'll kill him, my dear. I'm looking forward to him coming after you and I'm waiting," he answered viciously. "I've been waiting fifteen years to meet him again face to face. He's been a shadow in front and behind me for too long. I'm tired of his insolence, raiding my camps, interfering with my plans, but this time he's gone too far. When he took you, my dear, he signed his death warrant. I'll not give up now until I know he's dead." Loedicia shuddered at the enmity in his voice. Now she knew why Quinn hated him so.

From that evening on she avoided talking to Kendall as much as possible, but it didn't matter. He kept her beside him all the way, his eyes letting her know what he had planned for her.

The fourth day out, they bypassed Fort Presque Isle. Only a small garrison of men were there and Lord Varrick wanted to make Seneca country as soon as possible, so they continued to move on.

Some days later, in the early hours of the morning, as they topped a small hill, Lord Varrick stopped and breathed in deeply as he surveyed the scene that met their eyes. Spread before them near the shore was an Indian village almost as big as the one at Fort Locke. All along the lakefront, some few hundred feet from the edge of the sand, were dozens of bark huts teeming with men, women, and children. Kendall reached over and grabbed Loedicia's arm, pulling her toward him, making her stand in front of him so she could see better. As they stood watching, people started pointing, there was a shout, and all heads turned their way. Kendall gave Loedicia a push ahead of him and as they started down the slope four canoes left the lake, pulling onto the beach, painted warriors emerging from them and running across the sand toward them. As Varrick and Loedicia walked into the midst of the huts they were immediately surrounded by dozens of curious Senecas, their eyes wide and questioning.

Kendall held tightly to Loedicia's arm as the soldiers and Mohawks followed. He spoke to the Indians in their tongue and received smiles and nods as they led them to a longhouse in the center of the other huts.

Loedicia hesitated at the doorway of the longhouse, but Kendall's fingers tightened on her arm and he pushed her through, leaving the soldiers outside, and she stared wide-eyed as her eyes became adjusted to the darkness inside. Three men sat cross-legged about a sunken fire at one end of the lodge, their faces stern and unmoving, and above their heads hung a number of scalps and other trophies of war, but it didn't seem to bother Kendall. He raised his hand in a friendly gesture and began talking to them and Loedicia guessed they must have offered him a place at their fire because he sat down across from them, seating her beside him, as if he were an old friend.

She watched for a long time as they silently passed about a smoking pipe, each taking his turn, then handing it to the next. The silence was irritating and seemed as if it would never end, then suddenly one of the men, more elaborately dressed than the others, began speaking and Kendall joined them, talking at length, animatedly pointing at Loedicia as he continued to address them. Suddenly Kendall stood up, tall and impressive. He turned to her. "We stay the night," he announced as he reached down and pulled her to her feet. "Come."

She brushed the damp, sweaty ringlets away from her face. "Where are we going?"

His fingers hurt her arm as he ushered her back into the morning sunlight. "We've been assigned our own little bark hut, my dear," he answered sarcastically, a slight sneer twisting his mouth. "And it's time you lived up to your position."

She laughed almost hysterically. "My position . . . you couldn't care less about my position."

"On the contrary, Loedicia," he said, and she saw a gleam in his eyes. "Your position is very much my concern . . . or have you forgotten?"

Forgotten? God help her, no. She hadn't forgotten. He'd vowed to make her his mistress. She'd die first.

He took her to a small bark hut at the edge of the lake, talking to the people who crowded around them as they walked, gathering a group of Indian women with him on the way.

He stopped before a hut and turned her to face him, looking her over cynically. "You're terribly dirty, Loedicia," he stated with distaste, and motioned toward the Indian maidens. "These young ladies will see you get cleaned up." He saw the look in her eye and warned her.

"And don't think you can leave. They'd slit your throat before you got to the lake."

"I hate you!" she whispered viciously, tears in her eyes, but he only smiled, pleased with himself, as he turned and walked away.

The women took her first to the beach, where they hovered about as she took a bath, her first since the night she was captured, then they dressed her in leggings and a long shirt and brought food for her to eat.

As she moved about the camp with the women she became aware of a pair of eyes following her intently. She turned her head suddenly and caught one of the warriors watching her, his dark eyes glued to her. It made her feel uneasy and for the rest of the day until sundown, no matter what she did or where she went the man followed subtly, his eyes never leaving her. Who was he? Why was he watching her?

Shortly before darkness fell the man disappeared, leaving Loedicia to wonder. The women kept her with them until after the evening meal, then they returned her to the bark hut, lit a small fire in the center, and left her for the first time.

It was dark out now and she lay on a blanket watching the flames from the small fire in the center of the hut, wondering where Quinn was and if he was on his way to her and if, even if he came, he could ever get her back this time. She glanced toward the doorway, at the darkness outside, then suddenly her heart began pounding as Kendall appeared, his face dark and ominous. He never said a word as he moved forward and took a stick, poking up the flames, the scar on his cheek vivid in the firelight.

"What do you want?" she asked defiantly, breathlessly, and he looked at her, his eyes filled with lust.

"Don't you know?" he asked casually, and she cringed, moving hard against the side of the bark hut. "It won't help," he said, and his mouth twisted into a grin as he stood up and looked down at her. "Take them off," he ordered, and suddenly he was no longer smiling.

She pressed her hands across her breasts, shaking her head, her lips pressed tightly together.

He knelt down in front of her and his left hand shot out, grasping the front of her shirt above where her arms were crossed. "I said off!"

"No!" she cried, and grabbed his hand, trying to pull it from her shirt.

Instead his grip tightened as he stared into her eyes, his nostrils flaring angrily, then his right hand swung violently, catching her on the side of the head, and the force made her shudder and cry out.

Her head was swimming, her senses reeling, and she felt sick as she fought the darkness that was trying to engulf her. "You'll have to kill me first," she sobbed, gasping from the blow he'd dealt her, and he laughed viciously as he raised his hand to hit her again, but this time she was ready.

She tried to squirm aside and began kicking and scratching, grabbing his face, her nails digging deep into his already livid scar, drawing blood, and he cursed as she fought like a wildcat, forcing him to use his fist on her. He went berserk, hitting her again and again, laughing sadistically with every blow he struck as she tried vainly to fight back.

"I won't!" she gasped hysterically, blood streaming from her mouth, but he paid no heed as his fist continued coming down on the side of her head until she lay senseless, his hand still holding her limp body by the front of her shirt.

His eyes were glazed as he stared at her, then he released her, letting her fall back onto the blanket. She was unconscious and he felt a strange exhilaration as he stared at her. Slowly he leaned forward and began stripping her of her shirt and leggings. He stroked her soft flesh as he removed her clothes, enjoying the titillating sensations that made his breathing short and labored as her body was revealed to him, and he ran his hand excitedly from her breasts to between her legs, savoring the sensuality. He knew she'd look like this, her breasts high and firm, her body shaped like a goddess', and he felt the familiar bulge pushing against his buckskins.

He stood up and continued to stare at her transfixed as he began removing his own clothes. Loedicia began to regain consciousness.

Her head was pounding and she tried to move, but it was useless. She opened her eyes as best she could, trying to focus them, but it was hard and she had to fight the feeling of euphoria that kept trying to claim her. She could see as if in a haze and her mind was cloudy, her body trembling with fear as she watched Kendall pull off his shirt, then drop his pants and step from them, and she wanted to cry out. He couldn't! He couldn't . . . she wouldn't let him, yet he walked over and dropped to his knees, straddling her, and there was nothing she could do.

She gathered the little strength left to her and tried to move, to push him off, but he only laughed at her feeble attempt and shoved her legs apart and as if in a nightmare, she felt him force his way into her, pushing down, his flesh pressing against hers, and a painful cry escaped her lips and she whimpered like a baby as he raped her savagely, taking his time, making sure she was conscious enough to feel but not conscious enough to fight him. She wanted to die and wished for death, but it wouldn't come and he continued to abuse her as time seemed to stand still, satisfying his desires until his lust was finally satiated, then he left her crumpled in a heap, bleeding, hysterical, and only half conscious.

The Indian who'd been watching Loedicia all day had slipped into the shadows at dusk and was making his way along the beach, backtracking Lord Varrick's party. It was the same woman, he knew. The woman Captain Locke had announced he was going to marry. He'd seen her before he'd left the fort, the afternoon she and the captain had ridden in, and since Lord Varrick had her that meant something was wrong.

He left the camp behind, dodging in and out among the trees, over the sand dunes, following the stars and the shoreline.

Quinn had set his men at a fast pace, circling around

Fort Presque Isle, meeting with Telak and his men just north of it. They moved fast, resting as little as possible, so it was shortly after midnight when the lone Indian spotted them in a small grove of poplars near the edge of the lake.

Quinn stood near the water, paying no heed to the waves as they lapped at his moccasins. A storm was brewing off to the southwest and he watched lightning in the distance lighting up the sky, reflecting off the water, then suddenly he stopped, listening intently as a soft call broke the stillness of the night around him.

He hurried back toward the fire where the men were and raised his hands to his mouth, answering the call, and within minutes the Indian from the Senaca camp hurried up to the campfire and sat down to catch his breath.

Quinn's eyes darkened as he listened to the man, one of the Tuscaroras he'd sent into the Senecas' camp to spy on them only weeks before. He was one of Telak's best, but at the moment he looked pure Seneca.

"They arrived early morning," he said breathlessly as Quinn questioned him in the man's own language. "I see woman right away."

"Was she all right?"

He nodded, but his eyes looked wary. "Don't wait," he said warningly. "The Lord Varrick has eyes for her." Quinn knew right away what he meant. The Indian pointed to him. "You and I, we get her. I know how camp is, I have plan, is fine."

They put their heads together and although Burly shook his head, arguing that it couldn't be done, Quinn and the Indian took off within the hour, heading for the Seneca village with a promise to meet Burly and the rest of the men sometime after dawn at Birch Point, almost ten miles south of the Seneca village, along the lakeshore.

Loedicia stirred. Every bone in her body ached as she turned toward the fire and watched the dying embers. He'd been gone for some time now and she moaned every time she heard a noise outside, afraid he'd return. She reached up and touched her face, feeling the split, swollen lip and oversized jaw. Her eye was discolored and puffed almost shut and tears ran down her cheeks, burning the small cuts on her face as she reached out and dragged her buckskin shirt to her naked body and pulled it on slowly, all the time remembering as if through a mist Lord Varrick's body above her, making her submit to him.

She had wanted to die and even begged for death, fighting until she had no more strength to move. His attack on her had been vicious and now she whimpered agonizedly as she pulled the leggings up over her bruised legs, then lay back on the blanket, exhausted. Oh, God! Why? She felt dirty and sick inside, knowing what he'd done to her. Even if Quinn came now . . . he'd never want her . . . not now . . . not like this.

She lay for hours watching the fire, condemning herself for what had happened, admonishing herself for not fighting him to her death, but then that would have been impossible because he was a man trained in the art of inhumanity, trained to torture to the point of death, but no further. Trained to keep a man alive so he could feel the pain and he treated his women with the same devotion, keeping them alive so they knew the humiliation, the degradation. She watched the fire until it was almost out, afraid he'd come back. Afraid to shut her eyes.

Suddenly her heart turned over in her breast as a figure appeared in the doorway and ducked inside. She backed up, cowering against the wall, tears streaming down her face. "Get away," she whispered, her words jumbled, almost incoherent because of the swollen lip. "Don't . . . please . . . leave me alone."

The Indian knelt down and put two fingers to his lips, meaning for her to be silent. "Quinn," he whispered softly, and Loedicia drew in her breath quickly.

A Seneca Indian. He had to be, with the cropped hair, painted scalp, and feathers sticking from it, but he'd spoken Quinn's name and now he was motioning for her to follow him.

She tried to move, but it hurt. Her ribs felt on fire.

"Hurry," he said in English, and Loedicia managed to move a short way off the blanket and onto her knees. The

Indian reached out and grabbed her arm, pulling her to her feet, and she winced, almost crying out from the pain.

He motioned for her to be still and they made their way to the opening of the bark hut, his arm about her waist, practically carrying her to keep her from falling. He pulled her sideways as they moved out of the door and it was then she saw the soldier who'd been guarding her sprawled near the doorway, his red coat covered in the back with a dark stain.

They slipped to the back of the hut and melted into the shadows, moving from bush to bush, lodge to lodge, slipping past the guards, moving through the trees toward the beach. He kept his arm around her, helping to hide her face so that anyone seeing them would think they were an Indian couple.

On across the sand they moved, staying in the shadows, and suddenly, as they reached a bush near the edge of the water, a hand moved out and grabbed her wrist, pulling her into the bushes.

"Dicia!" His arms were about her and he held her close, not realizing his strength was hurting her, and she moaned low.

The Indian asked him something and Quinn whispered back, then abruptly she found herself pulled from the bushes as a shout went up from inside the camp. They were stumbling along the beach now, past the canoes, and Quinn started counting them as they went by, then he stopped at the fifth one, a small one, and pulled her to it.

He didn't wait for her to climb in but picked her up and set her in one end, then he jumped in the opposite end and the Indian who'd helped her shoved the canoe into the waves, pushing it through the breakers, off the beach until he was standing neck-deep in water.

"God speed," whispered Quinn to the man, and he smiled, then Loedicia watched, fascinated, as his head disappeared beneath the surface of the water as if he'd never been there.

Quinn handed her a paddle as she looked back at him. "Can you paddle?" he asked, and she looked back through the darkness behind him and saw the Indians on-shore pushing their canoes into the water.

She clenched her teeth and set the paddle in the water and began moving with his rhthym and the canoe left the shore, putting distance between them, then she looked behind Quinn once more, only to see the Indians floundering in the surf. Quinn had put holes in all the canoes except the one they were in and she sighed, relieved, then began paddling faster as the Indians, furious, their canoes sinking, began swimming after them.

They had been paddling for almost a quarter of an hour now and were about five hundred feet offshore when a strong wind began to blow up, making it hard to paddle.

"We can go toward shore?" she asked, her voice muffled in the wind.

He shook his head as he kept paddling and nodded toward the dark outline of the shore to their left. A light flickered, then went out, then another took its place, and he called to her.

"They're following and they'll continue to follow until they meet my men. And until then we can't touch shore or they'll take us." He paddled all the harder as the wind grew in intensity and the canoe began to bob on the water like a fallen leaf and thunder rumbled in the distance.

Loedicia felt the first drops of rain on her face, then shuddered as the deluge hit. With the rain came a violent wind that almost lifted them from the water, causing Dicia to drop her paddle as she clung to the sides and turned to face Quinn.

"Lay down in the bottom! Under the crossbars!" he shouted, trying to be heard above the storm, and she worked herself onto her knees, then stretched out on the bottom of the canoe as another wave hit, rain beating against them. Quinn stretched out too, trying to keep his Kentucky rifle beneath him in the bottom of the canoe, and lost his paddle too as they both clung to the bottom of the boat and the waves tossed them about, almost tipping them over.

Their heads met in the bottom of the canoe and he leaned his head against hers. "Pray, Dicia," he choked as a wave hit them and water splashed over the top. "Pray like you've never prayed before." His lips brushed her forehead as lightning forked the sky above them.

It was a long night and they were both exhausted as the first streaks of dawn fought to take over the night sky, dispelling the storm that was moving on toward the northeast. The air was cool, but the sun, peeping timidly at the edge of the horizon, promised a warm day.

Quinn reached out stiffly and touched Loedicia's head with his right hand. "Dicia," he whispered, and she stirred in the bottom of the canoe. "Sit up carefully," he said as he pulled his body back, inching it beneath the crossbars set at intervals. The same crossbars that held them in while the storm raged.

Slowly, every move painful, Loedicia too inched backward as he watched, then she moved slowly onto her knees and sat back facing him.

It had been dark last night and things had happened so fast. This morning was the first time he'd seen her face. He stared dumbfounded, shocked, his eyes bewildered. "Oh, my God!" he murmured, and his hand moved out slowly, touching her. His fingers moved gently across her eye to the cuts on her cheeks, then to her lip, where dried blood had already congealed in the swollen cut. "What has he done to you?" he asked helplessly, and tears came to her eyes, cascading down her cheeks and onto his hand, running wet between his fingers.

Her eyes fell before his gaze and she looked away, unable to face him. It was too late. He'd never want her now. He'd come too late and she breathed deeply, trying to hold back the sobs. "I wanted to die," she finally said, her voice quivering. "I wanted him to kill me, but he wouldn't. I fought until I couldn't move anymore, but he made sure I stayed alive, that I was conscious enough to know, then he . . . he . . . I wanted to die!"

He stared at her, anguish flooding him, anger branding his heart, and he moved cautiously across the space between them. He reached out and took her face in his hands, looking deep into her eyes, and he winced. "He'll never touch you again," he said through clenched teeth.

"Not as long as I have a breath in my body." She looked
at him blankly.

"He doesn't have to," she said simply, her voice dead.
"He already has." She pulled her head from his hands
and looked out over the horizon, turning her back to him.

Quinn was helpless. His hands dropped to his sides as
if she'd slapped him in the face and for the first time in
his life he didn't know what to do. He'd failed her when
she needed him most. He turned and looked out over the
water, moving back to the other end of the canoe, and as
he scanned the horizon on all sides his heart sank. All
that surrounded them was water, and not a sign of land.

"What do we do now?" asked Loedicia after a few moments of silence as she too scanned the horizon.

"We drift," he answered, and reached down at his belt
for a small pouch he carried and took out line and hook.
"Have you forgotten what I taught you?"

She shook her head. "No," she answered as he broke a
small piece of leather fringe from his buckskins and fastened it onto the end of the hook he'd taken from the
pouch.

That first day was awkward for both of them as Quinn
tried to overcome the barrier Kendall's attack on her was
putting between them. She avoided him all day, keeping
her back to him so he couldn't see her face, but in the
evening as the stars began to glimmer in the deep indigo
sky and a gentle breeze moved the canoe along, dipping it
gracefully, Quinn moved closer to her.

"Dicia?" he said softly, but she kept her head turned
from him as she looked out into the vast darkness.
"Damn it, woman, don't punish me anymore," he blurted
out huskily. "Do you know what went through me when I
realized I'd fallen into Ramsey's trap . . . when I saw the
fort in ashes? Now, when I see you turning from me . . ."
He took her by the shoulders, forcing her to face him.
"I'm sorry . . . my God, do you think I wanted this to
happen to you? I love you!"

She stared at him and her mouth quivered. "You can
still love me, knowing what he's done to me?"

He cupped her chin in his hand, trying to see her face

in the darkness, and he leaned forward, kissing her bruised, cut mouth softly, not wanting to hurt her any more than she was already hurt.

"Does that answer your question?" he asked softly, and she leaned forward, pressing her head against his shoulder, and cried until there were no tears left. The rest of the evening she lay in his arms, remembering other nights like this, nights on the trail when she'd slept in his arms, and the bruise on her heart slowly began to heal.

# 17

For the next three days and nights they drifted aimlessly, eating raw fish Quinn managed to catch and thankful they were on fresh lake water and not a sea of salt, but the sun in the daytime reflected off the water with a savage intensity, so hot that most of their days were spent lying facedown in the bottom of the canoe to keep from burning to a crisp and their nights were spent under the stars in each other's arms, praying there'd be no more storms.

Luckily, the weather was still warm. September was well under way and although the night air was cool, the lake temperature hadn't began to drop yet and the evenings were balmy.

Early on the fourth morning, shortly after sunrise, Quinn dropped his line over the side and waited for a nibble.

Loedicia watched him as she reached up and touched her face. The swelling had gone down on her eye, turning the deep purple to a faint blue; the small cuts were healing, leaving only bruises under the skin; her lip was back to its normal size, and only a small scab remained at the edge of her mouth. She was starting to look normal again and she smiled as Quinn felt her eyes on him and glanced toward her.

"What shall it be this morning?" he asked flippantly. "Would m'lady like perch or pike?"

"Oh . . . pike this morning," she said as she glanced off toward the horizon, and suddenly her face fell. "Quinn . . . Quinn . . . look." She pointed excitedly and as he followed her finger, scanning the horizon, he saw it too and breakfast was all but forgotten.

They used their hands as paddles, moving the canoe through the water, each of them with one arm over the side.

"Land!" he whispered breathlessly as the canoe rode the surf toward the sand that was waiting to stop its forward plunge, and as the edge of the canoe touched ground he was over the side in seconds, dragging it from the water, then almost collapsing in Dicia's arms, dragging her onto the sand beside him.

He rolled over in the sand, laughing and hugging her to him, the stubble of beard on his chin scratching her as he kissed her ecstatically. "We made it," he sighed as she lay on her back and he gazed into her violet eyes. "We made it."

"To where?" she asked, and he stared at her, then looked about him at the trees, the landscape, and where the sun was in the sky.

"To the western shores of the Erie, I'd say, my love," he answered as he sat up and pulled her up beside him. "I hope you speak French."

She frowned. *"Oui,* but not too well."

"Some is better than none," he answered. He stood up a bit gingerly, testing the muscles in his legs, rubbing them vigorously, then he reached down and took her hands, helping her to her feet.

It was strange to stand and walk again after the days in the canoe. Her leg muscles were sore and weak, not only from idleness but from the bruises Kendall's beating caused.

Quinn retrieved his Kentucky rifle from the floor of the canoe, then pulled the canoe far up onto the beach and hid it in some bushes at the edge of the woods. She hurried to help him and reached out to grab a branch to pull over the top of the canoe when suddenly a hard pain cramped her abdomen and she doubled forward with a moan.

Quinn was beside her and he turned to stare at her as she looked up at him, her eyes wide.

"Oh, my God!" she cried, gasping as she felt the blood gush, and her eyes moved from his face to her legs. Quinn's face went white as he saw the blood seeping down to her feet and the dark stains dropping into the sand.

"What is it?" he asked, and she reached out, her fingers tight on his arm.

"It's the baby," she cried, her voice breaking. "That's what I was going to tell you the night you left." Her fingers dug into the flesh on his arm as another pain swept through her. "I want the baby, Quinn," she whispered. "I can't lose it!"

His face fell, then his jaw set hard, and he picked her up in his arms, carrying her across the beach toward the edge of the woods. He found a spot where the grass was soft and set her gently on the ground.

She clung to him, her face contorted with pain, and he took her hand in his, holding it tightly.

"Dicia," he said as he stared into her eyes, and the look on his face frightened her, for his eyes were hard and cold. "Dicia . . . how long?" She knew what he meant.

"I knew shortly after we left Reading," she answered, and saw the pain in his eyes and felt his fingers tighten on her hand and she felt sick.

"Is that why you married me without putting up a fight," he asked harshly, "to give my bastard a name?" She cringed as his eyes flashed angrily.

She couldn't lose him, not now. She had wanted to tell him about the baby the past few days, but it hadn't seemed the right time after all that had happened and now his reaction frightened her. Her hands moved up as another pain left her breathless and she grabbed the hair on his head, tightening her fingers like a vise.

"I married you for the same reason I waited for you that night in Reading," she answered stubbornly, gritting her teeth. "Because I love you." She pulled his head down until their lips touched. "And don't you call our child a bastard!" She kissed him shamelessly, tears running from her eyes, and he surrendered to her plea, kissing her back long and hard, then he made her as comfortable as he could on the grass at the edge of the sand and set about making a camp.

Using some saplings nearby, he made a leaf shelter above her, then built a small fire a short distance away in the sand, all the while fussing over her like a mother hen. He stripped the bloody leggings from her, took off his buckskin jacket, and removed his frontier shirt from beneath, ripping it into pieces. He washed her gently with one large piece, then wadded the sleeve into a pad and placed it between her legs to catch the blood, his face compassionate at the sight of the bruises, then he wrapped the leggings about her like a blanket.

The bleeding had slowed down, but the pains were still hard and she clenched her teeth, closing her eyes in agony.

He touched her face gently, then kissed her cheek. "Be patient," he said, "I'll be right back." He started to leave, but she grabbed his arm.

"Where are you going?"

"I think I can help. If I can just find what I need . . . I have to do something. Trust me."

Her fingers slowly loosened on his arm and he stood up, took his bearings, then headed into the woods behind her.

He'd been moving over an hour when he saw the smoke; he dropped to the ground, then moved forward slowly on his stomach. The Indian village was spread out by a small stream and life was going on as usual with no thought that an outsider was near. The wind was with him, carrying his scent away from the village, into the woods behind him. Quinn knew by the headdress of the men and the ornaments they wore that it was a small group of Missisaugas, and since they were friendly with the Senecas, he had to be cautious.

One bark hut was only a few feet from him and he hunched up, watching from the tall grass and bushes as an old woman left her small crockery pot upside down on top of a stone to drain, then went in the hut, emerging a few minutes later with an armload of blankets she threw on the ground to air out in the sun.

While he watched, two small children ran up, grabbed her arms, jabbering excitedly, and pulled her away toward the other end of the camp. This was his chance. He moved quickly, dropping to the ground again, slinking along on his stomach like a snake to the back of the hut, then he reached out, pulling one of the blankets toward him. With one swift movement he reached out again, pulled the pot from its rock, then moved stealthily back into the long grass, disappearing as quickly as he'd come.

As soon as he was out of sight of the camp he stood up and headed back toward where he'd left Loedicia, stopping on the way to kill a rabbit, running it down and catching it with his bare hands so he wouldn't have to use his rifle and warn anyone in the vicinity that he was around, then he picked some leaves from a low shrub near the edge of a marsh. He'd been gone longer than he'd intended and worry lines creased his forehead as he plunged once more into the brush.

Loedicia had lain quietly, fighting the pains that bored into her abdomen, praying nothing would happen to Quinn, and twice she held her breath as she heard rustling in the leaves, then relaxed as she heard the scampering movements of ground squirrels and small animals behind her shelter. Once a skunk paraded close by and later on a raccoon came to the edge of the water to wet its food and it stood looking at her curiously, then took off again through the underbrush.

Minutes dragged by into an hour and still he wasn't back. Where had he gone? What was he doing? She had no way of telling time, but it seemed he'd been gone forever. Another hour must have passed and now she was chilly even with the sun moving high into the sky.

She checked the pad between her legs and realized the bleeding had stopped, but the cramps were still bad enough to bring tears to her eyes.

A rustling behind the shelter brought her up short and her hair stood on end. This wasn't a small animal and whoever it was was trying to be quiet, barely making a noise, then she sighed as Quinn stuck his head around the corner and moved over, kneeling quickly beside her.

He took her hand and kissed it as he threw the blanket down, setting the crock on top of it, the leaves he'd picked stuffed inside. "How is it?" he asked anxiously, and she tried to smile.

"Not as bad now that you're here," she answered, and his eyes stared into hers, love seeming to vibrate in the air between them.

He uncovered her legs and took a look at the pad, realizing her bleeding had stopped, then wrapped the blanket about her to keep her warm.

"You'll have to excuse the bugs in the blanket," he said as he took the leaves from the jar. He walked to the edge of the water and filled it, then came back to the fire. "I stumbled onto a small camp of Missisaugas a few miles from here. They can't be too friendly and I didn't have time to let the blanket air out, but I shook it vigorously most of the way and it shouldn't be too bad."

She moved onto her elbows, trying to see what he was doing as he sat down and began breaking the leaves into the crock of water.

"It's a brew Telak's wives have used," he explained. "It should work." He set the crock at the edge of the fire to heat, then began building a spit to cook the rabbit on.

"If I have my calculations right we should be about fifty miles or so from Fort Detroit," he said as he worked on the spit. "And there's not a friendly Indian for miles." He saw her frown. "Don't worry, Dicia, my love," he said soothingly. "It takes more than a few hundred miles of enemy to stop me." He winked at her intimately. "Right now my main concern is you."

He took a stick and stirred the brew as steam began to ease off the top, then he finished the spit and started skinning the rabbit and set it on to cook. This done, he moved off toward the canoe and she saw him doing something in the bushes. When he returned he was working on a wild gourd with his knife, hollowing the pulp from it to make a cup.

When the brew was through steeping, he dipped the gourd in and scooped some out, then blew on it until it cooled.

The taste was bitter as it trickled down her throat, but she managed to gag down a whole gourdful.

While the rabbit cooked, Quinn left again for a few minutes and came back with a handful of small apples, which helped get the bitter taste from her mouth.

Within an hour after drinking the third gourdful of the foul-tasting brew, Loedicia began to relax and the pains became less and less frequent and toward evening they stopped completely. She lay quietly, watching Quinn gather enough wood to last the night and then banking the fire to keep any wild animals away. He walked over and stood looking down at her.

"Feeling better?" he asked, and she smiled.

"I think I'm drunk."

He stepped over her, toward the back of the shelter and lay down, stretching out behind her, and he lifted her head up and rested it on his shoulder, his arms about her.

"You told me once you liked getting drunk," he said against her ear, and she cuddled closer to him, content to be in his arms.

For days they stayed close to the lakeshore in the camp he'd set up. Quinn used the skills he knew and made himself a bow and some arrows and they lived off the land, content to be together and alive. Loedicia had no more pains or bleeding and the danger of losing the baby seemed to be over, but Quinn still made her rest and stay off her feet as much as possible.

One morning Loedicia stirred in Quinn's arms and opened her eyes to find him staring at her intently, a puzzled look on his face.

"Do you think you could do it again?" he finally asked as she stared up at him.

"Do what?"

He reached up and put his hand in her hair, running his fingers through it. Although she had cut it short when she'd run away, it was now below her shoulders. "If I cut it short and find some black walnuts do you think you can pass as a boy again?"

She stared at him dumbfounded. "Why?"

"I'm not going up through the great falls. Too many people know me. Our best way out of here is south through Fort Detroit and around the Sandusky past Fort Junandat, then up the shore trail to the Ashtabula. That means about three hundred miles or more through hostile territory. Territory where a woman as beautiful as you, my love, would not be safe. The only way I can get you through is if the people we meet think you're a boy."

By late afternoon the transformation was completed, including some alterations in her shirt and leggings so they looked like a boy's buckskins instead of a woman's and she was wearing rabbit-fur moccasins Quinn had made for her. He laughed as he looked down at her, remembering the first time they'd met, and he reached out and pulled her into his arms.

"I'm going to have a terrible time remembering you're a boy," he said as he looked into her violet eyes.

She stood on tiptoe and pulled his head down, kissing him hard on the mouth. Although she'd slept in his arms every night, so far he hadn't made love to her. Now he kissed her passionately, his body responding to her as it always did.

"If you keep doing that I'll never remember you're supposed to be a boy," he answered huskily, then put his hand under her chin. "I want you to talk only Hindi and French," he explained. "And if I treat you harshly or sound angry I won't mean it, but you'll be my servant, a lad I picked up on the docks of New York, and these people out here are used to a man ordering his servants about. And for God's sake, when we get around people don't look at me like you always do or you'll give the whole thing away."

She smiled impishly. "And how do I look at you?"

"Vixen," he whispered, and he kissed her again, then they set about breaking camp.

The canoe was left behind, but he rolled the crock up in the blanket and tied it with a strip of rope he'd made from a vine he'd found close by, then he tossed it to Loedicia.

"I hate to have you carry this," he said, "but in case we meet anyone I want everything to look authentic." She caught it, then looked at him with approval.

"I don't mind at all, master," she said in French, then she smiled, blurting out a round of Hindi at him, and he knew she understood.

The first day they put almost fifteen miles of rugged country behind them, moving through the forest at a steady pace, Quinn in the lead. The trees dwarfed them and the undergrowth fought them as it became thick and they had to tear their way through. There was no Indian trace to follow yet as there had been when they'd crossed the Alleghenies and they had to make their own way in a land that was new even to Quinn. He'd never been here before, although he'd heard men speak of Fort Detroit and it was the last place he really wanted to go, but it was better than going to Niagara, where everyone had heard of him and most of them knew him on sight. At least out here there'd be more of a chance that no one would recognize him.

He'd dry-shaved with his knife after landing onshore and had kept his beard off and Loedicia had trimmed his hair as best she could, but the buckskins they wore were dirty and worn.

They stopped for the night at a rock overhang, built a small fire, and cooked two squirrels Quinn had shot with his bow and arrow. The sound of a rifle would have brought every curious Indian within its sound running and he wanted no part of them if he could help it. The squirrel meat was tough but better than nothing and when Loedicia was finished, she wiped her fingers on her buckskins, then spread the blanket close to the rock formation below the overhang.

She lay back and stretched out, watching him bank the

fire for the night, then he stooped down to slip under the overhang. His eyes caught hers and he stopped, looking deeply into their violet depths. "I told you not to look at me like that," he said, and she sighed.

"I love you," she whispered, and he could stand it no longer.

He stretched out beside her and reached out his hand, moving it up inside her buckskin shirt, feeling her softness as he caressed her. He leaned over her face, afraid for a moment after Kendall's attack that she might repel him, but instead she moved beneath his hands sensuously as she'd always done, her nipples taut and firm, and he sighed, his body throbbing.

"I'll be gentle, Dicia," he whispered against her mouth. "But I can't wait any longer. I love you beyond all reason." His mouth covered hers passionately as she surrendered to him, the night closing still and dark about them.

Fort Detroit was set on the west bank of the St. Clair River. It was a crossroads and meeting place for every Indian tribe in the vicinity as well as for every trapper and adventurer who trekked westward.

Quinn and Loedicia arrived, tired and hungry, late one afternoon in late September. The weather had turned rainy and Loedicia was a shade or two lighter than the original color she'd been when they'd started their trek, but Quinn said it only made her look more like a real Hindu.

There were no white women at Fort Detroit, but Indian squaws were everywhere as Quinn, with Dicia at his heels, moved past the gates of the fort and into the stream of life that centered there. A few people looked at them curiously, then went on about their business, but in general no one paid much attention to them.

Quinn had managed to collect some beaver, squirrel, and rabbit pelts on the trip overland and his first stop was at the trading post, where he turned them into supplies and gold for the rest of their trip.

"Going far?" asked the wizened old man at the trading post.

Quinn answered in French, not wanting his right destination known. "Heading for Kaskaskia. Got a friend out that way. Told me the land's good thereabouts. Ever been there?"

The man shook his graying head. "Nope. But I think that friend of yours was havin' daydreams. But if you need directions there's a man over there." He pointed across the room. "Come up from that way two, three days ago."

Quinn glanced quickly across the room and he stood motionless as he stared at the man. He was a British soldier, a major, and as Quinn stared at him he felt an urgent tug on his arm and looked down into Loedicia's face, which had turned white under the stain.

"What is it?" he asked in French as he bent close to her.

"That soldier," she gasped. "I know him."

His eyes widened. "You . . . ?"

"He was in Boston when I was there. His name is Captain Roth Chapman. He used to come and see me when I lived with Uncle Thaddeus."

"It can't be. Besides, that man's a major, not a captain."

"But it is him. I remember he left Boston shortly after the governor's party where I met Kendall. He stopped by the house to say good-bye . . . said he had a special mission."

"To check on the frontier forts, no doubt," acknowledged Quinn disgustedly. "How could we be so lucky?"

"He must have been promoted. I wonder if he heard about us," she whispered softly so only he could hear, then glanced at the trader, who was looking at her rather strangely.

Major Roth Chapman finished his mug of ale and set it down, then his eyes roved about the room, looking over the people. They were quite an assortment. Suddenly they stopped on a man he hadn't seen before and he frowned, looking into the man's blue eyes. He was a blond giant and his eyes were the most startling blue eyes he'd ever seen in a man. As he stared, mulling the description over in his mind, something clicked, then quickly he glanced down at the brown-faced boy with the violet eyes who was standing beside the giant and the whole thing fell into place. He looked stupefied. It had to be. There could be no mistake, but what were they doing here? They were supposed to be dead.

He watched them leave, then paid for his drink and followed them out, walking some distance behind them.

"He knows us," she argued as Quinn headed for the gate.

"How could he? You look like anything but a lady."

"Did you see him look at us?"

"It's not common to see a black boy this far west."

"All right!" she said angrily. "Don't believe me, then, but"—she glanced behind them—"he's following us right now!"

Quinn grabbed her arm and stopped her as Major Chapman walked up and the three of them stared at one another for a minute in silence.

Then, finally, "It is Loedicia, isn't it?" asked the major, and Dicia looked up at Quinn as if to say, I told you so.

Quinn's jaw set hard and his hand moved slowly to the knife in its sheath at his belt.

"Shall we talk?" the major asked, and Dicia took Quinn's arm, squeezing it lightly.

"Quinn?"

"Where?" Quinn asked, his voice cold and unfriendly.

The major looked about, then walked out of the gate with Quinn and Loedicia sauntering after him some twenty or thirty feet behind. He moved to the side of the trail and stood next to a tree, watching them approach, his face expressionless.

"Well?" asked Quinn as he and Dicia stopped a few feet from him.

The major held out his hand in a friendly gesture and Quinn took it hesitantly. He felt the man's hand clasp his hard and firm and he was puzzled.

"I always did want to meet you, Captain Locke," he said as both Quinn and Loedicia stared dumbfounded. "But what the hell are you doing here?"

Quinn released the major's hand. "I don't understand," he said, gesturing, bewildered. "Maybe you'd better explain."

"You mean why I haven't called out the guard?"

"Why haven't you?"

The major looked at Loedicia and touched one of her dark curls for a moment, then took his hand away frowning. "I remember the night of the governor's party," he answered. "I remember a beautiful young woman who shivered with fright when Kendall Varrick looked at her. . . . I remember the look in her eyes when he forced his attentions on her and I remember the terrified look on her face when I dropped by her uncle's house just before leaving Boston and she told me she was to be married. . . ." He hesitated as if thinking it over. "Before I call the guard, as you so delicately put it, I want to know what really happened." He eyed them both curiously.

Quinn looked at Dicia, who looked back at the major.

"I ran away," she said simply.

The major studied her a minute, then looked at Quinn. "You know the governor's put a price on your head?"

"My cousin's had a price on my head for years."

"They say you kidnapped her."

Quinn looked down into Dicia's eyes as she looked up at him and the major saw something pass between them so intimate he felt at a loss to describe it.

Quinn glanced back at the major, his face stern. "Loedicia's my wife, Major," he explained. "We got lost on the lake and ended up on the French side. It stands to reason I can't go back by way of Niagara."

"So you're going around the lake?"

"We're going to try."

"How long have you been gone from Fort Locke?" asked the major, and Quinn studied him, puzzled. He thought back, trying to count the weeks and days.

"About a month, maybe a bit less. Why?"

"Then you don't know."

"Know what?"

"There is no more Fort Locke and your Tuscaroras have scattered, Captain. They've moved farther into the valley, closer to the Cuyahoga River. A runner came into Kaskaskia just before I left, said Lord Varrick had burned Fort Locke to the ground. Word was that you and Loedicia were dead, drowned in a storm on the lake, but there was no mention of your being married."

Quinn's face was hard. "Major," he said, his voice harsh, "Lord Varrick is my cousin. The money I took from him should rightfully have been mine. He sold land in the Indies that had once belonged to my father. I was entitled to it. As for Dicia—"

The major put his hand on Quinn's arm. "Don't," he said. "It's not necessary. I won't turn you in. If you're what Loedicia wants, then I won't stand in her way." He looked at her tenderly. Her face was still darkened by the walnut stain, her eyes shining. "You see, I was falling in love with her myself."

Loedicia's eyes fell under his gaze.

"I'm sorry, Loedicia. I didn't mean to embarrass you," he said. He looked back at Quinn. "May I say, Captain Locke, that you have yourself one hell of a woman there."

Quinn eyed him curiously; he was wary.

"Now," asked the major. "Where will you go?"

"I have to see Fort Locke for myself," said Quinn, and the major nodded.

"I thought as much," he said. "But it's dangerous country to travel in alone."

"Not for us."

"I insist you go with me," he added. "He calls you Dicia, right?" he asked her, and Loedicia nodded. "I'm going to hire a guide and his black boy to take me back to Boston," he continued, leaving them no room to argue. "Of course if they suddenly disappear on the way . . ." He saw the look of protest on Quinn's face. "I won't take no for an answer. It'll give you some protection. I've got twenty men with me, all from Kaskaskia. They'll never suspect a thing."

"You'd do that for us?" asked Quinn, and the major sighed.

"I'll do it for a beautiful young woman I once knew in Boston," he answered, but Quinn was skeptical.

"We're both going the same way," the major reasoned. "It'd be silly for the two of you to try to go alone." They sat down under the tree at the side of the trail and argued about the situation until Quinn was finally convinced. Then they made their plans.

Two days later, twenty redcoats and their commanding officer, handsome Major Roth Chapman, marched out of Fort Detroit with a rugged frontiersman in the lead and a young, slightly built black boy in buckskins walking at his heels.

# 18

Quinn was apprehensive. "Are you sure we can trust him?" he asked her their first night out as they sat a bit away from the campfire. "What if he suddenly decides to collect that reward? After all, you heard him. He's in love with you."

"That's why I know he won't," she answered. "He knows I'd never forgive him if he betrayed us and he's not like that. Besides, we can leave whenever we want and he knows it."

He reached out and took her hand so no one would see. "My God, I love you, Dicia," he whispered softly. "Having to keep my hands off you is like dying inside."

"We can sneak away," she answered impishly, rolling her eyes, and he frowned.

"Will you stop that, you little vixen," he whispered through clenched teeth as one of the men looked at them rather curiously, and he turned his back as she giggled under her breath.

As the days moved on, so did they, but their pace was slow with a bunch of clumsy soldiers who were anything but woodsmen, even though they had spent a few years on the frontier. Loedicia stayed as close to Quinn as possible, but there were times when he was off by himself, scouting. When this happened Major Chapman kept her close to him so she wouldn't have too much contact with his men, a situation Quinn began to resent.

"He spends too much time with you," Quinn observed irritably one afternoon as he and Loedicia walked together, leading the column of men through a narrow strip of land across a swamp as they neared the Maumee River.

"He's a friend, nothing more," she argued. "I love you, not him."

"But I can't even sleep with you," he answered angrily. "I can't touch you or . . . damn it, Dicia, when I'm off scouting, anything could be happening back here."

Her eyes flashed. "You're not very trusting, are you?" she asked as she glanced back to make sure the soldier following her was far enough away not to hear him.

"I trust you, but not him."

"Quinn, we said we'd do it," she pleaded. "Please . . . you have no reason to be jealous."

But it did no good. Whenever they stopped he watched her like a hawk and when he'd return from a scouting trip his eyes told her more than words could, yet the major seemed to be keeping his part of the bargain. At any time she and Quinn could have walked off and no one would have tried to stop them.

They crossed the Maumee River into Miami territory and Quinn's eyes kept a sharp lookout on the trail ahead. The Miamis were a suspicious lot, hating the white man's encroachment on their land. Back in '64 they'd moved farther west, at least most of them, but a few hotheads like Little Turtle made journeys into the old territory every now and then just to let everyone know they were still around. Their old territory mingled now with that of the Wyandots and the two tribes were anything but friends.

That evening, as they made camp, Quinn could stand it no longer. He had to talk to the major. Roth was standing some distance from the fire, looking off toward the sun as it dipped like golden fire below the horizon, when Quinn walked up.

"Let's talk," said Quinn unceremoniously, and Roth whirled around.

"Oh, yes," he said, startled at first, then motioned with his hand. "Shall we walk?" he asked, and Quinn nodded. "What is it?" asked Roth as they strolled away from the camp toward a small hill.

Quinn cleared his throat, not knowing how to begin. "I want to ask you to spend less time with Dicia," he finally demanded as he bent down and pulled on a blade of grass, then bit off the end, chewing it nonchalantly.

Roth stopped, looking at him, then nodded as he said, "You're jealous?"

"She's my wife!"

"And she's expecting a baby," added Roth. "And if any of my men discover it we'll all three be in trouble."

Quinn frowned. "She told you?"

"She didn't have to. I'm not blind and neither are my men. Right now they probably figure he's just getting a bit fat, but we aren't going to be able to conceal it forever. Then what do we do?"

Quinn had no answer.

"She doesn't know I know," offered Roth, then turned on Quinn sharply, his eyes distressed. "Look," he said softly, "I won't pretend with you. I fell in love with her back in Boston. . . ." He saw the look on Quinn's face. "That's right," he confirmed. "I'm in love with your wife, but that's as far as it goes. She has eyes only for you . . . well, fine. That's how it should be."

He hit the dirt from the sole of his boot, knocking his foot against a tree. "At the time we made plans, Quinn, I didn't know she was expecting. I just wanted to help so she wouldn't end up with her scalp as some warrior's prize, but now . . . how far along is she?"

Quinn bit his lip and frowned as he thought back to Reading. The end of June. "About four months," he said, and saw the startled look on the major's face.

"And we're making less than ten miles a day through this godforsaken land," he answered irritably. "She'll be

six or seven months by the time we even get close to civilization at the rate we're traveling."

"So what do you want me to do?" asked Quinn. He
didn't like having to arbitrate. He was always used to giving orders, no questions asked, and he was never used to
taking orders.

"First of all, I want you to do one thing, please," ordered Roth. "Trust me. When I said I love your wife I
meant it, but I'm also a man of honor. She's in love with
you and I won't interfere even though it's killing me and
when I said I'd help the two of you, I meant that too, but
the situation is getting rather touchy." He saw the indeci-
sion on Quinn's face and he sighed. "You know, by all
rights I should hate you, Quinn, but I can't. Maybe I see
the same thing in you that Loedicia sees, I don't know."
He took a deep breath, then sighed again. "But you're going to have to trust me if we intend to get through this."

Quinn didn't know what to say. What did you do with a
man who tells you he's in love with your wife, then in the
next breath asks you to trust him? He scratched his head.

"All right," he finally said, then glanced back toward
the camp, where Dicia was busy gathering firewood.
"Look," he added, "we should be reaching Fort Junandat
in another three or four weeks. She shouldn't be showing
too much before then. We'll cut out there and head for
Fort Locke."

"But you can't go the rest of the way alone. It's almost
two hundred miles and there's not another fort between
Junandat and Fort Locke."

"I have friends," Quinn assured him. "We can make it."

"But what about Loedicia?"

Quinn's eyes narrowed. "You think I'm not thinking of
her?"

"I didn't say that. But what if she's not strong enough?
That's a rough trail for a pregnant woman." His face
reddened. "Have you ever delivered a baby, Quinn?"
Quinn stared at him, his eyes uncertain, then suddenly his
jaw hardened and his eyes grew dark.

"I can take care of Loedicia!" he said stubbornly.

"And kill her in the process?"

Quinn's face went white, but his eyes conceded. The major was right. He couldn't let his stubborn pride hurt the only thing he'd ever loved. "All right. What alternative do you have in mind?" he asked acidly.

"That's better," sighed Roth, knowing how hard it was for Quinn to capitulate. "As you said, another month and we reach Fort Junandat. I suggest that you two stay with us and instead of taking the shore trail, we take the Great Trail between the Huron and Mohican rivers and head straight for Fort Pitt. The trail is easier and we can make better time. We can go on to Philadelphia from there and it should cut at least a month or more off our time. When we reach Philadelphia, Loedicia can get proper care until the baby's born."

Quinn knew he was right but wished he weren't. "And what happens when we reach Fort Pitt?" he asked. "They'll know who I am. There are bound to be men there who've seen me. We'd never make it to Philadelphia."

Roth Chapman scowled as he thought this over. "You don't have to enter the fort. We can tell everyone you prefer the wild."

"And your men?"

"My men?"

"You don't think they'll know she's a woman by then?"

"We'll have to keep her buckskins loose, maybe she won't show too much." He reached out and took Quinn's arm in a friendly gesture. "It's the only way, Quinn. You can't take the chance. You can go back to Fort Locke later. Right now your main concern is Loedicia."

"Don't you think I don't know that?" he added. "She almost lost the baby once already."

"Then you'll go along with it?"

He watched her back at camp as she moved about helping get things ready for the evening meal, which would consist of a young doe Quinn had shot earlier in the day. "Do I have a choice?" he asked, and Roth smiled.

"We can be friends."

Quinn hesitated, then held out his hand. Roth shook it as Quinn said stubbornly, "Shall we say friendly enemies?" and Roth laughed.

"You're a hard man, Quinn Locke," he answered. "But I like you." They turned and walked back to camp.

The temperature had dropped and the leaves turned color and began falling, setting the countryside ablaze as they made their way around Sandusky Bay, only about a week away from Fort Junandat. They were bundled in the winter clothing they'd bought before leaving Fort Detroit, but at least they were warm, if not fashionable, and sometimes winter came early to the lakes.

Thanks to Quinn's scouting, they'd managed to slip by three Indian settlements on the way and so far there'd been no trouble, but two days earlier, about nightfall, Quinn had noticed a Wyandot brave watching them from the bushes, and although nothing had come of it, everyone stayed alert.

They moved across the Sandusky River shortly before dark and made camp on the opposite bank just as a slight rain, mixed with snow, began to fall.

Quinn put the soldiers to work cutting saplings and making shelters. The men grumbled, disgruntled, but they followed his instructions and by the time it got dark there was shelter for all of them ringing the huge fire in the center of camp. Each shelter faced the fire and as they settled down for the night Quinn stood for a minute watching everyone settling back into the leafy bowers that were beginning to be covered with the first light snow of the season. He bit his lip. He watched Loedicia move back into the shadows of the shelter they were to share and he wondered.

He hadn't been alone with her for so long. It began to snow harder and he made up his mind. Taking the bedroll from just inside the shelter, he opened it and shook out his blanket, then let it hang as a flap on the shelter, holding it in place with a branch so that no one could see inside, then he lifted the flap and slipped in beside her.

"Dicia?"

She reached out and took his hand as he stretched out. "You did that on purpose, didn't you?"

He sighed. "Good God, woman, a man can take just so much!"

"But it's cold and snowy."

"Shall we warm things up a bit?"

She giggled lightly. "I love you," she started to whisper, but her voice was lost as his mouth found hers in the darkness and he kissed her deeply, sensuously, then began loosening the fur wrap she wore.

"Dicia . . . Dicia, you drive me insane," he moaned against her mouth. "I worry about you, yell at you when I don't want to because I'm frustrated . . . because I want you so badly . . . to touch you, kiss you, caress you."

She opened her buckskin shirt, pulling back the laces, and he buried his face in her breasts, holding her against him, and time stood still for them as he made love to her into the wee hours of the morning.

Afterward, as he helped fasten the front of her shirt and pull on her leggings in the confined quarters and she laughed at his clumsiness, he touched her face, kissing her mouth softly.

"Are you cold?"

She laughed lightly. "I could lie in a freezing snowbank and it would melt when you're making love to me," she whispered.

His hand moved across her abdomen, feeling the softness of her skin, then it stopped, caressing the bulge that was becoming more apparent as the days went by.

"Are you sorry?" he asked softly, his eyes troubled, and she smiled in the darkness as her hand covered his.

"Never," she answered. "He'll be our son, Quinn, yours and mine. A child of love."

"And if it's a girl?"

"Then we'll have a boy the next time."

He shook his head. "Dicia . . . Dicia . . . what am I going to do with you?" he admonished her seriously. "I have no home to take you to, no security, a price on my head, and you talk about raising a family."

Her arms went about his neck and she breathed deeply, contentedly, and kissed him full on the mouth. "You sound too serious," she said lightly, then ran her hand through his hair, down the side of his face, feeling the tenseness in his jaw. "At the moment, my love, all I care about is that you're with me and I love you. The rest will take care of itself."

"I always said you were a vixen." He sighed and kissed her back passionately, not caring that the snow outside had stopped and the temperature had begun to drop again, covering the ground with a frosty blanket of icy crystals.

The next morning the sun broke the horizon, shining on the wet, bedraggled leaves overhead, and as the ice on them started to melt, everyone began to emerge from his makeshift shelter.

Quinn built up the fire, then headed down to the river to wash up and get some water for breakfast and Roth cornered Loedicia a few minutes later as she crept from the shelter, her face flushed and glowing. The men glanced furtively at her, frowning.

"You fools," Roth blurted out as he knelt down and helped her from the shelter. "What did you think you were doing last night?" Loedicia's face reddened as she remembered the lovemaking.

"We are human, Roth," she whispered, embarrassed. "Besides, no one knows."

"Oh, don't they?" He gestured toward his men. "Look around you. . . . The noise you two made was just enough to get the men to wondering. Young boys don't giggle or moan ecstatically, whispering until all hours of the morning." He paused and exhaled disgustedly. "We'd better go see Quinn. I think we're going to have to do some pretty tall explaining unless you want my men to think Quinn has peculiar taste in bed partners."

Her eyes fell, then she looked up at him sheepishly. "I'm sorry," she apologized. "We didn't think. . . ."

He gazed down into her violet eyes, at the saucy tilt of her nose and the sensuous curve of her lips. "I guess I can't really blame him," he confessed as he took her arm, and they headed toward the river to find Quinn. "If you were my wife I'd do the same damn thing." She blushed as she looked away from him. "But I'm afraid the situation's becoming hopeless."

The river was about two hundred feet from camp with a low bank that overlooked the sandy, rocky edge where water cascaded into a deep pool surrounded by huge boulders. Willow bushes lined the river, and the water, after the night's rain and snow, had overflowed its usual course, making new paths across the sandy bottom. In order to reach the river they had to go to the right, out of sight of camp, and squeeze through a growth of underbrush that clustered on the bank of the river before coming into the open where Quinn was, and as they ducked their heads, pushing branches aside, moving through the bushes, they stopped suddenly, standing motionless as a scream shattered the quiet morning and Roth clapped his hand on her shoulder, holding her back, keeping her from stepping into the open.

Quinn dropped the jug of water and whirled around as the Wyandots hit the camp, scattering the men in every direction. He reached down and pulled his knife, ready to climb the bank and spring into the fray, but it was too late.

Loedicia watched, horrified, as an arrow thudded into Quinn's side and a ball of shot embedded itself in his chest, spattering blood all over the front of his buckskins and fur robe. The knife slid from his hand and the impact threw him off balance, twisting him sideways, and he fell into the willows in the water, his fur robe catching on the branches, holding him, his head face down, water covering it.

She started to scream, but Roth pressed his hand over her mouth and pulled her back against him, her head against his chest, his other arm about her, holding her tightly against him so she wouldn't run to Quinn.

Screams and gunfire echoed from the camp, but Roth moved quickly. He set off in the opposite direction, carrying Loedicia with him, his hand still over her mouth. He moved into the bushes, keeping under the overhang of the bank, wading into the river, which was shallow as he went upstream.

Loedicia kicked and fought as he dragged her away, but he had no choice. The Indians hadn't seen them yet and if luck held, they wouldn't. He moved swiftly, sloshing qui-

etly through the water, hoping it wouldn't get too deep,
then after a while he moved up into a small crevice between two boulders where it was dry and stopped.

He held Loedicia close, turning her to face him, his
hands holding her head to keep her from looking up, covering her ears to block out the sounds of battle from back
at camp, as he pressed her head against his chest.

She held her head tightly against him, her teeth
clenched, trying to erase Quinn's death from her mind, but
it was no use. He was dead! She'd seen him fall, the blood
on his chest, the arrow in his side, his face contorted in
pain as he fell into the water, and she shivered as she
started sobbing.

"He's dead!" she sobbed against him. "He's dead . . .
Oh, God, he's dead." All Roth could do was soothe her
and whisper, "Shh quiet . . . They'll hear us . . . shh."

She took a deep breath and held back the sobs, but the
tears still came, wetting his shirt. He felt their warmth as
he held her and he felt sick. He'd have given almost anything before if she'd wanted him to hold her like this, but
damn it . . . he wouldn't have given Quinn!

Back at camp, the men were putting up a fruitless
battle. They were outnumbered ten to one as the Wyandots hacked their way from man to man, ripping, gouging,
scalping. The soldiers hardly had a chance to get to their
muskets.

In the willows at the edge of the river Quinn felt the
water cover his face and held his breath. His side hurt and
burned like hell, making him sick, and his chest was on
fire. He tried to get loose, but his fur robe was caught in
the willows. His mind was foggy, but he knew he had to
get to Dicia. She was up there somewhere with the yelling
and screaming, with the blood and Indians.

He raised his head, trying to focus his eyes, and his hair
prickled as he saw one of them headed his way, his scalp
lock glistening in the morning sun, the paint on his face
streaked, making it a grotesque mask. He had to get loose.
He had to get to Dicia! He pulled his arms frantically, slipping them from the fur robe, fumbling with the ties in

front, finally ripping them when they wouldn't give. But the effort was too much and the current too swift.

As his arms slipped free from the robe, he felt the current catch him and pull, but he was too weak to fight it and as he rolled over, his body pulled into midstream, he looked up and the last thing he saw before losing consciousness was the Indian, tomahawk in hand, pulling the fur robe from the willows, shaking the water from it as he watched Quinn float downriver, his body bobbing haphazardly, and the Indian grinned, wiping his bloody hands down the front of his buckskins as agonized screams pierced the chill morning air from behind him.

The sun was dipping down on the horizon, almost ready to give up for the day, when the last noise from camp was stilled and Roth finally moved from the crevice, gently helping Loedicia, holding her in his arms, moving back from the water until he found a place for her to sit.

"Stay here," he said softly, "while I look around."

She reached up and took his hand as her legs buckled beneath her. "He's dead, Roth, Quinn's dead," she muttered, her eyes swollen from crying, and he patted her hand, telling her to be as quiet as possible.

She covered her mouth and sat rocking back and forth in agony, seeing again Quinn's body lodged in the willow branches, floating face down in the water.

Roth crept cautiously a short way downstream and stood listening, but all he heard was the sound of the birds and the squirrels rustling among the wet leaves. He pulled his coat tighter about him and turned, making his way back to her.

When he reached her she was sitting quietly, staring at the river, tears streaming down her face, a faraway look in her eyes. He knelt down beside her. "Dicia . . . Dicia?"

She turned her head and looked up at him and he wanted to die too. The agony in her eyes made him wince.

"Come on," he said softly. "We'll go back to camp." She shook her head.

"It won't do any good," she answered as she licked the salty tears from her lips. "They're dead. I know . . . they're all dead."

"We have to go back. We have to be sure."

He reached down and helped her to her feet and they made their way back along the river, following the overhanging bank, sloshing back through the water. When they were within about fifty feet of the spot where they'd been when the attack started, Loedicia froze.

"I can't, Roth," she pleaded. "I can't."

He sat her down on the ground, leaning her back against the bank, then he slowly worked his way to the bushes where they'd been hidden, first making sure the Indians were all gone. He didn't want to go either, but he had to. He took a deep breath and listened. Everything was quiet, even the birds, and the ominous smell of death hung in the air.

Slowly he crept up to the camp and for a moment he didn't dare look and kept his head turned away, then hesitantly, his heart pounding, he looked around. The sight turned his stomach and his face went white. He'd seen men die before, but not like this. There wasn't even anything to identify. Their hands! Their faces!

He stepped forward, walking toward what was once a camp of laughing, talking men, into a bloody tangle of arms, legs, and bodies. Tears rolled down his face. He stood for a minute, his feet almost touching what was left of one of his men, but he couldn't tell which one. Bending down, he took a small locket from a severed hand and a lump filled his throat. He took two more steps and picked up a letter, the address smeared with blood. Then his eye caught something and he moved closer toward the fire.

Quinn's fur robe was stretched out over the torso of a man and he leaned over gingerly, picking up one end, then he let it drop again as his stomach began to churn, and he crumpled the letter in his hand, shoving it in his pocket with the locket.

Damn them! he said miserably to himself. Damn them all!

He stood for a minute, wanting to run. Wishing he had something to wash away the odor of death, which clung to his nostrils and seeped into his lungs. But he was a soldier and instead he squared his shoulders, holding his hand over his mouth as he tried to think rationally.

Only he and Loedicia were left. There was nothing he could do for these poor devils, not even a decent burial, but maybe the two of them could stay alive. He began to hunt as best he could among them, but there were no weapons, no supplies. The only thing the Indians hadn't taken were a few tin cups and the wet blanket that hung over the shelter Quinn and Dicia had shared the night before.

He grabbed the blanket quickly and picked up two of the cups, then, unable to stand it any longer, he stepped over the remains of his men and headed toward the river's edge, where he knew she was still waiting, stopping only long enough to see the empty willows where Quinn had fallen, then he moved quickly, not even looking back, hoping someday he'd be able to forget the slaughter he'd just seen.

Dropping the blanket and cups on the ground, he sat down beside her, his face ashen. She turned to look at him.

"I was right, wasn't I?" she asked, her voice breaking.

He nodded.

"And Quinn?" she asked, then saw the look on his face. "You saw Quinn?" She reached out and grabbed his coat, clutching it until her knuckles were white. "Where is he? I want to see him! I've got to see him!" She began to cry hysterically, but he grabbed her wrists, holding them tightly as he stared into her violet eyes. Those beautiful eyes that had looked at Quinn so lovingly.

"You can't!" he demanded harshly.

"But I have to . . . just one more time."

"Dicia . . ." He shook her gently. "You don't realize!" He hated what he had to do. "There's nothing left to see!"

She drew in a quick breath, her eyes wide, and she bit her lip as she understood what he meant. "Oh, my God! Then how do you know?" she asked breathlessly. "How do you know it's him?"

"Most of the bodies were stripped," he explained sadly, "and so was his, but the fur robe he'd been wearing was there, flung on the ground partially covering him, and the willow bushes by the river where we saw him fall were empty."

He let go of her wrists and her hands flew up, covering her face, but this time she didn't cry. She sat for a few minutes covering her eyes, then suddenly her hands dropped and she sat back on her heels as if exhausted.

"It does no good," she whispered softly. "I've been crying all day. I could cry for the rest of my life and it won't bring him back."

Roth didn't know what to say or do, he could only sit and watch her.

She reached out and touched the blanket he'd brought, remembering her last night with Quinn. "He asked me if I was sorry," she went on, her voice hushed. Slow tears began to run down her cheeks, tears she couldn't control. "I wish I could die!" she finally wailed hysterically. "I wish I could die!" Roth reached out, pulling her to him, his arms about her, trying to comfort her.

He was worried. They'd moved back upriver, heading for the other end of Sandusky Bay so they could reach the lake once more, but she only seemed to stumble on, barely aware of her surroundings, unconscious of the snow that had started to fall again and the fact that they had no food. She was like a walking dead woman, thinking and feeling nothing, and he had to lead her like a child.

She had slept all night in his arms, unfeeling, uncaring. When Quinn died it was as if something inside her had died too. He had to snap her out of it somehow.

They'd had no food for two days and were both getting weak. He stopped and sat her down, leaning her against the trunk of a silver maple, and she lay back, shutting her eyes. He stared at her, trying to think of some way. She seemed to be in some sort of shock. She talked to him, but it was as if he weren't there, as if she were talking to the air.

He sat down beside her, contemplating what to do, then he reached over and took her hands. "Dicia?" he whispered, and she turned to look at him, her eyes a dead stare. "You've got to pull out of it." He rubbed her cold fingers with his equally cold hand. "It's not accomplishing anything and you're only making matters worse."

"He's dead," she repeated again as she had for the past two days, her voice barely above a whisper. "I loved him and he's dead."

He squeezed her hand. "That's right. He's dead and so are the other men back there and we can mourn forever, but it won't change things."

She closed her eyes and leaned back against the tree again. "But you don't know," she moaned. "You just don't know."

"Then tell me about it, Loedicia," he demanded, and she opened her eyes, startled, and looked at him. "That's right," he insisted urgently, "I want to hear all about you and Quinn from the moment you met. Tell me!"

She closed her eyes again, then hesitantly at first, as evening shadows filtered in among the naked branches above them, she poured her heart out, telling him everything that had happened since she'd left Boston, leaving nothing out. Suddenly she opened her eyes as she finished her narration and stared at him, but they weren't the eyes of a dead woman anymore, they were alive and glowing.

Neither of them said a word as a sliver of moon began to clear the horizon, silhouetting the stark, black maze of branches overhead.

"It's going to be cold tonight," Roth finally said, breaking the silence, and he reached out, pulling her to him, cradling her in his arms.

"I'm all right now, and thank you, Roth," she said, and he felt her warm breath on his neck as she sighed. "I'm sorry."

"Sorry?"

"For not wanting to accept it. It seems like so much has happened and Quinn's death coming like it did . . . I have to fight it, Roth. I can't let it kill me and the baby." Tears rolled down her cheeks again, but this time they were tears of acceptance. "I have to have Quinn's son," she said. "I can't have him, but I'll have his son and he'll grow into a man his father would have been proud of." She hesitated a minute and there was a catch in her throat.

"Oh, God, Roth. Why couldn't Quinn have lived? Why?"

"I guess none of us will ever know," he answered, and he tried to hold his eyes open as long as possible because every time he shut them he saw Quinn's fur robe and remembered what was beneath it and he shuddered. But after a while, exhausted and weary, they both slept.

The next morning saw a change in Loedicia that astounded him. Once he'd fallen asleep he'd slept like a dead man and he hadn't even felt her crawl from his arms, but by the time he woke, as the sun streamed down warm in his face, breaking the cold spell, she had gathered wood, built a fire, and was roasting the roots of a plant that grew nearby.

"Well, lazy," she called as he stirred and moved his aching muscles, then rubbed his hand across two days' growth of beard. "Do you want breakfast or are you going to sleep all day?"

He sat up straight, blinking, then he stood up and walked over, looking down at the fire she had kindled, at the long, pointed spears holding the large bulbous roots on the end. They were baking slowly over the fire, where two cups filled with hot liquid bubbled, and Loedicia held another stick with a fish skewered to the end.

"Have a taste," she said as she pulled it from the fire steaming hot and held it out to him. Her face paled for a minute as she watched him take a small piece of fish from the skewer. "I'm going to miss him terribly, Roth," she said, and tears rimmed her eyes. "But I know I have to go on. He'd want that."

He smiled, relieved for the first time in two days, as he let the piece of fish melt in his mouth. She was going to be all right.

Loedicia had been an apt pupil when Quinn had taught her how to survive in the wilderness and now, determined to do what she felt he'd want her to do, she used all her skill to keep herself and Roth alive. They followed the lakeshore by day, eating fish they caught and roots and wild plants she scrounged from the cold, damp ground, teaching Roth as they went.

Skilled in military tactics, he knew little about surviving

on less than nothing, but he learned quickly and as they
trudged slowly along, putting miles behind them, Loedicia
knew somehow they'd make it and so did he. His only
problem now was what they'd tell everyone when they
reached Fort Junandat.

# 19

Quinn was starting to regain consciousness. His body
ached all over like a toothache and his head felt as if it
were unattached, floating in a state of limbo, then he felt
a soft, cool hand on his forehead. Slowly, one at a time, he
opened his eyes, but they didn't seen to want to focus.
Then, as he tried to speak, the darkness about him melted
away, leaving a warm glow of light that rested on a young
Indian girl sitting beside him.

She was undoubtedly a Wyandot, and couldn't be much
more than seventeen years old. Her black hair was pulled
into a long braid down her back, almost to her waist.

He watched her intently as his eyes became accustomed
to the firelight in the bark lodge. She moved across the
lodge gracefully, her movements like a creeping cat's as
she took a small cup from the floor by the fire and ladled
some broth into it, then came back to where he lay on a
bed of pine needles.

Her French was passable as she spoke to him and it was
then he noticed her pale green eyes and realized she wasn't
a full-blooded Indian. "Just a sip," she said in French as
she knelt beside him and reached down to hold his head
up so she could get some liquid into his mouth.

He sipped cautiously, spilling some onto his chin, and as
it trickled onto his throat she wiped it away with a small
piece of cloth from the floor beside her.

The bark hut smelled rank and stale, but the scent of
the pine needles beneath him mingled with it to dilute the
stench, making it bearable. To his surprise, the broth she

gave him was quite tasty, but he choked twice before managing to empty the cup.

"Who are you?" he finally asked when he realized he was still able to talk.

"My name is Chatte," she answered. "My father is Pierre LeBeau. He traps on the River Sandusky. That is how he found you."

Her French was mixed with Indian dialects, but it was understandable.

"How bad am I?" he asked.

"We took a ball of shot from your chest, an arrow from your side, two ribs are fractured, and your left leg broken."

He closed his eyes. "And the others?"

She hung her head. "All dead, m'sieur," she answered, then looked back at him. "My father went up the river until he found what was left of your camp, but there was nothing to bury. Scavengers had visited it during the night."

Quinn's eyes went dead as if the life had gone out of him. "Oh, God!" he murmured almost beneath his breath, and tears rolled silently down each side of his face into the pine needles. "Are you sure?" he asked as he watched her take the cup back to the fire.

She wiped her hands on the front of her buckskins. *"Oui.* I am sure, m'sieur," she answered as she walked back to him and knelt down again, then leaned back on her heels. "There was someone?" she asked.

"My wife," he whispered hopelessly. "And she was carrying our child." He stared overhead at the ceiling for a few minutes, then shut his eyes again. It wasn't true! It couldn't be! It was all a nightmare and he'd wake up any minute to find Loedicia beside him, cuddled close, her curly hair tickling him as she snuggled her face against his neck, kissing him softly. He'd be able to put his arms about her and hold her, caressing her softly as he had last night.

He tried to move his hands, to wake himself up out of this horrible dream, but he couldn't move, as if someone were sitting on his arms.

"I want to wake up. . . . I have to wake up," he mumbled as he tried to gather enough strength to move.

The Indian girl began to protest violently and his eyes flew open again. It was real! It wasn't a dream and he could feel her strong young hands pushing against him to keep him from moving and the low caress of her voice as she tried to soothe him. Everything his tortured mind suddenly remembered was true. Standing by the river hearing the cries from camp, his face in the water, then as he floated into the river current he remembered seeing the Indian, his scalp lock glistening. It had all been real.

He'd wanted to reach her and now she was dead. She and Roth and all the others . . . and what was it the Indian girl had said? Nothing left to bury? Oh, God! What had they done to her?

For the first time in his adult life Quinn cried for something he loved. The woman who meant more to him than life itself. He cried tears of anger and frustration as well as of sadness, knowing nothing would ever be the same for him again without her.

Chatte explained that he had been there three days already when he first regained consciousness and it was another week before he was even able to sit up. During that week Chatte's father returned with a huge bundle of pelts.

He was a robust, dark-haired Frenchman who'd taken a Wyandot woman as his squaw, treated her like a queen, and mourned her early death three years before, then continued raising their daughter the best he knew how.

Chatte was a friendly young thing, a step away from womanhood, a sloe-eyed beauty, warm and affectionate, always wanting to please, and she nursed Quinn with a determination, as if she didn't dare let him die.

"She is funny that way," said Pierre one evening as he sat cross-legged in front of the fire watching Quinn. "Even the small creatures in the forest dare not die when Chatte takes care of them. And if they do, she has the sad face for days." He smiled. "So you have no choice but to mend, m'sieur," he continued. "Even though I know in your heart you feel at this moment you would rather die."

Quinn was leaning against the side of the hut with a fur

robe wrapped about him to keep him warm and he stared at Pierre LeBeau. "What is there to live for?" he asked as he looked down at his leg, still in splints, and breathed deeply, feeling the pain in his chest, ribs, and shoulder. "Even when I get well, what do I have left?"

"You think she would want this, this Dicia you speak of?"

"Dicia's dead!"

"So you would be dead. While life abounds about you, you would rather sit lifeless and do nothing. Let your life end too." The man shook his head. "This is foolish. Even if you never marry again there are people to whom you can give your life. People who need you. Things you can do. What did you do before you met this Dicia?"

"That's gone too."

"But surely there's some reason for God to spare your life."

Quinn frowned and looked away, watching the open flap at the doorway of the hut, where snowflakes had begun to fall lazily. "Maybe there is," he said ominously. "If Kendall Varrick hadn't taken her, none of this would have happened." He stared, his eyes alive with hate, then he looked back at the Frenchman. "Maybe there is a reason I'm alive." His face grew hard as Pierre watched him closely.

"Revenge?"

"He'll pay with his life this time," stated Quinn, and the other man winced at the enmity in his voice.

"Who is he?"

Quinn turned to the fire and watched the flames intently as he told Pierre about Kendall Varrick. "It wasn't the Wyandots that killed her. Not really," he said as he finished his narration. "I've lived long enough to know their ways. I can't blame them. It was him. He couldn't bear the thought that she was with me."

"This cousin of yours, he is an influential man?"

"In some circles."

"Then you must be very careful."

Quinn's eyes glistened, his mind miles away. "I'll be

careful, Pierre. But I'll slit his throat from ear to ear with pleasure."

"And if they catch you?"

"Then I guess I'll hang, but at least I'll know he won't be there to gloat."

Pierre shook his head sadly. "Hate is a hard thing to live with, my friend."

"But a reason for living," asserted Quinn. "I have to stay alive now if for no other reason than to see Kendall doesn't."

So young to be so bitter, thought Pierre. Maybe it was good Chatte would nurse him. Maybe in time she could help him forget this woman who seemed to possess him so fully. Never before had he seen a man so torn with grief and so willing to die for the love of a woman. He had studied Quinn the past few weeks and for a man like this to love came hard, but when it came . . . ah, for a man like this to lose that love was tragic.

Perhaps the love of another woman would stir him. Yes, maybe it was well Chatte was young and pretty, and she'd been restless lately, like a bitch in heat. Maybe the two would do well for each other and as winter gripped the earth in its deadly cold he watched patiently as his young daughter nursed this giant of a man whose emotions, except for hate, seemed to have died with the death of his wife.

Not quite two weeks after the massacre at Sandusky River, Loedicia and Roth trudged wearily down the trail, then almost broke into a run as they spied the walls of Fort Junandat in the distance.

"We made it," said Loedicia, half running, and her laughter was almost hysterical. Then suddenly she stopped and stared ahead at the wooden walls and the forest surrounding them.

"What is it?" asked Roth as he stopped beside her. He had almost a two-week growth of black beard and as she looked at him for a moment she was reminded of Burly and it brought back all the memories of Quinn.

Tears welled up in her eyes, but she ignored them.

"What do we tell them?" she asked, and he stared at her for a minute, then frowned.

"The truth?"

"That you were helping a man to escape? A man wanted by the crown? They'd hang you."

"Then we tell them I captured Quinn and was bringing you both back."

She shook her head. "No! Not that. I won't dishonor Quinn in death."

"Then what?"

She moved over to the side of the trail and sat down and he followed. "Let me think," she said, then sat for a few minutes watching the winter sky as snow began to fall. "I know," she finally said. "Tell them I'm the wife of a trapper you hired to guide you through to Fort Pitt. I'm a mulatto, and now that my husband is dead you've promised I can continue with you to Philadelphia to be with relatives I have there. No one here knows us and who's to say different?"

"Let's hope so," he replied, "because we don't have time to argue the point. Look." He pointed to the fort, where a small group of soldiers was emerging. "I think we'll have an escort the rest of the way."

While they waited for the soldiers they settled on a name for her. She would be Mrs. Jacques Moreaux. It had been the name of a Frenchman who'd been a friend of her father's back in India.

"I suggest we don't tell him you're pregnant, however," offered Roth, "and you'd best stick to speaking French or broken English. Otherwise they'll never believe your husband was an ordinary trapper and not a man of some importance."

"*Oui, m'sieur,*" she answered as the soldiers approached them slowly, muskets drawn.

Roth stood up and it seemed incongruous under the circumstances as he saluted and introduced himself. Loedicia almost laughed. He looked like anything but a major with his tricorn hat on crooked, held down by a dirty old muffler, and his filthy coat with the inside hem hanging. His uniform looked ready for the rag pile and his holey gloves were wrapped with rags from his uniform lining to help keep his hands warm.

Fortunately, when they arrived at the fort the commanding officer believed them. He remembered when Major Chapman and his men had stopped here on the way west some months earlier, but he had no men to spare to escort them back east and matters were still far from settled a week after their arrival.

It took almost two weeks of arguing on Roth's part, and insisting that General Gage himself was anxiously waiting in Boston for his report finally swayed the man and made him change his mind about letting them leave, but he still wasn't very cooperative and swore they'd never make it with winter coming on. To make matters worse, because Roth had insisted they could travel light, the officer supplied them with only a guide, some warmer clothing, and enough supplies, including snowshoes, to last them to Fort Pitt, but no farther, as he claimed it was all he could spare.

They started their long trek eastward on a crisp November morning with snowflakes falling heavily and a biting wind at their backs. They hoped to make the Huron River within three or four days, but by nightfall of the first day, with snow piling up rapidly on the ground, Roth knew the long cross-country journey was going to be harder than anticipated.

He hadn't shaved his beard on the advice of their guide, a half-breed named Joe Roaring Mountain, who was nothing like his name implied. Slight of build but muscular, with a face like granite and a disposition to match, he was quiet and efficient, never saying more than what was needed in a soft voice and in broken English, but his eyes were alert, missing nothing. He was proficient on the trail and could set up camp in less than an hour, but his social graces left much to be desired and he kept to himself as much as possible.

"Looks like we're going to have a jolly good time," Loedicia said to Roth in French their first night on the trail as she scooped almost a foot of snow from the shelter Joe had built for her. "He's about as talkative as a deaf-mute."

"Let's hope he's unobservant as far as we're concerned," he replied. "When you tripped and fell this afternoon you let out a few choice words in Hindi and I'm sure Mr. Roaring Mountain knows it wasn't French."

She looked over at the man as he finished his supper near the campfire. Snow was still falling, heavier now, but he seemed oblivious of the fact as he cleaned his hands. They watched as he banked the fire, then moved back into the confines of the shelter he'd made and curled up. Each carried a rolled-up elk hide, which he'd used for their shelters, with a blanket apiece, and he pulled the blanket about himself, then turned his back to them.

"I take the first watch," said Roth as he fumbled in his pocket and came up with a pocket watch. "I'm to wake him at one o'clock." He pulled the fur robe tighter about him.

"Be careful," Loedicia said as he hefted it, straightening it on his shoulders.

He stopped and stared at her. At the violet eyes reflecting flames from the fire, at the sensitive lips, a hint of seductiveness in their movement of which he knew she wasn't aware. He stooped down. "Are you going to be all right alone?" he asked, and she nodded as she reached out and took the blanket, pulling it around her.

He had held her in his arms while they slept all those nights on the trial because they both knew the best way to keep warm was the warmth from each other's body and she had to admit she'd miss the security of his arms. It wasn't the same as it had been with Quinn, but it kept her from being lonesome.

He reached down and tucked the blanket around her, then stood up and walked across camp into the shadows of a tree where Joe had told him to stand. The howl of a wolf floated to him from off in the distance amid the heavy falling snow and he sighed. They had a long way to go and the weather was going to get worse. His boots were covered with an outer layer of hides laced as far as his knees and he felt like a stuffed turkey as he pulled the robe tighter, lifting the hood up over his tricorn hat.

He glanced over to where Loedicia sat alone under the

shelter of the elk hide and his heart ached as he remembered the first day he'd laid eyes on her. She'd been giving a dressing down to a man who was beating his horse with a whip and Roth smiled as he thought of the fire in her eyes as she'd tossed her long, dark curls behind her, yelling at the man angrily. Roth had come to her rescue when the man had threatened her with physical violence if she didn't mind her own business and he'd ended up escorting her back to her uncle's home.

It seemed like ages ago yet not even a full year had passed.

The fire burned down and snow continued to fall as he stood watch, thankful he'd taken Joe's advice about his beard, for his chin and cheeks felt cozy and warm. He had so much time to think as he took his eyes from her and stared back at the fire and he wondered what was going to happen if and when they finally reached Philadelphia.

The days dragged on and they moved steadily eastward, sometimes walking knee-deep in snow, and by December 1 they were well into the Ohio Valley, near the Pickawillany Trail. Supplies were running low, they were fighting frostbite, and as the temperature dropped well below zero, game started becoming scarce. But still they kept on. Christmas Day was spent huddled in a cave in the side of a hill to escape a blizzard that raged outside, adding more snow to the drifts that already covered the landscape. They ate wild rabbit and dried corn mush, and drank melted snow with pine tar and honey in it, a concoction Joe claimed would ward off the chills; however, when the new year arrived, a week later, it ushered in a thaw that brought warm and balmy weather, forcing them to shed the extra furs and carry them in bundles strapped to their backs.

Loedicia was starting to show more each day now and walking was becoming increasingly difficult for her, so it wasn't any wonder when Joe stepped over to Roth one evening while they waited for a rabbit to finish cooking on the spit.

"I must talk to you," he said softly, his deep voice resonant in the quiet forest.

"Talk," answered Roth, but he shook his head. "Come with me," he said, and the two men walked a short distance away, where Loedicia couldn't hear them.

The half-breed turned to Roth, frowning. "Why you not tell me woman carries a child?" he asked angrily, and Roth's jaw tightened as he stared into the man's dark eyes.

"I didn't know," he answered lamely.

"You lie! You know woman well. I see in your eyes." He waved his hand at Roth, flicking his fingers in front of his face. "I watch you with woman. . . . she more than friend. She have your baby."

Roth sighed. "All right, all right," he whispered, not wanting Loedicia to hear. "She is more than a friend, but she was married to another. It's his child she carries and I promised her the child would be born in Philadelphia."

"And if we cannot reach Philadelphia and the child comes?"

Roth gasped. "It can't!"

"The weather will turn cold again, it will slow us down, especially since the woman cannot move fast. We are still a long way from Logstown and Fort Pitt is twenty-five, maybe thirty miles beyond. Philadelphia is further."

"How long?" asked Roth.

"Another two months, maybe more, if the woman can keep up."

"Any chance of getting horses?"

Joe frowned. "Maybe . . . at Fort Pitt."

"How about any settlements along the way?"

He shook his head. "Horses are not plentiful." Then his eyes narrowed. "What happens if woman has child on trail?" Roth's eyes widened.

"I don't know anything about birthing a baby."

"Then we go slow, find horses, be careful. I will lead you, but if time comes I will not help with child."

"At least you're honest," said Roth, and he looked back at Loedicia, who sat by the fire rubbing the small of her back. She'd been taking everything well, but he knew it was getting harder for her every day and he prayed to God they'd make Philadelphia in time.

The second week in March, with a gusty wind pushing

at their backs but with horses beneath them, they rode wearily into Philadelphia. Roth rode close to Loedicia. Her stomach was swollen and distorted now with the baby and her once-slim body sat awkwardly as they jogged slowly down the street, but her eyes shone with determination.

"We made it, didn't we, Roth?" she sighed as they rode past the first houses, and she saw the lights flickering behind glass windows.

He leaned closer to her as the wind carried her words away and he reached out, putting his hand over hers as she held the reins. They'd come through a few towns and settlements since leaving Fort Pitt, but the horses had taken almost the last money Roth had brought with him, so they were unable to get any new clothing, only a bit of food, and he was glad it was dark out so no one would see what a sorry sight they made.

"Yes, we made it," he answered, and he felt her hand tense beneath his.

"I think it's just in time too," she said breathlessly. "I've been having pains ever since we crossed that bridge a few miles back." He looked at her sharply.

"Now?" he asked, startled.

"Now," she confirmed as the wind picked up its tempo, swirling the dark curls that framed her pale, thin face.

Roth called ahead to Joe, who wheeled his horse about and pulled up next to him.

"You know your way around Philadelphia?" Roth asked quickly, and the man nodded as he glanced at Loedicia, who hung tightly to Roth's arm as another pain swept through her body. "Then find us an inn as quick as possible," he continued. "We made it just in time."

The half-breed frowned, then motioned for them to follow as he moved ahead of them again, leading the way.

The Green Lantern was not the best of inns and the proprietor was skeptical about letting them in because they looked so disreputable and filthy, but while they were arguing his wife stepped into the room, took one look at Loedicia's swollen body and face contorted with pain as her labor began to intensify, and the argument was quickly over.

The room they gave her was small but clean, with a straw ticking for a mattress, a big feather-down pillow, and a fireplace, which was soon blazing cheerfully as the wind continued to howl outside.

They'd been fortunate, very fortunate, for the inn-keeper's wife was a midwife and promptly started ordering everyone about, taking command of the situation with a firm, experienced hand.

A short while later, Roth, shed of his topcoat, went in to see Loedicia. The innkeeper's wife had stripped off her dirty buckskins and put a nightgown on her and she was tucked in bed with a clean sheet and blanket covering her. He pulled up a chair and sat down beside her, then reached over, taking her hand. She had mentioned Quinn very little since that night two days after the massacre when she'd poured her heart out to him, but now, with his child on the way, the weary months of the journey behind her, she began to cry softly and bit her lip as pain wracked her body and her fingers dug into his hand.

"My God! It hurts!" she gasped breathlessly through clenched teeth as a moan forced its way out.

He leaned over, brushing a wisp of hair from her forehead, trying to soothe her.

When the pain was over, she eased back on the pillow and tried to relax. "I wish he were here," she whispered as the tears rolled down her cheeks. "He'd have been so proud." Then she began to sob as another pain made her gasp and cry out. "Oh, Lord," she sobbed as she held her hand on her stomach, feeling the contractions, her forehead beaded with perspiration. "I loved him so much . . . so much," she said in a choking voice. "Why was it him, Roth? Why? Why did I have to fall in love with him? Why did he have to die? I can't do it alone," she gasped, as he held her hand tighter.

"You're not alone, love," he comforted her. "I'm with you all the way."

The pain eased a bit and she breathed hard, then turned

toward the window as a gust of wind flew against it, rattling the panes of glass.

"It's March, isn't it?" she asked, her breath short and labored, and he nodded. "What's the date tomorrow?"

He shook his head and looked over at the innkeeper's wife, who was watching them while she counted the time between Loedicia's pains. He'd lost track of the days somewhere in the wilderness and looked to her for an answer.

"Today's the twelfth of March," answered the woman, and Loedicia smiled through her tears.

"Tomorrow's my birthday, Roth," she cried breathlessly as another pain started. "I'll be . . . twenty . . . tomorrow . . . oh, God, the pain . . . Quinn!" This time the innkeeper's wife came over and pulled Roth away as Loedicia let out an agonized scream that tore into his heart, almost making his knees buckle.

The woman leaned over the bed and held Loedicia's arms, talking to her, trying to help her any way she could, then suddenly she turned to Roth, who stood in the middle of the room staring at them, his face ashen.

"Go now!" she yelled as she continued holding Loedicia. "This is woman's work. Go!"

Roth stared helplessly at the woman for another second, then turned quickly and left as Loedicia's agonized moaning once more filled the room.

He sat in the taproom, a mug of ale in front of him, his fingers grasping it nervously as he lifted it to his lips. You'd think it was his baby she was having. His stomach was tied in knots and he felt sick as he remembered the torment in her violet eyes as she cried for Quinn and the tortured sound of her voice as he left the room. Why did it have to take so damn long?

He glanced over as the door opened, bringing Joe Roaring Mountain in, accompanied by a draft of cold night air. The half-breed walked over and sat opposite Roth at the table, his face expressionless except for his eyes. There was warmth in them as he watched this young officer. On the long journey eastward he'd taken care of the young woman with compassion and gentleness, and although love was written in his eyes, he'd kept his distance from her, treating her like a lady, a quality Joe admired in a man.

"I have sold one of the horses," he said as he leaned back in his chair. "It will pay for your rooms here." He took some coins from his pocket, putting them on the table.

"But I owe you so much," Roth said, shoving the money back toward the man.

Joe shook his head. "No. I will take the other horse. It is enough."

Roth reached out and toyed with the coins. "Thank you," he said softly, then sighed.

They sat staring at each other, then Roth, self-conscious beneath the man's gaze, downed the rest of his ale. "You don't have to stay now, you know," he said to Joe, figuring the man was probably anxious to be about his own business.

But the half-breed surprised him as he said, crossing his arms and holding his head high, "I will wait and see what the child will be," and a look of mutual respect passed between the two men and Roth understood.

In the wee hours of the morning, after an arduous night, Loedicia, tired and weary, gave birth to a little girl, then completely exhausted, her body aching from its labors, she fell into a deep sleep.

# 20

It had taken Quinn most of the winter to heal his physical wounds, but the wounds in his heart were harder to heal. It was close to dawn as he stretched on the bed of pine needles, then sat up and held his head in his hands.

He glanced back at Chatte sleeping peacefully beside him and he swore softly to himself. What was the matter with him? Nothing like this had ever happened to him before. He'd watched her every day as she'd nursed him. The way she moved her eyes, the seductive tilt to her hips as she walked, the way she leaned close to him, brushing her breasts against his arm. She was just realizing what it was to be a woman.

He knew she'd been wanting him to make love to her for weeks now, but something had been holding him back. It was ridiculous. He'd watched the swing of her hips as she walked and at night when she'd stretch out on her pine-needle bed he'd watch the sensuous way she'd twist her body and he knew it was an invitation, yet it had aroused no desires in him. There was an emptiness inside that confused him.

He'd always been able to take women or leave them, according to his moods, until Loedicia had come into his life and then for the first time he'd found a woman he couldn't keep his hands off. A woman he couldn't leave, who had the power to break down the reserves he'd taken a lifetime to build, a woman who'd showed him what love was really all about, but she was gone now. He'd finally accepted the fact that Loedicia was dead. But with her death had he died too?

He rubbed his forehead and continued to stare at Chatte as she turned her head restlessly in sleep. Last night he'd decided that if he came into physical contact with her body the old desires would be there once again as they used to be, but now, as the sun began to creep into the bark hut, he knew he should never have kissed her.

She'd responded quickly to him as he thought she would and he tried to put feeling into his caresses, but it did no good. He kissed her harder, almost brutally, but there was nothing. He was unable to make his body respond to her ardor as it had with Dicia. Just to be near Dicia had made him warm and heady as if he'd been intoxicated. Chatte was soft and returned his caresses with a fierce passion, wanting fulfillment, but there was no pleasure for him and he'd been unable to give her any.

What a sham he'd made of things. Wouldn't he ever be able to take a woman again? He'd heard of men like this, but he'd thought people only made them up. He was frustrated beyond anything he'd ever experienced.

Chatte stirred as a ray of sun fell across her face and she looked up at him, her eyes warm from sleep and sad.

He lay back on the pine needles beside her and she rolled over onto her stomach, then held her head up, looking down into his eyes.

"I have disappointed you last night," she said quietly, and he didn't know what to say. She leaned over and kissed him. "I'm sorry, Quinn. I have never had a man. What did I do wrong?"

He reached up and cupped her face in his hand. "You did nothing wrong, Chatte," he answered huskily. "It's me." He paused for a minute and stared at her. "When I look at you instead of seeing your green eyes I want them to be violet." Then he touched her long, straight black hair. "And there should be short, dark curls I can wind about my fingers," he said in a choked voice. He dropped his hand and lay staring up at the ceiling. "Damn it! I can't forget her," he cried, and he closed his eyes.

Chatte watched him with love in her eyes. He was a strange man, hard and bitter. "What will you do?" she asked.

He sighed. "It's time for me to move on." He opened his eyes and sat up again as she watched him. "I've been here too long as it is. The weather's broken and spring'll be on its way soon." He stood up recklessly and walked to the door of the hut and breathed in the crisp morning air. "Must be well into February by now," he went on. "If I leave now I can make it to Virginia by the time summer sets in."

She stood up and followed him to the door. "Where is this Virginia?" she asked sadly, and he turned to her.

"I have to go," he uttered helplessly as he saw the tears in her eyes. He reached out and cupped her chin in his hand. "Someday, my little one, you'll find a real man who can give you what I seem to have lost and you'll give him what you were going to give me and it'll be good because he will have it first."

She put her hand up and held his wrist as he held her chin. "I wish I could be her for you," she whispered softly. "I would give so much. . . ."

He nodded. "I know." He leaned forward and kissed her tenderly, knowing it was what she wanted and cursing himself because it was all he could give her.

Pierre arrived with another batch of pelts while they were eating breakfast and he frowned as Quinn told him of his decision to leave.

"Why to Virginia?" he asked, and Quinn's jaw set hard.

"I have friends in Virginia."

"We are your friends."

"These friends can help me reach my cousin," he answered, and he saw the look in Pierre's eyes.

"I was hoping . . ."

"I know what you were hoping, but it's no use. Besides, I've sworn that I won't rest until the day my cousin's in his grave."

Pierre shrugged as he glanced at his daughter. He was a good man, was this Quinn, but then perhaps this was better. He was restless, a man born to lead, and the life of a trapper would be alien to him.

That afternoon Quinn took a last-minute inventory of his supplies, then reached out and shook Pierre's hand, thanking him for saving his life and bringing him back from the dead, then he turned to Chatte.

"Would you walk to the bend in the river with me?" he asked, and she nodded silently.

She walked beside him gracefully, taking two steps to his one. "Will you ever return?" she asked as they reached the bend, and he stopped, looking down at her.

"Don't wait for me, Chatte," he answered. "You have too much to give."

"But no one to give it to."

"Your father told me he's taking you to New York this summer," he said. "You'll meet men there."

Her eyes fell under his gaze. "They will never be like you. They will not accept a half-breed. They will not understand."

He took her hand and raised it to his lips. "I love you in my own way, Chatte, as a friend, always remember that, but I can't undo what's been done to my heart any more than I can undo what I've done to yours. I only pray you'll forgive me and forget me quickly."

She bit her lips bravely. "There is nothing to forgive and I will remember you only as long as you are here," she lied. "Go and don't turn back, for I will do the same." She reached up suddenly, pulling his head down, kissing him on the lips longingly, then she turned and walked slowly away.

Quinn watched her back as she moved farther and farther from him, then he too turned and walked away. He couldn't see the tears that streamed down the young girl's cheeks as she walked back to her father.

Some days were still bitter cold and snow still clung to the countryside, but Quinn managed to go on. He stayed clear of the rest of the Wyandots as he moved down the Sandusky River, following its curving path into the heart of the wilderness. Each day brought a new sign of spring as he worked his way southward. He was sitting on a log, fishing for his dinner one afternoon, when the redwings flew into the cattails in a small marshy area a few feet away, the first harbingers of spring, and he knew the robins would be close behind. The redwings' cheerful "*charringing*" echoed through the tall trees all afternoon and he sighed as he cooked his fish over a slow fire and listened to it.

The sap was in the trees and they were budding as he left the Sandusky River and headed for the Scioto, and it seemed as though spring would be early this year. Already the days were warmer and the air smelled fresh and clean.

By the middle of March he was in Shawnee country and he moved slowly, covering his tracks. He had a job to do and it was essential that he stay alive and not end up scalped by a Shawnee.

By the time he reached the Kentucky River spring beauties were breaking through the dead leaves of winter and the other wild flowers of spring were pushing their tender shoots through the warming earth. Spring had come early. Spring with its warm breezes, the animals coming to life, chipmunks scampering amid the huge trees trying to stay clear of the squirrels, who chased one another incessantly.

That's what he liked about this part of the country; spring came weeks before it did in the northeast.

Quinn stood for a moment on the banks of the river, taking his bearings. What a glorious land this was, and he remembered Tom Jefferson's dream and George's words as he had stood at the edge of Telak's village. A nation so big . . .

He no longer had Loedicia, but he still had this land and he breathed deeply. America was his, the colonies were his, he was a part of them. He'd fought for them before Loedicia'd come into his life, he'd fight for them again. And, by God, he was going to make sure he didn't lose this too.

He reached down and scooped up a handful of earth, let it sift through his fingers, then with a determined look on his face, he plunged back into the thicket and moved downriver.

He was moving slower than usual now because he'd picked up Shawnee signs about two weeks before, indicating they were headed in the same direction, and with the trees greening there were too many places for them to hide. He'd even quit building fires at night, but with the warmer weather he didn't really need one. He skirted some bushes, then stopped suddenly, the hair on his head prickling. Up ahead he could hear the sound of axes echoing along the riverbank, filling the air, sifting through the newly born leaves bursting forth on the trees overhead. There were men ahead, but who were they? Indians? Hardly. The Indian sign he'd seen earlier was a war party. If they'd been moving a village there'd be women and children along, but he'd seen tracks of warriors only.

But what white men would be here in the wilderness miles from civilization? He took a deep breath and crept forward, then dropped to his stomach and slid across the ground as he came to a clearing. He raised his head, barely hidden by some dead weeds left over from winter, and surveyed the scene.

A group of men were studiously at work cutting logs and building a rectangular stockade while other men stood watch, Kentucky rifles ready. He glanced back, away from the Kentucky River and toward the woods beyond, and he saw an Indian dart back into the trees. There was only one thing to do. He put his hands to his mouth and a shrill trilling call pierced the air, stopping the axes in midair.

All the men in camp stood motionless, listening, for the call of the night heron was out of place in the middle of the afternoon. They expected to see a Shawnee brave burst from the trees beyond the camp, but instead they saw a shock of blond hair the color of faded dandelions rising from the brush, moving forward slowly, like a phantom, as Quinn stood up.

He stopped a few feet from what was to be the stockade, then moved into the rectangle as a man who seemed to be the leader said, "Don't stand there waitin' to be shot in the back, get the hell in here or ain't you no idea there's Shawnee in them woods?"

Quinn glanced behind him, then over to the tall stranger with the slow, easy drawl. "I been tracking those Shawnee for weeks now," he said, "just to make sure I could keep out of their way. Looks like you weren't able to." He motioned with his head, glancing at some wounded men propped against what was to be the stockade wall.

"They cut into us almost two weeks ago about three miles east of here," answered the tall one. "Killed two right off. We tried to hold 'em, but they only gave us a reprieve and three days later they hit us again. Lost two more men and ended up with five wounded in all. Took us over a week to get here, but we figure with the river behind us and a solid stockade we should be able to hold 'em off."

"And who is 'we'?" asked Quinn, his eyes studying the men intently.

The tall stranger smiled a half smile and quietly introduced his men. "And my name's Daniel," he said, holding his hand out, "Daniel Boone." Quinn stared for a second, then reached out and took his hand, a surprised look on his face.

"I think we have a mutual friend, Mr. Boone," he said, relieved. "You know George Rogers Clark?"

Daniel held on to his hand. "Yes, I know George, but who are you?"

"The name's Locke, Quinn Locke," he answered, and saw Daniel's eyes narrow as he released his hand.

"I understood Captain Locke was lost on Lake Erie sometime last summer."

"Hardly," answered Quinn. "Can we talk?"

Daniel looked at his men. "Over here," he said, and motioned toward the fire.

The rest of the men eyed them curiously but went about their business at Dan's orders and once more the steady thud of the axes broke the stillness of the afternoon.

"Sit down," said Dan, and gestured at the ground beside the fire, where some squirrels were roasting on a spit. "How is it you're still alive?" he asked as he turned the spit to let the flames cook the succulent meat.

Quinn took a cup of Indian tea offered by Dan, then told his story.

"Then Lady Aldrich is dead," commented Dan, and Quinn's eyes narrowed. "They still have a price on your head, you know," Dan continued. "That is they will when they find out you're still alive. And now . . . when they find out the lady's dead, things are going to get pretty rough."

Quinn frowned. "She was my wife, Mr. Boone," he said, "and no one knows more than I what I've lost."

Dan studied his face. It was hard and determined. "You intend to find your cousin?"

"And make him pay," answered Quinn as he stood up and walked to the edge of the stockade, looking off toward the woods, where the Indians were hiding. "And after that I intend to do my damnedest to see this country free of Britain's stranglehold, but I have to stay alive to do it." He turned and walked back to the fire.

Dan stood up. "That's a rather difficult task at the moment," he said. "There's close to fifty Shawnees out there and I don't think they intend to let us leave here alive."

"But you intend to leave, don't you?"

Dan smiled sheepishly. "One way or another, yes, as soon as these men get settled."

"Would you care for company?"

He studied Quinn. George had told him about the man the last time he'd seen him, which was less than two months back when he was recruiting men for this trip, and he liked what George had said, but at the time the whole world thought Quinn dead.

"A man who's survived what you have must have a charmed life. You should be an asset to have along," he answered, "but I hope you ain't in no hurry 'cause I don't know just how soon we'll be able to get away. Richard Henderson, the gent I'm workin' with, is on his way here with more men and some cattle and horses but I don't know as we'll have to wait for him, he probably won't show up till the end of April and that's a bit long to hang around, but I can't leave for a spell. Not till the stockade's finished anyways."

"I can wait," answered Quinn, and Daniel nodded knowingly, glad he wasn't the man Quinn was after, because his eyes looked deadly, his face like granite. Once he got started, a man like this would be hard to stop.

It was late at night and spring was well set in as Dan and Quinn slid their raft quietly down to the water, then turned to bid the men good-bye. The Indians were still out in the woods in full force, but Dan couldn't wait any longer. They'd drift down the Kentucky River until they felt it safe to move overland, then they'd travel the rest of the way on foot.

The men had christened the stockade Fort Boonesborough and Daniel'd laughed as he helped them set the logs in place. Quinn had gotten along well with the men, doing his share, but the only one who really got to know him was Dan. As they worked side by side they became good friends and both learned respect for each other and now, as they moved onto the raft, lying flat on their stomachs, and it was pushed silently into the water, they looked toward each other knowingly in the darkness. They had many miles ahead of them and both knew it wouldn't be easy.

The current pulled at them viciously, dragging the small raft into midstream as they held on tightly to their handholds, starting their haphazard journey. They were tossed about in the fast-moving waters with not even a moon to light their way. They'd chosen complete darkness for their escape hoping to get past the Indians unseen, and so far they were successful.

The men that were left dug in behind the walls of the stockade prepared to hold it at all costs until Henderson got there and Dan returned, bringing even more men, knowing full well the dangers that lay ahead of them, but their main concern tonight was the two men on the raft as they watched the woods for any signs of activity in the Indian camps.

They floated through the dark night, only stillness about them, hoping they'd encounter no shallows or rapids. As they moved downstream the river suddenly erupted into a small pool and the raft swirled in a circle as it landed in the center of the deeper water and Dan poked Quinn, motioning for him to look at the bank.

A small group of Shawnees were camped about twenty feet from the river's edge and had a fire going, but as the raft spun around, then headed back into the mainstream, beginning to pick up speed again, they were soon out of sight.

"Close one," whispered Dan, and Quinn nodded.

They lay prone on the raft, holding on to the handholds, plunging forward steadily. Sometimes, slowed by a diminishing current, they'd drift and bob gently, then suddenly plummet forward, buffeted off rocks as they hit frothy rapids. All night they drifted on, both men quiet with their own thoughts, their eyes searching the darkness for any sign of the Shawnees.

Morning came bright and clear and with it the rakish call of a kingfisher as it dived toward its prey, and before the sun could even break the horizon, they hit a shallow, rock-filled rapid that splintered the raft, throwing them off, and they waded ashore in water barely above their ankles.

"Well, that settles that," said Dan as they shook water from their clothes and checked to make sure their powder was still dry. They glanced up as the kingfisher once more made a pass at the water above the rapids, this time emerging with a beakful of wriggling fish, then he streaked off through the trees.

Quinn smiled. "Looks like the fishing's good."

"How far you reckon we might be?"

"Must be at least ten miles, maybe more. This is your neck of the woods, Dan, you know it better than I do."

And he was right. Dan had been here before, many times, but not to this particular spot.

They fixed a quick breakfast of baked fish skewered on sticks with dried corn mush to help fill their stomachs, then headed east toward what Dan called the Wilderness Road, which his men had just finished cutting out of the countryside.

Twice during the days that followed they skirted Indian camps before finally reaching the familiar surroundings of Castle Rock, then moved on to the Yellow Creek arroyo. They moved fast, stopping only long enough for a quick meal and a short nap. Dan was pleased when they finally reached the Wilderness Road and he saw the tracks of the small army of men and animals, and he knew Henderson was well on his way.

Quinn had been in this territory only once before, about three years ago, when he and George had scouted some land near the Clinch River, then moved into the Cumberland Gap, but he'd never been as far as the arroyo. Most of his time was spent closer to the Great Lakes, as most men called them.

Crossing the flat land of Powell Valley, they moved on to the Clinch River ford and Moccasin Gap, then hit the great road to Virginia. It had taken them less than three weeks to travel the distance most men traveled in over a month, and in the first week in May they sauntered into Fort Chiswell on the way to Roanoke, both men extremely pleased.

However, there were problems. Quinn didn't dare use his real name. He and Dan decided that for the time being, Quinn Locke would stay dead. Dan would introduce him as Cherokee Jones, a name he'd picked out of the air.

"Looks like the whole British Army's out in force," said Quinn warily as they moved on through the gates.

People were crowded about in small groups, whispering excitedly, so engrossed they didn't even seem to notice the two new arrivals until suddenly one man, a bearded settler, spotted Dan.

"Dan! Well, bless my soul, Daniel Boone. You almost got by me," he exclaimed, and the group he was with turned and stared at the two men. "Didn't expect to see you for at least two more months," the man continued, and he reached out, shaking Daniel's hand vigorously.

"What's all the excitement?" asked Dan as he looked about, bewildered by the scene they'd stumbled into, and he gestured toward all the people clustered about.

"That's right. You wouldn't hear," exclaimed the man. "We just got word this mornin'. There's been shootin' up in Boston. They sent troops out to take away the guns and ammunition at Lexington and Concord, and Sam Adams, John Hancock, and the rest wouldn't give it to 'em. We're at war, Dan'l, and everybody's up in arms. Word was slow gettin' here. It happened nigh two weeks ago, but now everybody don't know what to do. Even the soldiers here is befuddled."

Dan turned and looked at Quinn and there was a mutual understanding between them. It had happened. They'd talked of it often on their overland journey and both were convinced war was inevitable.

"How are things going so far?" asked Quinn, and the settler eyed him suspiciously.

"Eli, this is a friend of mine, Cherokee Jones. We traveled part of the way together," explained Dan.

The man shook Quinn's hand. "You're a friend of Dan'l's, that's fine," he said, then answered Quinn's question. "We hear tell the British got their pants stomped off the first round and they's men from all over headed for Boston and more men who's gettin' ready."

Both Quinn and Dan glanced at the redcoats standing about, nervously, restless as they looked at the crowd.

"How many of you are leavin'?" asked Dan, and Eli grinned furtively.

"About twenty men are aimin' to head out soon as we can slip away," he whispered, trying to hide his mouth with his hand without being too obvious. "The soldiers ordered us to stay put, but me and a few others got itchy feet."

Dan straightened as he glanced about at the men, women, and children in the small fort. "Who's in charge of this army in Boston?" he asked, and Eli shrugged.

"Ain't nobody knows. But the fight's started, Dan'l, and we ain't gonna let it be."

He nodded, then turned to Quinn. "You'll be going to Niagara?" he asked, but Quinn frowned.

"I think . . . maybe I'll head for Philadephia," he said slowly, and Dan was surprised. "I have a feeling they'll be calling another congress of the colonies together," he explained, "and I'd like to be there."

"Then you've decided against going after your cousin?"

"No . . . let's just say Philadelphia's on the way, so why backtrack? Don't worry," he assured him, and his eyes grew hard as steel. "I'll never give that little venture up until he's six foot under." Eli glanced at the two men curiously, wondering what the hell they were talking about.

That day, some twenty men, one at a time, slipped from the fort and met in the woods, then headed east. And among them were Daniel Boone and Quinn Locke, otherwise known as Cherokee Jones, but neither man was headed for Boston. Each had his own private part to play in the war ahead.

# 21

Loedicia stirred in bed, then slipped from the straw mattress and crept quietly to the cradle and sat on the floor, gazing at the soft pink bundle sleeping peacefully in its depths. She was a beautiful child with her father's blond hair, like soft down on her wee head, what promised to be her mother's violet eyes, and as Loedicia reached into the cradle and put her hand to the baby's, the tiny fingers clenched it tightly, holding on for dear life.

Rebel, that's what she was and that's what Loedicia had named her. A child set apart. For a child whose parents were rebels, what better-fitting name than Rebel Locke?

She removed her finger gently from the baby's grasp and stood up, then moved about the room as she dressed. It was barely dawn and she'd be expected downstairs in the inn to start serving breakfast. She was still at the Green Lantern where Rebel had been born. The proprietor and his wife, Polly, had been kind enough to give her work and she laughed as she thought about what Aunt Agatha and Uncle Thaddeus would think if they knew she was working as a serving girl. But it paid for her and Rebel's room and gave them a bit of coin to spare, and Loedicia didn't care. She was no longer the spoiled, naive girl she had been less than a year ago. She had learned what life and love were all about, she was a woman.

She walked to the window and looked out at the sunrise. It was such a beautiful Monday morning for April. Suddenly she leaned out as a group of men came running down the street, following a man on horseback. She tried to catch what they were shouting about, and she stared dumbfounded as the words echoed in the morning air.

"War! 'Tis war! At Lexington and Concord!" they were crying, and she drew in her head, standing stark still, a startled look on her face.

By the time she came downstairs the place was in pandemonium. It had happened. The redcoats had fired on the militia and they'd fired back and there was no more question as to what was going to happen next. Already hundreds of men were on their way to Boston to back up the militia. It had finally come to an end, the wondering and waiting.

Loedicia stood for a minute watching the confusion before her as excitement over the news spread like wildfire and she thought of Roth. He'd left for Boston the week after Rebel's birth and she wondered now if he'd be in the fighting. He'd looked so smart, almost his old self as they'd said good-bye. His beard was gone and he'd managed to get a newer uniform.

"You look human," she'd said as he stood in the doorway, hat in hand.

He rubbed his chin. "I must have looked like a grizzly bear."

"Thank you, Roth, for everything," she said softly, and he reached out, cupping her chin in his hand as he stared down into her eyes.

"I'll be back as soon as I can, Loedicia," he said. "So don't you run away." He leaned over to kiss her lightly on the lips, but instead, as his lips met hers, his hand dropped from her chin, his arms went about her, and he drew her to him, holding her close as he kissed her long and hard.

"Good-bye," he murmured breathlessly as he looked down into her face, then he'd kissed her again, more passionately, and was gone.

She stood now, watching the people milling about, remembering his last good-bye. She'd stared at the door after he'd left and tears came to her eyes because she hadn't returned his kiss. He'd kissed her, but she hadn't kissed him back.

She put her hand to her mouth, then shut her eyes as she began to cry. She liked Roth. He was good and kind and she loved him as a friend, but nothing more. There was no spark, no warmth deep down inside. None of the magic she'd shared with Quinn. He said he'd be back, but somehow she hoped he wouldn't, because she knew he deserved more than she could give him.

Polly, the innkeeper's wife, caught her suddenly by the shoulders, interrupting her daydream and startling her.

"Here, little missus," she quipped gaily. "There's some gents down by the far end needs waitin' on, so we'd best get about our work. The news is good, aye, but the work goes on, more so." Loedicia nodded as she straightened her apron quickly and walked to the back of the room, where a group of men were seated at a table.

Suddenly she stopped short and stared, her face turning white as she looked into a familiar pair of dark eyes scowling under bushy brows. The man's mouth, almost hidden by an immense black beard, opened wide, and he shouted as he spotted her at the same time.

"Hell's fire!" Burly exclaimed as he stood up. "Dicia!" Before she could say a word, he was out from behind the table and hugging her in his huge arms, almost breaking her in two.

"Here now!" hollered Polly. "Let the missus down," she yelled, and began pummeling Burly with her fists, but he laughed raucously.

"Hold to, m'lady, she's a friend," he explained as he set Loedicia back on her feet and looked into her pale face.

"If she be a friend, fine, but she's still got work to do. You can visit with her later."

"Now!" countered Burly, and Polly frowned.

"But who's to serve my tables?"

Burly reached into his pocket and took out a few gold coins and opened Polly's hand, slapping them in it as he winked. "You," he answered, "and I'm payin' you to serve 'em. How's that, m'lady?" he said, smiling, and Polly shook her head.

"All right, off with you," she said. "But mind you, don't keep her all day."

Burly took Loedicia's elbow and looked down at her. "Where can we talk, lass?" he asked, and her heart turned over as he called her lass and she was reminded of Quinn.

"I have a room," she managed to say, and moved toward the stairs as the men Burley'd been with stared at them dumbfounded, then started calling after them suggestively.

"Make sure you get your money's worth," yelled one.

"Need any help?" called another.

"Hell, he don't need help," yelled the third. "He's big enough to give any gal what she wants." All three laughed loudly.

"Don't pay no heed to them, lass," he said as she blushed, and he eyed them angrily and their voices faltered. "They never saw a real lady, that's all, so they don't know how to recognize one." Loedicia smiled sheepishly.

She stopped as she reached the door to her room and

turned to him. "We'll have to be quiet," she said. "The baby's still asleep."

His dark eyes studied her face. "A boy?"

"A girl," she corrected, then remembered her words to Quinn the night before he died, about having a boy the next time. But now there'd be no next time and her heart ached.

Burly was amazed as he stared at the wee babe wrapped in the worn blanket and she woke up as he stood watching.

"She wants her breakfast," said Loedicia as the baby began to cry lustily, and she unfastened her bodice, picked up Rebel, and put her to the breast as they talked.

Burly's eyes saddened as Loedicia told him everything that had happened and when she finished, he walked to the window and stared out, watching the commotion in the street below.

"Can I help in any way?" he finally asked as he turned to face her.

The baby had fallen back to sleep, so she stood up and took her to the cradle, gently laying her down, then she fastened her dress as she walked over to stand beside him.

"Oh, Burly," she whispered, tears in her eyes, "you've done more than enough just by being here. It's so good to see a friendly face."

"What happened to this major gent what brought you all the way from Junandat?"

"He had to get back to Boston, but he said he was coming back." Her face suddenly looked sad. "I don't want him back, Burly," she said vehemently, and he was puzzled.

"But . . . from what you've said . . . he must care for you, and if he said he'd be back . . ."

"That's just it," she blurted out. "I know he's in love with me, but I'm not in love with him. I love him, yes, but it's different. I love him like a friend. Like I love you. He's been good and kind to me, but that's as far as it goes. I can't give him the love he wants and I'm so afraid he's going to ask me to marry him if he comes back."

"And you wouldn't?"

"How could I?"

"If he's as nice as you say, you could do worse."

"He's too nice," she answered wistfully. "Remember how Quinn and I used to fight? I don't think Roth would even talk back to me. He can't do enough for me and I feel guilty because I've been unable to return his feelings." She shook her head. "I hope he doesn't come back, Burly, I don't know what I'd do."

"Can I interfere?" he asked sheepishly as the baby made a gurgling sound.

"How?"

"Look," he said, "you don't love him the way you loved Quinn, but does that really matter?" He nodded at the baby. "That little one needs a father and you can't go working in a place like this, you're a lady, you don't belong here. Things could work out for you, you know. You could make him a good wife. Maybe in time . . . as you said yourself, he's good and decent. Don't just throw the whole thing aside, lass. Think about it first, and if he does come back keep an open mind."

She smiled and reached out, hugging him. "You're a dear," she said. "But tell me, how long will you be around?"

"With this mess goin' on, I don't know. I hear they're having another congress set for June. Maybe I'll head out and see if I can find George. Maybe . . . I don't really know what I'll do with myself. Maybe I'll stick around awhile and keep an eye on you," he said, and she grinned. She was so happy to see him again, even if he did bring back memories that were painful.

Two days later, on the morning, of Wednesday, April 26, amid all the turmoil, Major Roth Chapman rode into Philadelphia alone. He'd been sent by the governor to gauge the temperament of the people and the sentiment of the town, but his first stop was the Green Lantern Inn.

Loedicia's heart fell as she opened the door and looked into his face.

"You look surprised," he said as he walked in, and she closed the door behind him.

"I . . . I didn't expect you."

"I told you I'd be back."

"But the fighting . . .?"

He put his hands on her shoulders. "Aren't you glad to see me?"

"Yes . . . but . . ."

"We've got problems," he said suddenly as his hands dropped, and he walked farther into the room.

"What kind of problems?"

He took a deep breath. "Lord Kendall Varrick."

Her face went white.

"You met too many people in Boston, Loedicia. Someone spotted you here one day at the market and you were recognized. Word's gotten back to him. That's why I'm here."

"But he can't do anything. What can he do?"

He took her by the shoulders and moved her to a chair near the baby's crib, making her sit down. "He's on his way here, Loedicia," he replied, and saw her frightened eyes. "He's about two days behind me."

Her hand flew to her throat. "Oh, God!"

"He's already informed your aunt and uncle that he intends to hold you to your promise of marriage, since Quinn Locke is dead."

She shook her head violently and grabbed the lapels of his coat. "I can't . . ."

"Your aunt and uncle intend to force the marriage as they tried to once before."

"I can't marry him. I won't."

He knelt beside her and reached out, cupping her face in his hand as he looked into her tear-filled eyes. "You won't have to," he said soothingly. "You're going to marry me."

She stopped shaking her head and stared at him.

"I'll be good to you, Dicia. You know how much I love you . . . how much I've always loved you."

"But . . ."

"As my wife he'd have no claim on you. It's the only way."

Tears rolled down her cheeks. The decision had finally come but not the way she thought it would.

"I won't let him get his filthy hands on you," he cried as

he stood up and started pacing the floor. "I've almost ridden my horse into the ground to get here in time. I've left my regiment on a trumped-up assignment I've talked them into sending me on. You've got to marry me, Loedicia. Now, today!"

"Roth . . . Roth," she said as she stood up. "I can't marry you."

He stopped pacing and looked deep into her eyes. "Because you're not in love with me?"

She hung her head, tears running unchecked down her cheeks. "Yes. I love you as a friend, but I'm not in love with you."

"But you don't hate me, do you?" he asked as he walked over and put his arms about her, tilting her face up. "I don't repel you, do I?"

She reached up and touched his face. "No, you don't repel me," she answered softly, and she thought of Lord Varrick, remembering the beating at his hands. "You could never repel me, Roth."

"You can't run away this time, Loedicia," he told her. "You have the baby to think of." She knew he was right. "And as my wife there'll be nothing he can do. After all, I'm an officer in the British Army."

"But it wouldn't be fair to you," she answered. "You deserve a woman who can return your love. I have nothing left to give anymore."

"I'm willing to take that chance, Loedicia. Please . . . you have no alternative."

She stared into his dark, flashing eyes. He was young, perhaps close to thirty, handsome, and he'd told her his family were successful English merchants who sent him an allowance every month. Along with his major's pay it was enough to take care of a wife and child.

"What of little Rebel?" she asked, and he smiled.

"I may not have been there when Rebel was conceived," he answered huskily, "but I was there when you carried her and when she was born and I almost feel as if she's my own. Don't you worry about Rebel. She and I will get along fine."

"But won't people think it strange, a British soldier with

a daughter named Rebel? And if they find out who I am . . ."

"Please . . . let me worry about that. Right now is what counts."

"What can I say?" she said, and he kissed her gently on the lips.

"Say yes, Loedicia, please," he begged. "Give me a chance. I can make you happy. I know I can."

She sighed as she realized she was cornered. Marriage to Roth was her only alternative, not only for her sake but for the baby's.

"All right," she said, and a sob filled her throat. "I'll marry you, Roth." He kissed her long and hard, not seeing the tears in her eyes or knowing the ache in her heart.

The rest of the day was almost like a dream. He called Polly from downstairs and told her they were getting married and she was ecstatic. She'd become very fond of Loedicia.

"He will make you happy, missus," she whispered as Roth left to find a preacher. "He will make you forget the other one."

"I'll never forget him."

"Don't be too sure. The years do strange things to us. You're not meant to stay a widow. Now smile. I'll see no tears for the young major."

"But I thought you didn't like British soldiers."

She leaned close to Loedicia. "I hate them. But, then, he's not like the others, we both know. He's a man first, a soldier second." Loedicia had to agree.

Before Roth could return with the preacher, Burly knocked on the door and when Loedicia told him everything he frowned.

"You mean Kendall Varrick's due in two days?"

She nodded.

"That major of yours really believes in taking chances, doesn't he?"

"Lord Varrick wouldn't dare do anything to a British soldier."

"Right now, Dicia, the status of a British soldier in Philadelphia is lower than the lowest gutter rat's. As it is, your major is taking a chance just by being here. If anything did happen to him who's to blame it on Lord Varrick? And I'd better stay out of Varrick's way too. Hell's fire, they still have a price on my head."

She reached out and put her hand on his arm. "I never realized. I'd forgotten."

"Don't worry, lass, I keep out of trouble's way. Few people even know who I really am. I told 'em my name was Smitty and those that do know me keep their mouth shut. Which reminds me, I better not let your major catch me here."

"But he won't do anything," she said. "You've got to stay long enough to meet him, Burly."

"How do you know he won't have me arrested?"

"I told you what he did for us. Please?" she begged. "He'd like to meet you, I know."

He finally consented and sat down to wait while Polly returned from downstairs, where she'd been hunting for something to give Loedicia to get her out of the old black dress she'd been wearing.

An hour later, when Roth returned, dragging a preacher at his heels, he was surprised to have the door opened by a tall stranger whose countenance was almost frightening, but he almost forgot Burly, who was standing and holding the door, as his eyes fell on Loedicia.

Polly had managed to find a yellow dress with lace at the scooped neckline and because it was a bit big, they'd tied it about the waist with a green sash. Her hair was cascading in curls onto her shoulders and the yellow dress made her eyes even more violet. She looked beautiful.

Burly ushered in the wizened preacher, then shut the door, and once more Roth was aware of him and whirled about.

Loedicia stepped forward as she saw his puzzled face. She touched his arm lightly with her hand. "Roth, remember when I told you about Quinn I also told you about his friend Burly?"

"You're Burly?" Roth asked, and Burly nodded. "Good God, man," Roth gasped, surprised. "Don't you know they're still looking for you?"

Burly grinned. He liked the major. He was tall, good-looking, had honest eyes. Something rarely anymore seen in a man. He shook the major's hand, assuring him he could take care of himself.

"But how about you?" asked Burly. "You boys aren't any too popular about town at the moment."

Roth's jaw tightened. "I too can take care of myself," he said, and Burly said he'd string him from the nearest yardarm if he didn't take proper care of Loedicia. But the warning was a friendly one and both men knew it.

They were married quietly in Loedicia's room with Polly and her husband as witnesses and Burly watching, then Polly brought a special bottle of wine from the cellar and they drank a toast to the bride and groom, after which Roth had to leave to report to his regiment.

"They don't even know I'm in town yet," he said, smiling as he kissed Loedicia, and promised to be back as soon as possible.

Polly and her husband followed him downstairs where one of the customers was doing double duty in the taproom. Loedicia and Burly were now alone.

"He's a good lad," said Burly when the door had closed behind them.

"Too good for me," she answered, and he looked at her, scowling.

"Nonsense!" he exclaimed. "He's got himself a real lady for a wife."

Her eyes filled with tears. "Oh, stop it, Burly. We both know I'm no such thing. Ladies don't carry on the way I do. They sit in drawing rooms and drink tea and crochet dainty doilies, they don't gallivant into the wilderness and get themselves pregnant and marry outlaws and . . . Let's face it, Burly, I'm no lady."

He took her hands as the baby began to fuss and led her to the rocking chair and made her sit down. Then he went to the cradle, lifted the baby out, and walked over, putting her in Loedicia's arms, then he stepped back and surveyed the scene.

"Now, if that isn't the picture of a lady, you can strike

me dead," he said, smiling, and she laughed through her tears.

"Oh, Burly, you're incorrigible," she murmured, and the baby started crying frantically, searching for food.

Burly kissed Loedicia on the forehead. "I'll say good-bye now, lass," he said, "and you take care. And if you need anything I'll stick around for a while."

"Be careful," she warned. "Remember Lord Varrick knows you by sight."

"I'll be careful," he assured her. Then he said good-bye to the baby, kissed her again on the cheek, and with the promise to stop by soon, he left the room.

She fed the baby and put her to sleep, then stared out the window.

The day slipped by quickly and the closer it came to nighttime, the more frightened she became. Except for the night Kendall had raped her, no man other than Quinn had ever touched her and she wasn't certain just what to expect. She didn't even know if she could do it or not. Love with Quinn had been such a vital part of her existence, but could she give herself to another man? What kind of lover would Roth be?

It grew later by the minute and still he didn't come back. At first she thought maybe he couldn't get away from his regiment, then she began to worry, remembering Burly's remarks about British soldiers not being welcome in the city. She was torn between her worry for his safety and relief that she didn't, as yet, have to face the inevitable.

It was almost eleven. The baby was sleeping soundly, so she put her nightgown on and climbed into bed, sure now that she probably wouldn't see Roth again till morning, and was surprised, minutes after setting her head on the pillow, to hear the key she'd given him earlier in the lock.

The room was lit only by a candle beside the clock on the mantel. As he stepped in, at first she was tempted to feign sleep, but her conscience got the best of her. He had married her to keep her out of Kendall's hands, but he'd also married her for love.

He slipped off his jacket, threw it over the back of the

rocking chair, then pulled off his boots, setting them next to the chair. She lay on the bed watching, her heart pounding, then he stepped over to the bed and looked down at her.

"I'm sorry I'm so late," he apologized, whispering softly so as not to wake the baby, "but I wasn't out drinking and I wasn't in a fight, but I do have a surprise for you."

"Oh?"

"How would you like to live in a small house all our own with someone to help with the baby?"

She stared up at him, bewildered. "But how?"

"That's my surprise," he whispered as he sat on the edge of the bed. "I went to see some people who were close friends of mine before they came to the colonies. He's a shipbuilder and they're quite well-to-do." He reached out and took her hand, holding it affectionately. "I used to spend most of my time at their home when I was a boy, back in England. I knew they were in Philadelphia somewhere, but it took a while to find them. I was hoping they'd let us stay with them, but they had a better idea. They have a small furnished cottage on their property and they insist we stay in it. She's even hired a woman to help with the baby. That's what took me so long. I've got her all moved in, ready for morning."

"You mean we're moving in tomorrow?"

He let go of her hand and brushed one of the curls back from her forehead. "Would you like that?"

"You mean a regular house with rugs on the floor and china in the cupboards?"

He smiled. "And a soft featherbed," he whispered as his dark eyes looked directly into hers, and she felt herself tremble as her face flushed. She knew what he was thinking and she felt strange inside.

He stood up, slipped off his shirt, and she stared up at him. The muscles in his chest rippled beneath dark, curly hair as he tossed the shirt to the foot of the bed. His body was as trim and well toned as Quinn's had been, although he wasn't as tall. He took off his pants and tossed them after the shirt, then lifted the covers and slid in beside her, wearing only his underwear.

She felt his body next to hers, warm and vibrant as he lay on his back breathing deeply and her heart started pounding, then fear ran through her as she heard him breathe a deep sigh.

Slowly he lifted his head from the pillow and turned on his side, resting his head on his hand, leaning on his elbow as he looked into her face. "I love you, Loedicia," he said huskily, and he bent down, his mouth covering hers, and she wanted to die. But then, as he kissed her deeply, sensuously, the fear left. This was the kiss of a man in love and she didn't mind it now. It was nothing like it had been with Quinn, but at least now she wasn't afraid anymore. She tried to respond. His hand moved beneath her nightgown and he began to caress her gently, his hands fondling her. She wanted to respond. She wanted to feel the same ecstasy she'd felt with Quinn. She wanted Roth to bring her to the heights of rapture that Quinn had brought her to so that her body felt as if it were filled with liquid fire that penetrated every nerve and fiber, tingling deep inside, making her lose herself in his arms, but it wasn't happening. There was no magic. His hands were only a pair of hands, his lips on hers brought only a mild response.

It wasn't fair! She couldn't cheat him like this. He loved her. He'd put his life, his career in jeopardy by marrying her. He deserved more than a halfhearted, passive attempt at returning his love. If nothing else, she had to pretend. She had to!

She began to think of Quinn's hands on her and the way they made her feel sensuous and abandoned. She pretended it was Quinn's lips that parted hers, exploring the sweetness of her mouth, and she began to move responsively under his hands, her body yielding to his caresses, warming to him. He was an ardent lover, gentle yet passionate, and her body began to beg for fulfillment so that by the time he moved over her she was ready for him and gave herself wantonly, only he never guessed it was really the ghost of Quinn she gave herself to.

But even pretending, it wasn't the same because he wasn't Quinn, and afterward, although he seemed content and satisfied, there was an emptiness inside her, for she'd been unable to reach the pinnacle of love she'd had with Quinn and her loins still ached with longing.

He lay on top of her, his body still pressed against hers, and she could still feel him inside her. He buried his face in her neck, kissing it tenderly, and his voice when he spoke was soft and endearing.

"I didn't hurt you, did I?" he asked, and she opened her eyes, staring at the candle, feeling his body above hers, his lips on her neck. He was trying to be so gentle.

"No," she whispered.

"I never want to hurt you, Dicia," he said softly against her ear. "I only want to love you and make you happy."

"I know," she answered, and there was a sob in her voice, but she didn't think he noticed as he pushed himself up and she felt his naked body slip from hers.

He rolled over beside her and reached out, pulling her to him, his arms about her, and he bent to kiss her forehead. He didn't see the tears that rolled down her cheeks, but as he held her close he felt them against his bare chest and a pain stabbed at his heart. Would he ever be able to make her forget Quinn? God, he loved her so much, and he held her against him until he knew she was asleep.

The next morning their carriage pulled up the long drive to the Newell home, a large stone house on the outskirts of the city with maple trees lining the drive, leaded-glass windows, and a beautiful green lawn filled with daffodils, narcissus, and tulips.

Beside the main house and toward the back, across a small, well-kept lawn, was a matching guest cottage of stone and Loedicia caught a glimpse of it through a willow tree next to the path to the door.

"It's such a big place," she exclaimed. She held Rebel in her arms, cuddling her close. "I feel out of place. Even Uncle Thaddeus' house was nothing like this."

"But we'll be in the cottage," he answered, and she smiled. He looked so handsome in his uniform and he seemed so happy in spite of the hostility they'd encountered when they were leaving the city. She had seen him become tense a few times when the shouts became obscene and abusive, but other than that he'd stayed calm.

He reined the carriage up to the front steps, got down, and took the baby from her, then helped her down. She was wearing the yellow dress she'd worn yesterday, with an old bonnet Polly had given her, and she felt like anything but a titled lady as she walked up the front steps beside Roth. She felt like a poor relative in such elegant surroundings.

The door was opened by a maid, who ushered them into the drawing room, where Mrs. Newell was waiting. "We don't have tea, my dear, it's the times," Mrs. Newell explained liltingly after Roth had introduced them. "But we do have some crullers and cool cider. I know you'll enjoy them."

She was a motherly woman with gray hair, a warm smile, and a fluttery disposition.

She smiled broadly as she chucked little Rebel under the chin and looked into her lovely eyes, which almost matched her mother's. "Roth used to be at our house all the time when he was a boy," she prattled affectionately. "I'm only too happy to take care of his little family." She looked at Loedicia. "He's told me all about you, my dear, and I only hope the two of you can find happiness. But I'm afraid with times what they are, it won't be easy." She glanced at Roth. "He's a good man," she said. "Even though he is on the wrong side of the fence."

Loedicia was startled.

"Mr. and Mrs. Newell, Dicia, are staunch rebels," he explained. "As are most of the Philadelphians. However, they've overlooked the fact that I'm a soldier."

"First and foremost he's our friend," Mrs. Newell confirmed. "Now, Roth, after you have a glass of cider see that your little family gets settled. Ondine has the house all ready." She turned to Loedicia. "A friend of mine recommended her in glowing terms. She's a real gem and she's got a heart of pure gold. Says she can't wait to get hold of the little one here. She just adores babies."

Loedicia was overwhelmed by Mrs. Newell's friendliness and warmed to the woman quickly.

"By the time Roth sits in on our congress and learns just what's going on," she concluded as she saw them to the door, "he's going to have a different outlook on this whole affair. Mark my words. I knew the boy and I think I know the man he's grown into." She glanced at Roth. "He's no king's puppet."

Roth smiled as he leaned over and kissed her cheek. "I do believe you're trying to turn my head," he said affectionately, and as they left the house and headed for the cottage Loedicia thought how strange it was. Here she was, formerly a widow of a man outlawed by the British, a man who spoke openly for a break with the crown, and she was now married to a major in the very army her first husband had opposed, a major sent here to weigh the temperament of the town and let General Gage know how the congress progressed. Now they were being befriended by people who felt as Quinn had felt. What a topsy-turvy world.

Roth opened the door and Ondine came running from the kitchen, all smiles and chatter. She relieved Loedicia of the baby, fussing over her like a mother hen as she ushered them into the parlor, then she disappeared upstairs with her bundle, cooing all the way. As they stood in the room facing each other the soft dulcet tones of a lullaby drifted down.

"Do you like it?" he asked.

"It's beautiful," she answered as she looked about. "But I feel out of place. It's been so long since I've seen crystal chandeliers and Persian rugs." Suddenly she remembered the biting sarcasm she'd directed at Quinn when she'd first seen his house.

"Nothing is too good for you," Roth stated boldly, "and someday I'll see you have a place of your own, grand and glorious."

"I don't need riches, Roth," she answered softly. "I never did. I guess that's why I didn't make a very dignified lady. I was content no matter where I was as long as I was happy in my heart."

"I'll make you happy again. I swear I will," he said almost angrily, then he reached out and pulled her toward him, into his arms, kissing her deeply, his only thought to make her forget the man whose shadow stood between them.

The next day, however, brought Quinn's memory back to him even more vividly as he stood in the small office at regimental headquarters and faced Lord Varrick, whose eyes blazed angrily at the younger man.

"When?" Lord Varrick shouted. "When did you marry her?" Roth stayed calm, only his clenched fists revealing his anger.

"We were married two days ago, April twenty-sixth, at the Green Lantern."

"It's a lie!"

"You asked the proprietor. That's how you found me."

"What proof have you? They could lie for you."

"What do you want me to do, drag the preacher in here just to satisfy your doubts? To hell with you. She's my wife, legal and proper, and there's nothing you can do about it."

"Don't be too sure. I happen to be a very good friend of General Gage's, young man." Lord Varrick sneered. "Major or no major, marriages can be annulled. We'll see what he has to say about this." He turned to leave, but Roth's voice stopped him at the door.

"I'm glad you brought that up," he said coldly. "Since the general and I are cousins it might be of interest to him at that."

Kendall's eyes narrowed. "What are you talking about?"

"I thought you knew," answered Roth deliberately. "Thomas Gage is my father's first cousin. Our families are quite close. In fact, he helped me get my first commission in the army and was quite effective in securing it for me. I think maybe he would be interested in my marriage."

Kendall's face turned white, then red as he stared at Roth. His eyes grew dark and the scar on his cheek became more prominent. "Perhaps he would at that," he answered viciously. "I'm sure he'd be pleased to learn his favorite cousin's son married the widow of a man with a price on his head. A woman who married the scoundrel who kidnapped her—"

"Oh, I see," interrupted Roth. "She's good enough for you, but not me."

"Loedicia was promised to me," he shouted angrily. "I've had her once, I'll have her again. She's mine and belongs to no one else!"

"You'll have her over my dead body!"

"That can be arranged too!"

"You're theatening me?"

Kendall smiled savagely as he opened the door, then glanced back at Roth. "Let's just say that at the moment the people of Philadelphia have little love for the color of your uniform, Major, so under the circumstances anything can happen." He left, slamming the door behind him.

Roth stared after him, his face hard, his jaw set firm. He'd hoped by mentioning the fact that he was related to General Gage Lord Varrick would back off, but the man was shrewd. He knew the general would never approve of his marriage. Well, to hell with all of them. He was his own man.

He turned to the window that overlooked the street and watched Lord Varrick leave, his two cohorts, a half-breed named Squint and a backwoodsman named Ramsey, with him. He'd introduced them when he'd first walked into the outer office and Roth hadn't liked their looks. Now, after Lord Varrick's threat, he liked them even less.

The days moved on. Roth was an ideal husband and a good father to Rebel, who grew pudgy with Ondine's loving care, and social gatherings at the house brought the young couple out of seclusion and into the stream of life.

The second week in May, Dr. Franklin arrived in Philadelphia and bells rang loud and clear as the city went wild. Everyone was throwing parties in his honor and Loedicia and Roth met him one evening at the Newells'. Loedicia was awed. Quinn had spoken of him often and of the part he was playing in the rebellion. He was a very important man and it pleased her to meet him, but she was also surprised to discover that Roth already knew him.

"I'm glad to see Roth's got some sense anyway," said Dr. Franklin as Roth introduced them, and he looked at Loedicia from head to toe.

She was wearing a velvet dress Roth had bought her a few days before. It was violet, to match her eyes, the décolletage trimmed in lace. She looked exquisite.

"At least he can pick women even if he can't pick sides," continued Dr. Franklin as he kissed her hand.

"And what is that supposed to mean?" asked Roth.

"It means, dear lad," said the doctor as he enjoyed Loedicia's physical attributes over the top of his little square glasses, "that you are a much better judge of women than of politicians. Why else would you be wearing the wrong uniform?" He nodded to General Washington, who was across the room talking with Mr. Newell and some other men. "Now there's the uniform to wear. There's dignity behind it. I know you, my boy. Stay in Philadelphia long enough and you'll change colors. You're too smart." He smiled and winked at Loedicia. "He had to be smart to catch you, my dear," he whispered, and took her arm and ushered her away as Roth's eyes twinkled.

He was at it again. Dr. Franklin always did have an eye for the ladies and Roth smiled as he walked over to join Mrs. Newell at the punch bowl.

As the days went by, Loedicia saw a subtle change in Roth. He seemed restless. Sometimes in the evening he'd sit and stare off into space; at other times he'd pace the floor, then stop and think, his mind miles away.

One evening she stood in the front window watching him as he entered the grounds and rode his horse slowly up the drive. He looked strong and handsome and yet sad. She was beginning to love him, but it was nothing like the love she'd had for Quinn. He was good and kind and he treated her like a princess, but she knew marrying him had been wrong. Not for her but for him. With the passionate love he had to give, he should have married a woman who could give him the same love in return. Not the restrained imitation she had been giving him. She cringed as she remembered the previous night and she could guess why he looked sad and forlorn today.

It had been late when they'd gone to bed, but it hadn't mattered. He'd begun to caress her and make love to her and once more, as she had every other time with him, she'd closed her eyes and pretended it was Quinn.

She began to respond passionately, her body wanting him . . . not him . . . the man she was imagining him to be. She'd played the part too well and suddenly, as he moved on top of her and started to press his lips against hers, her voice throbbed and she whispered Quinn's name against his mouth.

He stopped, his mouth against hers, his body pressing on hers, and she could feel his muscles tense. He stared down into her eyes as they suddenly flew open at the realization of what she'd done, and he drew his head back.

"My God!" he whispered softly, his voice husky. "Haven't I made you forget him yet? Don't you have anything left for me? I'm not Quinn, Dicia, I'm Roth. It's my body you feel, not his. It's my lips kissing you."

"I'm sorry," she cried as tears filled her eyes. "I'm sorry, Roth. I didn't mean—"

"You've been pretending it was Quinn all along, haven't you?" His eyes were dark and compelling. "Does it always have to be Quinn? Can't it be me just once?"

"I didn't want you to be cheated." She sobbed softly as the tears streamed from her eyes. "I had to pretend. It was the only way I could give you what you need . . . what you want . . . but if you don't want me . . ."

"Don't want you? Oh, Lord," he moaned, and buried his head against her neck, kissing her beneath the ear, his breath warm on her skin. "I want you so much I ache inside. But just once, can't it be me, Dicia?" he whispered slowly into her ear. "Can't you accept my hands, my lips?"

She felt his body against hers, searching, reaching for fulfillment. He lifted his head, leaned on one hand, then cupped her face in his other hand so she had to look at him, and he stared into her violet eyes.

"Loedicia, I'm Roth," he whispered, and kissed her lips passionately. "My lips can caress you, my hands can hold you, I can give you what you want if you'll only let me."

She looked into his face.

"Let yourself go, Dicia, let yourself love, let me show you what we can have together." Suddenly she wanted him to kiss her. She wanted him to caress her. It would never be the same as it had been with Quinn, but her senses began to cry for him and she felt a quickening in her loins. She began to move beneath him as she stared into his eyes and he sighed, relieved, as he kissed her deeply, letting his body possess her as it never had before.

She watched him now as he rode up to the door. No wonder he'd been restless. What man enjoy's competing with a ghost? Last night, as she lay in his arms afterward and let him kiss and fondle her, she'd made up her mind that from now on she was going to try to be the wife he needed and wanted and she was smiling as she opened the door for him.

He stretched after he dismounted and threw the reins to one of the stable boys, then he walked up the steps, took her in his arms, and kissed her thoroughly.

All through dinner, however, he was quiet, as if something were bothering him, but Loedicia didn't press him. She hoped it wasn't because of last night because she was determined that last night would never happen again.

Finally she could take it no longer, the silence was unnerving. "What is it?" she asked as they left the table and walked to the sitting room. "Something's bothering you, Roth. Is it me?"

He turned to her and shook his head, then sighed. "You know it isn't that," he answered. "I married you with my eyes wide open. What happened last night . . . well, it worked out anyway, didn't it?"

She flushed self-consciously as he took her hand. "Loedicia, I have to talk to you," he said seriously, and pulled her to the sofa, where he made her sit down. "How can I tell you?" He held her hand, rubbing her fingers affectionately. "I've sent a letter and resigned from my commission," he blurted out huskily, then waited for her reaction, but she only stared at him. "They've made General Washington commander in chief of the Continental Army and I've accepted a commission with him," he continued slowly. "I'll be a major in the Philadelphia Light Horse."

She was speechless. He stood up and slowly paced the

floor as he explained. "I used to talk a lot with Quinn on the trail," he said, pacing back and forth. "Then, when I returned to Boston and saw how things were . . . I've sat in the State House and listened to those men and I've talked with them socially. They're not rabble, and what they say makes sense. It's been eating at me for days, but I didn't know what to do and then today . . ." He stopped and looked down at her. "Today, after they confirmed Washington's appointment, a man from Virginia named Thomas Jefferson gave a speech and I saw all my doubts crumbling. Quinn was right, Loedicia. This country belongs to the people in it, not a king who's never even set foot on its soil. And someday it can be a great nation." He sat down beside her. "I wish you could have heard Mr. Jefferson."

She reached out and put both her hands on his. "Is that what's been bothering you all these weeks?"

He sighed as he stood up once more and walked to the fireplace, then turned to face her. "I should have discussed it with you first."

"It's your decision, Roth, not mine."

"But it affects you. I'm a turncoat, Loedicia. Some people will call me a traitor. Don't you see? When my family hears of it they'll probably disown me. I was planning on buying you a beautiful home like this someday, only bigger, with more servants. Now we'll be paupers. I'll have nothing but my major's pay for us to live on. . . . I've felt miserable about it ever since the doubts began because I promised you so much. I wanted to make you happy."

"I told you before," she protested as she stood up and walked over to him. "I don't need money to make me happy."

She stared up into his face and the look in her eyes made him all warm inside. There was love in her eyes. He reached out and took her hands, holding them in his, clasping them to his chest.

"Loedicia?" he asked, hardly believing it possible, and she tilted her face up to his, her lips slightly parted.

"I had nothing but love when I was with Quinn and it

was enough," she whispered as she brought her mouth close to his. "It will be enough for us too." His eyes looked deeply into hers, then he kissed her longingly, and she accepted his lips, kissing him back passionately, pushing Quinn to the back of her heart into her memories, where the dead belonged.

# 22

At that moment, at the other end of the city, Quinn whistled a gay tune as he rode in. He'd acquired a horse in Virginia and had made better time than he'd expected, but it had been a long journey. It had been a few years since he'd been in Philadelphia and he was surprised how the city had grown.

He'd stopped off at Monticello on the way, in the hopes of catching Tom before he left, but he'd been gone for weeks, so he traveled alone, using the name Dan had bestowed on him. The fringed frontier shirt, black waistcoat, and buff pants he'd managed to acquire were well worn by now and his black tricorn was covered with dust. He'd replaced his moccasins with riding boots when Martha Jefferson had given him the horse, but they too needed a good polishing.

Few people paid attention to him as he rode in and he was glad. The fewer people who saw him, the less chance of recognition, at least until he learned what the atmosphere was. He saw few lobsterbacks and those he did see seemed to be avoiding contact with anyone. Good. Things were looking up.

If he had Tom figured right, he knew exactly where he'd be staying and within an hour after his arrival he stood in front of a door in one of the better inns, took a deep breath, then knocked. It took some minutes, then the door swung open and the tall, thin, red-haired man holding the knob stood transfixed, his eyes like saucers.

"My God in heaven!" he blurted out as his mouth fell. "Where the devil . . . you're dead!"

Quinn grinned. "Am I, now?" he asked. "They didn't tell me."

"Oh, damn it, Quinn, come in here," he exclaimed, and Quinn stepped into the room while Tom pumped his hand in greeting.

It was almost an hour before Tom had the full story and he whistled softly. "When George sent word back about your marriage I was flabbergasted," he said. "And then the next thing I knew they said the two of you were dead."

Quinn had been sitting in one of the easy chairs in Tom's room and now he stood up, walked to the door, and stared out into the growing darkness. "I've been going by the name of Cherokee Jones," he explained. "It's a name Dan Boone thought up."

"It'll do," answered Tom. "And you'd better keep using it a little longer because there are still people around who don't care whose blood's on the money they put in their pockets."

"You think they'd turn me in?"

"I heard Lord Varrick was down here talking to the military some weeks back," offered Tom. "Maybe he's got wind you're on the way."

"He couldn't possibly know."

"Who else knows you are alive besides Boone?"

"The Frenchman and his daughter."

"Then I wonder why Varrick was here. He made a call at regimental headquarters," said Tom, "then he left for Boston a few days later, but I heard he left his two henchmen behind."

"His henchmen?"

"A half-breed and a backwoodsman. We rode by headquarters the other day and they were lounging around outside. One of the men we were with pointed them out. They didn't look any too friendly."

"Speaking of friends. Have you any idea what happened to Burly?"

Tom scratched his head. "I heard someone spotted him

in town before Lord Varrick showed up. He was calling himself Smitty, then he suddenly dropped out of sight."

"Maybe he went to Boston."

"Maybe."

"What's happening, Tom?" asked Quinn as he sat down again. "The whole country's taking sides, yet nobody seems to know where to go or what to do."

"We settled it today," answered Tom. "The congress has appointed General Washington to command the Continental Army and he's going to need every man he can find. Which brings me to you."

"Me?"

"We're still going to need a fort out there," he explained. "George is out there somewhere and a few others, but we need what you had. If the Indians stick with Butler and Johnson, which they no doubt will, the frontier will be a bloody mess."

"That part of my life's over," stated Quinn, and Tom scowled.

"Don't be ridiculous," he disagreed. "It's just begun. I want you to go see General Washington tomorrow, Quinn. He'll keep your identity secret and no one else in the city knows you by sight. We've only got a handful of men on the frontier. We need you."

"But my men are scattered."

"Let word get around that you're back and they'll be there."

"Where? I can't go back to the Ashtabula."

"Why not?"

Quinn sighed and stood up, walking back to the window. Could he do it? Could he start all over again? Tom was right. Brant's Indians would turn the frontier into a bloodbath and no settlers would be safe. Maybe he ought to try. What was it Dan had said when he told Quinn about losing his oldest son? The world goes on living no matter who dies, and we happen to be a part of that world.

Maybe a new fort was what he needed. It wasn't a new woman, he knew that. He closed his eyes for a minute and remembered Chatte. He'd avoided women since then. No woman could take Dicia's place, but maybe if he kept busy, had less time to think . . .

"All right," he finally agreed as he turned to face Tom. "I'll go see General Washington."

"Good," replied Tom. "And by the way, I want to find some different clothes for you tomorrow. They're having a social in the general's honor tomorrow evening and you're going with me . . . as Cherokee Jones, of course."

"Of course," said Quinn, and Tom smiled, relieved.

"It's good to have you back, Quinn," he said, and insisted he stay the night.

The next day Quinn spent with Tom at the State House, listening to more speeches and resolutions and to General Washington's plans, while across town at the headquarters of the Philadelphia Light Horse, Major Roth Chapman was introduced to his company, outfitted in a blue uniform, and spent his first day as a Continental soldier.

That evening, as they dressed for the party honoring General Washington, Roth watched Loedicia primp in front of the mirror as he slipped on his uniform and straightened the front of his shirt. Her skin was beginning to lose the deep tan it had acquired while she was in the wilderness and was becoming soft and creamy, and her hair, down to her shoulders again, was piled high with a cluster of curls hanging down to the nape of her neck. He had never seen her looking lovelier and the violet dress, his favorite, made her eyes seductive and sensuous. No wonder everyone spoke in hushed tones of the major's lovely wife. All they knew of her was that she was beautiful and he called her Dicia. No one except Mr. and Mrs. Newell had the slightest suspicion of her real identity and it was the way both of them wanted it. Lady Loedicia Aldrich was dead. She'd died with Quinn Locke on Lake Erie and it was better that way.

As he watched her now, smoothing the waistline of her dress, he thought momentarily of Quinn and the massacre and the long trek cross-country, and a physical pain made him flinch. She was forgetting Quinn. Last night and the night before proved that, but how long would it take?

There were still times when he knew by the look on her face that she was remembering.

She turned to look at him and as she smiled he pushed all thoughts of Quinn to the back of his mind and walked toward her.

"Do I look all right?" she asked, and he didn't have to answer. Instead he took her in his arms and kissed her long and hard. "We'd better say good night to the baby," she whispered as his lips left hers. He smiled, kissed her again, and it was some minutes later that they left the house and walked toward the Newells'.

The evening was going well. Music and chatter filled the stately mansion, spilling over into the gardens that surrounded it, and the night was filled with the scent of roses. Everyone who was anyone was there. Loedicia stood near the punch bowl with Roth while Dr. Franklin, his usual inimitable self, was bestowing compliments on her that would have turned the head of any other woman, but she passed them off coquettishly without hurting his feelings, then they moved on to talk to the general and she was pleased when he congratulated Roth on his decision to join the Continental Army.

"We need men of his caliber," he stated as they drank a toast to freedom, then they mingled with the crowd while more people arrived. Military men, delegates, businessmen, friends. Time passed quickly and it was so crowded Loedicia was unable to keep track of everyone, although she wanted to meet them all.

About an hour after their arrival she and Roth stood talking with Colonel Harrison and two of the Virginia delegates when one of the men from Virginia motioned to them.

"I told you I saw Tom Jefferson a bit ago," he said to Colonel Harrison. "He's standing a few feet behind us talking to General Washington and he's got that big blond fella with him. The one he had with him at the State House this afternoon."

They all turned to look. A tall red-haired man was standing a few feet away talking to the general. He was lean and wiry with thin lips, an aristocratic nose, and an

air of the elite about him, but it was not Mr. Jefferson
whom her eyes stayed on. They wandered to the man
standing next to him and she stared openly.

All she could see of him was part of his body and the
back of his head, for he was in conversation with the general, but it was enough to stir her and make her hair
prickle uncomfortably. He was tall, broad-shouldered, and
slim-hipped, his hair the color of faded dandelions, and it
contrasted well with the deep green velvet coat he wore.
His buff trousers were tucked into highly polished riding
boots and she could see the hint of a white ruffled shirt at
his throat and cuffs.

"Shall we go say hello?" suggested the colonel, and
Roth agreed. He'd been wanting to meet Mr. Jefferson
personally after hearing his speech the other day.

Loedicia couldn't take her eyes from the tall stranger's
back as Roth took her arm and they started across the
room.

The man laughed and his head tilted back a bit as they
moved through the crowd, but she still couldn't see his
face.

"The blond gent's named Cherokee Jones," offered one
of the Virginia delegates as they approached, and suddenly, when they were less than ten feet from them,
Colonel Harrison called a greeting to Tom. As Mr. Jefferson looked toward them the tall stranger also turned and
Loedicia's face went white.

Their eyes met and it was as if all the air had been
forced from the room. Quinn's heart turned inside him and
he gasped audibly as Loedicia's legs trembled beneath her
and the blood seemed to drain from her body.

Roth too turned pale as he reached out to steady her,
but it was too late.

Her heart began to pound and she couldn't breathe, as
if she were being crushed, and as she stared into Quinn's
blue eyes the world suddenly revolved about her and without any warning she slumped limply to the floor as a lady
standing nearby screamed and another gasped, holding her
hand to her breast.

Everyone took a step backward except Quinn. He

moved quickly across the short space that separated them as Roth knelt down beside her.

"Dicia!" they both cried at the same time, then they looked at each other across her fallen body, neither able to believe what he was seeing.

Quinn's arms went under her and he began to pick her up as Roth managed to compose himself.

"Bring her," he said hurriedly as Quinn stood up, cradling her limp body in his arms. Roth led the way through the shocked crowd to the front door, down the walk, past gaping couples who'd stepped out for a breath of air, out to the small stone cottage. He opened the door and led him to the parlor, where Quinn laid Loedicia gently on the sofa while Roth tucked a pillow under her head.

As Roth straightened and Quinn's arms loosened from about her, Loedicia's eyes began to flutter, then slowly they opened and Roth recoiled at the expression on her face.

"It is you . . ." she whispered breathlessly, staring into Quinn's face in disbelief, and tears welled up in her eyes, spilling onto her cheeks. "Oh . . . my God. . . ." She reached up and touched his cheek. "I thought you were . . . I thought you were dead," she sobbed ecstatically, and he pressed her hand as it rested on his cheek and they stared lovingly into each other's eyes.

"Dicia," he whispered huskily, his hand caressing hers, then he bent forward and kissed her, softly at first, then, as her arms came up about his neck, holding him close she kissed him back. Roth closed his eyes in agony and walked to the window, his back to them.

It was over. He clenched his fists as he listened to the two lovers behind him caressing each other, whispering endearments as Loedicia told him about the baby, her love for him spilling over into her voice. She was lost to him again and there was nothing he could do.

"I thought I'd never see you again," sighed Loedicia as Quinn took his lips from hers, then moved back, helping her into a sitting position. Then suddenly, as Quinn took a deep breath and started to say something, Ondine rushed into the room yelling hysterically.

"Missus Chapman, honey," she cried anxiously, her generous bosom heaving. "You all right? I was so worried when I looked out and saw you bein' carried home. Land a mercy, Missus Chapman!" Her hand flew to her breast.

Quinn looked at Ondine, then at Loedicia, then his eyes rested on Roth, who had whirled around from the window, and both men stared at each other, unflinching.

"Did I say somethin' wrong?" Ondine asked, staring stupefied at the three of them.

"Your mistress is all right, she won't be needing you," said Roth as he walked over and took Ondine's arm, turning her to the door. "Go tend to the baby, please." She frowned.

"But the little one's sleepin'."

"Then do something in the kitchen," he ordered irritably. "We'd like to be alone!"

She glanced about, sensing the sudden tension that had come into the room. "Yes sir, Major Chapman," she murmured hesitantly, and left the room, a puzzled look on her face.

Roth watched her leave, then turned slowly as Quinn said harshly, "Mrs. Chapman?"

Roth took a deep breath and looked at Loedicia, whose face had been flushed from Quinn's kisses but had now suddenly turned white.

"I guess I'd better explain," he said. His stomach tied up in knots as he ran his hand through his dark hair, watching the helpless look in Loedicia's eyes. He wanted to cry, but instead he held his head firm.

"What happened?" asked Quinn angrily, and Roth sighed.

"We were on the way to the river to see you when the Indians came," he began, trying to stay calm. "When you were shot and fell into the river by the willows, I grabbed Loedicia and dragged her away before they spotted us. We made our way upstream and hid in a rock crevice." He walked to the window and stared, as if he were once more standing between the two boulders and listening to the tortured sounds from camp. "All morning long we listened to the sounds of the men dying, knowing what was happening yet unable to do anything about it." His voice broke and he turned to face them. "I didn't even have a weapon, but I knew I had to keep Dicia alive. Hours went by and when it finally became quiet we ventured out and made our way back toward camp. I left Dicia in the bushes and went on alone." He swallowed hard and took a deep breath, his eyes misty. "Parts of bodies were scattered all over, it was sickening." He winced. "Everyone was dead. I found what I thought was the remains of your body beneath the fur robe you'd had on."

He saw the questioning look on Quinn's face.

"Your body was gone from the willows," he explained, "and there was some blond hair . . ."

"One of your privates had blond hair," Quinn reminded him.

"I assumed the bloody mess beneath your robe was you." He stopped for a minute and turned back to the window, nervously twisting one of the buttons on his uniform. "Dicia was in shock at first, but when she pulled out of it we made our way to Fort Junandat. I promised her the baby'd be born in Philadelphia, so we left Junandat as soon as possible with a half-breed named Joe Roaring Mountain as our guide. Sometimes I thought we'd never make it, but we did. The baby was born the day after we rode in, on March thirteenth. I left a few days later for Boston. While I was gone someone spotted Dicia and got word to Lord Varrick. I got back two days ahead of him and talked her into marrying me to keep her out of his hands."

So that's why Kendall was here, mused Quinn, then he took Loedicia's hand and held it tightly as she looked at Roth, a pained expression on her face. Quinn stared at the two of them for a moment, then realized Roth was waiting for an explanation from him. "Ironic, isn't it?" he said. "By the time I heard the Indians it was too late. All I remember was turning back toward camp, then the next thing I knew my face was in the water and I was spluttering to get air. I hurt like hell and as I pulled my head from the water and looked up, an Indian was bearing down on me." He squeezed Loedicia's hand. "I knew she was back

at camp and I had to get to her, so I managed to free my
arms of the fur robe. But the current was too strong and I
was too weak. A Frenchman found me some days later, a
few miles downstream, and his daughter nursed me. I had
broken ribs, a broken leg, a hole in my chest, and another
in my side. The Frenchman told me he scouted the camp,
but there was nothing left to identify. He couldn't figure
how I was still alive." He looked from Roth to Loedicia
and reached up, cupping the side of her face in his hand as
if he couldn't believe it was really her. "I thought the two
of you were dead," he said, then dropped his hand and
continued. "When I was well enough, I took off and
headed south. Thought maybe I'd find George before
hunting down Kendall. I ran into a man named Boone, a
friend of George's, and we headed east together. When we
reached Fort Chiswell we learned about what happened at
Boston. I've been on the road ever since, up until yesterday."

He stopped talking and the room grew awkwardly silent
as they stared at each other, then the silence was broken
abruptly by a knock at the front door.

Roth bit his lip and turned toward the window as Ondine hurried by in the hall, then ushered General Washington into the parlor. He stood for a moment, taking in the
scene. Quinn sitting on the sofa holding Loedicia's hand.
The stunned look on her face as she looked from one man
to the other. Roth's empty eyes as he stared at them both.

"I'm sorry to interrupt," the general casually remarked,
"but I was a bit concerned."

Roth swallowed hard, then took a deep breath, trying to
still the ache in his heart. "I'm sorry, General Washington," he apologized. "It's just—"

"There's no need to pretend," interrupted Quinn. "General Washington knows I'm not Cherokee Jones."

"But I didn't know the major knew," added the general.

Roth stood with his feet planted solidly. "I've met
Quinn before, sir," he answered, and his voice sounded almost like a sob. "I happen to be married to his wife." He
looked hard at Loedicia, who drew in a quick breath be-

cause the look on Roth's face was not the look of a man who'd married merely for convenience.

"Roth, please," she pleaded, then as Quinn too looked at her, suddenly aware that what he thought was a marriage for Loedicia's protection was in reality far more, she stood up, glancing from one to the other apprehensively. "You were dead," she said to Quinn. "I was all alone and Kendall was coming. . . . I thought you were dead. . . . Roth was kind. . . ."

"Kind?"

She saw the heartache in Roth's eyes. Right now she wished she were dead and she remembered the way he'd made love to her only last night and the way she'd responded, and her face suddenly became flushed and warm.

"By the look he's giving you," remarked Quinn coldly, "I'd say it was more than kindness that prompted him to marry you."

Her eyes began to glow angrily as her face reddened even deeper. "That's not fair!" she cried.

"What is fair?" Quinn asked, enraged. "That you enjoy the arms of another man?"

"Don't blame her," Roth snapped. "Blame me."

"All I want to know," said Quinn, "is what went on between you two."

"What usually goes on between man and wife?" answered Roth.

"Then I'm right. You didn't marry her just to protect her."

"I married her because I love her. You knew I was in love with her," answered Roth, and Loedicia sighed as she glanced at the general, who was watching the confrontation, his face disturbed.

"Make them understand, General Washington," she pleaded as she touched his arm. "I thought I'd never see him again and Roth was . . . he was—"

He put his hand on hers and he eyed both men sternly as he interrupted her. "Gentlemen, please!" he said. "There's no need for all this. I think I see the situation properly." He turned to Loedicia. "I assume you, my dear, are the former Lady Loedicia Aldrich. Am I right?"

She nodded. "Yes, sir."

"And when you thought Quinn was dead you married Major Chapman, right?"

"Yes."

"Then what, sirs, is all the argument about?" he retorted, looking at both men. "Since Quinn Locke is still alive, your marriage to the major is null and void. It's as simple as that."

"Is it?" asked Roth bitterly. "Just like that I can shut her out of my life?" His jaw set angrily. "I brought her cross-country. . . . I was with her when the baby was born. . . . I've held her in my arms as my wife. . . . I love her . . . yet I'm to forget all that?"

There was agony in the major's face. What he said was right, Loedicia knew. He could no more forget she was his wife than Quinn could. Legally she was still Mrs. Quinn Locke, but she was also Mrs. Roth Chapman. Each man saw her as his wife, but what of her?

"And you, my dear?" the general asked, and she stared at him, stupefied. There was no question in her heart. She was Quinn's and always would be, yet the thought of hurting Roth brought tears to her eyes.

"Which one of us are you crying for, Dicia?" asked Quinn sarcastically as tears rolled down her cheeks, and she turned on him heatedly.

"I'm crying for both of you," she sniffed furiously as she wiped the tears away with the back of her hand. "Damn you, Quinn Locke, I love you and you know it," she cried. "I love you in a way I could never love any other man, but I love Roth too. Not the same way. There's no fire, no sparks, but he's been good to me and I don't want to hurt him. If he'd been a horrid husband I could hate him, but I don't . . . or can't you understand that?"

He stared at her, frowning, then he glanced at Roth's pale face. Major Roth Chapman was no ordinary man. He'd been in love with her for a long time, but he'd been honorable about it and Quinn knew it. "I'm sorry, Roth," he apologized. "Suddenly I feel like a damn fool. I expected you to do something I could never do."

Roth ran his hand through his hair and turned to look

out the window again so they wouldn't see the tears in his eyes. He tilted his head, looking up at the trees outside and the stars beyond.

"I should be thanking you for taking such good care of her instead of cursing you," Quinn continued. "What can I say?"

"May I have a few minutes alone with her?" he asked, his back still to them, his voice barely audible. Quinn glanced at the general, who nodded.

"We'll be outside," said the general, and Quinn looked at Loedicia's tearstained face, then followed the general into the hall. The general shut the parlor door.

Loedicia stared at Roth's back and her knees felt weak. Why did she feel like this? What could she tell him? She walked over slowly and stood behind him.

"Roth?"

He turned, took one look, then pulled her into his arms, holding her tightly against him. "How can I let you go?" he asked huskily as he buried his face in her neck, and she felt the warm tears on her skin.

He held her close for a long time, caressing her, then slowly his arms loosened from about her and he drew back and looked into her face. "I'll always love you, Dicia," he said as he gazed into her eyes. "If he hadn't come back ... but he did and I can't hate him for being alive." He cupped her chin in his hand. "The last few nights I made you forget him, if only for a little while, and I'll always remember that," he whispered. "For a while you gave your love to me and not to him. God! I wish it could be for always, but it can't, so I'll bow out gracefully. All I ask is one kiss to keep me for the rest of my life."

Her eyes filled with tears as he leaned forward and his lips touched hers, softly at first, then he kissed her passionately, sensuously, until he almost took her breath away.

"Don't ever forget me," he whispered breathlessly, pulling his lips from hers reluctantly as he gulped back the sob that was creeping into his throat. He took his arms from about her, leaving her standing by the window trembling as he walked to the doors hurriedly and flung them open.

Quinn and the general were standing by the front door and now they walked back to the parlor.

"Take good care of her, Quinn," Roth said bitterly as he glanced at Loedicia, who still stood with her back to them. "I told you once before you had one hell of a woman and it still goes."

Quinn glanced from Roth to Loedicia, who'd turned to face them, and her face was flushed, her eyes misty, then he looked back at Roth. "What can I say, Roth?" he said. "I'd give almost anything—"

"Except Loedicia," interrupted Roth curtly, then his eyes hardened and his voice sounded strained. "But let's forget it, shall we? It's over and I've lost. Where do we go from here?"

General Washington cleared his throat. "You realize we have another problem on our hands, don't you?" he asked both men. "Everyone think's Loedicia's your wife, Roth, and Quinn has a price on his head. I told Quinn already that Lord Varrick's back in town—"

"I know," interrupted Roth. "He knows I married Loedicia. He was here in April. Ironic, isn't it? He said he was going back to Boston to see that the marriage was annulled."

"Well, when he finds out Quinn's here too there's going to be hell to pay. There's only a few men at British headquarters and I think you'll find them being escorted out of town in the morning, but they couldn't stop him anyway. They never have."

"We can arrest him," said Quinn.

"For what?"

"Can't you think of something?"

"Unfortunately there are loyalists left in town who could use the incident against us. An army that uses its power for personal vengeance loses some of its prestige. Besides, someone may get the notion to collect the bounty on you. I can't have that."

"What should we do?" asked Roth.

The general sighed. "We pretend this didn't happen," he said. "I've given Quinn a commission. He's a colonel in the Continental Army now and has promised to rebuild

Fort Locke. We need him out there, but he isn't scheduled to leave for a few days yet. In the meantime, if word leaks out that the man I'm sending into the wilderness isn't really Cherokee Jones, all our plans will have been for nothing. Even the men we're recruiting won't know who he really is until the day they leave and we're trying to keep the whole expedition as quiet as possible so he'll have no trouble along the way. The fewer people who know about it, the better. Mrs. Locke will stay here for now—"

"Not without Quinn, oh, no," she interrupted, shaking her head as she walked over to Quinn and tucked her arm through his, hugging it to her. "I lost him once, I won't lose him again."

The general scratched his chin. "All right," he said finally. "Mr. Cherokee Jones will have to become a houseguest of Major and Mrs. Chapman for the remainder of his stay."

"Do you know what you're asking, General?" retorted Roth. "It's bad enough I have to give her up, but to keep her under the same roof and not be able to—"

"Do you want her dead?" asked Quinn sharply, and Roth looked startled. "If Kendall gets his hands on her again she's as good as dead," he explained as he squeezed her arm. "I remember what he did to her the last time."

"Then it's settled," said the general. "Quinn should be able to leave in less than a week's time."

"Quinn?" asked Loedicia. "What about me?"

He stared at her, frowning. That's right. There'd been no thought of Loedicia at the time Quinn had promised to go.

"If he goes, I go," she added stubbornly. "I won't be separated from him again. I won't!"

General Washington's forehead creased deeper as he glanced at Quinn. If Loedicia didn't go, would Quinn go without her? Probably not. But how could she go? If he remembered right, she had a small baby. Now what?

"How old is your baby?" he asked, and saw her eyes fill with apprehension.

"But I have to go," she begged. "I can take her with us. She's strong, healthy . . ."

"Through wilderness?"

"Indian women travel hundreds of miles through wilderness with babies." She looked up at Quinn, her eyes pleading.

"You know what it'll mean," he said. "You've done it before, but this time it'll be harder with the baby."

"I don't care how hard it is," she answered. "I want to go back. . . . I want to see the house again and stand on the veranda and look at the lake with you. . . . Please, Quinn, don't you want me?"

He looked down into her eyes. Want her? My God! He turned to the general. "With good horses we should make it in about a month, maybe less," he said. "Loedicia and the baby go with me or I don't go."

The general sighed. "All right, but you get an escort, Quinn. I'm sending as many men as I can spare to go with you, plus men you'll need when you get there to start rebuilding." He straightened up, squaring his shoulders, and turned to Roth. "Let me congratulate you, Major," he said as he started slowly toward the door. "Things could have been messier than they were. You take defeat gracefully. May I always call you a friend?" He put his hand out to Roth and they shook hands. "Now, shall we join everyone at the house for drinks?" he suggested. "You can't drown your sorrow, Major, but you sure as hell can take the edge off it." He put an arm about Roth's shoulder and led him out of the parlor and on out the front door, closing it softly behind them.

Quinn and Loedicia watched them go, then turned to each other, and he scooped her into his arms, looking down into her face.

"Do you know how I feel?" he asked, his eyes boring into hers. "I feel warm and weak and alive and . . ." He drew her even closer. "And a man again." He kissed her deeply, thoroughly, and his body was responding to her as it always had. "Now you're going to show me our daughter," he whispered against her lips. "And then I'm going to make up for all the nights we've spent alone." As he picked her up in his arms and swept her up the stairs Ondine watched from the kitchen, her eyes wide in horror and astonishment.

The way Missus Chapman was carrying on! She shook her head in disbelief as she walked back to the kitchen. You really had to keep your eyes and ears shut when you were around white folks or you could get yourself in a heap of trouble.

Quinn set Dicia on her feet at the top of the stairs and she reached out in the dark and grabbed his hand, pulling him toward an open door on the right, where moonlight streamed through a window into the room, falling across a cradle set beneath it. Quinn held his breath as they reached the side of the cradle, then he bent over and looked down into the small face, so soft and delicate in sleep.

"She's beautiful," he murmured. "So perfect." He stared at her quietly for a long time, then he reached down, touching her little hand as it lay back against the covers. "How old is she now?"

"Three months."

"She's so tiny."

"But strong," whispered Loedicia. "Just yesterday Roth . . ."

She stopped abruptly at his name and Quinn waited for her to continue, but she didn't.

He turned his head slowly to look at her. "Roth what?" he asked quietly, and she continued, her voice faltering, face flushed.

"He . . . he held her hands and she pulled herself up until she was standing," she finished slowly, hesitantly, then suddenly she turned away from him and walked to the door as she remembered how the baby had laughed and Roth had hugged and kissed her because he'd been so proud.

"Just think," he'd said happily. "Only three months old and standing already. She'll probably walk before she's a year."

His words came back to her so clearly and she wished she could blot out their memory as she stood by the door and stared into the darkened hallway. Quinn left the baby's side, walking up to stand behind her.

"Dicia? What is it? What's the matter?"

"What kind of a woman am I, Quinn?" she asked desperately, her back still to him. "What kind of woman tears the heart out of a man as I've done with Roth!"

"You'd rather it be my heart?" he asked, and she whirled around.

"But I feel so helpless. He loves the baby and . . . and he loves me."

"I love you too."

"But . . ."

"But?" His eyes darkened in disbelief. "But what?" He stared at her intently. "Dicia, are you in love with him?" he challenged, and she had no answer for him.

What could she say? What did she feel for Roth? She turned without saying a word and walked across the hall, through the door of the bedroom she and Roth had shared, and stopped in the middle of the room and stood staring at the bed, its outline barely discernible in the darkness. The bed where she'd lain in Roth's arms and he'd made love to her. She'd been so thrilled to see Quinn again she hadn't even taken time to sort through her emotions and realize that Roth meant something to her too. There were memories she couldn't erase. She could feel Quinn's eyes on her as he watched from the doorway, then he stepped into the room and confronted her.

"I asked you a question, Dicia," he said stubbornly. "Are you in love with him?"

But instead of answering, she let out an agonized moan, then turned to him, flinging herself at him, burying her face in his chest, her hands clinging to the front of his shirt, and she began to cry softly.

"Last night he made love to me," she murmured against him, and he felt her tremble. "He made love to me and I loved him back. Last night I loved him, I know I did, yet . . . I love you. . . . I know I love you. I'm so mixed up!" She tilted her head to look up at him. "Do you know what I'm trying to say?" she asked, and he stared at her, trying to understand, but it was so dark he could barely see her face.

"You're trying to tell me you're in love with both of us?" he asked, incredulous.

"I don't know," she sighed. "Maybe it's just compassion . . . maybe it's all the memories." Her voice lowered. "Maybe I do love him, but in a different way. . . ."

Quinn tensed as he reached out and cupped her chin in his right hand, holding her head so she had to look up at him.

"Different?" he asked cynically. "Love is love, Dicia. How could it be different?"

"I don't know! I don't know!" she cried. "All I know is I don't want to hurt him! I feel guilty about what I'm doing to him."

"Guilty? He had you to himself all that while. Isn't that some compensation?"

She stared at him, her eyes hesitant, but she could think of nothing to say to justify herself.

"Or maybe that's what's wrong," he said, savagely misunderstanding her silence. "Is that it? Is that it, Dicia? Is that what's wrong? Maybe it isn't enough for you. Maybe you want more. You liked his lovemaking, you told me so, didn't you?"

She opened her mouth to protest, but no words came out.

His fingers tightened on her chin until it hurt. "Well, didn't you?"

"Yes . . . yes . . ." she finally whispered helplessly, tears running down her cheeks. His fingers eased and he caressed the side of her face and her whole body flushed warm inside, tingling all over as he pulled her closer in his arms and she felt him hard against her.

"Maybe that's what you want. Is that it, Dicia? Do you want him to make love to you again? Do you? Do you want him now?" he asked huskily, then his voice lowered. "Or maybe you remember my lovemaking and you want me. Do you, Dicia? Do you want me?" His hand moved from her cheek to her throat and his fingers began caressing the nape of her neck. "Who do you want, Dicia?" he said coaxingly, and she could feel his breath warm on her face as his fingers continued to caress her.

Her heart was pounding. She loved Roth. Somehow, some way she knew she loved him, but she loved Quinn more. Her love for Roth was a quiet, gentle acceptance. Like something you get used to. The love she had for Quinn was like a fire within her, raging wildly, untamed. Like a violent storm that went on forever, never letting her rest, always there to stir her even when she fought against it. Like now! Right now her whole body was on fire. Any man could take Roth's place, but, oh, God, no man could ever replace Quinn. No man!

Quinn shook his head. Her silence was maddening. She had to answer. Why did she just stare at him? Why couldn't she make up her mind? Why couldn't she say something?

"Please, Dicia," he demanded, forcing the issue. "You have to choose and it might as well be now. You have to, Dicia, because you can't have both of us!"

She stared at him, feeling vulnerable, letting his words sink in, knowing he was right, knowing in her heart there was only one choice she could make yet hating herself for making it.

She shut her eyes for only a second, then sighed submissively, opening them again as she melted against him, her decision made.

"Oh, Quinn, I don't want both of you," she whispered softly, and her arms went about his neck, dispelling all his anger and frustration. "You should know that." Her lips moved up to his. "There could never be anyone else, ever. I love you . . . I want you." She pressed even closer, moving seductively against him, and she could feel his body alive and eager, making her all warm inside. This was what she wanted. This was what she'd hoped for every time Roth made love to her, but she knew now that only Quinn could give this feeling of euphoria to her.

"Make love to me, Quinn," she begged, brushing her lips against his passionately. "Make love to me and help me forget everything. Help me forget what a cruel, selfish woman I am for loving you . . . help me to forget I have a conscience, I need you!" He sighed ecstatically as his mouth covered hers and she moaned blissfully as his hands reached behind her and he began unfastening the hooks on her dress.

Kendall Varrick paced the floor of his room at the inn, cursing softly to himself. News travels fast. That stranger, Cherokee Jones, was Quinn, blast his hide! Why did he always have to show up? He should be dead. Handling Roth would have been hard enough, but Quinn! He lay down on the bed and stared at the ceiling.

Somehow he had to get Loedicia back. His eyes blazed. She belonged to him and he'd have it no other way. Just the thought of her excited him and brought an ache to his loins. He'd have her again, by God! But how?

He mulled the thought over all afternoon until darkness began to creep into the room. He could get no backing from the military because the few remaining soldiers had been escorted out of town early that morning. Whatever he did he would have to do on his own. General Gage had been furious when he'd learned of Roth's marriage and had ordered him back to Boston to have the marriage annulled, but now that Roth had turned traitor there was no way to enforce the order.

Kendall remembered Roth's vow that the only way he'd get Loedicia back was over his dead body. Well, that could apply to Quinn too. But even with Quinn dead, how could he get out of Philadelphia with her? There had to be a way. She'd become an obsession with him and he had to have her. He had to!

He suddenly stood up. It was the only way. He walked to the wardrobe, slipped on his cloak, and left the room to find Squint and Ramsey.

It was well past midnight as the three men made their way across the dark lawn, leaving their horses tied to a nearby tree. Thankful the Newells had no dogs, they slipped to the side of the small cottage and started jimmying one of the side windows.

"Don't make so much noise," cautioned Kendall as Squint forced the latch.

"It's a strong one," he protested, but the latch finally gave and the windows swung open.

All three men climbed stealthily in. This was undoubtedly the parlor. The bedrooms would be upstairs. They made their way slowly into the hall, moving cautiously so they wouldn't bump into furniture, then crept silently up the stairs.

There were two bedrooms off the upstairs hall, one on each side. One would be Roth's room, the other for Quinn, Loedicia, and the baby. Kendall opened the door on the left and listened. All he could hear was a man's deep breathing, but as he glanced toward the bed he could see Loedicia's face where the moonlight streamed in at the window and his heart beat faster.

She was there, beautiful and sensuous, not a stitch of clothing on. The covers were just below her waist and she was on her stomach, with one arm flung across Quinn's bare chest as he lay on his back sleeping.

Kendall held his breath as he looked at her, then slowly he stepped into the room, the other two men following close behind. He motioned to Ramsey, who drew a knife from his sheath, then Kendall brought a blanket from under his arm as Squint stood by to help.

Ramsey tiptoed toward Quinn's side of the bed, raised his knife, and took a deep breath, starting his downward plung toward Quinn's chest, but he wasn't quick enough.

Quinn had heard the door as it opened and by the time Ramsey reached the bed he was wide awake, his feet hitting Ramsey in the chest as the knife made its descent.

Ramsey gasped, the wind knocked out of him, as Quinn shot up in bed, toppling Loedicia to the floor. She woke, looking into Kendall's face as she hit the floor and saw the blanket fall toward her. Instantly, she rolled under the bed.

The place was bedlam. Kendall cursed as he tried to grab her, but he was too large to fit under the bed to go after her.

Quinn grabbed Ramsey as he started to double over and picked him up, throwing him at the half-breed, Squint, and both men fell back against the dresser, scattering its contents about the room.

Kendall, unable to reach Loedicia, lurched up and started across the bed as Quinn whirled around. He was on top of Kendall in seconds and the two men grappled across the bed as Ramsey got his second wind and Squint pushed him off his chest while the naked Dicia cringed beneath the bed.

As Squint and Ramsey made a lunge at Quinn the door flew open and Roth, clad only in underwear, dived into the fracas with Burly following close behind. Burly had arrived on their doorstep that morning shortly after the soldiers had been escorted from town and Quinn had been elated at seeing his old friend. Now Burly plunged into the midst of the battle, fists flying.

Dicia could hear breaking furniture and glass as well as grunts and groans as each man picked an opponent.

Kendall was breathless as he and Quinn rolled off the bed onto the floor and were almost stepped on by Roth and Ramsey, fighting toe and toe.

"I've been waiting for you," grunted Quinn as he struggled with Kendall, trying to keep the man's hands from the pistol he had stuck in his belt. Kendall pulled it out, but Quinn was too quick. He hit Kendall's hand, sending the pistol flying across the floor, but in doing so, he lost his balance just enough to give Kendall the advantage and Quinn flew backward as Kendall shoved him.

By now Loedicia had stuck her head out from under the bed and although it was dark, the moon shining through the open windows gave her a good view of Kendall as he sprang from the floor and crouched, falling on one knee, his hand reaching inside his coat.

She saw the flash of the knife in the moonlight and held her breath, knowing Quinn was naked and unarmed. As Kendall drew his arm back, ready to throw the knife, her eyes fell on the pistol, not two feet from her. Quickly she reached out, grabbing it; she still lay on her stomach, the rest of her body under the bed. She could barely move but she managed to cock the hammer and point it at Kendall.

As his arm started forward she gritted her teeth, her heart pounding, and pulled the trigger.

The noise of the shot almost deafened her and the kick, as the pistol was discharged, knocked her head against the side rail of the bed, but seconds later, as she opened her eyes, she saw the knife hit the floor near Quinn's feet as Kendall, a shocked look on his face, stared in disbelief, then slowly slumped lifelessly to the floor.

As the sound of the shot filled the room, startling everyone, the fighting ceased and everyone stared at Kendall's body, sprawled on the floor, blood seeping from a gaping hole in the side of his head. The ball had entered near the eye.

Loedicia lay transfixed, the pistol still smoking in her hands, and a heavy silence filled the room. Then slowly Quinn grabbed his pants from the bedpost, slipping them on as the four other men disentangled themselves.

He pulled a blanket from the bed, walked over and dropped it across his cousin's still body, then knelt down beside Loedicia and slowly took the gun from her trembling hands.

"He's dead?" she asked as she stared up at him, and Quinn nodded as she relaxed, her eyes closed.

"He was going to kill you," she whispered softly as she opened her eyes. "I couldn't let him kill you."

"It's all right," he assured her as the room suddenly came to life again.

Ramsey and Squint made a break for the door, surprising Burly and Roth, almost knocking them down, but they were no match for the angry pair, who forced them to stop in their tracks.

Quinn took a sheet and helped Dicia from under the bed, wrapping the sheet about her, then they confronted the men.

"Well?" asked Quinn, his voice deadly as he stared at Ramsey.

"It was Lord Varrick's idea," answered Ramsey nervously, his eyes searching the moonlit-filled room, trying to avoid the anger in Quinn's eyes. "He figured the major would be asleep across the hall. It was supposed to be so simple and quiet."

"The major was asleep downstairs," offered Roth at his ear. "But steps in old houses make noise and my bed was right under them. The maid and the baby are asleep across the hall. At least they were before all this started. Ondine's probably hiding in a corner shaking half to death by now."

"None of this was supposed to happen," retorted Ramsey.

"In other words, I was to get a knife in the chest while I was sleeping and he'd carry Loedicia off without her raising a fuss?"

"He planned to grab her before she had a chance to yell."

"Thank God we're all light sleepers," stated Quinn as he put his arm around Loedicia. "Take them downstairs and tie them up," he said to Roth and Burly, "and we'll get dressed. I have a feeling we're going to have some tall explaining to do." He glanced at the blanket that covered Lord Varrick's body.

By morning, everything was straightened out to everyone's satisfaction. Ramsey and Squint were sitting in jail, charged with attempted murder, Lord Varrick's body was disposed of as quietly as possible with a note of his demise forwarded to General Gage, and things were almost back to normal.

Four days later, with an entourage of thirty men and Burly, Quinn and Loedicia, wearing buckskins, with little Rebel's Indian cradle strapped to the side of Loedicia's saddle, prepared to leave Philadelphia.

Everyone stood in front of General Washington's headquarters saying good-bye and confusion reigned as everyone checked to make sure nothing had been forgotten.

"Well," said the general as he shook Quinn's hand, "I hope everything goes well. We'll give you about a month to get there, then start spreading the word, the men'll show up, you'll see. Since this new fighting in Boston, I too will be leaving in a few days. It looks like we have a war to win." He glanced down at Loedicia, holding the baby in her arms. She looked deliriously happy. "And I wish you

Godspeed, my dear," he said. "And take good care of this husband of yours. He's important to us out there."

"He's important to me too," she answered as she looked at Quinn, her eyes shining, then she glanced away quickly as the clatter of horses' hooves interrupted them. Roth rode up, dismounted, saluted both of them, then stood beside the general.

The smile that moved on his face was a bit forced but not because he disliked Quinn. On the contrary. He'd have been happier if he could have hated the man, but he didn't. He extended his hand. "Good-bye, Quinn," he said firmly as Quinn shook his hand. Roth looked quickly at Loedicia, then back to Quinn. "Take good care of her and don't let anything happen. Remember, she means a lot to both of us."

Quinn nodded as he grasped Roth's hand in both of his. "You take care of yourself, Roth," he answered. "And thanks again . . . for everything."

Roth straightened a bit too rigidly and looked down at Loedicia. His eyes fell to the baby in her arms, pink and happy, and he reached down and touched the side of her face. It was petal soft like her mother's and she stared up at him with those big violet eyes. As he touched her face Rebel grabbed his finger, hanging on as she cooed.

He looked at Loedicia and thought he saw tears in her eyes, but maybe he was mistaken.

"Good-bye, Dicia," he said softly as he reluctantly disengaged his fingers from the baby's hand. "I don't suppose we'll ever meet again, but always remember, if you and Quinn need anything at all, I'll be around. At least I hope I will." His voice was strained, as if he were holding something back.

Suddenly he leaned down, kissed her lingeringly on the lips, then turned abruptly, without saying another word to anyone, walked to his horse, mounted, and rode off without looking back.

General Washington stared after him and swallowed hard, trying to clear the lump in his throat. "There's a man I'm proud to have on our side," he said as Roth disappeared down the street.

Quinn put his arm about Loedicia and they too watched him go. "He's a better man than I'll ever be," stated Quinn, and Loedicia felt him squeeze her shoulder a bit harder. She knew what he meant. Quinn would never have been able to walk away from a woman he loved, not for anything.

"Well," said the general, sighing as he turned to face them, "the horses are skittish, the men are eager and getting nervous, and the good-byes are over."

Quinn helped Loedicia strap Rebel into her hanging cradle, everyone mounted, and with Burly proudly leading the way, they left Philadelphia, headed for the frontier.

The general watched them slowly make their way down the street, his face somber as he wondered how things would work out for them. It was too bad the war had started because now, with Lord Varrick dead, even though Quinn wasn't a legitimate heir, he was the only heir to the Locksley estates. Well, maybe someday.

Quinn glanced over at Loedicia as they rode side by side down the streets of the city, out onto the road that led away from town. How much he loved her. His eyes moved to the shock of blond curls bobbing up and down at the side of her saddle. Rebel seemed to be enjoying her ride immensely, gurgling and waving her arms as they jogged along. She was a beautiful baby with eyes just like her mother's and he smiled proudly.

"What are you grinning about?" asked Loedicia as she looked over at him, and his eyes twinkled as he gazed back at her.

"I was just admiring my family," he said proudly, "and thinking how fortunate I am."

Loedicia glanced down at the baby's head and her eyes grew warm and soft. "She is adorable, isn't she?"

"Like her mother."

She glanced at him quickly and their eyes met and held. He reached out to her and she took his hand as their horses moved closer together, then he leaned over, his mouth covering hers, and he kissed her thoroughly as they rode along.

"I love you," he whispered against her lips. "I've always

loved you. I can't even leave you alone when you're trying to ride a horse."

"Who wants you to?" she answered coquettishly, and he sighed.

"I always said you were a vixen," he said softly, and he kissed her again as they rode off into the wilderness to raise their family and fight their fight for freedom. He was her bastard, her rebel, her husband, but most of all he was her lover and her world was complete.

## About the Author

The granddaughter of an old-time vaudevillian, Mrs. Shiplett was born and raised in Ohio. She has been married to her husband Charles for more than thirty years and they have lived in the city of Mentor-on-the-Lake for more than twenty-five years. She has four daughters and two grandchildren and enjoys living an active outdoor life.

She is also the author of REAP THE BITTER WINDS, THE WILD STORMS OF HEAVEN, and DEFY THE SAVAGE WINDS, which continue the sweeping saga of her historical romantic series. All are available in Signet editions.